Brody

A.S. ROBERTS

DEFAULT DISTRACTION

Jeanette
make sure you
have no
regrets!

Best Wishes

Other books by this author

The Fated series

Fated
Inevitable
Irrevocable

Undeniable

Coming soon

Default Distraction series

Brody

Rafferty

Cade

Luke

In the end, we only regret the chances we didn't take, the words we didn't say, the relationships that seemed too intense to take a risk with, and the decisions we waited far too long to make.
In the end, make sure you have no regrets.

~ Brody Daniels

Dedication

This, as always, is dedicated to my husband. Thank you, for putting up with the weekends I lock myself away to write. Thank you, for understanding when I listen to the voices in my head, more than I listen to you. Thank you, for being you and loving me unconditionally.

I love all love stories, but ours is my favourite.

I love you.

To my nan, Vera. Thank you for teaching me how to love.

It's also dedicated to the strong women behind me. Thank you for having my back. To Sarah, Debi, Kirsty, Crystal, Tammi and Cassandra. This book would never have been written without you. It means so much to have friends like you.

Thank you!

Prologue

BRODY

Twenty-six years ago

MUSIC BLARED OUT from the kitchen. I knew that Mom had turned it up again. I opened one eye and looked at the houses on either side of us. Any minute now they would start to close some of their windows, as they always did when Mom played her music loudly.

I loved music, I loved that it made her happy, it meant Sissy and I could be happy as well.

I didn't care that no one liked my mom, not really, anyway. She was my mom and I loved her, especially on days like today. When she was singing and dancing, it made me happy. I felt all warm inside and my tummy felt full up.

I heard a window slam, like I knew it would, and I closed one of my eyes to go back to my cloud watching. I put my curled fists together, one on top of the other, to make a telescope shape and I looked up again. Together with my sister we blanked out the shouts being aimed at our garden and went back to our make-believe world.

It was safe there.

'Look, Brody. That one there looks like a white, fluffy princess.' I felt her small elbow hit my ribs as she nudged me. I rubbed at my side and followed my sister's pointing finger. I couldn't see anything but cars, Superman's cape, and one that looked like a very hairy dog.

'It does, Sissy,' I agreed, to keep her smiling.

I turned my head to look at her next to me and grinned. She looked really pleased with herself and smiled back at me. I watched her as she poked her tongue through the small gap where she had lost her baby tooth, worrying with the hole it had left behind.

I felt sad that the tooth fairy hadn't come for her. She'd lost it at school after her tooth had come out in an apple she'd bitten into. The tooth fairy had never come for me either, but I didn't care. The kids at school had laughed at her when she hadn't been left any money under her pillow. I'd called them names and had got a bruise on my face when Harry had hit me. But his eye looked worse after I hit him back. I'd made sure that I placed a dime under her pillow that night, after she'd cried herself to sleep.

The adults at school didn't like my mom and most days the children there didn't like me, but they weren't going to be cruel to my sister. I was big for my age, big enough to take care of us both and I would.

I had pinky swore I would.

I lay back into the cushion of the long, uncut grass in our back yard and sighed as I lowered another peanut butter and jelly sandwich into my mouth. I pushed the jelly that was escaping and running down my chin back onto my tongue with one finger. As my finger left my mouth I made it pop and my little sister giggled beside me at the noise.

Dad would be back sometime today and I was looking forward to seeing him. I had said my prayers every day he'd been away. I knew it would be better this time. My worried tummy turned over, and I placed my hand over it, feeling my skin. My school shirt was too small and didn't touch the top of my grey school shorts. Another thing that the kids in school made fun of, at least they used to, until I hit them and then they'd stopped.

I knew that when my dad came home, it was going to be better.

I had prayed every night that it was going to be different this time.

'Brody, come here and help me.' Mom's voice travelled over to me and I stopped daydreaming.

My head shot up from its soft, green pillow and I looked at my mom standing in the doorway. I knew that look and it frightened me. I watched as one of her feet suddenly stepped forward to stop herself from swaying and I wanted to be sick. I felt Sissy's small hand as she

2

grabbed mine. I knew she was scared, watching Mom. I was too, but I couldn't show it. Dad said I was the man of the house when he wasn't here and I always looked after her.

'I'm just coming, Mom.' I jumped up quick, ran over to her and held her arm. Then I helped her out onto the grass where we were sitting and made her sit down. I ran back inside to bring out the last of our picnic and to turn down the music. Before I went back outside I looked around the kitchen, and there it was. The bottle was brown and looked harmless but to me it meant arguing, being hungry and dirty. I grabbed it and poured the contents into the sink. Then I turned on the faucet and watched the tablets disappear down the drain. I opened the overflowing garbage bin and pulled out some stuff to hide the bottle underneath, hoping that it wouldn't be found by anybody.

'Fucking God!' I swore quietly. I was angry, but was nervous of saying a word that I knew I'd get a smack for saying.

The prayers I'd said since dad had been away seemed to have worked. Mom had been happier. Our clothes had been washed regularly and she'd cooked most nights. The day he was coming back my mom had taken her tablets. Praying was no use. No one was listening to me. I'd tried so hard to be a good boy.

Couldn't God see how me and Sissy were hurting?

There wasn't a fucking God, just like there wasn't a tooth fairy.

I looked back out to the garden. Mom was lying down on the grass, singing along with the song she had playing on the radio and Sissy was sat beside her looking small and scared. I picked up all the food I could carry in my arms and took it outside. I needed to get her to eat before Dad came home. I knew it would help, maybe I could make her better before he got back?

'Mom, what do you want to eat?' I asked her as I dropped the food down on the grass.

She didn't reply, the only words coming from her mouth were the words she was singing.

'Please, Mom. Please eat,' I begged as I lifted her heavy head up off the grass.

Up and down our small road of military houses, we could hear doors slamming and excited voices.

'Brody,' my sister whispered. I looked at her as she began to shiver, even though the sun was out in our yard. We both knew what was coming next.

I heard our front door slam and my eyes shot up to my sister as she scurried closer towards me. I let go of my mom and cuddled Sissy.

'I'm home,' came my dad's cheerful voice.

He didn't hurt us. Dad was a big man, but he wasn't violent. But him and my mom together, they shouted and screamed at each other, and she hit him until he held her arms behind her back.

When she had taken her tablets, it was always this way. We knew they loved us, but deep down inside they were hurting us. I was okay, I was the man of the house when my dad was away, so I was fine. But I hated watching them fight and being mean to each other. What really hurt me was watching Sissy struggle. She had no friends at school and stuttered her words when she wasn't talking to me.

Living like this hurt so much and it never seemed to stop.

Sometimes, I had to go under my bed to drown out the sounds of them shouting and then of them kissing. I'd heard a neighbour down the road talking about my mom and dad and she'd said, "It's like they can't live with each other, but they can't live without each other." I had poked my tongue out at her and run off.

'There you all are.' His voice sounded happy, but I couldn't turn my head to look at him, instead I hung it down. I was ashamed I hadn't been good enough to make it better this time.

Mom had stopped singing and was now asleep in our yard.

I pulled Sissy closer to me and hugged her. I moved my mouth closer to her ear and whispered, 'It's okay, we'll be okay. I'll look after you. Pinky swear.' I wrapped my little finger around hers.

Together we looked at our linked hands and went back to our make-believe world.

Amy

Twenty-three years ago

'Pick up your bag.' I could hear by the sound of my mum's voice that she wasn't happy with me. I didn't understand why. I'd been quiet for nearly the whole car ride. I hadn't asked her any silly questions. I'd been sitting like a lady sits too, as I'd deliberately tucked my hands underneath my legs so I didn't fidget. I had kept my knees together and crossed my feet at my ankles. My legs had begun to ache ages ago, but I didn't want to make her angry with me, so I had kept them still and ignored the pain, even though they begged to dance to the music that was playing on the radio.

I looked down to the floor of the taxi at the small pink rucksack by my feet. I made the material wrinkle a little with the side of my pink

4

and white trainer. All my favourite pens, my reading book from school, and my CD player had been shoved inside, as my mum had hastily run around our house in London, packing for the surprise she had promised me.

I grabbed the handle at the top of it, not wanting to upset her anymore, and with the sudden fear of losing all my special things.

I took a quick look out of the window to see where the taxi had brought us to. It was funny, the houses on the street were small and very close together, whereas our house was big and tall. There weren't any paths here and there wasn't anyone driving down the small road. I grasped my small bag to my chest and jumped down to the ground through the open car door.

'Come on, Amy. Pay attention, you silly little girl. It's your own fault that I get so cross with you.' My mum had stopped in a shop doorway and I heard her take a deep breath as she grabbed hold of the door handle. I looked upwards at the sign above the shop. It was so pretty, painted in lilacs and purples with gold writing. The sign read "A stitch in time." I wondered what it meant.

But most of all, I wondered why we were here.

I pulled my eyes away from the sign to look at my mum again as she pushed the door further open. She was carrying a suitcase with all my clothes in it, but I knew her case was still in the taxi, the same taxi that had its engine still running. I looked back at the white car and the driver that sat in it, ignoring us.

'And tidy yourself up... Do you want to meet your nanny looking like that?'

My nanny? I remembered hearing my nanny mentioned a long time ago. I'd thought I hadn't got any other family apart from my mum, but I'd decided it didn't matter as I had my childminder Jessica's family. I spent a lot of time with them. I wondered if she knew we had gone away.

I looked down at my clothes and smoothed down my denim skirt with my hands. I couldn't see anything wrong with it, but I did it out of habit anyway. I looked further down and checked my long white socks were still pulled up to my knees and that the patterns on them were straight. I hated my mum being cross and disappointed with me and I didn't want to be told off again.

I heard the bell ding its welcome as she pushed the door open wide and stepped inside. Hesitantly I followed, looking behind me to take one more look at the taxi.

'Hello... Vera?' I heard my mum calling to someone.

I turned around quickly to see a friendly looking lady rise from behind the counter. Her hand came up to her mouth as she gasped in surprise.

'Oh, my goodness... Sandra? What a surprise to see you. Is that Amy?' The smiling, older lady squeezed herself through the small gap between the two counters into the middle of the shop, wiping her hands on her apron. She put her hand into the apron pocket and pulled out a bright white, lace-trimmed hanky, which she dabbed hurriedly to her eyes and then put back again. Once she reached us she bent down in front of me and took my hand in hers. The skin on her hand was worn and so soft. I immediately knew I wanted to feel more of her warm hands, so I dropped my bag on the floor to reach out to touch the soft, freckled skin with my other hand.

I looked at her kind face, to find she had smiley blue eyes.

I liked her immediately, but I could sense that my mum didn't.

'Hello, Amy.' She smiled back at me. 'My, you've grown up into a pretty young lady. Now let me think, you're ten now, aren't you?' I nodded back at her. 'You won't remember me, but I'm your nanny. I'm so pleased to...'

My mum, tutting her impatience, stopped my nanny talking to me.

'Yes, yes, yes... Look, I hate to break up the family reunion, but the taxi meter is running outside. So, let's cut to the chase... I've brought Amy to stay with you for a while.'

I watched as my nanny looked at my mum. Her eyes widened with surprise. I looked between the two of them, confused at my mum's words.

'You know I'm more than happy to see Amy. But she doesn't know me anymore, Sandra. You haven't brought her by in what six... nearly seven years. How does she feel about staying here?' My nanny stood up to address her concerns to my mum.

'She's fine. Look, I must run. I'll be in contact soon. I've had a job offered to me in New York and I've accepted it. Children aren't part of the contract and you always said to bring her around whenever I could. So, here we are... Do as you are told, Amy. I will be very disappointed to hear otherwise.' She glanced at me quickly and looked away. 'I'll see you both soon, I promise! Have fun. Ciao'

No, Mum. Please don't go...

I'll be good...

I'll try to be better.

I promise... please don't leave me.

My silent pleas went around and around in my head, but my lips never dared to release them into the shop I stood in.

6

BRODY

My mum turned quickly on her very tall stiletto heels and walked out of the door. She didn't kiss me or hug me, she just left. Although that wasn't unusual, as I was used to her not making a scene in public, I felt the pain deep inside my heart as she left me. My tummy felt funny, and as the butterflies flew around it, I felt sick. But I knew not to call her back, she would be really cross with me if I did. Tears began to make their way down my face and my nose began to run. I lifted my arm to wipe away the snot and stared at the white sleeve my arm presented. I faltered, knowing how much my mum would shout if she saw what I was about to do. My nanny's warm hand gripped mine slightly tighter as if she could feel my pain. Once again, she reached down into her pocket to pass me her pretty lace hanky that I had seen her dab her eyes with earlier.

The bell above the door shook with the finality of my mum leaving as the door closed behind her. I watched in disbelief as she got into the waiting taxi and it pulled away. She never even turned her head to wave goodbye.

'I cannot believe that I gave birth to her!' my nanny spat out. She spoke like she'd forgotten I was in the shop with her.

I looked to where my hand was being caressed by the softest fingers I had ever felt. My nanny bent down to me.

'Now, you're not to worry, Amy. You're safe with me. You will always have a home here. I promise you... Always.'

I stared into her kind blue eyes. Not breaking that contact, I finally wiped my wet nose up the sleeve of my white top. The shiny trail it left on the material was my way of wordlessly showing my mum that I no longer cared about her or her rules.

One

Amy

Present day

'**BLOODY HELL... IT'S** cold enough to freeze the balls off a brass monkey,' I heard Lauren's voice exclaiming as she came bursting through the shop door, and I felt a smile pull at the corners of my mouth. I felt lighter just hearing her voice.

Unfortunately, I then heard the glass panes rattle in their rotten, wooden frames. The door had slammed behind her, as it caught on the cold gust of wind that was blowing down the lane. I closed my eyes and gripped the wooden pole I was holding a little bit tighter, waiting for the glass to fall out onto the floor. The door signified just how precarious my life was. Luckily, the smash of glass never came. I let out the breath I was holding.

'Whoops! Sorry, Amy! That was close, wasn't it?' Lauren grimaced as she spoke to me.

I nodded at her and sighed as I hurriedly finished tidying away the pieces of scrapbooking papers that I had pulled out for the last customer. Then I closed the well-worn wooden drawer, by lifting the brass cup handle and sliding the wood back into place at just the right angle. I jumped down backwards off the steps, holding tight to the long pole that served as a handle. I had sold a few papers to her, and she had even bought some other bits and pieces as she had looked around my nan's shop.

I just wished it was enough.

"A Stitch in Time" had diversified several times over in the last ten years. It no longer just sold haberdashery items. If you had a need for it in your life, then one of the sectioned glass counters, or one of the many different sized wooden drawers that were built floor to ceiling along all the walls of the shop, probably contained it. Unfortunately, as much as I had enjoyed talking to the lady and watching her with a sense of pride, as she stood and took in the beauty of my nan's old Victorian shop, she had been one of only three customers I had seen all day. Her purchase and the promise of her returning with her friends wasn't going to be enough to keep the wolf from my nan's shop door.

One customer hadn't even bought anything. I wondered, not for the first or even the second time today, just what had brought him into the shop in the first place. I had been behind one of the counters when he had walked in through the door. After hearing the bell signalling someone's arrival, I had shouted out a greeting to them.

"I'll be with you in a minute, please feel free to have a look around. Hopefully something will catch your eye."

I had finished what I was doing and stood up, to find the back of a male figure completely dominating the space. My fingers grabbed onto the edge of the counter as if my body knew instinctively that I was going to need steadying. I leant forward and allowed my eyes to quickly take him in. Black Chelsea boots, black slim-legged jeans hugging muscular thighs and a very well-defined gluteus maximus. His short wool coat was of course black, it was expensively cut and accentuated his broad shoulders. Finally, my eyes had reached his head to find it was covered with a black beanie, with just an occasional piece of dark brown hair curling up and around the edge.

Please turn around.

I desperately wanted him to turn so that I could see his face.

He seemed completely oblivious to me as his body revolved slowly and his head twisted from side to side looking all around the shop. At last he had rotated enough for me to glimpse the only part of his face that was exposed between the turned-up collar of his coat and the beanie that was pulled down so low that it covered his eyebrows.

The air was sucked from my body as my eyes found his for the first time. My reaction to his presence was visceral. I had never met anyone with eyes the same colour as his. I watched fascinated as his oh-so-long eyelashes came down just the once as he blinked at me, effectively severing our connection. Finally, he began to smile. I couldn't see it, but the corners of his eyes creased just a little and I knew it was there hidden behind the fine black wool of his coat.

'Sorry... I was out walking, exploring, and your shop looked warm and inviting.' His voice was rich and warm and I was mesmerised. In fact, his voice was almost as captivating as his teal coloured eyes. He placed a hand to his forehead and pushed the beanie up, just slightly. I was entranced by the long fingers on his hand, it seemed that all of them had at least one ring on.

'Oh, that's no problem.' I smiled back at him, suddenly very pleased I was wearing one of my decent hoodies, one without holes in the elbows. I was trying to place his accent, it seemed to be a mixture of tones that my ears recognised but my brain could not, however much it tried, filter through.

'How old?' I heard teal eyes ask.

A little stunned, my voice stuttered. 'Well, my birthday is just around the corner...'

He suddenly raised a ring-covered, cold-looking hand. 'Sorry.' He smiled after he had managed to interrupt me. 'I'd love to get to know you... But this time I was asking about the building.'

'Oh... You meant my nan's shop. Its Victorian,' I answered, as I felt an embarrassed burn hit my cheeks. 'Please feel free to have a look around and let me know if anything takes your fancy, won't you?' I heard the words that left my mouth and visibly cringed inside. I rolled my eyes at myself.

His teal eyes sparked to life with obvious amusement. Flustered, I turned around quickly to tidy a non-existent mess behind me. As I busied my hands, I heard his boots connect with the tiles on the floor. I knew he had moved closer to the counter I was hiding behind when his cologne hit my deprived nostrils. I closed my eyes and momentarily inhaled the bergamot and cinnamon spices that had been warmed by his skin.

He smelt like Christmas. It must be my imagination?

Dear God, I was losing it!

'Thank you for your hospitality... But the thing I like the look of, the one thing that's caught my eye, I'm sure ain't gonna be for sale.'

Did he mean me?

I wasn't sure, and couldn't trust myself not to make a fool of myself yet again.

Like a coward I stayed with my back turned towards him and only glimpsed behind me when the click of his boots quietened. The almost threadbare matting at the doorway had masked the sound of his steps. and as I looked over my shoulder he pulled the door closed behind him.

Obviously expecting me to turn, I saw a smile once again light up his eyes, 'Thank you, Ma'am.' He caught my eye and nodded at me.

He was American then? He obviously thinks I'm old enough to be Victorian too! *The thoughts ran quickly through my head, but I refused to open my mouth again in case I made an even bigger fool of myself.*

He winked one beautiful, amused, teal coloured eye at me and left the shop.

I immediately felt bereft as the draft of cold air not only took away the hottest man I had ever laid eyes on, but also the smell of Christmas that had entered the shop with him.

'Earth to Amy, I have news!'

Lauren's voice brought me back to the present and I shook my head to once again focus on her, but I couldn't stop one small sigh sounding out loud with the memory. After my feet had hit the floor I had frozen in place. I now turned around to face her and the sight of my cousin brought a much-needed smile to my face. She was almost a mirror image of me and it was obvious that we were related, "like two peas from a pod" our nan often remarked. We had the same chestnut coloured mane of hair, and apparently the shape of our faces ran in the family, but our eyes were different shades of brown, hers light and mine so dark they were very nearly black. Strange how you can almost look identical to another person, but have such a completely different outlook on life.

She had jumped to sit up on the counter that ran down in front of the side wall. Since she had been tall enough to get herself up there, it had become her contemplating place in the shop. Our nan had long since given up asking her to not sit on the ancient counter.

'Where did you go to?' she teased.

I shook my head at her.

'It doesn't matter. Come on then, spill it,' I said and returned her smile.

'I need your full attention before I do,' she stated as she pointed towards the opposite counter, waiting for me to jump up on it to sit down.

I walked towards the door, shot the bolt across and turned the sign to closed. However, I resisted turning off the fairy lights that decorated the main window, just yet. I had taped them delicately around the panes of glass in the window and threaded them amongst the small display of knitted woollen gloves, hats, and the neatly folded crocheted blankets. The pretty coloured lights gave the run-down shop an extra sparkle and my nan had been right, her homemade knitted crafts had sold quite well.

I knew there wouldn't be any more customers today. It was Friday and the start of the last weekend before Christmas, nine days before the day itself. The weather was freezing and people had disappeared inside their houses. I wasn't even sure I'd open the shop at all next week. Lauren had already asked for my help at The Fairy Garden for most of it. I could earn more there as a waitress for a few hours than my nan's shop would take all day and I was almost counting the tips that I could make. People were always more generous at Christmas time. I turned and leant my bum against the counter and looked at Lauren expectantly.

'Well?' I questioned as I crossed my arms over my chest.

'Ok, you're going to be shocked at what I'm about to say, but before you go off on one, please understand that I. Have. Thought. About. It.' She was placating me with her hands as she spoke.

'Go on then.' I felt my brow furrow, questioningly.

'Okay, you know that group, band, whatever they are... that have been doing up Falham Manor for the last couple of years?'

I opened my eyes wider, pondering on her words. 'Of course, I do live here too, you know... and it's Raff's band. They're called Default Distraction,' I replied, shaking my head at her strange description and stupid questions.

'Well... Winter called me a few hours ago and she needs my help with their opening day.' I didn't say anything, I just stared at her trying to work out what the hell was going on inside her head and equally, for that matter, what the hell was going on inside of Winter's?

'She needs your help with what?' I couldn't believe she'd asked her for help, knowing the history between Lauren and Winter's older brother, Rafferty.

'Half of her chefs have come down with some sort of lurgy. You know the shit and vomit sort of lurgy. They can't go near the kitchen, let alone the food. She needs help preparing the food for the big open event they're having on Sunday.'

I took in what she was saying, for a moment. A few years ago, Lauren had very courageously opened a beautiful tearoom in the old coach houses of Falham Manor. They had been sold with most of the other out buildings of The Manor itself. The Fairy Garden was now going from strength to strength. It drew people in from far and wide. Part of the attraction was to sit in the beautifully well-designed comfort of the place, the other was to sample some of Lauren's homemade, traditional English cakes and pastries. She had taken a huge risk and it had paid off.

I was beyond proud of her.

We should have known then, with the sale of the outbuildings, that The Manor was also in trouble and would eventually have to be sold too. It was happening all over the country, when upper-class families no longer had the money to sustain their substantial properties. It had been a shock however when we had learnt, via Winter, that The Manor had been bought by Default Distraction. I knew no more about them than a few songs I had heard on the radio and that Raff, who we had grown up with, was part of the group.

Lauren had been floored by the news. It meant he was finally coming home, when it had taken her years to come to terms with the fact that she had thought he was never coming home.

I shook my head at her. 'I can't believe Winter would ask you. I mean, I know you're a superb cook and are probably the very best person to help her. But, let's face facts, you've been steering clear of the actual Manor house for the whole of the time they have been doing it up... I'm sorry, Lauren, but we both know why, don't we?' Her eyes misted over and I immediately felt like a bloody bitch for making her face up to the biggest heartache of her life.

'I know, but she's our friend and she needs help. I've decided I need to do this and I need to show...'

'What?' I interrupted. 'You need to show Raff that you no longer care, is that it? And if it is...Why? Why would you put yourself through that?' I could hear the concern in my voice as I almost pleaded with her to rethink her decision.

She shook her head at my words. 'No, you're wrong. I really need to show myself, once and for all, that *I've* moved on.' I watched as she copied my body language and crossed her arms over the top of her thick cream jumper.

I wasn't sure, she might be able to fool herself, but not me.

I caught the look in her eyes, it was her stubborn look. Now wasn't the time to keep questioning her motives. The look was one she had been mastering since childhood. She had pulled it out the very first time we had met, as she had told me in no uncertain terms that our nan was hers and her little brother Mark's only, and they weren't going to share her.

The memory still made me smile.

'What does Toby say?' I watched the stubborn look slide right off her face at the mention of her quite recently acquired boyfriend's name.

'I haven't told him yet... It's my business, not his.' Stubborn was replaced by a fleeting look of concern. I heard myself sigh as I realised I had made her feel uncomfortable.

'Forget I said anything,' I added as I pushed myself away from the counter I had been leaning on, to walk the few steps across to where she sat. As I arrived next to her I took hold of her left hand in both of mine and held it tightly.

'Look, take no notice of me. What do I know? I may have been married once, albeit for a short time, but I know that I've never really been in love, ever. As you know, I'm not sure it even really exists… well not for the likes of people like me.' I felt myself shrug my shoulders to drive the point home. 'As well as poor romantic decisions, I am also the queen of making appalling business decisions… instead of taking the opportunity of a lifetime when you wanted me to go into business with you, I stayed here to run Nan's shop, thinking my business degree would turn a failing business into a thriving one. So, what the heck do I know?' I twisted my head to the side as I looked at her, to try to convince her of what I was saying.

'Oh, come on! You never thought that Nan's shop would get any better, even you're not that stupid,' she laughed.

'Oi! You cheeky bugger. I could go off you, you know.'

'No, you're stuck with me. We both know the reason you stayed here at the shop. It was for love, not for any business reason.'

'Yeah, you're right, that's the sort of love I do believe in.' I smiled in acceptance at her words.

'And what do you mean, people like you? Love can be just around the corner for us all, just waiting for our right moment to meet *the* right person.'

I shrugged my shoulders at her. It was a long-standing argument between us, that just at this minute I couldn't be bothered to reopen. She stood firmly on her side of the fence and I stood on mine, even if I did occasionally try to peer over. I changed tack a little.

'So, let me ask you… Are you helping Winter for business reasons or for love?'

'Definitely business,' she said adamantly.

'Then if you need my help, I'm all yours. I know it may surprise you, but I could do with the extra money.' I knocked my shoulder against hers.

'Pack a bag then, you're moving up to The Manor,' she added.

'God, they won't know what's hit them. With the two Harper girls and Winter Davenport in the same place at the same time.' I laughed, knowing it would be hard work helping Winter and running The Fairy Garden at the same time. But I knew we would have fun together.

Still holding hands, we both separately contemplated what the next few days were going to mean for us. I had a few days of much needed freedom as my nan had gone into respite care to give me a break and Lauren was going to face the man who had left, taking her heart with him.

Two

Amy

FINALLY, I REACHED the bottom of the narrow staircase. I kicked open the door with the toe of my fleece-lined boot and manoeuvred my case into the back of the shop, using my shin. Luckily, my suitcase had wheels on it. I dragged it around the corner of the back counter and out into the middle of the floor.

Lauren had left after we'd had a hot drink. I just had a couple of things to do and then I was going to follow on up to her flat, which was sat in the roof space above her tearooms. We had decided it was best if I had my car with me, with all the work we had to get done over the next forty-eight hours. So, I was going to follow her in our nan's old soft top Triumph Herald.

I pulled out the handle of my case, walked up to the locked front door, and began to carefully tape the note to it that I had written in bold black lettering.

**MERRY CHRISTMAS AND A HAPPY NEW YEAR TO ALL OUR CUSTOMERS, OLD AND NEW.
WE WILL REOPEN IN JANUARY.
LOVE FROM
VERA AND AMY**

The weather had turned even colder in the hour it had taken me to pack up enough clothes to last me the week. Now I had moved closer to the windows, I could feel the chill on my exposed cheeks. I could also see that the earlier sleet had now turned into flurries of snow. I squinted through one of the small panes of glass, thank goodness the lane was still clear enough to drive safely. But I had to hurry, it was dark and cold, and I knew the snow would only get heavier as it had probably set in for the night.

I patted the pockets of my long, black padded coat, just feeling through the thick layer of down for my keys. I found them as the metal banged against my right hip and I pushed my hand in to retrieve them. With my other hand, I pulled my case up close behind me. It was only then that I realised I still hadn't turned off the fairy lights in the window. I lowered myself down sideways in the small space of the shop doorway. I felt around to find the switch that would plunge me into the darkness that had devoured our country lane.

My concentration was broken suddenly by a sharp, metallic rap on the door. The sound made me jump and my heartrate quickened in panic. I stepped back on instinct and suddenly found myself flailing around in mid-air as I went backwards over my case and fell down hard onto my backside.

'Shit!' I exclaimed, and instinctively my hand came up to my heart as I tried to calm it down. Luckily, although I had fallen onto the hard tiles, my padded coat seemed to have protected me from the worst of the fall.

My eyes, opened wide in fear, searched through the circular glow of the fairy lights and found the beautiful orbs of teal eyes. From the other side of the door I saw his eyebrows lift and then he lifted his hand to apologise for startling me.

'For Christ's sake. What the bloody hell?' I murmured under my breath as I stood back up quickly, trying to save face and not look like a complete bloody idiot.

I slid the bolt across and jerked open the door. Automatically, he took a step forward and I found myself almost nose to broad chest with the most captivating man I had seen in a long time.

'You frightened the life out of me,' I reprimanded him.

'Yeah, I saw… sorry. Are you okay? Not hurt or anything?' I heard the laughter in his voice and saw his eyes crinkle at the corners and once again I knew he was amused by me.

It seemed I was an endless source of entertainment for teal eyes.

'Can I help you?' I was speaking to his eyes only, as the tall figure in front of me was still covered head to toe in the same black clothes he had been wearing earlier.

'Yeah, well I was sorta hoping you could, but it looks like you're closing up for the day. I can always come back tomorrow.'

'Unfortunately, I'm not opening again until the new year.' I broke eye contact with him, bent my knees a little and grabbed hold of the handle of my case and stood it back up. 'So, if you want something, it's now or never as they say.'

Why's my heart still racing? He must have frightened me more than I initially thought.

'Are you going away for the holidays then?'

'You could say,' I answered with a small smile.

'It figures,' he stated.

'It does?' I questioned him, bemused by his statement.

He nodded his answer and started to shift around, looking uncomfortable.

'So, if I can get you anything, it truly needs to be now. The weather is getting worse and I really need to get going.'

I watched his head glance to the side. 'Well my hands are freezing. I'd forgotten just how cold English winters could be. I could do with a pair of gloves...'

I followed his eyes to the four pairs of fingerless gloves that were still in the window. They certainly didn't fit the image he had going on. The four pairs were all that was left of the geometric snowflake pattern I had made with the display of gloves earlier in the week. A pink pair, a multi-coloured striped set, a pair of yellow ones with large white daisies all over them, and a pair of turquoise blue ones with a mitten pouch. The pouch could be pulled over your exposed digits and by buttoning them up on your palm they turned into mittens.

It was my turn to smirk. I looked up at him in question.

'Sure, which ones did you have your eyes on?'

'You can choose. If they work, I couldn't give a damn.'

After hovering my hand for a few seconds over the bright yellow ones with daisies, I realised I couldn't be that cruel and grabbed up the blue ones. They seemed the lesser of the two evils.

'There you are.' I held them out to him. 'They match your eyes, well almost.'

Did I really just say that? I felt my eyes beginning to once again roll upwards at my own words.

'Thanks, I appreciate the choice.' He smirked back. 'How much are they?'

'Eight pounds, please. They're homemade, my nan knitted them.' *I really am the queen of giving out superfluous information today.*

His eyes smiled again at my completely irrelevant explanation. I watched as he lifted his shoulders to make his coat rise, then he reached behind him into the back pocket of his jeans and pulled out his wallet.

Without looking inside, he pulled out a card and held out his hand to pass it over.

I looked at the black piece of plastic he was offering me. 'Sorry, we only take cash here.' I had wanted to update the shop and bring it into the twenty-first century, but some things my nan refused to budge on.

'Ah... Then we have a problem.'

'Don't tell me. You don't have any cash, do you?' I shook my head slightly, laughing a little at the fact that only I could get an actual customer who didn't carry cash.

He passed the gloves back to me. 'Not to worry, you know what they say. Cold hands, warm heart.'

Once again, I could see he was smiling at me. I desperately wanted to move his collar down and away from his face to get a better look at that said smile. I was sure it was as gorgeous as the eyes that were currently holding me spellbound. I shook myself free of my thoughts.

'Look, I'm really in a hurry. Take them, you can be my good deed for the day.'

I watched as he shook his head in response. 'I couldn't do that.' His warm voice washed over me, caressing me in its embrace.

'Oh, just take them and buy me a drink sometime.' I closed his fingers over the open hand that contained the gloves. As our bare skin touched for the first time, my whole body jumped in reaction.

I watched as his teal eyes momentarily opened wider with shock and then just as instantaneously recovered. 'Let me carry your case for you for now, ok?'

'Thanks.' *I think.* I reached down again to flick off the fairy lights with my left hand. Pretending I needed to see what I was doing allowed me to pull my eyes away from his.

How embarrassing? It could only happen to me. Pluck up the guts to ask a man to take me for a drink and watch him flinch in horror at the thought.

I realised he had moved away when I heard the wheels of my case as they encountered the road outside of the shop. Without looking towards him, I stepped outside and wrapped my long scarf once more around my neck as the bitter wind blew strongly around me.

'Where's ya car?' I heard him shout over the wind.

'Just around the corner, over there,' I pointed.

I took a few seconds longer locking up the shop. I ran my fingers over the cold, wet glass to clear the flakes of snow, just so I could read the note I had written and taped there. As I read my words a sense of foreboding ran through me. I felt tears spring to my eyes and sniffed suddenly trying to clear my head. Things were changing, I could feel that, and change scared me. I blinked, trying to clear my head, and pulled myself together.

Snap out of it, Harper.

My minor breakdown had given me a couple of minutes and it allowed me to walk behind teal eyes. I hoped that with the self-imposed space between us and the weather, we wouldn't have to strike up another conversation.

I got to the passenger door, pushed my key home and unlocked the two-seater car. I was sure I heard a deep growl carrying on the wind as he took in my mode of transport for the first time.

'Could you place the case on the passenger seat please and strap it in with the seat belt?'

'Sure.' He lifted the heavy case with ease and unceremoniously dumped it onto the seat. I observed the car lurch to the side with the weight and then I watched fascinated as he tried to fold his large frame up to lean inside to buckle it in. Very quickly he reappeared.

'I can't do the belt. There's not enough room for the case and me in there.' He smiled again with his eyes. 'Look, my car is parked just up the road, outside a friend's house. It would be a much safer way to travel in this weather. Are you sure I can't give you a ride?'

I followed one of his covered hands, as it gesticulated to a large vehicle outside of Jasmin's house. I realised for the first time that he had turned the fingerless gloves into mittens and swallowed down a laugh that threatened to escape my open mouth.

Looking at the dark vehicle it all fell into place. So, that was where he had come from. It made sense now. Jasmin's husband John was American and teal eyes had a similar sort of accent. I knew that all the Carpenters had friends and family staying. The youngest sibling Jack was getting married on Christmas Eve, a week tomorrow.

Our little village had never been so busy with people.

'No... I'll be fine thanks. I need the car with me.' I pulled open my door and held my long coat tightly to my legs so it wouldn't bunch up as I sat down. I jumped in quickly, eager to leave behind my awkwardness.

'Ok... Thanks for the gloves, hope to see ya around.'

I turned the key in the ignition. I was sure I saw a couple of other words form on his lips, but I couldn't gauge what they might be. Instead of being communication, they became puffs of hot air released into the freezing evening.

Thankfully, the engine started first time and drowned out the possibility of any further conversation. I breathed out a sigh of relief as he slammed the passenger door. The closing of the door was hopefully the full stop on my embarrassing behaviour.

'Not if I see you first,' I whispered into the cold air of the car. I carefully put the car into first gear and pulled away. I couldn't help but look to the small rear-view mirror to see him standing in the middle of the lane. He had his hands cupped over his mouth as he blew warm air onto his newly acquired mittens.

I smiled to myself, before I tore my eyes away and concentrated on the road ahead.

Three

BRODY

AS THE OLDEST car I had ever seen in my life started, the roaring engine coming to life cut off my words. Reluctantly, I slammed shut her creaking passenger door. Everything about the vehicle seemed and looked unsafe. I closed my eyes, shutting down my head.

Very slowly and cautiously she pulled away. *Well at least that was something.*

Even though I hated watching her pull away from me, I felt a grin break out on my face. I was stood smiling, fucking smiling. I had no fucking idea why. The way I felt was difficult for me to decipher. The shrink said it was normal. Normal when you've spent so long faking smiles to hide the pain inside you.

I laughed, 'Me! Fucking normal?'

I blew hot air onto my freezing hands and grinned at the homemade things with the button-up flaps. Looking at them touching the black cashmere of my Burberry jacket made me laugh out loud.

It felt fucking good and I nodded at the realisation. I pushed my hands down inside my jacket pockets and exhaled, watching my hot breath turn into a cloud of condensation.

It was the fourth time today that I had gone past her old Victorian shop and the second time that, not being able to resist, I had gone inside.

Just to talk to her.

I had no idea of her name. All I knew was that I had caught sight of her first thing this morning as I went on a run through the village. The way she smiled with her eyes and laughed throwing her head right back, like she hadn't got a care in the world, caught my attention. Hearing her joking with her neighbour had made me want to look at her, to study her. As I had carried on down the quiet lane, I had twisted my head to look around the edge of the hood of my sweatshirt and I'd taken a double take.

A fucking double take!

Not being able to refuse myself, I had circled what I now knew to be the war memorial and gone slowly past her shop again. I'd stopped outside to tighten up a shoelace that wasn't even loose and taken her in as she danced around inside the old place, singing. I had never seen a more naturally beautiful woman, with a thick, chestnut coloured mane of hair and a body with curves in all the right places. I had felt my mouth fall slack at the sight of her. Her beauty was enhanced by the happiness she seemed to feel in the simple things around her, it radiated off the whole of her body. She pulled me in, like the moon pulls the tide to make it turn.

I couldn't remember the last time a woman I'd just met warranted even a second look, let alone two visits just to talk to her, in the same fucking day no less. Normally, the women I met were just a diversion, a recreational fucking pastime. They came, they went and that was just the fucking way I liked it.

But talking with her made me feel unburdened. In the few minutes we had spent together she had made me remember that life could be simple. I liked it, and I wanted more of it. She held a promise of something I had never wanted, nor expected to want in my life. I needed to get to know her better.

I watched the fucking death trap of the thing she called her car finally leave the edge of the village. I felt my nostrils flare as I inhaled sharply and clenched my fists tightly as I fought off the urge to follow her, to make sure she didn't kill herself. *Stop it, Brody... you can't control every fucking thing.*

The wind blew so strongly that flurries of snow clouded my vision and she disappeared from my view far quicker than I wanted her to.

I was pleased for her that she had somewhere to go.

And pleased for her that it seemed to be somewhere she wanted to be.

What I couldn't get my head around was the jealousy that was collecting inside my gut as it rolled itself bigger and bigger like a snowball. But, instead of being cold like snow, the ball was red hot and angry. As it rolled around, it spat out its anger like sparks from a volcano.

I was angry and jealous that a woman I had only set eyes on today, wasn't rushing to spend time with me.

I'm even more fucked up than I thought.

Four

Amy

I **PULLED INTO** the courtyard about thirty minutes later, rested my forehead down onto the steering wheel and exhaled a huge sigh of relief. What should have been a ten to fifteen-minute drive tops, had been much longer due to the difficult conditions. The snow had gusted around in the narrow lanes, creating drifts on the banks either side. My little car, with absolutely no modern technology, had struggled. To add insult to injury, my windscreen blowers had decided ten minutes into the journey to completely pack up on me. I had spent almost the entire journey with my small front windows open to clear the screen. This had made the inside of my car the temperature of an igloo. Along with the flakes of snow swirling around, my long brown hair had been blown into my mouth, up my nose and a couple of times it had even restricted my view of the road ahead. I'd spent the last twenty minutes of the journey wiping the windscreen with the chamois leather, spitting, pulling pieces of hair out of all my exposed orifices and swearing in terror at the weather conditions. I'm sure it would have looked comical if it hadn't been so terrifying.

But it was the fact I couldn't turn my brain off that had seemed the most dangerous problem.

My mind was on constant repeat of the strange day I'd had. I'd even shouted at myself at one point on the drive over to "concentrate."

Reminding myself that I needed to focus on the task of driving and not day dreaming about the stranger with the beautiful eyes.

I looked up through the restricted view of my now frozen windscreen, to see the welcoming lights of Lauren's flat shining through the Velux windows. I felt a wide smile spread over my face.

God, I need this.

I was really pleased to be here. With my nan having put herself in a home to give me some rest, it would have been a sad and lonely Christmas by myself at home. I wasn't sure she had thought about that, although she had thought about everything else.

She was a bossy one, my nan. I had been informed she was going into the home for six weeks, she had arranged the whole thing herself with the help of Dr. Carpenter. He was our family doctor and the one who had helped to diagnose her dementia three years ago. Her dementia meant that some days she was perfectly lucid, on other much more exhausting days she was completely and utterly confused. On a funnier note her filter had almost evaporated, she now swore like a trooper and used words I hadn't even realised were in her vocabulary.

One lucid day, she had written down her exact instructions, in two letters. One letter, to herself, explained why she was where she was. So, on a confused day at the care home, the staff could let her read the letter written in her own hand. It would explain to her exactly what she was doing in the home and how she had made the decision herself to be there.

I hoped it would help.

In the other letter, which she had given to me, she had stipulated that I was only allowed to visit her once a week, but could phone her every other day, but only if I really needed to. Her letter also explained how she knew the opening of The Manor as a hotel and Jack's wedding would bring life back into the village. She wanted me to join in and be part of that life and then come to tell her all about it. After I had read her explicit instructions, she had sat down and taken my hand in hers.

"Life is for living, Amy. You never quite know when that gift will be taken from you. So, grab it by the balls and ride the hell out of it."

Hugging each other we had laughed at her choice of words.

Always thinking of everyone else but herself, she had insisted that I needed the few weeks to live exactly like a thirty-three-year-old woman should be living. She hated the fact she thought I had given up on my own life to take care of her. I knew it made her sad that I wasn't married with a family of my own. Many a time we had the same conversation about her going into a care home. But I wouldn't have it, she had given me a home when I had needed it and I wasn't about to refuse her one.

Other more jokey times, we had discussed the fact that I must have "needs" and that I should be making more of an effort to take care of my said "needs." Said with a twinkle in her eye, I had known exactly what she meant.

The Velux window I was staring at suddenly swung open. The exquisitely made up face of Winter appeared in the small opening.

'AMY! AMY!... are you coming up?' She beckoned to me with her twinkling, red manicured nails. 'We have Pinot,' she teased.

I laughed at her information and flung open the car door.

'On my way. Pour me a large glass,' I shouted back.

I left my case on the passenger seat. Although Lauren had a two-bedroomed flat, the guest room was only accessible by an outside staircase. It was like it had its own private entrance and I would drag my case up there later.

I slammed the door to my car, ignoring its creaking hinges. Then I grabbed hold of the wrought iron staircase that would lead me to being the young woman my nan wanted me to be. For the first time in a long time, I realised I wanted to be her, too.

With every step I took on the black, ornate metal, my excitement began to ramp up. The shackles of the everyday worries and concerns I normally carried around with me began to break and fall away. If the steps hadn't been icy, I would have run up the last few.

The door opened as I got to it and the warmth from the small flat swept out. Winter's hand grabbed my arm as if I might be having second thoughts and pulled me inside quickly.

'Give me your coat. Your wine is on the breakfast bar.'

I complied immediately, shrugging myself out of my scarf and coat and thrusting them into her arms. I kicked off my boots and looked around for Lauren. Then I walked the few steps to the small breakfast bar that served as a dinner table for two in the small, but well thought out, flat.

I loved Lauren's space. Although her flat was in the old servant's quarters above what would have been the coach houses, she had made the small amount of square footage work for her. The whole place had been modernised and was painted in what she called "Antique lace." In one corner of the open-plan living space was the kitchen/breakfast area and the opposite corner housed a desk and chair with storage for her business paperwork. The rest of the space was filled with an array of mismatching furniture, all very deliberate. She had incorporated different fabrics and patterns, all with the same cream and dark red colouring, to give the impression that the comfortable room had been put together effortlessly. When, in fact, it had taken her ages to complete. In the centre of the room was a floor-to-ceiling, completely cylindrical log burner, roaring flames could be seen from every angle through the large glass doors.

Finally, my eyes found Lauren, spread out in the middle of the floor on her stomach. Her jean-clad legs were bent at the knees and crossed at the ankles. Her bright pink fluffy socks rubbed together as she concentrated on her work. Papers, invoices and her open laptop surrounded her.

I looked behind me to find Winter hooking up my coat on a vacant peg next to the door. Moving quickly, I grabbed my wine glass and then sidled up behind our always immaculately turned out friend. I lifted her thick dark hair away from her ear and whispered into it.

'Look, I need to ask this… Do you think her helping you, is a good idea?' I didn't need to explain to Winter, she knew precisely what I was asking. 'Every time she has found out Rafferty might possibly be at The Manor she's found some excuse to lie low. Once she even made Toby take her away for a romantic weekend.' I pulled a grimace as Winter quickly looked at me and contorted her face into a pained expression. Neither of us were fans of Toby.

Winter turned very gingerly to check Lauren wasn't watching us and answered my question, keeping her voice as low as possible. 'She was adamant she wanted to help me.' We both guiltily looked in Lauren's direction again. 'The truth is, she's the only one I trust to help me in the kitchen… but if I felt she couldn't cope with it, I would have gone elsewhere. I don't want to see her hurt again…you know that. But it was seventeen years ago. Truthfully, I think her and Raff need closure, they both need to move on. Hopefully after this weekend they can.'

I crossed my fingers on my spare hand and lifted them in between us, raising my eyebrows as I did so.

'Come on, you two. Stop whispering. What are you waiting for?' We both turned automatically and plastered "butter wouldn't melt" smiles on our faces as we moved towards Lauren. 'I've checked and reworked the spreadsheet. If all three of us pull our weight, this is all doable, just.' She finished speaking and pulled a face. 'I know you both think I'm anal, but I've made a separate list of jobs for us all. Things that need checking, collecting and hours that we're all going to actually need to work in the kitchen at The Manor, and in The Fairy Garden.' Lauren jumped up from the floor and made her way to the printer that was sat on a shelf by her desk. She picked up several pieces of paper from the tray beneath it and made her way back. She handed out the relevant sheets to us both and I briefly swept my eyes over my timings, jobs and shifts for next two days.

'Well there's not a lot of time for sleep.' I looked at them both and laughed. 'But as Nan says, "I can sleep when I'm dead." So, I'm up for it,' I added as I bent my knees and sank cross legged to the soft cream carpet.

They both sat down with me.

'We have tonight to chill out and the next two days to show the world what we're made of,' Lauren said and lifted her glass of wine towards us both.

I looked at Winter and we lifted ours to join her.

'All for one,' she said.

'And one for all,' we replied as we gulped large mouthfuls of wine and gave in to some of the apprehensive, hysterical laughter that was beginning to build up.

Five

Amy

WE MUST HAVE *been bloody mad. Drinking on a school night, when we knew what the next few days held.*

Was the first thought to go through my head, on the wave of pain created by the alarm from my phone. It was five a.m. I slapped my hand around on the empty pillow next to me to shut it up.

Finally, I found what I was searching for, pushed the right button with my eyes closed and it stopped. The relief I felt as the noise subsided was immense.

If I was lucky I'd had three hours sleep, tops.

Sharing two large bottles of wine and a double measure of Baileys should have knocked me out for the count, but I had been fuelled with excitement and adrenalin. After our chilled evening, the three of us together had pushed and pulled my case up the stairs to the guest room. With the alcohol we had consumed, we were lucky to have made it at all without breaking our necks. Several times we'd stopped, as our feet had slipped on the metal rungs, or as we were consumed with hysterics at how ridiculous we would look if anyone walked past. It had taken far longer than was normal to get the case up to my room, as all our strength had left us time and time again. But it was moments like these with my best friends, that I wouldn't miss for the world. By the time I got into the warm, comfortable bed, I had struggled to sleep.

Finally, as fast as I could, I forced myself out of bed to get on with my day. One shower, a bottle of water and two headache tablets later, I made my way downstairs to the tearooms.

I paused on the steps a third of the way down, gripping the cold, black metal and inhaled a deep breath of fresh, crisp air. The world was completely white. Behind the outbuildings, I watched as the tall evergreens moved under the weight of the snow that had fallen. It was like they were shivering with the chill of it. The only sounds that could be heard were the intermittent crack of a branch and the trees occasionally relinquishing their burden to the ground around them. It was magical. I could see no footsteps, or tyre tracks, breaking the perfect covering. It was as if the world had cleansed itself of the whole human race. The world was silent and it was breathtaking. The Manor and surrounding countryside looked like a Christmas card. It was beautiful, and for those few seconds that I stood there I felt selfish, pleased that no one else could share what I was seeing right at that moment.

I took it all in and committed it to memory. Breathing it in deep and filling my head with the beautiful sight. I knew that the next couple of days were going to be utter bedlam. I could draw on the peaceful feeling the fresh fallen snow gave me, time and time again, and I knew without a doubt it would be needed.

I continued down the steps, hesitantly breaking the snow, feeling it compress, crunch and finally give way under my shoes. I could see that Lauren was already inside the tearooms. They were already lit up with the twinkling, white fairy lights that were strung up high, and looped across every available window, mirror and flat surface that wasn't used to serve or eat from. The large arched French doors that opened out one side to the Victorian walled garden and the carpark on the other were steamed to three quarters of the way up.

'Morning!' I shouted as I pushed the main door open. I stepped briskly inside banging my snow-covered heels on the doormat and then I dropped the latch behind me. I knew it was only me and her this early in the morning. I had taken in that much as I'd let my eyes sweep over the itinerary she had printed out last night.

Gorgeous smells hit my nostrils as I entered. She'd already been busy.

'In the kitchen,' Lauren shouted back.

I walked towards her voice, taking off my coat and putting it away in the small staff room as I went. The kitchen was absolutely boiling. I could feel my face break into an involuntary sweat as the heat hit me.

'Bloody hell, how long have you been here?' I lifted up my arm to check the ancient watch on my wrist. It was just after half past five. I wasn't late. I scanned the worktops and cooling racks, they were already heavily laden.

A guilty looking Lauren, with flour all over her face and in her hair, turned to answer me. 'A while.' Then she smiled.

'You haven't slept at all, have you?' I questioned, crossing my arms on top of the camel coloured, bobble cardigan I had placed over my white blouse.

She shook her head in response. 'Once you and Winter left, I sobered up quickly, my brain wouldn't shut up. The tearooms are completely booked out today from ten a.m. right through until we close. I knew just how much needed to be baked.' She paused for a moment trying to read my expression as I stood in the doorway shaking my head. 'So, I came down and got on with it.' She turned back around to face the worktop in front of her, and once again squeezed the icing bag with just the right amount of pressure. Continuing like the expert she was, she set to decorate the cupcakes set out in front of her.

'How do you expect to last the next few days on no sleep at all?'

'Don't be so dramatic, Amy... I'll be fine, we're in our thirties not our seventies,' she answered, throwing a smile at me over her shoulder.

'Point taken.' I shrugged my shoulders at her. 'Have you had breakfast?' I asked as I walked further into the furnace-like room.

'No, not yet. I've just got this and one more batch to decorate. Then all the cakes, pastries and deserts will be finished. So, when I leave here in... What's the time?' She shook her head, seemingly bewildered by her inability to read the hands on the steamed-up clock face.

'About twenty to six,' I replied, still puzzled by her motives for working all night.

'Ah, okay. So, when I leave here in about three hours everything should be ready for the day ahead.'

'You can finish decorating the cupcakes, you're much better at that than me. I'll cook us breakfast and we can sit down and eat together. Then, you are off upstairs for a rest and a shower before you join Winter over at The Manor.'

'Well, I...'

I held up my hand to her. 'Not taking no for an answer.' I pulled out my schedule for the next few days from my cardigan pocket and I pinned it onto the neat corkboard displaying health and safety posters. 'Anyway, we're still waiting on deliveries to complete the sandwiches...and you know as well as I do that freshly made sandwiches are always better than those made earlier.' I grimaced at her. 'Nothing worse than an immaculately cut finger sandwich with curled up, dry edges.' I raised my eyebrows at her.

'What would I do without you?' she asked, and I knew she wasn't questioning my sandwich making knowledge, but my skills at keeping her calm in the emotional crisis that I knew was threatening to consume her.

I could hear the phone literally ringing off the wall in the back office next to the kitchen. God knows where any of the extensions were hiding.

I gently placed down the cake stand I was carrying into the middle of the table of four, not wanting to appear in a rush in front of the customers.

'Anything else I can get you?' I asked with a smile. I watched as with mouths full of deliciousness, they all smiled back their answer and shook their heads.

I moved away as quickly as I could through the bustling room.

Opening the door, I flew in as quickly as my feet would take me, just as the phone stopped ringing.

'Typical!' I exclaimed, slamming my hand down on the desk.

I heard the answer phone click into action. After hearing Lauren's welcoming greeting, I heard a voice relay exactly what I didn't want or need to hear. A message that told me what Lauren's finely tuned spreadsheets had absolutely no leeway for, a problem. When we hadn't any available time to allow for contingencies, let alone problems. The message was from the fishmongers and the male voice explained that their delivery van had broken down and they wouldn't be able to schedule a delivery for the next three days. On the plus side, he would stay open for us to come and pick up our order, if we arrived in the next two hours.

I poked my head around the door and peaked into the tearooms. Everything was going well. All the staff were in and the food had been prepared for the next few hours of bookings.

So, I made the decision.

Winter and Lauren would be well under way now preparing and cooking for tomorrow. They needed the delivery and so did the tearooms. I would go and pick up the salmon for us and the many other things I knew Winter was bound to have ordered for tomorrow's opening.

I just hoped it would all fit into my small car.

It would just have to, even if I tied it to the roof.

BRODY

FOR THE FIRST time in a very long time, things felt right with my world. *I wasn't fucking telling the guys that they'd been right about putting down some roots here! Fuck no!* I thought, as a shit eating grin spread over my face. I hadn't known it, but I'd been searching for this comfortable feeling for a long time, who'd have thought I'd find it in the country of my childhood?

My bare forearms were crossed over themselves on top of the steering wheel. I could feel the hard, leather-covered wheel underneath my chest as I leant as far forward as possible. I was staring through my large windscreen, just gazing at the countryside around me. This part of the country was seriously fucking beautiful. Some of the snow that had fallen for most of the night had started to melt in the bright midday sunshine. Other parts of the road hadn't seen any sun at all, and the snow had turned to ice in the shade. The feeling of contentment had increased as I was out driving around in my brand new Land Rover. I was fucking pleased with the new vehicle. I had several other cars garaged in America that I never drove, but this one meant more than all of them put together. I'd wanted to own a Land Rover Defender since I was a small boy living in the UK.

It brought back happy memories of spending carefree days with my family. Memories that for far too fucking long I had buried deep inside.

Truth be told, I was also driving around just trying to stay away from all the madness and the unrelenting preparations going on at The Manor. I just wanted the place up and running. Falham Manor was going to be the first of many hotels we were about to renovate and open in the UK and Europe. It was our "getting older and for various reasons wanting to put down some roots" plan. A plan that after what felt like a million fucking years on the road, we all desperately needed. The Manor, as the locals called it, was going to be our home base here, our template, our flagship. So, rightly or wrongly, although we had a fantastic management team in place, we were more involved with this one than we would be with any of the other renovations we had planned. Eventually, I even hoped to build myself a home, hidden somewhere in the acres of grounds that had come with the place.

Raff's sister had been given the contract for the opening event, it would give her small catering business the injection of cash it needed. After fucking years in the world of the cut throat music business, we looked after the few members of family and friends we had, before all others.

Yesterday, we had all been called in to attend a last-minute meeting. Winter had told us that three chefs had gone sick with some goddamn awful sickness bug. She had also done a fantastic job of convincing us that she had already sorted the problem out and guaranteed that nothing we had planned for the opening would be compromised. She reminded me a hell of a lot of her brother, Raff. He was always in charge of us, always the grown-up when through the years we had needed him to sort through some serious fucking shit. Only thing was, he hadn't been too receptive to her emergency plan and who she had called in to help her. I knew exactly why.

I was happy to leave it to the people we were paying to get on with it, and not to get too involved. In fact, I had only just about managed to attend the meeting, in between my many goddamn visits to the nearby village of Falham.

I squeezed my eyes shut quickly, trying to remove her from my head. It was fucking useless. An image of her had taken root, like writing a song consumed me. I still couldn't get her out of my head, even now. It was another reason for me driving around. Everything about her I had committed to memory. Her eyes, the way her rich brown hair shone as it curled around her shoulders. The woman inspired me. I remembered the way she had reacted to me, and I had gone over and over the few words we had spoken. Even though I knew she thought she had embarrassed herself in front of me, she couldn't have been more wrong. I could hear the slight amusement in her voice at our back and forth banter. If I was honest with myself, I had enjoyed the few minutes I had spent with her yesterday more than anything I could vaguely recall. She intrigued me so much that I had wanted to go back to the little shop again today just to check that she hadn't returned and opened it up.

I had no idea what the fuck was up with me?

I had wanted two things as a teenager, to write and sing my own music, and to own a Defender like my dad had driven around on the base. I had achieved them both and now it appeared I was hell bent on something else.

I wanted her.

But, I had no idea who she was. The whole thing was fucking crazy.

What had really fucked me up and caused me to spend a very sleepless night, was that I had no idea who she was with now. Who was the ungrateful bastard she had rushed off to be with last night? He sure as hell hadn't married her. For the first time ever, I'd looked at a ring finger to check. No ring on her finger, so as far as I was concerned she was available.

Was he good to her? I wasn't so fucking sure. She looked like she could do with someone to look after her. If I found out he wasn't good to her, or didn't look after her the way I could see she needed, he was going to find himself with one hell of a fucking fight on his hands to keep hold of her.

What man would allow his woman out on a night like last night, driving around in that unsafe crock of shit. If she was mine, I'd have driven over to pick her up.

If she was mine?

I'd never allowed anyone I'd ever been with before to think I was even monogamous, let alone let them think they were mine. Because I had never been, nor did I want them to be. It came with the job. As did everything dysfunctional. We'd had everything thrown at us from a very young age, money, drugs, alcohol, and sex in various forms, but rarely anything real. It had been so bad at some points that I couldn't tell night from day. It had taken a couple of deaths, and the promise of more to come, for us to sort out our shit. But after we'd all made it through to the other side, we made sure we looked after our own.

I wanted her, and with all the years I had spent with the world at my feet never hearing the answer no, I was a spoilt bastard. I wasn't prepared to take no for an answer.

When The Manor had been officially opened, and we had time to concentrate on something else, I was going to find her.

I made myself that promise.

I heard myself exhale loudly as I tried once again to get my mind onto something else.

I looked up at the shining road ahead, squinting behind my Aviators, and I spotted something else on the road except me. I could see the back end of a small, pale blue car on the right-hand side of the road. After slowing down as I came nearer, I realised it had probably lost control on the ice. Some of the narrow English lanes had ditches to either side of them, for rain water, and the front of the car had gone down into one. As exhaust fumes were still blowing out, I could see it had only just happened. I peered harder to get a better look at the stranded vehicle.

'FUCK NO!' I exclaimed, slamming my left hand down hard on the steering wheel.

Unbelievable. It was hers. My heart accelerated quickly until it was banging hard in the confines of my chest, at the thought of what I might find.

I clicked on my hazards and slowed down to a stop. Not thinking about anything else, I flung open the door and jumped out to help her.

'You OK?' I shouted as I wrenched open the creaking door. Holding the door open wide and gripping onto the roof, I bent down to her. My eyes took a quick look around. Thank fuck, I couldn't see any blood. Relief flooded my system as she started to turn to look at me, and I started to smile at her in reassurance.

Then a strong fucking smell of fish hit me straight at the back of the fucking throat. My stomach convulsed and I coughed away the feeling to retch.

Fuck, I hate fucking fish.

Reeling, I moved my head to the left to breathe in some much-needed fresh air.

'I don't know what happened...' she answered. 'She was going along really well, I was taking it carefully when suddenly the car started veering to the left and the back end slid. It caused me to spin and I ended up here. I don't think I'm hurt.'

I listened to her explaining what had happened. She was shocked. She was talking fast, as if she was just trying to come to terms with it all herself. At the same time, I put my hand inside the car and switched off the ignition.

'Okay, just stay still a minute. I'm gonna get you out, but I need to know you haven't hurt yourself first. I want you to breathe in and out slowly and when you feel a bit calmer, I need you to concentrate on how your body feels.' I took hold of one of her hands in mine as she steadied herself.

Shit! I was struggling hard not to keep imagining how her body felt.

I became a lost cause when the zing of electricity where we touched, zipped up my arm and quickly around the whole of my body. I'd been on stage in some of the biggest fucking venues in the world. I'd consumed, injected and snorted some of the most expensive drugs in existence. But, as I stood there holding her small hand in mine, I had never felt so fucking alive. My eyes searched for hers through my Aviators just to see if she felt it too. Sure enough, her head snapped fully around, her deep brown eyes were staring straight back at me and her mouth had fallen open.

'I feel strange,' she muttered, looking at where our hands were connected.

'You do?' I checked with her again, trying to concentrate on what I needed to do to help her.

I watched as she blinked several times over as if her eyes were dry, or she was trying to clear her vision. 'No... No, sorry. It must be just the adrenalin leaving my system.' She pulled her hand away from mine. 'I'm fine, everything feels fine.' Reluctantly I let her hand go and stood up.

'That's good.' I cleared my throat. 'Look we need to get you out of the car. When you're ready, I want you to very slowly pull yourself up and out, using my hands to help you. If you feel pain anywhere, stop immediately.'

'Okay.'

Her hands came out of the door to find both of mine. I ignored the reaction I felt as our skin came into contact again.

'Okay, swing out your legs one at a time.' Immediately she complied with my instructions. I watched as black heeled shoes came into view, followed by shapely calves where her coat parted. Her calves were covered in what I could only hope, in my fucking dreams, were fine stockings. Her black skirt had ridden up high revealing a perfect pair of thighs, and I should know as I was undeniably a fucking leg man.

Fuck. Concentrate asshole!

I willed my dick to stop twitching, just so I could concentrate on helping her and not nailing her.

She edged herself to the side of the seat and after taking a deep breath she stood up right in front of me. For a few seconds, we just stood and looked at each other, with our hands clasped tightly together in the tight space in between us.

I inhaled quickly, the smell of musk hit my needy nostrils. FUCK! Now I know how she smells too. Her subtle perfume was perfect for her, not floral or fruity. The musk accentuated her natural scent, it was heady. I fought off the urge to run my tongue up her neck or over her wrist just to taste it on her skin.

What the actual fuck?

'Thank you so much for your help. I feel alright, a little shaken.' I didn't answer her, and again she pulled a hand away from mine as she turned to look at her car. 'I don't know what I'm going to tell my nan, this car is her pride and joy. Yet another thing she's going to lose.'

I had no fucking idea what she was talking about, as I was still struggling to bring myself to heel, but I agreed wholeheartedly about the fucking death trap of a car. 'Yeah, I think you're right. It'll probably have to be scrapped. We won't know what going down into the ditch will have done to the sub-frame, at least not until it's in a garage. But the car's old, so I predict it'll be bad.' What I didn't say was that I was gonna make sure the fucking thing was off the road for good, she deserved better, so much better.

'Oh.' She sighed with sad resignation and that small almost inaudible noise went straight to my cock.

I realised she was starting to shiver and for the first time I comprehended just how fucking freezing I was, in only a T-shirt. 'Come on, you could go into shock. We need to get you out of the cold. We're going the same way, I'll give you a lift.' I led her by the one hand I still held, around to the other side of my Land Rover. I could feel her feet slipping on the icy patches, the soles of those cock-taunting heels she was wearing just weren't coping. So, without even thinking I slipped my arm around her waist and pulled her closer to me. As her body relinquished its independence to mine, for a split second I froze. She felt good there, really fucking good. We felt in tune as we continued around the front of the car. I pulled open the door and took a deep calming breath. As I exhaled, I forced myself to behave like a fucking gentleman and not to let my basic instincts take over. Winning my internal battle, I released her and went to help her inside.

'WAIT!' she suddenly screamed. In response to her outburst, I opened her black coat to look up and down her body, just checking if she had been hurt in the accident and that I hadn't missed anything. All I could see was a pretty, lacy white bra through an almost see through white shirt. 'Thanks, but I can't go with you. I know you've been kind and helpful, but I don't know you from Adam... Look, I can ring a friend and they'll come and pick me up.'

I dropped the edges of her coat and they fell together again, effectively covering up my view.

'Seriously?' I felt my eyes open wide at her. 'You'd prefer to freeze than risk getting in the car with me?'

'Well that and there's the fish. I definitely can't leave here without the fish.'

A strange thing happened there on that ice-covered lane. She smiled at me. Her smile was seriously the best thing I had seen in a very long time.

Fuck my life. The girl I want lands in my lap and brings fucking fish with her. But for that smile, I'd do anything.

Without even thinking, I opened the glove box and pushed the condom box I had stashed in there to the back and covered it up with the car manual. Then I grabbed my ridiculously expensive leather driving gloves. I closed the glove box and walked back to her car.

I heard her giggle as I made the first of four runs back and forth, between her car and mine.

If only my dad could see me now, I was ruining my new car smell with stinking fucking fish and all for a smile, he'd die in his grave laughing.

As the last of the apparently sealed, polystyrene boxes went into the back, I peeled off my now stinking leather gloves and flung them on top, slamming the door as quickly as I could. It wouldn't help at all and I knew it, as a Defender didn't have separate compartments like most cars. Sure, they were fucking beasts, with a safety record second to none, but everything was in the same section. The smell of fish would invade everywhere.

I placed her warning triangle down behind her car, and phoned the police alerting them to the accident.

'Now will you get in?' I questioned, leaning my head to one side.

She laughed nervously. 'Ermmm.' I could still hear the hesitation in her voice. 'Yes. Thank you, the fish is really important. I need to get it to Falham Manor if that's okay with you?'

I walked to the passenger side and helped her up into the vehicle, holding her elbow.

'Yep,' I laughed. 'I know where that is... but you're more important, you could do with getting home first.' I moved quickly around to my side, jumped in and started the engine.

I pushed the gearstick into first and began to pull away. 'So, where do I take you?'

'Please, the fish first and then I can walk.'

'Like hell you will… I'll deliver the fish and then I'll deliver you.' My voice lowered to a growl and I glanced over to her quickly, wanting to get my point across. I removed my eyes much quicker than I wanted. In the weather conditions, I couldn't afford to take my eyes off the road for too long.

'I don't normally get into cars with strangers, you know? But I feel as though I know you? Or maybe we've met before?' Her face scrunched up as she thought and questioned me. I could see her out of the corner of my eye, still staring at the side of my face as we began to gain some speed up the narrow lane.

Here it comes! One by one my facial muscles began to tense up as she studied my profile, until I felt my tic spasm above my cheekbone.

3, 2, 1… and nothing.

She didn't recognise me. I slowly relaxed with every small and slow breath out. The knowledge that I was a nobody to her, made me happy and warm inside. I didn't think she'd recognised me yesterday either and it was fucking uplifting.

I. FUCKING. LOVED. IT.

Taking a huge risk, I lifted my Aviators away from my eyes and placed them in their holder above the mirror and turned towards her again.

'OH! It's you!' she shrieked as our eyes came into contact for the first time today. For a split second, I thought my risk had backfired on me. I stiffened up waiting for the normal, exhausting fucking reaction.

'It's you from yesterday. I know you weren't particularly taken with me when we met.' She threw a look over her shoulder to the fish in the back. 'Now I've ruined your plans for the day by crashing my antiquated car and spoilt the inside of yours. You must think I'm the most annoying person ever?' I took in her worried expression and at the same time I exhaled completely in relief and shook my head.

I laughed out loud. 'You couldn't have got that more wrong. I think you're the most refreshing person I've met in a long time.' In my peripheral view, I could see her studying me closely, confused by my last statement.

I felt my stomach lurch as the heating I'd switched on for her recycled the fucking fish smell straight back under my nose.

'Hold on,' I muttered. I couldn't fucking take anymore, I couldn't take in another breath. I flicked the switch and made the window open. Any amount of fucking cold air was worth suffering, to take away the all-consuming smell of fucking fish. Even at the risk of freezing my ass off. As the cool wind entered my side of the vehicle, I inhaled deeply trying to rid my nostrils of the foul stench.

Then I remembered something and leaning down I reached to the side of me, searching around with my fingers. Finally, I found what I was looking for. I pulled them out and put them on over the rings on my fingers, feeling the wool of the blue, knitted gloves snag on the metal.

I heard her giggle again as she took in the sight of me wearing them.

'Did you have no idea?' A quick look at her showed her gently shaking her head. 'I came into your nan's shop twice yesterday, just to see you. These... are definitely not my choice.'

I picked up speed as the road ahead widened and I pulled back the gearstick into fourth, loving the feeling of power I felt as we pulled ahead. Then I looked over at her again. Her eyes were still focussed on me in what looked like disbelief. Her cheeks had a flush of colour in them, making her look even more beautiful.

'You did?' she questioned.

'Uh, huh.'

'But I gave you an in, and you certainly didn't show any interest in buying me drink.'

I looked at her again and gave her a reassuring smile. Her cheeks gained a little bit more colour. 'I can think of much more effective ways of getting to know you, other than consuming alcohol.' I let those words just resonate for a few seconds.

'Oh yes, and what would that be?' I saw her fidget in her seat and then I saw the start of a frown on her forehead.

'Don't worry, little girl... I'm not the big bad wolf.' I smiled over at her. 'Well not right at this minute, anyway.'

I looked over at her again, waggled my eyebrows and laughed.

'I believe you.' She smiled.

'Well, now we've established that I'm not really a stranger, although I can't swear to not being just a bit strange.' I squinted and took one blue, fingerless-gloved hand off the steering wheel. Holding my index finger and thumb about an inch away from each other, I smiled at her.

'Wearing those... you'd have to be,' she replied, glancing at my hands again.

'Hmmm... Anyway, I hear there's a tearoom near The Manor, you gonna let me treat ya to a late lunch, we could get to know each other better there?' I gave her a quick wink as I let my eyes once again find hers.

She nodded back her answer. 'Yes, okay. I think that could be arranged.'

Her laughter filled the inside of the vehicle and it was worth every single fucking cent I was going to have to pay to get the fucking smell of fish out.

Seven

Amy

I WATCHED FROM the comfort of the oxblood coloured, leather interior of his car. I was under instruction to stay where I was to keep warm. I wasn't used to doing as I was told, nor was I used to being looked after. It was an unfamiliar feeling and one I realised quite quickly that I liked, unfortunately. I watched as he unloaded the fish and carried them into the back kitchen at The Manor.

My body had stopped shaking. I wasn't sure if the shakes had been from the accident, the cold, or the breathtaking man who had rescued me. I warmed my hands on the car heater as I watched him, in a loose white T-shirt, black slim-fitting jeans and heavy looking black boots, carry the boxes in.

I knew when we had met yesterday that he was going to be stunning, from the small glimpse I had seen, but now I was having trouble averting my eyes. The beautiful eyes that had captured me yesterday were still the icing on the cake. Now, I also knew that they were framed by thick dark eyebrows, which made them stand out even more. Today had revealed a square jaw, a couple of days' worth of stubble, dark brown, nearly black hair that was just long enough to curl slightly over his ears and at the nape of his neck. The list of his attributes, in my eyes, was seemingly endless. Those same eyes were now caught between his bare tattooed arms, as they flexed under the weight of the fish, and the severe expression he had on his face as he willed himself not to breathe in. I was drooling at the sight of him, but also wanted to laugh out loud at the expression on his face.

He was new around here, he felt like a breath of fresh air. Living in a small village meant we all knew everyone thereabouts and sometimes that was extremely claustrophobic. Although he had found his way to The Manor with ease. I was now absolutely convinced he had to be here for Jack's wedding.

Whatever he was here for, and for however long he was around, I made up my mind as he walked backwards and forwards, that for once, I was going to go with the flow. He had said I was refreshing and the way he had looked at me several times over, I had felt attractive for the first time in a while. I selfishly needed something to energise my dull, monotonous life. I didn't need attachment, or commitment. I also didn't need anything more than what we could both gain from a few days in each other's company and perhaps, if I was lucky, each other's beds.

The last load was now inside The Manor, all that was left in his car was the small package for the tearooms.

I returned the smile he was giving me as he jogged back to the vehicle. His hand found the handle and the door had just opened slightly when I heard a male voice call out to him.

'Daniel…' The door closed on a strong blast of cold wind and cut off me hearing anymore of the conversation.

So, that was my stranger's name. I let his name roll off my tongue. It felt surprisingly comfortable there. Daniel swung around quickly to talk to the guy who came running outside.

Maybe, The Manor had paying guests before the official opening. I knew there were quite a few Americans over and if it was ready to go, then you'd have to be mad to refuse the business. There I was again! My business trained head kicked in. *Turn off your brain, Amy.*

I couldn't make out the conversation, but found myself peering closer, trying to earwig at their interaction. The other guy was blond, around the same height as Daniel and he was also remarkably good looking. He had a checked shirt on over a T-shirt, and after spotting me staring at them both, his arm came up to give me a cheeky wave. They were obviously friends, I could see by the grin on his face that he was now teasing Daniel about me being in the car.

I moved back further into my seat as Daniel turned around to look at me, following his friend's wave. I wrapped my coat around me a little tighter and quickly averted my eyes.

'For goodness sake, Amy, grow up,' I mumbled into the empty car, hardly moving my lips in case he saw me talking to myself. 'You're a grown woman, you're allowed to be caught looking. Just own it.' Despite the pep talk, my head refused to turn back towards them.

Finally, the door reopened and he jumped in and on instinct I turned to look. Once again, I had difficulty tearing my eyes away from him. This time I was taking in just how well his jeans fitted as I watched them pull over his firm thighs. To me he was the absolute perfect package and then some.

'Okay, let's go back to yours, shall we?' he stated as we pulled away.

Yes please, I thought with a giggle that somehow I just managed to internalise.

'I'm staying above the tearooms you mentioned earlier.'

'Handy, that means you can't refuse me... so you're gonna let me take you for that late lunch?' he asked again as he turned right, steering the car down the long driveway between The Manor and the outbuildings.

Hearing the word lunch, I glanced at the digitalised clock on the dashboard. I was twenty minutes later than I had said I would be. I knew just how full the tearooms were going to be right now. I was wondering if Kirsty was getting concerned about where I was. We had enough staff, but not enough to cover for the extended break I had now taken because of the accident.

'About that, Daniel.' I looked up and watched as he turned his head in question, for a moment he just looked at me and then he smiled.

'What? Don't tell me I don't deserve to take you for a cup of tea after all that I've just been through.' He laughed although it sounded a bit nervous.

'What do you mean, all that YOU'VE been through?' I smiled my question at him.

'At least tell me your name?' Daniel didn't answer my question, but in a much softer tone he asked me his own question.

'Amy... Amy Harper,' I answered.

'Amy,' he copied. 'Well, Amy Harper, just in case you hadn't noticed I HATE fish.' He lifted the front of his T-shirt, still wearing the blue gloves my nan had made, and sniffed at the fabric. 'I now stink of the fucking disgusting stuff.' He grinned at me.

'Oh... For a minute, I thought you were going to say you were allergic to it.' I relaxed and laughed at him.

'Right,' he grinned mischievously at me as we pulled up in front of The Fairy Garden and he switched off the engine. 'Is that what I need to say, to get you to check me all over for a rash?' He winked at me to drive the point home.

Laughter burst from me as his hand came up to hold onto my seat. Using his grip on my seat he twisted himself sideways to check my reaction.

I looked quickly at his hand so near to my shoulder. 'You can try it,' I countered with a smile. 'What I was going to say was, that the tearooms are fully booked this afternoon.'

His forehead creased a little. 'That's a shame,' he sighed. 'How the hell do ya know?'

'My cousin owns the place. I'm in charge of it this weekend while she works up at The Manor with our friend Winter. The small packet of salmon still left in the car is for the sandwiches I'm going to need to make almost immediately.'

'So, that's it? I've rescued you and all that shit and you're giving me the brush off?' He smiled at me.

'It's not a brush off. It's just that I'm going to be in the kitchen for most of the afternoon.' I looked as he rolled over his bottom lip at me like a sulky child. 'Oh, come on... Do you think that's going to work?' I felt a grin spread over my flushed cheeks.

He nodded.

On impulse, I reached over and pushed his lip back up and into place, trying to completely ignore the strange feeling that travelled between us every time we touched. What I couldn't ignore though was the response my body had. I dropped my hand quickly and changed the subject.

'Come on then, I suppose you deserve a sandwich.'

'And cake?'

I shook my head at him, relishing just how light I felt joking around with him.

'Yes. You're a big kid! *And* cake.'

'You know it makes sense. Lead the way.' I watched as Daniel pulled the black beanie he had been wearing yesterday firmly down onto his head and then he jumped out.

By the time I opened the car door, he was there to help me down the step. I became aware as I twisted to get out, that my body ached from the accident and I winced a little.

'Maybe I should just take you straight upstairs?' He lifted one eyebrow at me in question as his hands found my forearms and he helped me gently down the step. Then he smirked as he saw me take in his words.

'Mmmmm... That's not happening. Lauren is counting on me. I'm not letting her down. That's the reason I went to pick up the fish today, she's relying on me this weekend.'

'Ah, that figures,' he mumbled as his face fleetingly took on a thoughtful expression.

'Sorry?'

'Nothing… Okay, right, I'll just stick around for a while after you've fed me, just to check you're alright.'

'You don't need to.' I stopped thinking about his previous comment and focussed on the fact that the last thing I wanted, was him feeling like he had been lumbered with me.

'I may not need to, but, Amy, please understand… I want to.'

With his hands still holding my forearms I looked up into his face. For a few seconds, I couldn't find the right words. It felt like his teal eyes were staring deep down inside of me. What he was searching for I hadn't a clue. But what I did know was, I liked him holding me and whatever he was looking for, I wanted him to find it in me.

'Come on then, "Oh knight in shining armour," follow me.'

Eight

BRODY

I **KNEW I** was comprehensively fucked.

I'd been sitting in the corner of the small, spotless kitchen, eating my own fucking weight in sandwiches with the crusts off, pastries and cubes of sweet jellies. I'd finally topped it all off with several pieces of cake. The food in this place was everything I'd heard it was, and I had stuffed my face with far too much. My plate had been refilled several times over. As a very grateful Amy had replaced the food I had already eaten as she busied herself around the kitchen.

But it wasn't the food that held my attention, but my own personal waitress. In fact, it seemed my new favourite pastime was watching Amy. I'd looked at her from every given fucking angle. The way she moved as she flew around the kitchen was the best fucking sight ever. Occasionally, I'd get a glimpse of her soft skin as her shirt rode up away from her skirt, as she stretched for something out of reach. But the unsurpassed view was when she was bent over in front of me. The sexist male in me knew he would kill to be the one who she allowed to run their hands over that ass.

What did they say? The best sort of women were cooks in the kitchen and whores in the bedroom?

Fuck me… the thoughts in my head are turning me into a sexist bastard.

I squeezed my eyes shut tight and cleared the thought, she was all of that and so much more. The white shirt, black above-the-knee fitted skirt, and cock-charming heels all made sense now. It was the uniform that all the staff in the tearooms had on. But the stockings I was absolutely convinced she was wearing, were all her. Yeah, after a hell of a lot of looking, I was still fucking going there.

I finished my last piece of chocolate fudge cake and licked around my lips in appreciation. Once again, my eyes looked to her shapely legs and I was convinced I could see the small bumps of the metal catches on her garter belt. I'd been knocking green bottles off a wall in my head just to keep my dick from making an appearance as we spent time together. She made me feel like a fucking fourteen-year-old.

We hadn't spoken much. She was too busy and, truth be told, I was far too busy gawping at her. I had found out that she had a degree in business management. She'd told me like I needed to understand that although this small area of Kent was her life and contained all the people she loved, she was capable of more, but had just chosen differently. She intrigued me and I wanted to know more about her, but for now it would have to wait.

'That was great, Amy, thanks.' I pushed my empty plate away from me and shifted my ass on the stool I was sitting on. I was trying to find a bit of space in my jeans, as they fought to contain my once again expanding cock.

Ten green bottles hanging on the wall. Ten green bottles… Come on, you fucker, don't embarrass me now! Who would have thought that watching someone bake could be so erotic.

'You're welcome,' she called over her shoulder as she rolled out some more pastry.

Her voice washed over me and I inhaled deeply. That was it, it wasn't *someone* baking. It was watching *her* baking that affected me.

I leant back on the stool I was sat on, trying to rest my shoulders in the corner of the room. It was fucking uncomfortable; my shoulders were far too wide to fit. But I wasn't prepared to stand up, she might think I was getting ready to go and that was far from the truth. In the seclusion of the busy kitchen with Amy, I felt content. In the warmth of the small room, I appreciated the peace and quiet away from the world. The busy world full of people that wanted a piece of me was no further than ten feet away. But here with a woman I hardly knew and one that certainly didn't know me, I was completely at home and comfortable.

'It's warm in here, I think you could lose the hat.' I watched her smile as she spoke the words that broke through my thoughts.

'I'm good,' I lied. I knew that when I did eventually peel myself away from the cool wall she would be able to see that my white T-shirt was soaked, but I felt the hat was necessary. Occasionally another member of staff would bolt in, collect the trays and dishes of food off the chrome racks and then disappear out through the door just as quickly. I had answered their greetings from under the hat, behind either stuffing my face or from the cover of the newspaper I had found on top of the stool. Their eyes had lingered on me for much longer than I wanted them to. I'd felt uneasy under their perusal but also euphoric, because I'd quickly realised what it meant. Although they all seemed to know Amy well, it appeared seeing her with a man was uncommon.

I was floating on air with that fucking insight. It shelved my fears from yesterday and the jealousy that had kept me awake last night. She had friends and family that cared about her. But no man in her life and I was fucking thankful.

'You still feeling okay?' I asked her as I crossed my arms over my chest and shifted on the uncomfortable fucking stool for what must have been the millionth time.

'Uh, huh... I'm...' She nodded her answer to me as she concentrated on what she was trying to achieve. Her hands were covered in flour as she rolled the pastry out onto the cold marble slab. As she pushed her hands forward again, shaping the pasty just the way she wanted, I watched as a piece of her thick hair that had been previously tied up and firmly placed under the small paper hat she was wearing, fell free. It fell straight into her line of sight. She turned to me smiling as she tried to blow the piece of errant hair away from her mouth and tried to answer my question. 'Urrghhh.'

'Hold on,' I said, laughing as the piece of hair waved around annoyingly in front of her face making her eyes cross together as she tried to blow it back to where it had come from.

I pushed myself off the stool, hearing it rock back against the wall in the corner with force, and I made the couple of steps over to her. She removed her hands from the pastry on the slab and turned to face me. She held her dirty hands up and out wide, like she was surrendering to her fate.

Oh baby, you know it makes sense.

I picked up the piece of hair between my thumb and forefinger and tucked it behind her ear. Having been given silent permission to touch her my fingers stilled, almost glued to the spot. Our bodies froze in the proximity to each other's and my eyes drifted down to hers. At first, she smiled in amusement at her predicament. Then the smile faded and her pulse accelerated under my fingertips. Her beautiful face had dustings of flour in various places and the pull was just too fucking strong to ignore anymore. I made my fingers move, running them down behind her ear and then out over her jaw. I realised that I was touching her more tentatively than I had ever touched another woman.

I had no fucking idea why.

Almost on instinct her eyes blinked and closed fleetingly, then they opened to find mine as she leant into my touch.

My fingers found their way to her chin and I lifted her face up to meet mine.

'You've got flour on here.' I kissed her gently on the cheek and heard a tiny sigh leave the small fissure in between her parted lips. It gave me all the permission I needed to carry on. 'And here,' I softly kissed her forehead, 'and loads of the fucking stuff on here.' I ran my lips down her nose, kissing the tip, and was rewarded with a small smile. 'God knows how, but it's also found its way here, too.' I twisted my head to the side, lowering myself down to reach the base of her neck, where her shirt ended and her skin began. Flicking out my tongue I ran the very tip of it slowly up to just below her ear, taking in the taste of her skin and her subtle perfume.

Changing the pace, I quickly sucked the lobe of her ear into my mouth and allowed my teeth to gently nip her flesh. The gasp that freed itself from her lips fed my soul with expectation and hope. I released her lobe with a small pop and moved myself in front of her again. I could still taste her skin on my tongue, the faint traces of her musky perfume tempted my taste buds. I restrained myself, with our lips barely millimetres apart. For a few seconds, we were immobilized by the strength of the connection between us and then I gave in and sank my lips to hers.

I'd been dreaming of kissing her since I first saw her, I was going to tease and tempt her to open up, but that wasn't how it went at all. As soon as our needy flesh found each other's, the urge to take was far too strong to fight. She crashed her body into mine. Her hands found their way up to either side of my neck as her pastry covered fingers held me to her, in our mutual desperation. With our mouths fused together, taking everything we needed from each other, I walked her backwards quickly, until we reached yet another work surface.

My arms wrapped tightly around her body, making her full, soft breasts push firmly into my chest. Standing there almost fused together as one body, I could feel how she was trying to draw in small gasps of air. Releasing my hold on her body, but not my mouth on her warm, full lips, I ran my hands down her sides until they found the globes of that full ass I had been wanting to touch earlier. Both of my hands moved on instinct as I began to inch up her black skirt. I picked her up and then sat her down on the work surface. I wanted her legs open wide enough to welcome me. I moved in between them as our tongues continued to duel. Then I ran my needy hands up the outside of her legs until I found where the fine covering ended and her hot skin began.

I fucking knew it! Fuck!

The awareness that I'd been right all along nearly had me unzipping my pants and freeing my dick to take her right there and fucking then. *Nine fucking green bottles...* All the time my mouth kept up its assault on hers and she answered me back as an equal.

'Ooops sorry!' we heard from the side of us, as another of the women working today walked in to collect more platters of the prepared food. 'Don't mind me,' we heard her call out as she exited with the required goods, and the swing door shut behind her.

Amy broke our kiss and I reluctantly let her. I leant my forehead to hers as we both drew in calming breaths. Then she began to giggle like a schoolgirl at getting caught. I smiled down at her again and drew her back into my arms. She stayed there for a few seconds, then she removed her hands from my neck and ran them down to my biceps, pushing me slightly away from her.

'That was...' She attempted to explain and I smiled at her lack of words.

'Yep, it was.' I winked at her reassuringly as our breathing slowly began to normalise.

'I'm sorry, Daniel, but I really do need to get on.' I released one arm from her body and lifted my hand to her face. I ran my thumb ring over her bottom lip and watched it pucker under my ministration.

I moved my eyes back to hers. *Eight fucking green bottles...*

'Yeah, I understand. But, you need to understand this, this is just the start of us, Amy. We both want this... I'm coming back later.' I lifted her back down to the floor, gave her a chaste kiss on her swollen lips, and confident she felt the same way, I started to back away towards the kitchen door.

'I'd like you to,' she answered almost on a whisper.

'Good. What time do ya finish?' My face broke out into a huge grin at her words.

'We close up at around seven, but I'll have some bits to do after,' she answered as I watched her smooth her black skirt back down over those fucking stockings. I fought to tear my eyes back up to her face.

'That's okay, I'll wait, because you're worth waiting for.' I gave her a smile, taking in everything about the flushed state I was leaving her in, and exited quickly out of the kitchen door, before I changed my mind about leaving at all.

Nine

Amy

I WATCHED THE door close after him and then moved my eyes to the window. Although the glass in the kitchen window wasn't transparent, I could see the moment his headlights came on as his car started and pulled away from the parking spot outside. I watched until the red of his tail lights dimmed to nothing as he drove away.

My heart was still banging in my chest, my knickers were wet and the top of my thighs felt damp.

'What the hell?' I asked into the empty room.

But there was thankfully no one within earshot to answer my question, nor sight to witness the state I was in. The sound of the busy tearoom filled my ears. *What had I very nearly done in here with all those people just a few feet away?*

I walked over to the sink we used for handwashing and just stood with my wrists under the cold water for a few minutes as I took in deep breaths and tried hard to collect myself enough to cool down. At first, I couldn't look in the small mirror above, but eventually I lifted my gaze.

The woman in front of me was no one that I recognised.

My cheeks and neck were flushed with colour. My lips were a dark red and full. Unconsciously, I brought my fingers up to touch them, they felt tingly and sensitive. My hair was messy as several other pieces had fallen out in our desperation for each other.

I had never been that frantic for anyone else. I was no innocent, I'd had relationships and had always enjoyed the physical stuff. But I had wanted Daniel to literally consume me here in Lauren's kitchen

'Oh, my God.' I spoke to the reflection looking back at me as I tidied up my hair back to where it should be.

I knew that, caught in the moment as I had been, I would have let him fuck me on the worktop he had lifted me to sit on.

'Who are you?' I laughed at myself as I watched my eyes open wide in realisation.

I felt younger than my thirty-three years and free for the first time in a long time. Excitement coursed around my bloodstream as I remembered how his touch had driven me to the point of combustion. I wrapped my arms around myself and inwardly squealed.

'And he's coming back,' I spoke to the once again pulled together woman in the mirror. I began to dry my hands on the blue paper towel.

'Has he gone?' Kirsty asked from behind me.

I spun around quickly to find her and Debbie behind me in the doorway. I nodded my answer to them and, trying to look professional once again, I looked around the kitchen to check we had everything necessary for the rest of the day.

'Wow… What can we say? He was rather gorgeous, Amy,' Debbie uttered.

I couldn't stop the huge smile I was trying to suppress as it engulfed my face.

'I know. Sorry, both of you. I know how busy you've all been out there, when I was in here…' I stopped, unsure I could explain exactly what I had been doing in the kitchen.

'You're right! It's disgusting, us out there working our hands to the bone and you in here nearly getting boned. It was only *nearly,* wasn't it? I mean you didn't do the nasty in here, did you?' Debbie carried on as she wrinkled up her nose in pretend disgust. 'It looked like a close thing to me,' she added.

The three of us burst out laughing as they walked over to the trays of sandwiches they appeared to both need.

'No, we didn't do the nasty in here. I promise you,' I replied.

'SANDWICHES!' came the shout from the other side of the door, reminding us just exactly what we were here for.

The girls grabbed the trays and started to exit.

A sudden burst of excited adrenalin took over me. I wanted all the cakes and pastries done for tomorrow. For some reason, I wanted the night off. I went back to the pastry I had previously been rolling out, picked it up and chucked it into the bin.

A voice from behind me interrupted my thoughts as I calculated how much I needed to make for the eight hours of opening tomorrow and the forty covers we had for every hour.

'Oh, by the way, I think you may need to disinfect that worktop too,' called out Kirsty as she poked her head back around the swing door. Laughing, I picked up the nearest oven glove and threw it at her fast retreating figure.

'There you go.' I counted out the last of the day's tips and pushed the large piles of coins and notes towards each member of the staff. 'Thirty-two pounds and seventy-five pence each. It's been a great day, everyone. Thank you so much for your hard work.' I stood up and pushed my chair back in to the table. 'I'll see you all nice and early tomorrow.'

I watched as ten hands came out to grab their money and then they all stood one by one to leave.

'Bye, Amy.'

'See you tomorrow.'

The shouts got less as one by one they streamed out the door and finally it shut with me inside.

The almost silence was welcome. All I could hear was the sound of the oven cooking the last of the goodies for tomorrow and the hoover of Mr and Mrs Smith as together they cleaned up the tearooms.

I looked up at the weight-driven wall clock. We'd done fantastically. It was only twenty minutes past six. As if on cue the door burst open and my eyes darted to it in panic.

'Oh my God, what a day… Is it wine o'clock?' Winter's voice rushed over me with the cold air that entered with her, and I relaxed a little.

'What's up with you, Amy?' Lauren asked as she came into the tearoom behind her. I watched as she gave The Fairy Garden the quick once over, taking in everything about her baby. Then she smiled as she realised all was well.

'I'm fine, all good here, nothing to say. Great day, excellent takings. All as it should be.' I knew I had said too much, but didn't seem to be able to stop myself.

They stopped dead in their tracks and turned to look at each other just the once. I watched them nod in understanding and then they turned back to stare at me. The longer they looked, the higher their eyebrows raised.

'Uh huh,' Lauren answered.

Winter walked over to me and pulling herself up to the tallest height she could in the ridiculous heels she nearly always wore, she began to walk around me. In defence, I folded my arms over my chest.

'What?' I questioned.

I could feel their eyes just taking me in. Winter had begun to move my hair around, lifting long pieces as she pretended to examine me.

'Enough.' I let out a small laugh as I pulled away.

'TOO LATE! Oh, Amy, what are we going to do about you? You have a love bite on your neck. What have you been up to?' She spoke in her best posh, reprimanding voice as I pulled away from her appraisal. 'We leave you alone for a few hours and you turn into a horny little bitch.'

In reaction, my hand came up to the side I knew Daniel had lavished attention on earlier and I knew I was caught. I'd been played into a confession by my best friends.

'Got something to tell us, cousin?' Lauren asked as she smiled.

'It was Kirsty and Debbie, wasn't it?'

They both nodded in unison.

'Sit down then,' I answered.

Over a glass of Pinot, I told them everything I knew about Daniel. The colour of his eyes, and just how attractive he was. I told them about the accident and the possible loss of my nan's car and how he'd rescued me after I'd gone into the ditch earlier today. I explained how he'd looked at me and the fact he had said I was refreshing. I tried to get over to my two best friends the chemistry that seemed to flare up between us just by our eyes finding each other's. They asked a few questions about him, but most of them I had no answers for. I told them he was American and that he was over for Jack's wedding.

'Should I have asked him more about himself? I don't even know how old he is,' I asked them both suddenly, worried by my lack of knowledge about a man I'm sure I would have allowed to fuck me in my cousin's kitchen, if we hadn't been interrupted.

'Seriously, Amy?' Winter laughed. 'You are in your thirties and an intelligent woman. We do not, I repeat *do not,* have to know every detail of all of the men we bed.'

'We don't?' I grimaced at them both. 'You both know how out of touch I am.'

I bit down into one of the pastries I had brought out with the bottle of wine and groaned at the rich taste and the way it melted in my mouth. My cousin was a seriously good cook.

'No. We don't.' She flung her head back and finished what was left of the wine in her glass. Winter was always one for the dramatic way to get her point of view across. Once again, her head tilted forward and her eyes found mine, just as my index finger pushed the last little piece of pastry, that had stuck on my lips, into the corner of my mouth, 'And you, Amy, by the sounds of it, need an orgasm that is given by a man's fingers, tongue or cock, not a food related one.'

I bit down onto the inside of my lips, effectively sealing my mouth shut as the urge to burst out laughing at her words became all-consuming. If I hadn't have done, the absolute perfect vision of Winter would have been covered, as I sprayed her with small pieces of masticated pastry. Her eyebrows raised as she watched me struggle. Luckily the urge left me as Lauren dipped into the conversation.

'I agree with Winter. He sounds gorgeous and just what you need, Amy. Whoever he is and wherever he's come from, if he's a one-time-only or a couple of weeks' worth of very welcome distraction...' She didn't finish her sentence. I watched as after she'd stopped speaking, she slumped back into her chair with a sigh at her own words.

'You just had to use *that* word, didn't you?' Winter chuckled at her.

I looked at Winter and raising my eyebrows in question, without using words, I asked how Lauren had got on today at The Manor. She grimaced, shook her head slightly and slashed a single finger across her jugular.

But the urge was strong and I just had to ask. 'And you, Lauren. How are you?... How did your day go? Did you erase the ghosts, by seeing him?' I shoved her shoulder gently with my hand, trying to push her into answering. 'How did it go?'

Lauren didn't answer me straight away, but took a large gulp of her wine and then, holding the stem, she wiggled the glass in front of Winter, like the empty vessel was now offending her.

Winter refilled it.

'Well I saw Rafferty, several times actually. I know that's what you're asking.'

'Well yeah! And?' I pushed.

'I think the only sentences we actually spoke went something like, "leave me alone, you just don't get it, do you? I'm *not* interested in you," and he replied, "I don't for one fucking minute believe that and neither the fuck, do you!"' She took another swig of wine to wash down the memory. 'It seems he's convinced I only took the job with Winter to get back with him... ARSEHOLE!'

'I know he's my big brother but... hear, hear.' Winter raised her glass to us both. 'Here's to the company of females, as my brother's bloody band have been nothing but bloody distracting all day,' Winter toasted.

'Really?' I questioned with a raise of my eyebrows.

'Yes,' she answered. 'Lauren and I did really well today, but we could have achieved so much more if they'd have just left us alone. We may even have to ask for your help up there tomorrow evening, if that's okay?' She smiled a thin-lipped grimace at me and I nodded quickly to answer her. 'Raff has been "helping" whenever she's around.' She used her fingers either side of her head to open and close quote her sarcasm. 'And I... well, I seem to have pulled the roughest, most foul-mouthed member of my brother's band.'

'You have?' I sat up, almost bouncing in my seat to listen to more of the story. 'Come on, tell me all. We know how much you enjoy a bit of rough, now don't we?' I smirked at her, eager for her to dish up her news, and loving the fact I was no longer in the spotlight.

There we sat for another thirty minutes as she told us all about the drummer Cade. He had pulled no punches when explaining what he would like to do to her and how much she was gagging for him in return. Him trying to hook up with Winter had meant Raff had hung around even more, apparently calling Cade "the biggest fucking male slut on legs" and telling him in no uncertain terms that "no fucking way did he stand a chance with his sister."

By the end of the story we were laughing at the whole predicament.

It all sounded like a comedy sketch, albeit a little more fraught.

I raised my glass at them both. 'Here's to us, the three musketeers. It could only happen, that us three could attract so much bloody male interest on a weekend when we don't even have time to sleep.'

'Only us. Cheers!' they called back.

We downed our glasses and I took my leave, the weighted clock telling me that it was now quarter past seven. I was running late for my date or whatever the heck it was.

Ten

BRODY

I HAD PULLED up outside the tearooms way before seven o'clock. I wasn't normally so fucking punctual, but tonight wild horses couldn't have dragged me away. I watched as several staff members, including the few I had met today, jumped into their cars to go home.

I could just about see Amy inside through the steamed-up glass and the glow of the decorative lights on the windows. My hand had found the door as I thought about getting out early, when another car pulled up. I let go of the door and leant my body over onto the steering wheel watching closely through the windscreen as two women got out of a Mercedes. I instantly recognised Winter, Raff's sister, and turned my gaze to the other one. She looked a lot like Amy, same hair, build etc. Then it clicked, it was Lauren. I had only seen her a few times in pictures before. Pictures that my best mate only got out when he was fucking hammered. But when Raff described her, it was like he was writing a song. He had described her every fucking detail and so fucking perfectly. I had long since seen her in my mind's eye, before I'd ever seen her in the pictures he held in his wallet and on his hard drive.

Apparently, he was over her, and in some strange fucking way I think he really believed it. We were all absolutely convinced otherwise. But it was a banned fucking topic and as the rest of us had only ever had fucked-up relationships with the other sex, who the hell were we to give advice?

When I had gone back to The Manor for a couple of hours this afternoon for a shower, I'd caught up with Luke and his little girl, Brielle. In amongst playing with her and her puppy Biscuit, Luke had caught me up with what was happening there.

So, it appeared the solution that Raff had first come up with three years ago, that Luke, Cade and I so desperately needed, was now biting him in the balls like a dose of genital crabs. He was back here with Lauren, although maybe subconsciously it had been the solution he needed, too. Luke told me how he'd had to pull Raff off Cade earlier as Cade had made several plays for Winter, just to wind the fuck out of Raff.

I'd laughed, listening to him describe the situation.

It all sounded like a normal fucking day at the office to me.

I looked back over at the tearoom. I'd told her I'd wait, so that's exactly what I did. With less bodies in the tearoom the windows had begun to clear.

Amy and her friends had stood and laughed together, over what I couldn't make out, and then they'd sat down at one of the tables with a bottle of wine. Instinct told me that I might be waiting some time.

But like a dog in fucking heat, I stayed there. I relaxed back into the warmth of the leather seat, crossed my arms over my chest and closed my eyes, trying to convince myself that I wasn't impatient as fuck.

I'd never waited for another woman before, why the hell was she different?

Every now and then I opened one eye just to check she was still in there.

It's okay, Brody, you just need a fuck that's all.

Suddenly she stood up and I briefly glanced at the time on my dashboard. It was fifteen minutes past seven. I sat up, desperate to know if she was coming out.

Desperate? Fuck, I was a pathetic fucker.

I saw her pull her coat on and my heart jumped up into my mouth. I'd been waiting for this moment since I'd closed the kitchen door on her earlier.

I opened the car door and stood down onto the newly fallen, crisp white snow. Carefully, trying hard not to scare her with any sudden movements, I made my way to the hood of my Defender, leant my ass against it, and crossed my arms over the top of my coat.

She stepped outside and pulled the door closed behind her. As she turned, I saw the moment she caught sight of me waiting for her.

'Evening,' I said, a cloud of steam leaving my mouth with that one word. It was so fucking cold.

'Hi,' she managed, in an almost breathless whisper.

I swear if the light had been better I might've caught sight of the blush I knew had crept over her cheeks.

'Sorry to keep you waiting,' she offered.

I smiled at her and pushed myself forward away from my vehicle. She seemed to freeze in place as I made my way over to her. I walked with very deliberate steps, drawing it all out just for her. Years on stage playing the crowd had its bonuses, and this was one of those golden moments. I watched her tongue come out to wet her suddenly dry lips as she watched me. If I hadn't fucking known before, I would have known right there and then just how much I affected her. I felt a smile pull at the corners of my mouth.

Finally, I was stood in front of her. She smelt of baking. *Who the fuck knew flour could be such a turn on?*

I caught hold of her chin and lifted her eyes to meet mine. 'No, you're not sorry.' I smiled at her and narrowed my eyes. 'You like the thought of me out here waiting for ya. It's probably kept your panties wet all the time I've been gone.'

Her eyes opened just a little bit wider in shock at my words and then I saw her smile.

'Cocky much?' she asked.

I flicked open the front of her black padded coat, threaded my arm behind her and pulled her to me. Then I grabbed hold of her ass with my hand, squeezing the muscular flesh, and pushed my erection against her. She gasped. 'Yep,' I answered. 'But then you knew that, you felt it earlier.'

She shook her head at me and tutted. Then realisation that what I had said was true came over her beautiful face. 'You're right. I liked the thought of you being here, waiting for me, wanting to be with me.'

I dipped my head down to hers as the snow once again began to blow wildly around us in the soft yellow glow of the one antiquated outside lamp. I brushed my lips softly against hers, feeling her take in a sharp breath at the connection.

'I've not been wet *all* day,' she spoke into the tiny gap between our parted mouths.

I fucking love her sass.

'No? Then I didn't do a very good job then, did I? I think you should let me have another try,' I whispered back. She smiled and nodded back her answer. 'I think it's best you get your pretty little ass up those stairs before I carry you up them.' I gestured my head over to the wrought iron staircase to the side of the building.

She followed my gaze. 'How did you know that's where we need to go?'

'I've been staring at this building that contained you for what feels like fucking forever. Now let's move, unless of course... you wanna give your friends a floor show?'

She looked back over her shoulder just in time to see Winter and Lauren stand to come over to the window. They both cleared the condensation inside in a circular shape, so they had a better view. I put my hand to my forehead to make sure my beanie was low enough down on my head and pulled my collar up higher. She lifted one hand to wave at them and grabbed mine with her other.

Slowly, we turned away from their prying eyes and made our way carefully towards the stairs, all the time I could feel her slipping. I looked down at her feet.

'Fuck this, Amy. God knows I love those heels on you, but you're going to break your fucking neck and that's not happening on my watch.'

Using the one hand I had hold of, I pulled her back to me, and our bodies crashed together. Before she knew what was happening, I quickly picked her up and put her over my shoulder.

'Oh my God! What the hell are you doing?' she squealed at me. I smacked her ass softly. 'Stop fucking wriggling. I'm saving you from yet another fucking accident.'

I climbed up halfway and then looked down at the two women who had come outside to watch. They were staring up at us. Lauren had her hand over her mouth laughing and Winter was gently clapping.

'Ladies.' I used my spare hand to give them a two-fingered salute.

'Daniel,' they both answered.

And I knew then, that I'd been important enough in her day for her to tell her best friends all about me. A broad smile took over my face as I galloped up the rest of the steps, hearing her scream with laughter and fear behind me.

As far as I was concerned it was the best fucking day I could remember and we still had all night to look forward to.

Eleven

Amy

EXHILARATION RAN THROUGH my body. Or was it complete and utter bloody terror.

I watched as we climbed higher and higher up the wrought iron staircase. It was narrow, steep and every step was completely covered in at least two inches of snow. Correction, that was every other step, I could see a very solid boot print sunk down deep on the ones in between.

Oh, my God! He's carrying me over his shoulder and only treading on every other step.

How strong was this man? I wanted to swoon, but upside down and still a bit concerned for my life all I managed was a quick look at Winter and Lauren as they both gave me the thumbs up.

Bitches.

'Key,' I heard Daniel demand as we stopped dead outside my door.

'I have it in my pocket. But I can't let go of you to retrieve it.'

'Trust me, I've got you. Get me the key.' He spoke with quiet authority.

I stopped breathing, closed my eyes and summoned up as much courage as I could. Carefully, I removed one of my hands that until only seconds ago had been gripping like a vice to the hem of his wool coat. Rolling my hip up and away from his shoulder, I felt his grip on me increase. I thrust my fingers into my deep coat pocket. I found the metal

I was looking for and pulled it gently out, placing it into his waiting open palm.

As my fingers brushed over his, my body trembled. I hadn't appreciated before just how calloused his fingers were. A delicious thrill ran over me at the thought of feeling them on my unexpectedly needy skin.

I heard the door release its hold on the frame and then we were inside. The warmth from the room touched the bare skin on my face. He unhurriedly pulled me back down over his shoulder and lowered me to the ground. I felt every muscle in his body go rigid with his slow deliberate movements. He leant his broad shoulders back and pushed them against the wood, effectively slamming the door shut behind us.

Finally, we were once again stood in front of each other. His left hand came up to pull off the black beanie he had been wearing. His hair was completely tousled as it fell back to his head. The beanie was then thrown somewhere behind me, with me still looking up into the most captivating eyes I had ever seen. His hands came up to clasp either side of my face and firmly but gently he held me just where he wanted me to be. The cold metal of his rings was in complete contrast to the heat contained in my face. Heat from a blush that had swept up and taken over my cheeks.

His mouth came down to consume mine. What started off as a flirty, in control kiss became something else in seconds. It was no longer a kiss to tease. His mouth demanded more and more and I reciprocated in every possible way. I moulded my body in tight against every hard sinew of taut muscle that belonged to this man. I had never been kissed like this before, with so much want and need. He kissed with experience, like he'd had enough practise to well-hone the skill. Knowing he was experienced was even more of a turn on, I knew he was going to take care of me. I tried to commit the feelings he dragged out of me to memory, if we only had tonight then I wanted to remember every single detail.

The taste of his open mouth and the feel of his tongue on mine.

The way it probed and took just what he demanded it should.

The way he took no prisoners and held nothing back in return.

My head began to swim with the heady lustful feeling that was rising quickly inside of me. My hands, in desperation, came to find the buttons on his double-breasted coat. With his large hands still on either side of my face I began to slip the buttons undone, one by one. Until at last, I could put my arms inside his outer layer and wrap them around his firm body. His body was hard, taut and muscular, and was now only covered by what felt like a thin T-shirt. But I wanted to feel his skin touching mine, everything we were both wearing just seemed like far too much. I pulled him to me as we continued to kiss, to take and to consume each other. Then I lifted my arms over the top of his and pushed the heavy material down his broad shoulders. I heard as the coat hit the floor with a dull thud and then I moved my hands towards his belted black jeans.

He freed my mouth.

'We have all night, Amy.' I felt his breath caress my throbbing lips as he spoke. His mouth moved down to my neck and I took in a sharp breath as his tongue ran up and down my skin. Goosebumps followed in his wake.

My hands continued their path, eagerly pulling at the leather strap at his waist and I heard the leather strike against the top of my hand as it flicked open, before I felt the sting. His jeans dropped further onto his hips as the belt released its hold.

'No rush.' A hand came down to mine, enclosing it in his. His fingers squeezed gently onto mine to halt my movement. His voice was a little louder this time and I stopped in my bid to free him completely of his jeans. 'But, we do need light. I want to see you when I make ya come all over my fingers, I want to watch you when I make ya scream with every sweep of my tongue, and I want to stare into your eyes when I thrust my cock inside you.'

I opened my eyes to find him staring back at me. I was marginally taken aback by his dirty mouth and words. But only marginally. His eyes danced in amusement as he took in my brief hesitance.

'There's a string of lights wrapped through and around the brass headboard,' I advised.

'Fairy lights.' He laughed out loud. 'Not enough, I want to see all of you.'

I sighed. 'The main light is behind you next to the door.'

He lifted an arm behind him and flicked the switch. The room that had before only been lit up by the snow-filled sky was suddenly illuminated by the spotlights that ran down the centre of the pitched ceiling. Luckily, they pointed into each corner and not directly over us or the big, brass-framed bed, where I was sure we would end up very soon.

I was thankful that the room had skylights. At least no one could see us. I was sure from his last few sentences he was confident enough not to give a damn, but I wasn't. It had been a long time since I'd been in this position and that made me feel self-conscious enough.

I watched his head turn to take in the room around us. His eyes rested on the leather wing-backed armchair in the corner of the room.

'Follow me,' he directed.

I followed him to the chair. He sat down heavily and his hands gripped hold of the arms. I stood in front of him, feeling a lot out of my depth.

'What shall I do with you first?' I watched his Adam's apple bob as he slowly swallowed. His eyes swept over me. 'Fuck... You're so damn sexy, Amy. I'm not sure you have any idea just how much I want you. You will, once I've finished worshipping you tonight.' One hand came up to find mine and he ran his thumb purposefully over the back of my hand. 'I want you to undress for me.' My eyes darted up to find his in panic. 'Let me change that, I need you to undress for me, Amy.'

That substituted word changed everything. I looked away from him, unable at that moment to look at those beautiful eyes, a little apprehensive at what I might find concealed within them. I swallowed deeply and took a small step backwards.

With a sudden flourish, I took off my coat and chucked it over by the door and then found his eyes again with mine. I could see a small lopsided smile pulling at the corners of his mouth, and that small in to how he felt, gave me all the courage I needed.

My hands lifted to my hair.

'Just your clothes, Amy... I want to let down your hair and remove those fuck-me heels. Then, at the very end, I'll strip you of the garter belt you've been cock teasing me with all day.'

I smiled at him.

I undid the pearl buttons of the white top I was wearing and let it shimmy off my shoulders and down my arms. I unfastened my bra and let it follow, revealing my breasts. I watched the lace skim over my nipples and took in just how hard they already were. Daniel dragged in air through his gritted teeth.

I was doing okay, he was enjoying what I was revealing.

'You're beautiful, Amy,' he whispered.

My hands went to the back of the waist band on my skirt and pulled the zip down. I pushed the black fabric over my hips and then threw it towards the blanket box. I hoped it would find it and not be in too bad a state to wear again. Then, inhaling a calming breath, I pushed down my knickers and tried to step out of them as daintily as I could. I went to throw them somewhere behind me but Daniel caught my hand and removed them from my grasp. Lifting them to his nose, I watched him inhale and the blush on my cheeks hit the very tip of my ears. I felt wetness pool at the top of my thighs as I watched him lick his lips.

'Intoxicating.' He added a final verb to my list of attributes.

And there I stood in front of the most handsome man I had ever seen in my life. I watched as very slowly and deliberately his eyes swept up and down my nearly naked body.

I knew I should be embarrassed. I was sure I would have been embarrassed if I'd have done this before for anybody else, but surprisingly I wasn't.

He had told me I was sexy and beautiful. The way his eyes caressed me as he took in every part of me was empowering.

I felt bold. I felt wanted, and it was an invigorating experience.

'I want to taste you,' he stated. 'Step up here. Place your feet on either side of my legs and hold onto the wings of the chair to stand up.'

With absolutely no second thoughts I did exactly as he had requested, until finally I was standing up straight on the chair with my legs open and on either side of his thighs. My hands held onto the leather wings, as per his instructions.

'Just look at you. I never expected a bare pussy, you must be a dream.' As his breath hit the sensitive skin of my hairless mound, my head fell back on instinct and my knees began to quiver. I was so very grateful to my nan for giving me the gift voucher to the local salon as an early Christmas present. Fleetingly, I thought over her words as I had opened the envelope containing my present. "A stitch in time, Amy." I smiled at the memory and how right she had been and then lost the thought as Daniel spoke again.

'Hold on, beautiful. By the way you're trembling I can tell this is going to be quick.' His fingers took hold of my suspender belt firmly as he pulled me towards his face to meet his mouth.

His warm, wet tongue pushed its way in between my folds and circled quickly around my hard, beaded clit. Around and around it went, the feeling was almost too much. Shockwaves ran up and down my body. My head flicked back up and I looked down in between us. His eyes were open wide as he devoured me. He looked up at me, silently daring me to look away. I couldn't. I wanted to watch him as much as it seemed he wanted to see me. I heard myself gasping for air, in between the 'Oh yes...' And the 'Oh God, right there!' that just spilt from my mouth.

My body was spiralling out of control.

'Oh God! Oh God! Oh God!' I continued like I was chanting a tribute.

He was right, it was quick. My body began to twitch as my orgasm reached the point of no return. As it pulsed through me, it made me convulse against him on every single wave. My engorged lips scraped against the stubble around his mouth, extending the exquisite feeling.

Suddenly he stood up and my hands were wrenched away from the leather as we moved as one. In the same movement, his hands had gone between my legs, forcing me open wider. My body continued to move involuntarily as my orgasm continued to pulse through me. His arms went under my thighs and, placing his hands on my bum cheeks, he carried me to bed. My hands found his hair and I threaded my fingers into the back of his head to hold on as he slowly laid me down onto the soft floral quilt cover.

As my orgasmic state drifted away, I looked down the length of my body to see his eyes shining with raw passion.

I released my hold on his hair and offered him my hand.

'Your turn,' I smiled.

He moved up and away from my body. He stood still, looking at my hand and smirked at me. 'Oh no! I'm not sure how you've done this before, but let me re-educate you. It's *your* turn, and it will be until I say differently. I want to sink balls deep into you and I will, but not yet... I want you every fucking way possible first.' He pulled off his light blue T-shirt as only men seem to be able to do, by pulling it up with both hands from the back of the neck. It swept up his body fast and then just as quickly it was slung to the ground. I gasped as it revealed his almost totally tattoo-covered body. The coloured inks had been designed to show off just how sculpted he was. 'Turn over and spread your legs wide.'

I wanted to look at him and touch his recently revealed body. His eyebrow lifted at me in question and I rolled over onto my stomach.

'I want to touch you.' I spoke into my forearms as I bent them and placed them under my chin.

'You will, but first I need to properly reintroduce myself to these fucking stockings that have driven me crazy all day.'

His hands took hold of my feet and he pulled off my shoes. His thumbs started to move in deep circles into the arches of my feet, as he massaged away my day.

'That's bliss,' I uttered. Then he placed a kiss in the centre of one of my soles and I pulled it quickly away.

His hand, now empty, moved and smacked my arse.

'Ohhh!' I let out in surprise.

'And that?' he asked. I could hear the smile in his voice.

'I'm not sure,' I replied. But I was lying, as once again I felt wetness at the top of my thighs.

I heard him laugh as he acknowledged my blatant lie. *Of course, he could see what effect it had on me.* I was wide open to him.

His other hand left my foot and together they ran slowly up the inside of my splayed legs as he touched my stocking-covered flesh. I started to writhe a little, wanting the touch of his hands on my skin.

At last the fine material ended and his fingers once again touched my deprived flesh. I let out another sigh. The bed dipped behind me with his weight, and I felt the heat of his body emanate over me as he leant down. The warmth of his lips brushed gently over the lace at the top of my stockings, and intermittently I gasped as he bit into the exposed skin at the tops of my thighs.

His hands opened my bum cheeks and his tongue ran down, from my anus to my clit. Then it followed the same route in reverse, repeatedly. Every time his tongue touched my puckered flesh he paused and I held my breath. And just like that he brought me to the edge again. At last he pushed two fingers inside me and began the rhythm I had been silently crying out for.

'You feel so fucking good inside. I can feel your hot walls tightening on my fingers. Come on, let go. I want to see your cum run down my fingers. I want to coat my cock with you.'

Once again, I began to moan as he continued to pump his fingers in and out. My orgasm appeared, almost blinding me with the white light behind my closed eyelids.

'Gorgeous, just like that.' He kissed both of my bum cheeks and then I felt his fingers gently pull out of me. I lay there for a few minutes completely spent.

Gradually, I became aware of movement behind me.

I rolled over and took in the magnificent sight in front of my eyes.

Daniel was completely naked. He appeared to have got rid of his jeans as I'd struggled to come back to earth after my last orgasm. His face was pained as he wiped his wet hand up and down his cock. Every hard muscle I had previously felt was exposed to me now. He was a beautiful sight, like something I had only ever seen before on the front cover of a book or in porn. His hand moved up and down his mouth-watering cock. As it reached the head he twisted his grip, showing me just what he liked.

I moved quickly up onto my knees, kneeling in front of him and sitting back on my haunches.

'Open,' he instructed, as he held himself out to my mouth. He wiped the crown of his cock across my parting lips, fleetingly I tasted him there and I wanted more. It was all the invite I needed.

I took him in as far as I could. I wasn't playing around with any preliminary crap. Although I'd enjoyed his direction and dirty mouth, I wanted to control these few minutes. I grabbed a tight hold of his well-defined arse and pulled him to me. His knees bent slightly as they hit the side of the mattress.

Two can play at your game.

I didn't dare remove my tight hold on him. In the short time we had been in this room he had shown that he loved to be in charge. I knew that given half a chance he would pull himself away and regain control, and I was having none of it. I dug my fingers into his taut muscular backside, and he lost it. I felt the head of his cock hit the back of my throat as he began to quicken the pace I had set.

I worked up and down his length, swirling my tongue around the head in the same way I had watched him twist his hand as he'd pleasured himself. His abdominal muscles tightened in front of my eyes with every sweep of my very determined tongue.

'FUCK,' I heard leave his mouth on a deep, primeval groan. 'I'm gonna come in that pretty little mouth,' was all the warning I had. I looked up at him as he threaded his fingers through my hair, making several clips spring free. His eyes found mine, they'd darkened as his pupils had dilated. He held my gaze as he pumped himself one last time to the back of my throat. His cum poured down the back of my throat and for the first time ever the urge to gag and spit was nowhere to be found. I swallowed and then drew back as I released his cock with a pop and wiped the back of my hand across my mouth.

'Where the fucking hell did you learn to do that?' He smiled his question at me, his face still showing signs of him calming down from what looked like a powerful orgasm. I felt proud I'd been able to give him such pleasure.

'I've been around too, you know.' I winked at him as I answered back with all the confidence I could muster. No way in hell was I going to tell him that he was the first man I had ever wanted to do that to. That felt like far too much information to give someone I hardly knew.

'Stop. I don't wanna know, forget I asked. Call me old fashioned, but I don't want to think about you with other men.' His dark pupils sparked to life with what looked like jealousy. I saw a small facial tic on his left cheekbone.

'You asked.' I let out a small laugh.

He had been frozen to the spot since his orgasm, as if moving might just be too much to handle and I understood. I mean how the heck he was still in a standing position I didn't know. But he moved unexpectedly, almost prowling like a wild animal does with its prey before it then consumes it. He placed his hands down on the edge of the mattress, and slowly I started to lie down backwards, releasing my legs from underneath me. On instinct, I began to move backwards on my elbows, and still he kept coming. I watched as his heavy cock came to life once again.

'Come here.' He pulled my legs to him and I fell onto my back. He knelt up in between my legs, with my wide-open pussy at his knees.

'Condom?' I questioned, already anticipating exactly what was coming next.

He reached over to the pillow, where he had already placed a few. I watched as he ripped open the packet assuredly with his teeth. All the time his eyes still possessed mine. He pinched the end of the condom between two fingers and rolled it down his length in one very well practiced operation.

'Eyes on mine while I fuck the sass out of ya.'

In one fluid movement, he leant down and firmly grabbed my hips. He pulled me up his legs and onto his cock. The wonderful sweet burn of satisfaction filled my senses as he entered me and an involuntary scream of pure pleasure left my mouth, just as a smile curled up the corners of his. As he pushed in yet again his mouth came down to find my needy nipples. Just before he sucked them into his warm mouth I heard, 'Told ya I was gonna hear you scream, beautiful.'

He held my hips to him and began to fuck me in what was the perfect pace for both of us. But something somewhere changed in those few minutes. Our eyes held each other's initially, almost in a dare. A dare that would determine which one of us would look away first. Which one of us would it be that could no longer bare the intimacy between two virtual strangers. Then the expression on his face changed and he moved us bringing his hard body down onto mine. He rocked in and out of me, faster and faster, and my hips met his thrusts every time. The sound of our flesh meeting together filled the room, along with our moans. He held his weight away from my body on his forearms, but he kept his face mere centimetres from mine as we watched each other.

Finally, taking his weight on his right forearm, his left hand tenderly brushed my hair away from my face. This no longer felt like an itch being scratched, but like something I'd never felt before. I was spellbound as, with our bodies instinctively talking to each other, we both came apart in each other's arms. Holding each other close, alarmingly like lovers.

My rules were broken and every promise I had ever made myself was lying in pieces around our sweaty conjoined bodies.

I'd lost myself.

I had lost myself to the feelings this man seemed to be able to pull out of me the moment his flesh touched mine.

Twelve

Amy

I WAS EXHAUSTED, but I felt euphoric and terrified in equal measure. I'd never spent a night like I had just spent with Daniel. It hadn't felt like a one-night stand, he'd read and understood every single signal my body had given him, and nurtured multiple orgasms from me. I was now wrapped up in his arms like he was holding his most precious possession.

For the second night in a row my head wouldn't let me sleep.

It wasn't the fantastic sex we'd been having for hours on end that kept my brain whirring, it was the way he was holding me, and the way that made me feel that kept me awake.

Anxiety flooded my system, making my heart pound and my throat feel constricted. I wasn't meant to feel like this. It all felt too dangerous. I suspected that the warmth and comfort that radiated from his body to mine, could puncture every piece of self-defence I had ever cocooned myself in.

I looked at him, only daring to move my eyes, reluctant to disturb him. His face was less than two inches away from mine. The only air I could breathe in had just been exhaled from him, and that was normally a complete no-no for me. I hadn't shared many men's beds, but normally I was a "turn my back and sleep right on the edge" kind of girl. But here, far too hot in his hold, it all felt *so* right. His left arm was underneath my neck and his right arm was loosely draped over me. His fingers were threaded into my hair at the back of my head, holding me close to him. His right leg was over the top of mine, trapping me within the confines of his body. His eyes were closed and his breathing had evened out a few minutes ago. I wanted to trace my fingertip over the muscles, to copy the ink as it swirled and danced over his skin as I tried to commit everything about him to memory. Instead, I forced myself to lie quiet and still.

It was scary just how much I had enjoyed my time with him. I had to keep reminding myself that this wasn't my life, this wasn't my bed and this wasn't what I needed. What I'd needed was some laughs and free flowing banter. To spend time with a man who showed me some attention and the bonus would have been a few days of no-strings sex, something I could look back on as a bit of fun.

I sensed that this whole scenario was so much more than the fun time I was looking for, and I knew it was going to have me running scared.

Through the four skylights above us, I could see the night sky as it began to come back to life in the way it does just before sunrise. Almost as if it anticipates the caress of the sun. Fortunately, I knew my time here with this man was running out. I had the perfect excuse, I had to be back down in the kitchen as early as I could manage. I just had to sort out in my head how the next half an hour was going to go.

Suddenly, his right arm moved up and away from me as he rolled onto his back and bent one of his knees up. The cream sheet he had over him rippled across his skin as it fell just a little bit further down and revealed more of his nakedness to my eyes. He was gently snoring as his breathing became deeper and I knew it was now or never.

As carefully as I could, I determinedly extracted myself. I tiptoed around the room, collecting the bits and pieces I needed to take a shower in the en-suite wet room. With relief, I found that my skirt had found the blanket box and I could see it was decent enough to carry me through another day.

Thirty minutes later, I emerged fully dressed. At first I didn't look towards the bed, and if I was honest with myself I knew I was scared that the pull to get back in would take over. I couldn't allow myself to once again feel what I knew was so out of my comfort zone, and unquestionably out of my reach. I grabbed my make-up bag from the table, having decided earlier to spend as little time in here as possible. I could do my make-up in the tearooms. I picked up my coat from just in front of the door and pulled it on, wrapping it around me like a shield. Then I put my plan into action. I walked confidently back to the bed, allowing my movement to make some noise.

I bent towards him, trying not to breathe in the smell of Christmas that seemed to envelope his skin, and gently brushed my lips against his. I refused to feel the connection between us.

'Hi... morning,' I whispered. 'I'm off to work, thanks for a fantastic night. Don't rush to get up, I'm working all day. Just do me a favour and make sure you close the door on your way out.'

His bleary eyes finally opened enough to find mine and his arms reached up to me. I moved quickly away.

'What are you doing, Amy?'

'I'm just saying goodbye. I need to go.' I moved up and further out of reach.

'That's not what I meant.' He sat up against the pillows and put his arms behind his head. I could just about see his penetrating, questioning stare in the dim light of the room.

'Let's not make this something it's not, Daniel,' I pleaded.

'Okay...' I could see him thinking on my words as I backed closer towards my escape route. 'So, let me get this straight. What you're saying is... thanks for the orgasms and for fucking me on almost every available surface in the room... Goodbye... and have a nice life?'

'Yes, that's exactly what I'm saying. It really was a great night, but I've got to go.' I kept my voice deliberately light, blew him a kiss, turned and vacated the room that smelt of us and the obscene amount of sex we'd had.

I moved down the metal steps as fast as I safely could. The clang of metal on metal rung out loudly in the still of the early morning as my heels collided with the wrought iron. Each reverberation reminding me I was running scared. I entered the tearooms and locked the door behind me. I didn't let out a breath until I was in the confines of the kitchen. I placed a hand over my heart and wondered what I had forced myself to walk away from. But I knew it was better this way.

I had a few rules. I didn't get close and I didn't connect with anyone. That way I didn't get hurt and I didn't get left behind.

I would be fine later. It would get easier. I would laugh with the girls and tell them just how mind blowing the sex had been, as we laughed and drunk far too much. I would describe his hard, tattooed, muscular body and how he'd satisfied my "needs'. I wouldn't tell them how he had made me feel as he held me in his arms, or how he had called my name looking into my eyes each time he'd orgasmed. Then I would tell them how I'd walked away, giving him his get out clause by leaving him in bed, and we would high five each other in our feminine solidarity.

I allowed myself just the once to wonder if I could fool my heart into believing the words I was going to tell them were true.

BRODY

I didn't move as she closed the door on me. I think my mouth fell open and I blinked a couple of times as I tried to work out what the fuck was going on and what fucking parallel universe I'd entered.

I heard the door slam underneath the flat and I let out the laugh that was building up inside me. I fell back onto the pillows, the same ones I'd only pulled out from under her ass not much more than an hour ago.

'Fuck me! Brody Daniels, you've just been fucking used.'

I was one of the biggest players I knew, and I'd just been played at my own game.

Not once since my mom had gone, had I been left by another woman. I did the leaving, not them. In fact, I usually didn't even bother staying around much after the sex, not even for a smoke.

But with Amy I had happily drawn her into my arms and fallen asleep. The way she'd cosied up next to me, she'd felt more than fucking happy to be there.

Felt? There was that fucking word again.

Feeling wasn't something I made a habit of doing, but being back in this country was starting to influence me. I was slowly coming to terms with my past, allowing the parts I had blocked out for what seemed like fucking forever, to gradually seep back in. I was dealing with the memories and even coping with how raw they made me feel.

But her? What the hell was up with her?

Something wasn't right. I could still see the expression on her face as she had said goodbye. Her face showed she was struggling with the words she was saying. Something or someone was behind her denying she wanted to spend more time with me. The more I thought about it, the more I was fucking convinced it was her.

She was running and she was running from herself.

'You can't kid a kidder, Amy.' I spoke out loud into the empty space around me, just as I saw the sky lighten through the skylights, the morning light was starting to creep into the room.

The guys would have a field day if they ever found out that a woman had walked out on me. Fucking hell, I was Brody Daniels for Christ's sake. I was the lead singer of one of the biggest fucking rock bands in the U.S. Women *threw* panties, and themselves, at my fucking

78

feet. They passed out when I sang, screamed and cried if I so much as looked in their direction.

This wasn't happening. She may be running from whatever it was we had both felt between us, but no fucking way was she running away from me.

No fucking way.

'Game on, Miss. Harper.'

Thirteen

Amy

'**S**HIT!' I EXCLAIMED, as one of the racks in the hot oven seared into the skin on my index finger. In reaction to the pain my grip immediately relaxed and the large tray fell with a crash to the floor.

I watched as the mini cinnamon swirls leapt and rolled to various hidey holes all over the kitchen. Hurriedly, I stepped over and around them making my way to the sink. Then I plunged my throbbing finger under the cold tap for the ten minutes required by my first-aid training. As I watched the cold water do its work, for a few seconds I wanted to burst into tears. I tried hard to convince myself it was the pain of the burn causing the pressure behind my eyes, not the absolute misery of walking away and denying myself.

Three hours ago, I had left him in the bedroom above me and for every second of those three hours I had been waiting for him to leave. Normally, the radio would be blasting out from the corner of the kitchen, but today I had kept it low in volume. I pretended to sing along with the songs playing and had even made my hips sway a few times. The truth was, I needed to hear the moment he walked down the stairs and took up my invitation to make this exactly what I needed it to be, a one-night stand. I looked at the clock again, checking the time. It was ten minutes past eight. But I'd known that without looking. I had watched nearly every single turn of the hands. I knew it was still early, but surely he would want to be on his way after our brief conversation earlier?

Questions had gone over and over in my head as I had baked my heart out this morning. I had replenished more than enough food for the day, but had been grateful to keep busy.

Why hadn't he just got up and left?

Had he fallen back asleep? And if so, why was he comfortable enough to do that?

What was he playing at?

'Bloody men!'

The longer he stayed, the more my heart filled with hope and all the scenarios ran around my head, skidding and colliding with each other in excitement. I allowed myself to think that maybe just this once someone wouldn't accept the words I used to push them away, that he might be the person who would force me to accept what he had to give.

I turned off the tap and pulled a blue paper towel from the dispenser and patted my fingers dry.

'Enough, Amy. Stop thinking about it, because whatever the answers are, they don't matter.'

Refusing to allow my head to turn once more towards the clock, I began to pick up the mess from the floor. I threw the pastries into a waste bag and then set about cleaning up the sticky residue.

'Right, that's it.' I spoke firmly, trying to convince myself.

As I started to wield the steamer around the kitchen, I decided right then and there, with a determined nod of my head, that I had other things to do today. Other things to sort out and yes, I had other things to look forward to.

As I steamed away the last of the mess off the floor, I finally heard the heavy clunk of his boots coming quickly down the stairs to the side of the kitchen and the slam of my bedroom door behind him. I held my breath and lifted my head, waiting for his engine to start. I caught sight of myself in the small vanity mirror above the sink, and offered my reflection a small smile, as I tried to convince myself I had done the right thing.

The smile never reached my eyes.

I heard his engine start and ducked my head so I wouldn't see the few tears that silently rolled down my cheeks, obviously in response to the pain in my finger.

The tearoom was once again bustling. Every table was full of people rejoicing the onset of the Christmas holidays, celebrating milestones with friends and family, or catching up with best friends in the warm ambience. I stood in the doorway to the kitchen taking it all in.

I looked all around the room several times, but my eyes always came back to table sixteen. Set back in a recess next to one of the huge arched windows, it had four comfortable armchairs set around a low, oval table. One man was sat there all by himself. He wasn't a local. I loved to people watch and he interested me. He was another good-looking guy who had the saddest eyes I think I had ever seen. He had medium brown coloured hair and a full, well-kept beard that appeared to have flecks of red in it. Every time the tearoom door opened he and I quickly glanced in its direction. I looked away in relief when I didn't find Daniel standing there and when it seemed his eyes didn't find what he was looking for, he looked back down to the condiments that he was fidgeting with. Finally, a young woman who was well wrapped up against the cold walked in and looked hesitantly around.

'Morning,' I heard Kirsty greet her.

'Good morning, I'm meeting a Mr. McKenzie here?' she questioned.

'Oh yes, follow me. He's waiting for you.'

I watched her pull off her bobble hat as she walked behind Kirsty. Long, thick strands of jet black hair fell beautifully down her back. Mystery man leapt to his feet, shook his legs to make his ripped jeans fall and extended a bare, tattooed forearm, towards her in greeting.

Blind date? How sweet. I managed a rather sarcastic smile.

'Amy, are you taking your break soon?' Debbie touched her hand to my shoulder as she asked the question, making me jump and taking me away from my thoughts.

'Yeah, but I'm just going to make a couple of calls first, so probably in about thirty minutes or so.' I looked at her questioningly.

'Okay,' she nodded. 'I'll wait until you get back to take mine.'

I tore my eyes away from the blind date couple and smiled my thanks at Debbie. The tearooms needed at least two of us women at any one time. The teenagers working here over the holiday were great, but the ship needed a steadying hand to run smoothly.

The phone in her room rang twice before the recognisable voice picked up. I closed my eyes and exhaled as I appreciated the warmth in my nan's tone.

'Hello, Falham 209278.'

It was our shop telephone number. Despite the fact she had got that wrong because of where she was, the enthusiasm in her voice lifted me. Today was obviously a good day. Like many other people, her dementia came and went like the rise and set of the sun. There was no formula or equation that would enable you to work out what sort of day or even what sort of hour you would get with her. But I had worked out months ago, she seemed to know when I really needed her to be her and not the confused old lady that was gradually consuming her vibrancy and personality. I could only assume that it was the strength of her love for me and the rest of our family that made her fight with everything she was to still be the matriarch we all needed and loved.

'Morning, Nan,' I answered, immediately feeling my heart grow a little lighter at the thought of talking to her.

'Amy, how lovely! I was just thinking about you.'

I closed the door to the office, letting the hustle and bustle around me disappear. I wanted to let her voice wrap around me like a comfort blanket. It had always had that effect on me as a child and it was still the same now that I was a grown woman.

'You were?' I sank a little further into the office chair with relief.

'Yes. How's the tearoom? Is it as busy as you and Lauren thought it would be?' She really was on the ball today, remembering a previous conversation we'd had.

'It's SO busy. I think even more than Lauren hoped for.' I pushed away the pain in my heart and tried to lose myself into our small talk.

'That's good. I'm really pleased.'

'My baking went well today, you'd have been proud. Well, apart from the complete tray load I dropped all over the floor when I burnt my finger,' I laughed.

'Oh, no! Are you okay?' she questioned, the concern in her voice making it rise in tone.

'Oh, don't worry. I'm fine.'

Then I heard it, that tiny moment when she had time to think. The instant when she had put two and two together and probably knowing my nan had come up with fifty.

'That's unlike you, Amy. What's going on?'

There it was, her opening question. I could lie to her, but it had never worked before, she saw right through me.

'I met someone yesterday.'

'Someone?' she came straight back with.

'Yeah…' I stopped talking when I became aware that my breathing rate had quickened. I could hear it echoing into the mouthpiece of the old-fashioned telephone in Lauren's office. 'Just a guy here for Jack and Lily's wedding,' I finished off after speedily composing myself.

'What's his name, this young man?' I smiled at the phone knowing her interest had suddenly increased.

'Daniel.'

'Ooooo, I've always liked that name, tell me more,' she probed.

'There's not much more to tell, Nan.' A small laugh left my mouth.

'Amy. I wasn't born yesterday, if the two of you had just had a conversation, you wouldn't have even mentioned him. Something has happened, I can feel it in my water.' I crinkled up my face in amusement at my nan's terminology. 'Now tell me what happened and just what it is that's upsetting you enough to call me from a quiet room away from others. You don't normally throw food all over the floor either, so I know it's something.'

The woman who had brought me up hardly ever missed a thing, even with her dementia.

I took a deep breath and carried on. 'We spent the night together.' I squeezed my eyes together tightly, leaving the words hanging on the line.

'Oooooo, go on… and make it quick, you know I need to know more. I'm with you today, Amy.' I heard her sigh with acceptance. 'I might not be next time you speak to me or come to see me.'

I mulled it over, and not for the first time either, just what it must be like to be our nan. Vascular dementia had been diagnosed shortly after her suffering a stroke just over two years ago. Rehabilitation had enabled her to regain the strength the stroke had robbed her of in her right side, but as those weaknesses dissipated, the weakness within her brain reared its unwanted ugly head. She had never smoked, or drank to excess, the only contributing factor that doctors had said went against her, was that she was overweight. She had one vice, her love to cook. To spend time with her family around the overly large dining table that took up most of the room in the living area we had above the shop, was her idea of perfect.

Nan had led a life that was fully involved with her family and the community around her, and watching from the side lines as that life was gradually chipped away was excruciating. Sometimes it absconded in tiny pieces and then on occasions in great big, very unwelcome chunks. My heart felt heavy, I knew I was losing her and I was nowhere near ready to let her go. I gave her what she was asking for.

'He's beautiful, Nan. He's tall, a few inches over six foot, and like one of those men we used to sigh over on the covers of the books we read.'

'Well…' She pushed into the conversation and I could picture her with her eyes closed, with a beautiful smile on her face and her hand over her heart like she did when she was overwhelmed. I carried on, letting her live vicariously through me.

'He has fairly short, dark hair that curls over his ears.' I stopped short of telling her that when he had exerted himself and his hair was damp, it curled even more. 'He has the most unusual coloured eyes I have ever seen, I can only describe them as like a teal colour. His whole body was covered in tattoos, colourful, artistic tattoos.'

I stopped, not really knowing what to say.

'He sounds breathtaking, but how did he make you feel, Amy?'

I knew it was coming, I knew she would ask. I thought back to how I had felt when he was holding me close, and to how he had made love to me, with his eyes capturing mine and how he had refused to release them.

'He made me feel… cherished and appreciated. Almost like we were meant to be.' My voice got quieter as I came to terms with the words I was speaking

'Oh, Amy,' she whispered down the phone.

I could feel stirrings of panic welling up inside me. *What have I done?*

'I can't wait to meet him, he sounds wonderful.'

'Nan, it was a one-night stand, he won't be back. He left this morning after I came down to work.'

'I don't understand. If there was the level of connection between you that you just described to me, why would he just up and leave? Your grandfather and I knew the moment his fingers found mine, the very first moment he took my hand.'

'That's just the way it is these days.'

'Don't you come that with me.' Her voice strengthened, as she began in her way to tell me off. 'Finding someone you connect with is the same now as it has ever been. It's the same as it was in my day, or as far back in time as we can both imagine.'

'We slept together, Nan. It was just sex. Admittedly very good sex, but just sex nonetheless. This morning I gave him a way out, Nan. I gave him the way out, before he came up with his excuses.'

'If you were one of those sort of women, Amy, that might be true. But you're not like that. You don't spend the night with every Tom, Dick, or even Harry. This must stop, Amy. Please, you must stop pushing everyone away, stop trying to keep everyone at arm's length… for me.'

Although we'd had the same conversation many times before over the years, this time the last couple of words resonated deeper within me.

'I'll try, Nan… for you.'

'When he comes back, which I'm certain he will, you make sure you do just that. Now, there was something else, hold on let me find my piece of paper.' I closed my eyes and grimaced. I concentrated hard on my breathing, making sure I didn't sigh with what sounded like impatience at the delay in our conversation. I could hear her searching her handbag for the exact scrap she was looking for. It had become one of her coping mechanisms, to write everything down. Her hope was that she would be reminded of it later. The only problem was her handbag was very often full, with varying pieces of paper all with things she felt she needed to remember written on them. Sometimes it made the whole situation worse. I had found her before with her bag emptied out, her lap completely covered in pieces of screwed up papers. She had been in tears as she tried so desperately hard to sort through them all. The same night I had emptied the lot in the bin, knowing that if I didn't we would be bound to go through the process again from start to finish.

'Oh yes, that's it.' She finally spoke and I smiled at the happiness in her voice. 'When are you going to tell me about Grandad's car and the fact you had an accident? You did, didn't you?'

I didn't question how she knew, we lived in a small village. Everyone knew each other's business around here. 'Your piece of paper is correct,' I reassured her, after I heard the doubt creep in momentarily. 'I was going to… I'm sorry. There was nothing I could do. She slid on the ice. I'm not sure whether the insurance company will pay out enough to cover the repair bill. I'm *so* sorry. I know how much that car meant to you. I know it's the last thing that Grandad bought for you.'

'Just as long as you're not hurt, that's the main thing. We really should have got rid of the car years ago, but it's always held a special place in my heart, because your grandad gave it to me... Unlike some of the other things he gave me.' I heard her sigh and knew she was talking about my mum. She took a deep breath and continued. 'But I still remember the way he loved me and what it felt like to be held in his arms, I don't need the car to remind me of that. I have all of you, and it's enough, its *more* than enough. Gradually we all learn to let go. It's one of life's lessons. We have to learn to let go of the people we love, when they can no longer be with us, whether it's taken completely out of their hands... or by their choice to leave.'

'I'm trying, Nan...I am trying.' I closed my eyes and whispered into the phone.

'Not hard enough, Amy. I want to be around long enough to see you happy and settled. You *need* to let go of the negative feelings that are eating you up inside, feelings like pain and resentment. Those can consume you and twist you. They can bring you down and stop you leading your life to the full. Stupidly, we all fight to hold on to things that are of no benefit to us at all, because we can't bear the thought of change. So, we push people away because we're scared.' I heard her take in a deep cleansing breath. 'Let it go, darling, let it all go and please learn to love yourself. Then and only then can you be loved fully and completely in return. You deserve that, I want that so much for you.'

More silent tears fell down my face as I listened to her words. She had a lifetime of experience to share, but no longer a lifetime to share it.

I missed her already.

'Wipe those tears away, Amy. If he has a connection to you, like you felt, he'll be back. Mark my words. You are far too beautiful to ignore.'

I wiped my face with the back of my hand and sniffed to clear my nose.

'We'll see, Nan. I love you.'

'I love you too, bye for now.'

'Bye.'

I didn't want to put the phone down on her, not knowing if she would be my nan next time we spoke. I wanted to be in the same room as her, so I could fly into her warm comforting embrace. But hearing the click and then the dead tone that followed, I placed the receiver gently down in its cradle.

After spending a few minutes mulling over her words, I picked it back up to call our local garage. Luckily the guys there already had my nan's car in hand and were just waiting on the insurance company's visit. Thank goodness, it was one less thing to deal with.

Fourteen

Amy

LETTING OUT A deep sigh, I pushed open the heavy door to my bedroom. I was utterly exhausted, but two twelve-hour days, two nights with no sleep, one of those with unlimited orgasms, would do that to you. As if to punish myself just a little bit more, the first thing I did as the door closed behind me was to inhale deeply, just to see if Daniel's cologne had left its presence, but I found nothing. The room was tidy and the bed had been expertly made, almost with military precision. It was as if he'd never been here at all.

I was physically and mentally spent, but first I had tonight to get through, before I would allow myself to dissolve into a bedridden, emotional heap. All I would need would be my own morose company, my duvet, a tub of Ben and Jerry's and a large spoon.

I kicked off my heels and after making a brave attempt to ignore the leather chair in the corner and just what I'd done in the said chair with Daniel, I sat down on the end of the bed and flung myself backwards. I stared up through the skylights at the clear, dark sky as one by one the stars began to appear.

I could only allow myself ten minute's rest. I had approximately one hour's reprieve before I was due to be picked up to help at The Manor this evening. Although I was mainly going to be behind the scenes, just making sure that the kitchen ran smoothly, I knew I needed to look the part. I was going to have to shower, re-do my make-up and rummage through Lauren's wardrobe for something suitable to wear. I stood up on throbbing feet that genuinely felt like they were on fire and could barely take anymore. But, I had promised Lauren and Winter, so I drove myself on. I really needed their company, I had spent far too long today in my own head. Tonight, after a job well done, I was going to have a couple of drinks to unwind and have a much-needed laugh with them.

One hour later, I was standing in the carpark waiting for my ride. Physically I felt revived, but mentally I felt fragile. At least I looked the part. I'd found a knee-length, black lace cocktail dress and it fitted like a glove. I'd made up my face, paying special attention to my eyes as I tried to camouflage the building emotion behind them.

A dark, expensive looking car pulled up in front of me and I got in.

The sleek vehicle swept up the main driveway to The Manor and I saw for the first time just what a superb job Winter had done. The long driveway had been transformed. This evening it had been lit with flaming torches. It was showy and very effective, casting the red brick of the Victorian manor with contrasting lights. The old building looked stunning. I knew that today a separate opening had been held for the corporate guests, which included hotel reviewers and national newspapers. She had explained that this evening would have a completely different feel to it. Apparently, the band had wanted it to be more relaxed and they wanted an evening to share with their families and extended group of friends. Winter had said that Raff had even hinted that Default Distraction were going to play a few popular covers and some of their best-selling hits

The car I was in pulled off the main drive and around to the back entrance.

Story of my life I thought with a smile, but I appreciated that my thought had given me my first lift of the day. I took one more look at the drive and then focussed ahead.

It was almost midnight when the final trays had left the kitchen. The food this evening had included fish and chips in newspaper with mushy peas, and jelly and ice cream. The trays that had just left were freshly

baked warm rolls, spread with local butter and stuffed to the brim with crispy bacon. The band had insisted that this evening everything was to be less formal than they'd scheduled for the daytime. Unfortunately for me, I hadn't received that memo. So, I had stayed put in the kitchen once I had worked out I'd be the only one in a little black dress, which showed far more cleavage than I had bargained for.

The adrenalin I had been running around on earlier was beginning to subside and fast. Every muscle in my body ached.

'There you are.' Lauren's voice found me as I pressed the start button on another full load in the dishwasher. 'Look at you... nice dress.' She smiled over to me as she teased.

'Oh, this old thing.' I smiled back at her. 'Sorry, I borrowed it. I *thought* I had nothing suitable with me to wear. Who knew I could have come in comfy jeans and a pair of Converse?' I stared at her, raising one questioning eyebrow.

I watched her grimace as she silently mouthed her apology. 'It looks better on you than it ever did on me,' she offered, trying to appease me.

I looked down at myself. I had, until I'd realised my choice of attire was completely wrong for the evening, been really pleased with the reflection I had seen in the full-length mirror of Lauren's spare room.

I lifted my eyes from the beautiful, black lace. 'So, what brings you to my lowly domain?' I opened my arms wide and gesticulated the kitchen.

'Well, Cinderella, Winter and I want you out of here. All the guests have gone into the ballroom to watch the band and we thought we could share a couple of glasses of bubbly together and then hopefully go to find our beds.'

'I'm a little overdressed.' I looked down at my boobs. Held in a decent bra they were filling up the majority of the space in between the plunging V neckline of the dress.

'You look beautiful, even stunning.' She smiled at me and I raised my eyebrows at her. 'I know. Not to worry, we'll hide you away in the drawing room, because God forbid anyone should get an eyeful of your tits.' Her laughter filled the kitchen. 'Come on, we deserve the celebration and we're dying to know how last night went?' She winked at me and grinned a broad knowing smile.

'I bet you do, but that will have to wait for another day. I'm too exhausted to talk tonight, just take me to the alcohol.' It was a lie, I just wasn't strong enough to go there this evening.

Lauren offered me a tight-lipped smile and took hold of my hand. As we left the back of the house and began to move forward down the empty passageway, the sounds of the band tuning up reached my ears.

The drawing room had two entrances. As we arrived through one door, Winter was closing the grander double doors behind her, on what had to be the ballroom. Next to her was a small silver drinks trolley. I could see two bottles of Champagne and three glasses. I smiled broadly at her as she began to push it towards the two overly large settees, placed either side of a roaring log fire.

I walked nearer to one and sat down quickly in an undignified heap.

'I'm knackered, completely cream crackered,' I declared as I kicked off my heels, bent my bare legs and placed them beside me on the comfortably stuffed settee. While Winter fought to release the cork from the first bottle, I absentmindedly rubbed at a sore spot on my right heel.

I was relaxed and comfortable. The excitement from the large room outside had to some extent invaded the smaller cosier one that contained just us three. My earlier feeling of absolute tiredness began to lift as we looked at each other with the recognition at just what we had managed to pull off in the last two days, and the enthusiasm from the happy people waiting outside began to filter through.

POP!

Finally, the cork wiggled free and shot off towards the ceiling. The three of us smiled at each other. Hurriedly, Lauren pushed the glasses under the stream of escaping Champagne. When the flutes were full, Winter thrust mine into my waiting hand.

'To us!' Winter shouted into the warm room.

'To us!' we called back, clinking the expensive glasses together.

I took a large gulp and relaxed a little more into the settee as I felt the bubbles come alive in my mouth. I swallowed quickly before they travelled up my nose.

'I don't know what to say to you both, other than thank you. But that doesn't seem nearly enough.' Winter drunk the rest of her Champagne down quickly and sat down opposite me.

'It went brilliantly, Winter. You should be so proud of yourself,' Lauren added. 'I saw you handing out your business cards left, right and bloody centre today.'

'Well, I couldn't have done it without you both, thank you from the heart of my bottom.' She smiled at us again and topped up all our glasses. I just managed to get my fingers over the top of mine, before she overenthusiastically filled it to the point of it slopping over the rim.

'The Fairy Garden had one of its best days ever today, Lauren... I'm so proud of you both and your achievements.' I lifted my glass to them both and took another sip.

I saw the moment they glanced at each other and without saying a word they both made their way over to my settee, to hug me from both sides.

'We're proud of you too, you know,' Winter spoke into my ear.

I smiled at their words, holding them close to me. Finally, they released their hold and sat back down on the settee opposite.

'So?' questioned Lauren as they both interrogated me with a stare.

I shrugged at them both.

'Okay, let us recap. When we last saw you last night, the very lovely Daniel was climbing the wrought iron staircase to your bedroom, doing the stairs two at a time. Let us remind you, *he* was carrying you over his shoulder as if you were as light as a feather.' Lauren placed an open palm over her heart, it was a mannerism of Nan's that she'd taken on as one of her own.

I shook my head slowly from side to side at them.

'Oh, come on, Amy, spill it. We need to hear it all.'

I had gone over the words in my head, practising what I was going to say.

'My night was amazing. Having never had a one-night stand before, I don't know what I was expecting. He was attentive and gave me exactly what I needed.' I forced the words out. Not wanting to think on them too much.

I watched them turn to look at each other again.

'Oh dear!' Lauren added to the now quiet room.

'Indeed,' replied Winter as her beautifully shaped eyebrows lifted so high they nearly touched her hairline. 'So, it was either bloody awful or the best sex you've ever had. He was that good, huh?'

'Yes, he was good. I had a really good night,' I answered as nonchalantly as I could manage.

'So, let's get this right. He's tall and good looking?' Winter asked, turning her body away from facing towards me and angling herself towards Lauren. Lauren in turn copied her, effectively shutting me out.

'Yes,' I answered, although neither of them even turned their heads towards me.

'He was *so* strong, we saw that by the way he picked her up,' added Lauren.

'We did,' Winter answered, as she feigned fainting like a southern belle.

I nodded in response, although they never looked my way.

'With that sort of strength, he probably has the most fantastic body?'

'Yes, he had a really good body.' I almost sighed as I answered, remembering the feel of his hard, muscular torso under my fingertips and my urge to constantly touch it. I'd once again added to the conversation, but still they effectively ignored me.

'We witnessed he had a sense of humour.' Lauren was adding up Daniel's list of plusses on her fingers as she and Winter carried on having the discussion between themselves.

'A man like that is sure to know exactly how to use all of those qualities to best effect,' added Winter, nodding her head.

'I bet he knew just how to use all of those skills.' Lauren sighed and leant back into the comfy cushions behind her, fanning her face with her hand.

'He did,' I added.

'He exuded confidence, I could sense a bit of a bad boy about him,' Winter continued.

'His body was covered in the most beautiful, brightly coloured tattoos and his fingers were covered in rings. Sex with him was amazing... the way he controlled my pleasure and then held me close afterwards was more than I could have ever imagined.'

At that point, they turned to face me, with wide grins. I knew I had been tempted into giving them the information they'd been after from the beginning.

'So, when are you seeing him again?' asked Lauren.

I looked at them both in disbelief. Lauren was full of excitement for me at the thought. Winter seemed a little lost in her own thoughts at our conversation.

'It was a one-night stand, we made no other plans. I told him to make sure the door closed behind him on his way out.'

Both of their faces contorted in front of me.

'So, you're telling us that you effectively kicked him out of bed and slammed the door shut on his face?'

'Stop it!' I was shaking my head at them both. 'It was a one-night stand. He's here for Jack's wedding, after that I'm sure he'll be on his way back home. By the looks of his clothes and the car he was driving, he has money. So, what on earth would tempt him to stay here in our sleepy little village?'

'Did he tell you all of that?' questioned Winter.

I shook my head a little. 'It's just what I got from our few conversations.'

'What sort of car did he have? Just as a matter of interest. Was it a sports car?'

'No, it was a Land Rover. A Defender I think.' I smiled at the memory of sitting in it with him, feeling warm and comfortable after my accident.

'Oh.' She nodded. 'Well, I for one think you'll be seeing him again...'

I looked at her in question, furrowing my forehead.

'I mean, we're going to the wedding, aren't we?' She smiled.

Just then a loud cheer went up next door. Instinctively my gaze left Winter and travelled towards the closed double doors. A beat was being tapped out on what appeared to be one drum and then the guitars joined in. I realised it was a tune I recognised. A voice joined in, masculine, deep and melodic and on some notes, his voice rasped. I was enthralled. So, it appeared that I did know some of their music after all. I began to sing along to some of the words he was singing and to mime the ones I didn't know.

'Oh, I love this one.' Lauren started dancing around the room, with her glass held high in her right hand. Winter jumped up to join her.

'Come on, Amy!' Lauren shouted.

I jumped to my feet, my earlier exhaustion had been left behind. I danced my way over to them, picking up the Champagne on the way.

The more Default Distraction played, the more we danced, the more we drank and luckily for me, with a glass held up high in one hand and bottle of Champagne in the other, the more I could forget.

Fifteen

BRODY

CUPPING BOTH OF my hands, and raising my bent elbows high into the air, I sang the last note into the microphone. Holding the chord for as long as I had air in my lungs forced my body to lean backwards. The stool I was resting my ass on teetered on two of its four legs. In a well-practiced pose my right leg was straight out in front of me, balancing my weight. Finally, with my head right back and with my eyes closed, I finished the song at the exact same time Cade once again hit the snare.

The song we had ended the short set with was a favourite of our fans, but the words I had written many years before and had just sang to the mainly strangers in the crowd, affected me every single fucking time. Behind my trademark aviators I knew there would be tears in my eyes, my body as per fucking usual was trembling with exertion and the fucking emotion of it. As with every other time I'd sung "Regret" I saw my mum and sister leaving. The pain of my heart being smashed into pieces, as I sang the words and relived the old movie clips in my head, was as excruciating now as it was when I had to live through it as a small boy.

My sorrow had been torturous enough to live with, but my dad's had been more agonising to stand by and watch. Watching was *so* much worse, especially as a child when the only tools you have in your arsenal are your arms. My short, skinny arms weren't nearly big enough to wrap all the way around him when he sobbed into his pillow every night.

Applause went up all around us. I opened my tightly squeezed eyes and with a loud sniff, I dragged myself out of my memories and back to the small stage I was sat on.

Slowly, I moved my body forward, feeling the beads of sweat run down my spine. I moved and my T-shirt fell into the dip, soaking up the moisture. I focussed and looked back out into the small crowd.

'Thank you…Thanks so much… We've been Default Distraction, double D's over and out.' I two-finger saluted them in the exact same way I would end any concert or gig of ours. No matter how big or small they were, they all mattered to us.

I got up off the stool and bent down to pick up the bottle of water to the side of me. Then I squatted down and unscrewed the top. Tipping the bottle back I emptied the contents down my hot, dry throat and then crunched the plastic container in my tightly clenched fist. I looked around the small stage we'd had made. Cade was talking to a small group of girls that had gathered around him. I had no fucking idea where they had appeared from, knowing him he had probably bussed them in. They seemed young, hopefully legal, and willing, and that made them without any doubt, his type. But following his line of sight, I could see his eyes were on Raff's sister. Winter had walked into the room with Lauren when we had begun to play our last song. I watched as the fuckwit placed his fingers to his lips and he blew her a kiss. Thank fuck the successful opening weekend was over, Raff had warned me that his sister was on the verge of walking out because of Cade.

But Cade was Cade, and looking at Winter, she looked jealous of him giving the group of girls his attention. So perhaps Raff had got the fucking situation between them wrong?

Luke stepped off the small stage and took Brielle from her new nanny's arms. So far, I hadn't had much to do with her, but she seemed friendly enough, even if she was young. If Brielle was happy, that was everything to all of us. Luke was her dad but after Cherise's death we had all made ourselves surrogate parents.

Raff had stepped down off the stage and was walking towards where Lauren had been standing earlier, his head was turning frantically as he sought her out. His parents were in the room and he offered them a quick nod on the way past. His father was a retired colonel, formally with the British army. They had been estranged for quite a few years but they were now trying to move past it.

I jumped down off the stage, hearing my boots hit the floor and then sat back down on the edge, watching the crowd.

I had no one to go to, so I stayed put.

As I watched, my mind wandered back to three years previously.

'How do you feel?' the doctor questioned me.

That was a good fucking question. I wanted to laugh out loud.

I could tell his eyes were on me as he waited for my answer. But I kept my eyes cast down, I hated places like these. Places where I felt laid out bare. Stark white walls and heavy walnut furniture offered no comfort to anyone sat in its confines, especially to someone like me. I could hear the London traffic rushing past outside the Georgian building, the sound getting louder and louder the longer I concentrated on it. Quickly, I lifted my eyes to the glass of the window and stared out of one of the slightly imperfect rectangular frames, watching a red double decker bus go past. A blue coloured bird caught my eye, as it swooped down and pulled a sunflower seed from the bird feeder hanging on the one solitary tree outside. I closed my eyes and sighed, shutting my head down, hoping not to overwhelm myself.

'Is there a way I'm supposed to feel?' I asked as I shrugged my shoulders. I didn't look back over the desk at him, choosing instead to play with the sole and heel of the Chelsea boots I was wearing. My leg was bent at the knee with my ankle bone laid on top of my opposite knee. I tapped my fingers on the different materials and concentrated on the sounds they made. I could layer the notes they made on top of each other and began to play the new tune in my head.

I blanked him out again, just like I had blanked out most of my life.

'Hopefully you can come to terms with the diagnosis. By understanding it better, and recognizing how it affects you, I would like to think that you can make changes to your lifestyle and lead a happier, healthier life?'

I listened to his words, still laying out the new tune in my head. The notes went over and over, as I filtered him and his bright white fucking office out.

I hated being put on the spot as me. Life was much easier as the lead singer and main songwriter of Default Distraction.

'Thanks... But, don't betcha life on it.' I pushed myself up from the uncomfortable chair I was sitting in and made my way to his door.

'I'm not in the habit of betting with my life, Mr. Daniels. Can I suggest you don't gamble anymore with yours?' I let his words wash over me and then made the last couple of steps towards the door.

'I'll be seeing ya.'

Without waiting for his reply, I pulled open the heavy, white glossed door, placed my Aviators back over my eyes and re-entered the world wearing the only "costume" I was comfortable in.

As I strode out of the house in Harley street, London, a solitary flash bulb went off across the street. It had to be from the paparazzi.

Fuck! I responded as only Brody Daniels would.

I could see the stories in tomorrow's papers, "Brody Daniels, lead singer of Default Distraction, stuck up his middle finger in response to us waiting outside his doctor's office. With his trademark lopsided grin, he pushed the Aviators up higher on the bridge of his nose. Then he confidently ran down the steps and jumped into the waiting Limo, giving us no answers as to why he was in Harley Street."

Once the door to the car was closed and I was behind the blacked-out glass, I immediately flicked up the lid on the centre console and grabbed at the bottle of Dalmore that I knew would be waiting for me. The black metal seal had, as I had already requested, been removed. My fingers lifted the black stoppered plug out with ease and forgetting all about the cut-crystal tumbler that rested on the highly polished, mirrored glass, I chugged down several large gulps. With my hand still holding on tightly to the opened bottle I leant my head back into the leather of the car seat and closed my eyes. The warmth of the whiskey started to spread around my body and I began to relax into its familiarity. As it spread I slowly let out a long audible sigh and tried to come to terms with the diagnosis I had just been given.

How did it make me feel? How the fuck would I know? More pain than I could handle had caused me to shut that part of me down a long fucking time ago.

I spent two more minutes thinking before I chugged down half the bottle.

My unwelcome thoughts became haphazard.

Eventually, I no longer needed to ask myself the questions I feared hearing an answer to. As if by magic the amber liquid dampened down the fire of panic in my gut.

I passed out into the heaven of oblivion.

Someone patting me on the back brought me out of my memory. I cracked open more water as I received a few more slaps on the back as people walked past.

'That was great.'

'Thanks.'

'You've still got it, man.'

'Thanks.' I saluted them all with my water bottle.

It was all mindless talk.

Not for the first time my mind went back to Amy.

Was it possible to fucking miss someone you had only met two days ago?

BRODY

Stupidly, I felt more alone than I had in years, it was as if just being around her had reminded me what it was like to want and need someone.

'I'll letcha choose one, Daniels.'

The thoughts in my head evaporated as I heard Cade's voice. When I didn't respond, he kicked the side of my boot with his.

'Nah, thanks. I can choose my own. Thanks anyway, asswipe.' I didn't look up, I knew he was offering me one of the groupies that were hanging all over him as they each vied for his attention.

Thank God, he appeared to be keeping the whole fucking thing PG.

I stood up fast. I needed out of here, it all felt too fucking claustrophobic.

I nodded to Cade, Liam and Raff as they turned towards my sudden movement and I walked towards the double doors that Winter had been leaning against only a few minutes before. I knew the smaller, smart looking room to the side of the ballroom had another door that would take me towards the back of The Manor. I could jump into my vehicle and go for a ride.

I already knew where that ride would take me to. I had played every part of last night over and over in my head. But certain parts I'd replayed more than others. I could still see her bare pussy in front of my eyes as I'd pulled her towards me using her garter belt. I could still smell how much I'd aroused her. The way her ass had turned pink under my hand. The sounds that had left her mouth when I fucked her so hard she'd screamed. The bit I replayed the most was when I had fallen asleep holding her close to me. Never had I fallen asleep with anyone in my arms, apart from my dad.

I felt at peace with her wrapped up there, she eased my memories. Although I had no fucking idea what the hell I was going to come up with tonight to get her to talk to me. I had made up my mind this morning I wasn't giving up on her. I needed her and I felt in some way she needed me. I shook my head to dislodge the thoughts, because she probably wouldn't even fucking be there anyway.

Determined, I made the few strides towards the heavy wooden door and turned the handle. I walked in quickly before anyone followed me and closed it behind me as quietly as I could. The room was only lit by the flames of a blazing log fire. It had a warm and comfortable feel to it and I felt my tense body begin to relax. I peeled off my Aviators and hooked them into the neck of my T-shirt. My eyes began to adjust to the dim light.

I started walking through the room towards the door I needed. When the flames from the fire reflecting on something on the low table caught my eye, I stopped. I felt my throat hitch at the realisation of what it was. Almost on automatic pilot my feet moved towards the dark glass bottle with the flames of hell reflected in its shiny surface. I moved around one of the two large couches in the room to get nearer to the bottle. As I leant down to pick it up, my heart accelerated as my fingertips gripped its smooth neck. I exhaled through my open mouth as I comprehended that a small amount of liquid was still swishing around in the bottom.

Go on, do it.

My arm moved on its own, lifting the bottle so my eyes could register what my brain had already fucking concluded.

For fucks sake Brody… put it down.

The words of "Regret" were still running through my fucking head and I knew that right at this moment in time, I was yet again at another make or break moment. My addictions were piling forward in my head. Presenting themselves where they weren't fucking welcome. But even though they knew that, they continued to scream loudly telling me how they would make me feel better. They shouted out purposefully how they and only they could help me. Yelling, they set out all the reasons of why I should listen to them. How they would give me the release I needed. I gripped hold of my forehead in my struggle. With my body tensing up my facial tic returned. From my left eye, I could see the flick at the very bottom of my view.

Do it.

Do it.

Lose yourself…come back to the darkness. You're not strong enough to stay in the light.

You're not meant to live in the light.

Guilt and blame are your life, come back to the storm.

The feeling inside me was so intense, it was like drowning. The feeling of going under was pushing me to give in. I knew I needed to drown to soothe the pain inside me. To soothe the guilt, the blame and the desolation. My loneliness was all too fucking consuming.

My demon was too strong to fight.

Do it.

My right arm continued to lift the bottle almost in slow motion as I fought to swallow down the overwhelming battle inside me. My left hand had left my head and was now balled tightly into a fist, so tightly my fingernails dug deep into the fleshy part of my palm. I hoped my nails would cut into my flesh, marking me as the spineless, guilt ridden bastard I knew I was. Still my arm lifted. My mouth clamped shut and my teeth gritted together so fucking hard I felt my teeth might break under the pressure.

With the bottle raised to just a few fucking centimetres from touching my mouth, I finally gave in to the inevitable. I opened my nostrils to inhale the smell of the alcohol inside the darkened glass with the flames of hell on its side. I allowed my brain to recognise the stench of my demon.

But instead, all I could smell was Amy.

My eyes that had been squeezed tight in forced tolerance, flew open.

I inhaled again, still smelling her musky scent. My arm lowered the bottle away from my mouth in a sudden unwavering movement.

All I could smell was her. The neck of the bottle smelt of her, the air around me smelt of her. My heart accelerated again, but this time it wasn't in panic, it was in acceptance.

'Heeeey, issss mine…itsssss mine… and itsssss my friends', go get your own! Put. It. Down.' A slurred voice hit my ears as I placed the bottle back down on the table top.

'Amy?' My eyes that had gradually got used to the dull light in the room looked away from my demon from hell, towards where her voice had come from. I found her, and my body instantaneously relaxed. She was lay on one of the huge couches. She looked tiny, curled up in the foetal position with a cosy looking blanket over the top of her.

'Mmmm hmmm,' she replied, as I watched her arm flap the blanket away from her body. She revealed her gorgeous little body, barely wrapped in a black, lace dress. Her breasts were just about being contained within the deep V that seemed to go all the way down to her crotch. Okay, maybe I was exaggerating, but hell my dick twitched at the eyeful I was getting. 'Hellooooo, Daniel from my dweeeams.'

My previous internal fight was forgotten. I felt my head nod and my mouth pull into a wide smile. A small snigger left my mouth. She didn't know it but unwittingly she'd saved me.

I moved over to her and knelt beside her. Without even thinking twice I ran my fingers across her forehead and temple, lifting her chestnut hair away from her face. I needed to see her gentle brown eyes.

'Hi, Amy. You feeling okay?' I smiled.

'Oh… the best dreams…' Her eyes fluttered closed and she smiled a look of pure contentment.

'The best dreams, Amy?' I whispered into her ear as I got nearer to her, the pull of inhaling an even stronger smell of what I was sure was white musk had consumed me. I just wanted to be close to her, to hold her in my arms. I wanted to wrap myself around her like a shield, to defend her from whatever the hell she was running from. Equally, I needed her presence to save me from myself.

'Ooooo, you talk tooooo, itssss a loverly dreaaaaam.' I watched her eyes fluttering as she tried and failed several times to focus on me.

A sense of alarm coursed through my body, as I got a fucking idea of just how drunk she was.

'You'rrrre my protectorrrr... I made you go awayyyyy and close the door BEHIND YOU!... and nowwww you're BACK!' All her words were slurred and her voice raised in rhythm and tone as she overly pronounced everything that seemed to be important enough to her for me to understand. Just then, with the last word of the sentence, her hand uncurled from beneath her chin and she flung her arm open wide. The back of her hand cracked me across my jaw and instinctively made me pull away. Her movement gave me an even bigger fucking eyeful of her white, soft breasts, doing their best to fall out of her dress.

'Ooooo gooooodiieeee!' she exclaimed. 'I can feel you too... itsssss an errrrotic dreeeeeamm. They're the besssssst ones,' she slurred at me, smiling.

'I'll take your word for it, beautiful.' In an instant her smell, presence and humour had pulled me out of the deep, dark hole I had almost carelessly allowed myself to fucking fall back into. I seriously was a lucky fucker.

Without even thinking once, let alone twice, I slipped my arms underneath her and swung her easily up into my arms. She felt right there, so fucking right. Just holding her steadied my world. The loneliness and despair I had felt only a few minutes ago fell away.

I needed her and at this moment she needed me. I knew right then and there I was going to convince her that she needed me as a permanent fucking fixture.

I stood up tall and straight as she snuggled up close to my chest. One arm found its way behind me and the other hand she rested on top of my chest. I felt stronger with her in my arms, she supressed my demons and my fears. Her hand stroked gently over the top of my T-shirt until my nipple became hard under her fingers.

'Mmmm, you're soooooo hard.'

My dick twitched in response, and I managed to supress the laughter rumbling up inside me. Thankfully no one was in earshot, she almost sounded like she was starring in a fucking porno. That sigh, those words and the way she lazily spoke them were for my ears only.

'Are you rescuuuiiing me again, Daniel?'

I didn't answer her as we left the room, through the door I had been looking for earlier. If she let me, I wanted to always be around to rescue and protect her, the same way she inadvertently found the ability to salvage the wreck that was Brody Daniels.

Sixteen

Amy

MY BLADDER IMPLORED at me. Adjusting my position, I rolled over onto my back. Squeezing my eyes tighter together I tried to fall back to sleep. It was no good, there was no way I was going to be able to sleep without relieving the pressure. Without opening my eyes, I swung my legs over the side of the bed and tried to put my feet down.

Where the hell was the floor? My feet swung around in the cool air as I tried to find something solid with my pointed toes.

It must be the Champagne, I had misjudged where I was on the bed and was in the wrong position. I edged my bum further over the edge, finally my toes found the floor and I sighed with relief as they took my weight and I could stand up. I walked around the bed and tapping the bottom corner I set off in the right direction to find the toilet. Walking more steps than I thought I should be doing, caused me to feel a little apprehensive. Seriously, I was never drinking Champagne again, it literally went straight to my head. Finally, my outstretched hand found the door knob and I pulled on it, making the door open. I took the couple of steps I needed and stepped inside.

This isn't right.

I opened my eyes, desperately trying to see. I could feel things in front of my face.

I must be dreaming.

Suddenly my world became just a little brighter.

'You looking for something, Amy?'

I froze.

The few things around me were clothes, hanging in what I could only presume was a walk-in wardrobe and the voice was Daniel's.

What the hell had I done? I remembered dreaming about him talking to me, but that was it.

'Amy?'

This couldn't be happening, could it?

I blinked a few times and then stared straight ahead of me like a rabbit caught in the headlights. The smell of his cologne forced its way into my reluctant nostrils and I let out a deep sigh of remembrance as it captured all my senses, like semi-reluctant prisoners.

Perhaps I'm still dreaming?

But I knew I wasn't, my bladder was screaming at me to find the toilet.

Oh, my God! What have I done? How did I end up wherever the hell I am, and how did I end up with him?

'Amy? Oh fuck, don't tell me. Now she's sleep walking,' I heard him mumble in a sleepy, gravelly voice that went straight to my core.

The bed moaned as he shifted around on it and still I remained frozen to the spot, stood in the walk-in-wardrobe, surrounded by his clothes.

His ring-filled hands lightly found the tops of my arms and I shivered in response at the contact. My cheeks flushed as I allowed him to gently remove me from my hidey-hole. I relaxed into his touch, closed my eyes and permitted him to silently guide me.

'Okay, one foot in front of the other…that's right…careful…let's getcha back into bed.' His deep, caring voice caressed my soul with his tenderness and concern as he steered me from behind.

A few steps in, I carefully opened my eyes and took in the large bed we appeared to have been sharing. The sight that met my eyes wasn't just a slightly disturbed bed, made that way as we had both clung on to either side keeping a six-foot-wide chasm between us. No, it was a mess and the mess was in the middle. I didn't know what the time was and how long I had been in the bed with him, but we had obviously spent that time very close together.

'Oh my God!'

Suddenly we halted, he had stopped guiding me forward.

'Amy… you're awake?'

'It appears that way,' I managed to get out on a small squeak. 'What have I… what have we done?' Frantically I tried to sort through in my head anything I could remember from last night. The last thing I remembered was dancing around to Raff's band and dreaming I was speaking to Daniel. That was it. I remembered nothing more. I let out a sigh of resignation.

He didn't move a muscle, he just stood resolutely behind me. The only part of him that was moving was his large hands as he methodically rubbed up and down my bare arms.

'If you're asking if we had sex again… we didn't. Call me old-fashioned but I don't do unconscious women.' His hands stopped rubbing my arms and firmly he turned me around to face him.

He was almost completely naked in front of me, naked apart from a pair of black fitted boxers. I lifted my gaze up quickly from his boxers, then up over his sculpted tattooed chest and bravely I made my eyes find his. At the very first contact, I heard myself release a very audible gasp. His eyes looked heavy, tired and what I found in the very depths of them made them appear to be tortured.

'I don't understand,' I managed to put out into the electrically charged air around us.

'Let me recap for you. I found ya late last night in a room all by yourself, drunk. I could have left you, but I didn't want to.'

Where the hell had Lauren and Winter gone? I'd never forgive them!

I felt my brows furrow in question. His arms lifted from my shoulders and his warm fingers brushed my hair away from my face. His thumbs caressed my eyebrows almost ordering them to flatten down under his ministrations. Once my face had relaxed his hands once again found their place holding me.

'You were drunk. I was worried about you.' His voice had taken on a harsher tone. 'Drinking by yourself is a fucking game changer, whatever the reason you might think you have to do it…DON'T!'

My eyes widened at his reprimand. It was like a red rag to a bull.

'I was not drinking by myself!'

'It sure looked that way to me,' he accused.

'Just who the hell do you think you are? We have a one-night stand and now you think you own me! I'll drink whatever and whenever I bloody feel like it. I don't need anyone to parent me. I never have before and I'm not starting now.' I moved my arms, suddenly lifting them quickly and bringing them down on the broad forearms holding me. In self-defence class, it was a manoeuvre we had been taught to break someone's hold on you. My arms came down on his fast, but he never even flinched. His muscular arms kept their same solid hold on me.

106

BRODY

Ok, I'd only been to the class twice, maybe I'd done it wrong?

'We had more than a fucking one-night stand and you know it.' His right hand moved off my arm and he tapped his index finger gently on my temple. 'I felt it and so did you, that's why you ran the fuck away yesterday morning... I'm not letting ya run away again.'

My body very mildly started to shake. But still he continued.

'I found you by yourself and I didn't like the state you were in, I was worried about you.'

'Oh, right, yeah. So, you brought me up to your bed... so we could... well so you...' My voice tailed off, no longer sure what I was accusing him of.

'So, we could what, Amy?... Let's hear it, what did I do?' The corners of his mouth twitched with amusement at my words. Eventually the full lopsided grin took over his face, revealing his dimple. 'Come on spill it. I brought you to my bed, so I could do what?'

'So, you could have sex with me.' I watched the grin on his face fall away.

'Do you really fucking think that's what I have to do, to get someone to fuck me?' His head shook from side to side and I could hear him tutting at me in disapproval. 'Do I really seem like the sort of man who has to get women drunk so they'll fuck me? Let me assure you, I fucking don't. I get enough women willing to share my bed or any other fucking surface available and they always moan their consent to me, usually several times over. The women I have sex with are coherent enough to know I'm not starring as part of their erotic drunken dream... your words not mine.' Another flush went up my body and coloured every part of my face. 'Believe me when I say, I don't force women who have just thrown up all over me to suck my dick either, strange as that may seem.' He watched my eyes open in horror before he carried on. 'Neither do I balk at changing a woman out of her sick spattered dress and putting her into one of my T-shirts. Even though the whole of my fucking body was screaming at me to hold you in my arms with your bare skin against mine. It's called looking after someone you care for... Hell, I even cleaned your teeth.' He smiled at me.

I ran my tongue instinctively around my mouth, feeling the smooth, squeaky clean surface. Then I looked down at myself, taking in that I was indeed dressed in a very big, grey T-shirt with rolled up sleeves. 'I threw up on you?'

He nodded.

I didn't continue our conversation. I just looked up into his face. A strange compulsion came over me. I wanted to trust him, I wanted to fling my arms around him and hug him to me. But for now, I was scared. So, I took a deep breath and like every other feeling that had ever threatened to engulf me, I held it inside.

'I'm sorry, I don't make a habit of doing things like I've done in the last few days. I don't crash cars. I rarely drink, and especially when I haven't eaten since lunchtime. And I definitely don't have one-night stands.' I didn't know him well or at all really, but I could have sworn that his face took on a sense of pride at my words. 'The problem is you don't know me and I don't know you, do I, Daniel?'

I was sure he flinched slightly at my words, but it was momentary and then he was back, standing firm and resolute in front of me once again. 'Then let's spend some time together. Let me get to know you and you can get to know me, stop pushing me the fuck away.'

I shook my head at him.

'Is this what you do, Amy? Do you push everyone away who threatens to come into your nicely compartmentalised life?' He exhaled and pulled me just a little further into him, and I felt his warm breath on the top of my head. Then his hands gripped me just a little bit tighter. I didn't know how, but it seemed he could identify my fear.

'I recognise it in you, Amy. I've been there, hell I'm often still there teetering on the edge. I don't know what bastard did a number on you, but that was their fucking loss and as far as I see it, my gain. I don't see it as a problem, I see it as fun. I see it as something to look forward to. Let me in, let me get to know you.' All I could do was nod my head at him as he continued. 'Hell, it's normal life, isn't it, Amy? It's what happens all over the world when people feel a connection.' One hand found my chin and effectively forced my eyes back to his. I complied. I had been attempting to look away. I had been trying to find something else to concentrate on, something else to try to break the bond I already felt to a man I had only met a few days ago.

'I don't know about you, but I'd love a bit of normal in my life.' He laughed. 'We have a connection, Amy... Don't we? You don't have to own up to it, I can feel it when we're near to each other and when we touch it's like my skin catches alight.'

'Yes... I feel it too,' I answered, still trying to process through the words he had just spoken.

My body continued to shake in his arms. The stunning man in front of me, wanted to really get to know me. I was dazed.

'Come on, get back into bed, you're trembling.' His voice was deep and low.

'I can't.'

A loud exhale left his mouth as he took in my reply.

'Not taking no for an answer.' His body began to stiffen up in front of mine, although his hold on me relaxed.

He stood to his full height. 'You know you were almost right when you said I didn't own you. I don't own your mind, I'd never want to, either. I prefer a woman who can give as good as she gets. The sexiest women have minds of their own.' He inhaled before he continued. 'However, since the moment we met I have had a command over this gorgeous body of yours... you know it and I know it. Get back into bed.' His voice had become quieter but firmer, as he stared down expectantly at me.

My whole body reacted to his words. Every single hair on my body stood on end, my breathing was laboured and my heart was nearly breaking out of my chest in response.

'Don't cross me, beautiful. I will, if I have to, pick you up and put you there.' Finally, his hands left the tops of my arms and crossed over his chest. His fingers twitched as he fought to keep his hands to himself.

Slowly, I finally began to relax, his words were beginning to hit home. Feeling a little more confidant at the unusual circumstances I found myself in, I replied. 'I have no problem with you picking me up, God knows you seem to have been doing it a lot in the last few days. But before you put me back into bed, could you carry me to the loo first?' I smiled up as I teased him.

His eyes that had been dull and tortured before, sparked to life as he began to laugh at my words.

'I'm sure I can do that. Is that whatcha were looking for earlier?'

'Yes,' I muttered with embarrassment.

He placed his hands under me and once again swung me up, in one very easy movement.

When we arrived at the bathroom door he gently lowered me down. I quickly ran into the room, making sure the door closed behind me. Pulling my knickers down I sat down on the chilly seat and to the absolute relief of my bladder, I began to wee. As I sat there, for the first time ever, I realised that my clit was throbbing, having received no foreplay whatsoever. It appeared he was right. He, his words and his body, seemed to be able to control the way I felt. I liked the thought that he owned my body. I was shocked to realise I felt safe and comfortable with the thought. I stood up, washed my hands and in somewhat of a hurry I took a quick look in the mirror. Luckily, I didn't look like the sick mess I might have done. Apart from my eye make-up having made its way under my eyes, I was in quite a good state. I wiped a damp tissue under my eyes and then I pulled the door open quickly to find Daniel stood in exactly the same spot I had left him.

Not saying a word, he picked me up again. This time his front to mine. On instinct, my legs wrapped around his waist and he placed his hands on my bare bum cheeks. I gasped at how much I'd needed to feel his calloused fingers on my needy flesh. His hands were warm but some of his heavy rings were cold, and it felt exquisite. It appeared that he was as shocked as me that I'd deliberately left my knickers on the bathroom floor. I watched his eyebrows raise in surprise and question at the bare skin he found in his grip. I allowed my hands to find purchase on his shoulders and then, as our bodies crashed together, I accepted my body's need to wrap my arms around his neck, effectively pulling him closer to me. As he walked, holding me tightly against his bare torso, I summoned up the courage to place a chaste kiss to his lips.

'Thank you for looking after me.'

With as much care as he could, he gently lowered me onto the bed. By the light of the bedside lamp he had switched on earlier, I watched as his expression changed rapidly from tenderness to one of lust at the position we were now in. He had stayed in between my legs as we came down almost as one, to the soft bed now underneath my back. He kept his weight off me and on his forearms as he gazed down.

His eyes darkened as his pupils dilated.

'Always.' The one word he spoke resonated deep inside me.

My head was dazed with that one word, but my body expected something more, I wanted something more, and I could see that he was fighting with what he also needed.

'Goddamn it... Do ya know how much I want you, Amy?'

I sucked in my bottom lip and shook my head shyly under his darkening perusal.

'I find that weird, surely you can see how much you turn me on? If ya can't, you should definitely be able to feel it.' His hips thrust gently in between my legs, his rock-hard cock pushed into my mound, making me gasp. 'I can smell how much you want me.'

Without one coherent thought in my head I allowed my mouth to say exactly what I wanted it to. 'Then take me, just bloody take me. Please, my body feels like it's on fire.'

In one quick movement, he rolled away. I heard him push his boxers quickly down his legs, the tell-tale crinkle of foil as he ripped open the condom and then he rolled back. With his eyes once again holding me captive he sunk himself inside me in one swift thrust and we both groaned at the immense feelings our connection created inside us. Then he froze and as his tense face relaxed he smiled his lopsided grin at me.

'I thought we were going to get to know each other, Amy?' he asked.

'Tomorrow, Daniel. Please, tonight just fuck me.'

'Hold on tight, because I damn well want this more than I need my next fucking breath... I wanna be as deep inside you as I can.'

I could already feel my eyes rolling up into my head with every single thrust he made into me.

'Then do it,' I whispered, knowing I would grant him permission to do anything to me.

He lifted my right leg, placing his hand under my thigh and then he pushed my leg closer towards my chest. I felt myself open wider to him.

'Oh... I wasn't asking, beautiful. I was always going to take exactly what I needed from you and give you. Exactly. What. I. Know. You. Need. From. Me.' Every word he spoke to me came as he thrust deep inside me. The bundle of nerves that were screaming for attention felt the smooth crown of his large cock every single time. Within minutes I was falling apart in his arms.

'Let go,' he commanded and I came, shouting out words of encouragement to him.

'FUCK!' he roared, as his head convulsed forward in spasms and then it finally fell onto my T-shirt clad shoulder.

For a few seconds, I just held his body close to mine. My fingertips wandered over his muscular, sweat-covered back. He was beyond anything I could have ever dreamt about in my wildest dreams and now he was holding me close, like a lover. I had never experienced sex like I had now experienced the past two nights with him. I wanted more, so much more.

Suddenly he reawakened and pulling me to him, he rolled us both over so I could now collapse on top of his chest.

'I'm so fucking happy you're here, Amy. No more running away, promise me.'

I lifted my head away from the comfort of his heartbeat, to find him staring at me.

'Just don't give me any reason to run then.' I smiled back at him.

His hand swiftly came down on one of my bare bum cheeks with a firm whack.

'Hey!' I exclaimed, feeling wetness hit the top of my thighs as he soothed my enraged skin with a circular motion with the palm of his hand.

'I said, promise me.'

'I don't make promises, they're just words, they mean nothing,' I whispered.

'Actions speak louder than words, is that what you mean?'

'Mmmm... I suppose I do. I find it hard to trust people, when they find it so hard to keep their promises to me.'

'I'll remember that, I promise you.' He kissed the top of my head and squeezed me tightly to him.

Moving one arm from around me, he shifted us both around. Gradually, he helped me out of the T-shirt he had put on me earlier. Then in one decisive movement, he pulled me back down into his embrace and we connected, skin to skin. The touch of his flesh on mine ignited a deep want within me, but not just a sexual want. I realised I wanted to always feel this close to him. The thought was crazy, worrying and satisfying, all at the same time. But I couldn't think on it now, and as my cheek laid on his chest I heard myself sigh. I was already starting to drift off. But as he began to speak again, I heard the words as they resonated deep inside me.

'This reminds me of last night. I lay there holding you as you slept and I looked up through the skylights to see the stars twinkling above us. In that sky full of stars, all I could see was you.'

My heart leapt in panic and filled with something I'd never felt before. I spoke, trying to maintain a lightness to my voice to disguise my confused feelings.

'That's so romantic, maybe you should write songs,' I muttered as my eyes struggled to remain open.

I felt his chest hitch underneath me. 'Yeah, maybe I should...'

Seventeen

Amy

'**Y**OU ARE RIDICULOUS,'I muttered to myself as I walked down the driveway.

'This whole situation is bloody ridiculous.' If I hadn't been holding my coat so tightly around myself, to keep out the freezing cold temperatures, I would have waved my arms around in indignation.

It was just before eight in the morning and I was walking down the long driveway between The Manor and the outbuildings containing The Fairy Garden. Although the drive had been cleared and salted several times over for the opening yesterday, we'd had another light dusting during the night and the driveway this morning was now once again covered in ice. I was walking on the grass verge to the side of the driveway in three-inch heels. The same three-inch heels that were undoubtedly either going to be the attributing factor to me breaking my neck or going to be ruined by my stupidity. Nearly every step I took resulted in my freezing cold, stocking-clad feet burning with pressure, as they were once again forced against the pointed toe of my shoes. I was fighting against my heels disappearing into the ice underneath my feet. What was worse was the fact I was causing myself the excruciating pain deliberately, as like a child I ran away again. I wasn't proud of myself, in fact if I was my best friend I would be laying into me something awful over the way I was behaving.

'WHY, AMY?' I shouted into the stillness around me. As my voice disintegrated into the chill, the air around me changed suddenly. I could now hear the low purr of an engine behind me. A vehicle was coming down the drive. Without turning to look, I pulled the faux fur coat tighter around myself and made sure the collar was standing as tall as possible, so I could sink further into its covering depths. I was doing the walk of shame and it would be so *bloody* great if I could keep it to myself. I didn't want to share my embarrassment with anyone else. It would be a profound relief if I could complete this expedition, into what felt like Antarctica, with no one recognising me.

The low purr got nearer and finally it slowed to the pace I was walking. I knew if I threw a look over my right shoulder the vehicle would be there just behind me, deliberately going at my pace. Realisation hit.

It was following me.

Oh, fuck my life.

I didn't need to look.

I knew it was Daniel.

I could feel him, and now with every single painful step forward I could feel his anger ramping up. I was stupid. I knew I was stupid. Whatever had possessed me to leave his bed again this morning in the dark, was crazy.

I was certifiably crazy.

Deep down, I knew why the compulsion took over me.

I was scared, so scared of letting down my walls and letting him in.

What if he didn't like what he found?

What if I found in time an even greater connection to him and he just simply upped and walked away?

'Get in,' I heard almost growled at me through the open passenger window.

At the very moment he chose to speak, my right heel did everything I had been trying so hard not to let it do, it sunk further into the soil and my foot rose up without it. I froze as I willed my body to balance precariously on the left one. The car next to me quietened as its engine stopped when it came to a standstill beside me. Looking down I could see my right shoe had now been filled with snow, in the wake of my foot. I now couldn't put my foot back in.

Dear God, this could only happen to me.

Slowly, I glanced to the right.

Daniel was dressed in the same grey T-shirt he had put on and taken off me last night. The very same T-shirt that had been in between our bodies when we had once again given into the feelings of immense need that took over us whenever we were together. His muscular arms were fully exposed, showing me wonderful amounts of bare flesh and a myriad of tattoos on them both. Those same strong arms that I loved to feel wrapped around me. He was leant forward onto the steering wheel and I found it hard to tear my gaze away. Eventually, I composed myself enough and looked up to his face. At first glance his expression appeared stoic and unreadable, but on further inspection I appreciated it was more likely he was worried or even tired. The stubble on his face was the longest I'd seen it and I could see the salt and pepper effect over his jaw line. I watched as his eyebrows began to move in question at me.

'At least let me take you to wherever the fuck you're running off to… Get in.'

'I can't,' I finally answered in a small voice. Then I looked down at my feet and knew as I heard him shift on the leather seat he had followed my gaze.

A few seconds passed.

The laughter that spontaneously forced itself out of him was therapeutic and it almost cleansed us both completely of the awkward situation enveloping us. Once his laughter had faded away, his anger once again permeated the air and I looked away. The car door slammed and I knew he had jumped out to rescue me once again.

I didn't lift my eyes away from my feet until I saw his unlaced brown boots in front of where I was struggling to maintain balance. Then, as his hands found my elbows to steady me, I let my eyes travel up the worn, light blue jeans he had pulled on and then over the grey T-shirt that was stretched magnificently over the wide expanse of his chest.

'I'm beginning to think you're cursed in some way, Amy.'

'It's probable,' I replied with a sad resignation.

'Come on.' In one swift movement, I was grasped by the waist and hoisted once again over his left shoulder. This time I didn't question what he was doing. As he walked the few steps over to his waiting vehicle I watched as in front of my eyes the muscles in his backside flexed in his well-fitting jeans, all the time fighting with myself not to touch.

To my dismay, the view in front of my eyes was gone as quickly as it had appeared. I heard the click of the door as he opened the passenger side and I was unceremoniously dumped on my arse on the warmth of his heated seat. My coat was falling off me and my dirty dress was twisted to the side and much higher up my thighs than I wanted. I looked down and saw the exposed lace at the top of my thigh highs. I knew I was sans knickers, as in my hurry this morning, when I had woken up with panic clawing at my throat, I hadn't been able to turn on the light in the bathroom to look for them. I hadn't wanted to risk waking the gorgeous man by my side.

He slammed the door on me, taking out his anger and frustration on his prized possession. I watched him turn and walk back towards the stuck shoe. I quickly pulled the dress down as far as it would go, to cover up my shame.

'Don't worry, just leave it,' I called through the open window as I righted myself. I had no idea why. It was a typically English thing to say. I mean who in their right mind leaves one of their most expensive shoes in a pile of ice and snow?

Ignoring me completely, Daniel crouched down on his haunches and picked up the black shoe, shaking and banging it against his palm until it emptied. From the same crouched position, he turned his head when he heard my voice, to stare at me in question, his eyes once again meeting mine. I hardly knew him, but I could sense by his posture just how angry he was, his body was bristling as he fought to contain just how pissed off he was with me.

I had felt ashamed as I walked down the driveway earlier, but that was nothing to the way his look made me feel right now. He didn't have to say a word. I felt my shame and his hurt, deep down inside.

Slowly he stood to his full height. He made his way around from the grass verge to the driver side still holding my eyes captive with his. In a swift movement, he jumped up into the car and slammed his door. His hand passed me over my sodden shoe. I took it from him and watched as his fingers found the switch to close my window, effectively closing us into the fraught space of the car.

'I don't know what to say,' I spoke, trying to break through the heavy atmosphere as I looked down to my lap and to the wet shoe I was turning over in both hands. I started to physically shiver as my body started to warm up, or was it because of the feelings between us?

I didn't look up at him again, but I knew he was staring at me. I could feel the thick tension in the small space. The chemistry was once again ramping up between us, even with his anger and my stupidity. As a deep sigh left his mouth, he turned his body to face mine. In the edge of my peripheral view, I saw him bend his left leg at the knee and lean it against the centre console, as he repositioned his body. I knew he wasn't going to move the car until I faced him. I couldn't look away any longer, so I lifted my head and turned it slowly to fully take in the man who had come out in the cold to find me.

He had obviously woken up and finding I wasn't there, had left in a hurry. His hair was still mussed from sleeping and he had grabbed any clothing to hand, but it was once again his eyes that reeled me in. They looked angry, but most of all they looked pained. His tic on his cheek was spasmodically twitching as he tried to work out exactly what he wanted to say to me.

'Please say something, say anything. Shout at me, swear if you have to.'

'Shout? Swear? Will that make me feel better, Amy, or you?' His right palm smashed down onto the steering wheel, making me jump. 'I'm not sure what the fucking hell to say to you.' His voice was deep and controlled, although I could hear a hint of exasperation. 'I thought we'd gone over this last night?' His eyes questioned me. 'If you'd wanted to go home, after we'd fucked, all you had to do was say. I would have taken you. I wouldn't have wanted to, but fuck, I would've taken you.'

'I know.' My voice was small, as I took in how much I'd hurt him.

He rubbed his hands over his face as he tried to work out who I was. Silently, I wished him good luck. Even in thirty-three years, I hadn't been able to work it out. 'I'm confused, Amy, when we're together you're with me in every fucking way possible. When we touch, the chemistry between us is off the fucking rails. Do you agree? Or have I got this so far fucking wrong that I'm delusional?'

'No, you're right, everything you've said is right.'

'Then why do you wake the fuck up every goddamn morning and instead of cuddling further into me and sharing all the wonderful, awesome possibilities of being alive and together in each other's arms, do you panic and go with your first instinct and try to run as far away as possible?'

I looked at him in that moment, really looked at him. For all his obvious confidence, knicker-melting good looks, and money, he was equally as scarred by life as me.

He was as damaged as I was.

For opening up just that little bit to me and exposing his vulnerability, he deserved something in return. I wasn't sure what to say that would make him feel any better, but I wanted to try. As much as being with him frightened me, I realised that being without him terrified me even more. I didn't want to hurt him as his past clearly had. The only people in my life to ever fight for me before were my friends and my nan, but Daniel was here and fighting for a chance to be with me.

'I like you, Daniel. For the first time in a very long time, I want more. But with what's happened in my past and the way my life is just now, I'm just not sure I'm cut out for a relationship. When I'm with you, I want to be with you so much it scares me.'

'What the fuck did I do to scare you away?' His voice was once again pained as he questioned me.

'*You* didn't do anything, it's not your fault.' I stopped for a few seconds, mulling over just how much I wanted to expose to the man sat next to me. 'Me leaving in the morning is to protect myself.'

'At fucking last,' he added to our emotional conversation, a smile twitched at the corners of his mouth.

'What do you mean, at last?'

'I wanted you to admit that you were running from yourself. I saw it in you, because for most of my life I've been doing the same fucking thing.'

'Why?'

He exhaled deeply, shook his head and banged his open palm down on the steering wheel. 'Because I was dealt a fucked-up hand in my childhood. It's taken me too many fucking years to be able to stand being in my own company. I'll tell you about it sometime.'

'Oh.' The word was pathetic, it wasn't a lot to answer him with, but I had to add something to the conversation. So, that was how he saw through my façade. It takes one to know one, ran through my head.

'Look, I know this is intense between us. Hell, it's far too fucking fast to feel this…' for a moment he stopped to think, '… this way.'

I felt my eyes opening wider at his words. His warm hand came over the console and after throwing the wet shoe he found in my lap to the floor, he grasped both of my hands in his one. His thumb casually rubbed over my hand offering me comfort, as the tide of emotions swirled around us.

'Amy, do you at least want to try? I know that I fucking do and believe me I only normally want to be with a woman for the sexual release, I don't *do* relationships. Do you like enough of what you've seen and found with me in the last few days to give it a go?' His stare was intense to say the least, as if he was trying to show just how much this meant to him. 'What I'm really asking is, do you want to try the relationship thing with me?' For all his normal confidence and maturity, he sounded like a young man asking a girl out for the very first time.

I sucked in my cheek and bit down, teasing the soft flesh I found there. One of my hands left the confines of his, it came up to twiddle with a piece of my hair and curl it around my index finger. My heart was shouting inside of me to be heard, and for one of the first times ever my brain engaged and listened.

'I do,' I whispered.

Momentarily he shook his head and then he laughed out loud. The deep warming sound filled me up. At last the shivering that had overtaken me finally relented. 'That wasn't something I ever thought I'd want to hear from a woman in any fucking context, but here and now, from you. I'm fucking ecstatic to hear it.' His lopsided grin spread over his relieved face.

He physically relaxed in front of my eyes, sinking further into the leather upholstery. His hand moved up and took mine away from fidgeting with my hair, he lifted it to his mouth and turned it over to place a gentle kiss on my exposed wrist. Every nerve ending I had sparked to life and the sparks travelled straight down to my sex. I blinked slowly and clenched my core muscles, trying to alleviate the feelings he pulled out of me with that simple show of affection, or was it ownership? I wasn't sure, but either of them were fine with me.

'Okay, that's good, Miss. Harper. I wasn't prepared to accept any other answer, anyway.' His eyes met mine as he looked up from my wrist. He winked at me, then twisted his body back around and placed my hand down to rest on his thigh.

I laughed back at him as the car came to life when he placed his foot on the accelerator.

'So…' He spoke as his car began to once again travel down the driveway.

I looked back up at him, tearing my eyes away from my hand on his thigh.

'So?' I questioned.

'It seems that you and me, beautiful, are officially in a relationship.'

My heart skipped a beat at the words, beautiful and relationship. I grinned back at him.

'Prepare to be swept off your fucking feet. I need you in my life and I know that you need me just as much in yours. I'm pulling out all the fucking stops. I dare you not to fall in love with me, Amy'

He watched as his words resonated inside me and then he turned back to concentrate on the driveway in front of us, leaving me still staring at the gorgeous man next to me. I knew deep down that if he carried on the way he was going I would be there sooner than either of us needed.

Eighteen

Amy

I MADE MY way, as fast as my heels would allow me to go, up the wrought iron staircase. At the top I turned to give Daniel a wave before he pulled out of the carpark. He had pulled on his beanie and his sunglasses, while he had watched me climbing the stairs. My stomach somersaulted as he two-finger saluted at me and then with the same two fingers he blew me a kiss. His large car began to pull away and I made myself go into my room and not stay there to watch the red of his tail lights disappear.

The tearooms were closed today as they always were on a Monday and I was going to have a much-needed day off and take the time to sleep. With the door locked behind me, I hung my coat up, stripped out of my clothes, and dropped them to the floor where I stood. Lauren's sick-spattered dress would need dry cleaning anyway.

On the way to the shower I switched on the digital radio and began to hum to the tune that immediately started playing.

The shower was refreshing and just what I needed. I spent the longest time in there under the strong spray of water. However, it wasn't without its problems. I had soaped up my body in the same methodical way I had done for years, but for the first time ever, every piece of skin on my body reacted to my own touch, as though it was crying out to feel Daniel's caress. I allowed my hands to run over my needy skin a few times and remembered once again what it felt like to be in his arms. I knew that I could have quite easily made myself come, but I wanted to save myself for his touch only. I stepped out, listening once again to the radio and sung along with the song. The coarseness of the towel as I rubbed myself dry was a welcome diversion.

I stepped out into the bedroom and walked around to the oak wash stand, rubbing the towel over my wet hair. Holding onto the ceramic knob I pulled open the drawer and found just what I needed, a thick pair of Tartan pyjamas. I dressed in their warmth quickly, without undoing any buttons. As my head appeared out of the neckline, a piece of paper hanging from the letterbox caught my eye. I finished dressing, pulled out the paper and sat down on the bed to read the words.

I know you eat lunch (unlike breakfast and dinner) and I know where to find you.

I'll be back to pick you up at 1pm.

We're going on a picnic.

Wrap up warm.

I ran my eyes over the words, twice. I couldn't believe he had already been back to post the piece of paper.

He's coming back, today?

Despite only a few minutes ago feeling like I could comprehensively sleep for a week, I jumped up off the bed and ran to retrieve my phone from my coat pocket. Checking the time, I realised I had five hours. I had plenty of time. Feelings of excitement ran through me, followed quickly by nausea.

Am I really going to do this?

Yes… I really am.

The red icon on my green message box, indicating I had six messages, caught my eye. I opened them all quickly, to find that Winter and Lauren had been messaging me on and off since this morning.

"Where are you?" was repeated several times over.

I sent them a quick "All okay. I'm back at the tearooms, speak to you later." Then I set my old and often unreliable phone hopefully to silent, knowing they were bound to come back with more questions. I knew what those questions would probably be about and, not quite knowing all the answers myself, I took the easy way out. But I was still annoyed that they'd left me drunk on a settee, so I would catch up with them later.

I turned off the radio, set the alarm on the clock on the bedside table, jumped into bed and pressed the button to the side of me. Motorised blinds closed instantaneously on the four skylights above, and as the room fell into darkness I immediately fell into a deep sleep.

BRODY

I hadn't felt this fucking excited since the double D's first got to the top of the U.S. charts, and that was a lifetime ago.

So much had fucking happened between then and now.

I was sick of drowning in remorse, she made me want to climb out of the dark pit I had built myself. She made me want to live and that realisation was everything.

I'd pulled away from the tearoom earlier and began the short drive back to my bed. My brain had been on overdrive wondering where the hell I was going to take out the first woman I had ever had a relationship with. The same fucking woman who had consumed my every waking minute since I'd first seen her in her nan's old shop. I'd been to meetings, had important phone calls, and written down the basics for three different fucking songs in the last few days, and not for more than five fucking minutes had she left the forefront of my mind. The three songs I had the basics of were all love songs, I'd written four for the band before over all the years we'd been together, but now I'd scribbled down three in the last three days, it was fucking crazy.

Suddenly, all the words in my head were about her.

A building off to the right, through the tall trees and far away from the main drag of the drive, caught my eye. The sun was low in the sky and was shining on the windows of the building. Having never even noticed it before, I pulled over to investigate. After freezing my nuts off running for about a mile over the snow and ice covered garden, I found it was better than I could have imagined. Peering through the windows like a fucking kid staring into a sweet shop, I'd discovered it was just what I needed for today. I drove quickly straight back to the tearoom and pushed the piece of paper through the letterbox. I'd seen the English equivalent of an American mailbox the first time she had run away from me, when I'd stared hard at the door just willing her to walk back through it.

It took me an hour to track down the key to the building I had found out was called Lake View. I'd enlisted a few of the staff from The Manor to do some extra cleaning and made sure that they would light the large open fireplace in the main room. I knew the place was going to be absolutely fucking perfect. I wanted time with her where we could get to know each other and luckily for me, it was also away from any audience.

I was now back in the kitchen and filling up a wicker basket thing that one of the kitchen staff had found for me, with different foods I wanted to treat her to.

'Well, look what the fucking cat dragged in.' I heard Raff's voice behind me and smiled. 'If it isn't Daniel.'

I swallowed, placed the knife I had been cutting bread with slowly down onto the board, and turned towards my accuser and his implied accusation. I leant my jean-covered ass down onto the polished metal preparation area and sighing in acceptance, I crossed my arms across my chest.

My eyes found him pulling up a stool behind me and I knew he wasn't leaving until we'd had a conversation that I wasn't yet prepared to fucking have. He sat down and mirroring my defensive body language, he also crossed his arms over his chest. I stared at him, letting his questioning gaze wash over me.

I knew that face, he meant business.

I held up my open palm to him. 'Just slow the fuck up, I know where this is coming from.' I put my hands into the front pockets of my jeans and shrugged my shoulders at him. 'I never lied to Amy, she heard Cade calling out Daniels and she just took it from there.'

He moved his head from side to side and pulled his mouth into a slight sneer as he mulled over my reason.

'Yeah, I'm reasonable, I can see that. We all call you Daniels, instead of arsehole, from time to time when we talk to you, but what about now?'

'Oh, ha fucking ha, you're a fucking comedian. Whadaya mean, what the fuck about now?' My voice rose in volume in defence.

'You're packing up a picnic, and it's for Amy, don't fucking tell me anything different.'

'It could *be* for anybody,' I snarled at him, pissed that I'd been caught out.

'Winter guessed that the "Daniel" Amy was talking about, was you. She and Lauren had a conversation with Amy after you slept with her the first time. Then last night, she disappeared from the drawing room next to where we played. The room that you were seen escaping into after our set. We looked around for about an hour before Winter put two and two together and we all realised she must have gone back to your room with you.'

'Yeah, I was escaping. Hell, if it means that much to you all to know my business, you might as well know that we didn't do much fucking sleeping… either night.' I knew I was being a bastard, so I upped the fucking stakes, and made myself an arrogant bastard.

'Fuck, Brody! Don't play fucking games here. What the actual fuck do you want with her?'

I uncrossed my arms quickly, rubbed at my hair on my head and started pointing my finger at him and his fucking accusations. 'Believe me when I tell you I'm not playing around here. This has the possibility to be so different from anything else I've ever had.' I watched as his eyebrows raised in question and surprise. I crossed my arms again to stop my accusing finger pointing at him. 'She hasn't a clue who I am, and it's seriously the best fucking thing ever. I know I will have to tell her. Eventually.'

'Soon,' he pointedly interrupted me.

'Yeah, okay, fucking soon. I do know that. But just for a few days I want to be the guy she's just met, the one who makes her heart flutter and her breathing quicken, just because I'm me and not some rock God. I want her to *want* to be with me for what she finds in here.' I smashed my closed fist into my chest. 'I'm sick to the fucking back teeth with the false fucking shit that's been in our lives and that comes into our lives on a regular basis, because we're in a band. Tell me you understand that?'

'You know I do.' His body language relaxed as he empathised with me.

'Then just give me a few days.' My voice was quiet and almost pleading in its tone.

'Look, I grew up around here, with people like Amy. They're not used to having people like us around.' I raised my eyebrows at his "people like us," not quite sure exactly what it was he was getting at, but my brain quickly came up with a thousand reasons why their quiet civilised lives really didn't need us in them. My stomach churned over. I'd only just found her and I wasn't prepared for the fucking fact she may not want me to stay. Raff carried on. 'I didn't have a lot to do with her when we were younger, as you know I didn't hang around here very long. But, she means the world to Winter and she's Lauren's cousin. So, you could say she's like part of the family, just don't hurt her. I do know that she has dealt with more shit in her life than a fucking pig farm.' He looked up and caught the look on my face. 'Yeah, I know you have too, but I'm serious. Do the fucking right thing by her, have your couple of days and then tell her who the fuck you are and let her make her own decision about it.'

I nodded resolutely at him. He walked up to me, and we man hugged for a few seconds as we slapped each other on the back.

'So, how's it going?' I countered as he pulled away, eager to put him under the spotlight and to remove it from me.

'How's what going?'

I smirked at his brazen attempt to pretend he wasn't once again trying to get the woman he had never stopped loving.

'Lauren,' I added, to jog his selective memory.

'Oh… Lauren. Mmmm… Well she's just got engaged and it's not to me.' Pain overtook his features as he spoke the words.

'Fuck,' was all I could offer in answer.

'Yeah, see ya later. Have fun, but do right by her and be good to her, take it from me you may never get the opportunity again.' I could hear the regret in his voice.

I watched as he walked towards the kitchen door. I had no advice to offer, I wished I had. As the aluminium door swung shut behind him, I turned back to my previous occupation and carried on making up our lunch.

Nineteen

Amy

'YOU CAN OPEN your eyes now.' His fingers slowly peeled away from holding my hands firmly in place. His arms came down and he wrapped them around my body, holding me close to him, his front to my back. I felt his chin gently resting on the top of my head as he allowed me to take in the view.

I was filled with anticipation, so I slowly opened my eyes and eventually stood looking in absolute awe at the beautiful building in front of me. I knew by the architecture and the shape of the arched windows that were represented everywhere, that it was part of the same estate that included The Manor and the tearooms. Although I lived nearby I had never seen this place before, it was picturesque. The mainly iced-over lake that sat behind it, offering a background that surrounded it like a frame.

We had been walking through the layers of snow for about twenty minutes. All the time my snow boots had been crunching through the bitter cold, Daniel had been guiding me. As soon as he had picked me up in his car, he had taken me into his arms and pulled me tightly to him as if he was trying to convey all the feelings that were coursing around his body. Then he had kissed my forehead and wrapped his scarf around my eyes like an excited schoolboy trying to keep a secret. His cologne had engulfed me like a warm blanket as soon as I had inhaled. Although I was now getting colder with every second that passed, his obvious excitement and the fact that his hands had been connected to me in some way for the whole of the journey, had kept me going.

'Will this do for our first date?' he whispered into my ear, the warmth of his breath caressed my sensitive skin with a promise of what our first date as a couple would entail. Electrical charges ran through me, warming me up and making me shiver all at the same time.

I nodded. 'You certainly pull out all the stops when you date a woman, don't you?' The air left my body and sent warm clouds into the air around us.

He laughed gently into the crevice of my neck. 'I've no fucking idea. I've not dated since school and even then, I hung out at the diner with everyone else. This with you, is different.'

Before I really had time to think over his words, he was once again pushing me forward to enter the two-storey, red brick building. His hands left me and he walked to the side of me to open the door. The beautifully glossed, navy blue wood and glass panelled door swung open to reveal a room that seemed to be trapped in history. Heavy drapes were at every window, all the wooden furniture was made from mahogany and its warm burgundy colour embraced the room. To one end a huge stone fireplace dominated most of the entire wall, the fire was lit and heat billowed out into the room. I stepped across the worn flagstones and entered the room. Immediately feeling the heat, I started to remove my coat and gloves as Daniel closed the door behind us. I placed them down over the back of the huge settee in front of me.

'Is this okay?' A nervous voice asked from behind me. I heard him sniff. 'It smells a bit... what do you Brits say?'

I sniffed into the air and laughed. 'Yes, it's a bit musty. But it will definitely do. I can't believe you found this and have gone to all this trouble for me.'

'Would it be too corny to say that you're worth it?'

'No, it wouldn't.'

I spun completely around and finding his arms already open and by his side, I walked straight into his embrace. He kissed the top of my head as both of his hands found my bum cheeks and he squeezed.

'What's with all this head and forehead kissing, my lips are still in the same place as this morning, you know?' I closed my eyes momentarily as the thought that was flying around my head was traitorously expelled by my mouth. I tentatively looked up to see him throw his head back as he roared with laughter.

'Do you know how hard it is?' he finally replied.

I looked at him quizzically as his head once again came forward and he looked down at me, shaking his head at my doubt.

'Enlighten me,' I answered and his grip around me tightened.

'As soon as the car door slammed shut on us this afternoon, I wanted to lift you onto my lap and impale you so fucking fast onto my dick, you'd have felt me for the rest of the day. It makes no fucking odds to me that people could have seen you through the windows.' He let out a long sigh as if he was imagining the absolute feeling of satisfaction we both got from him being inside me. 'We're now shut and locked in a remote building all by ourselves. The open fire was a necessity, but it makes me want to strip you of every single piece of the warm fucking clothing I asked you to wear.' He stopped and widening his nostrils he quickly inhaled. 'After I'd got ya naked, I could watch as your blood rushed to your breasts, making them heavy and sensitive. That would be closely followed by your nipples turning the raspberry colour I fucking love, as I pinched and rolled them between my fingers. That gorgeous sight would drive me to my fucking knees, where I'd be able to smell that bare pussy of yours. Lifting your legs over my shoulders, I would push my long tongue through your wet folds and then it would find its way home, where I would pump it in and out of you so fucking fast, you would begin to shake in response. I'd then restrain you against the wall using this hard, muscular body that you want to touch every time I'm close to you. And you would stay restrained by me as I slid my dick inside you, not waiting for you to adjust to me. I swear to you that I would pound in and out of you until the ice on that lake outside shattered and the wildlife around here knew just how much you loved God... How are ya liking my reason so far?'

My eyes had widened as his story went on, and my knees had got to the point of being so sensitive, that if his arms hadn't been wrapped around me so tightly I was sure I would have collapsed, as I pictured every scene he spoke of.

I took an audible intake of breath and exhaled it before I was calm enough to speak. 'Okay... You certainly have a way with words.'

'Mmmm hmmm... Trouble is, beautiful, we don't have a good track record. Every time we sleep together, you follow it with a panic attack and leave, even though ya say you won't.' I started to try to pull out of his embrace as he reminded me of my stupidity. But his grip tightened around me as he finished what he wanted to say. 'See you want to run, even now. I just want some time to get to know you. I want time for you to get to know the... the real me.' I leant my head against his chest, finding his heart beating fast under my ear and I started to once again relax in his arms, at his words. 'And running from me again, from here? I seriously, I mean fucking *seriously* don't rate your chances out there, Calamity Amy. From what I've witnessed in the last few days, you would end up lost in the snow or face down in the lake.' I looked back at him quickly to see a grin sweep over his mouth and then it travelled and lit up the whole of his features. I smiled back. The man holding me to him, the man prepared to try to have a relationship with me, was breathtaking. His trademark beanie was still on his head, the odd dark curl of hair peaked from underneath it. His strong square jaw was covered in even thicker stubble. I just stared into his eyes as they darkened in colour and lost myself in the depths I found there.

Finally, I decided to make the move he was holding himself back from. I stood up on tiptoe as he looked down at me and clasping his face in both of my hands I pressed my lips to his. After a few seconds of our flesh connecting I removed them and placed my heels back to the floor. He was right, any connection between us meant I wanted so very much more.

'Thanks, for your self-control… I think.' I smiled at him.

Twenty

BRODY

'**C**OME ON THEN,** get your ass in gear, the lunch is over on the rug in front of the fire.' I smacked her backside as she moved slowly in front of me. It seemed every fucking time I knew we were meeting up, made me even more excited than the previous times. I was really looking forward to spending this afternoon with her.

Casually, I grasped my bottom lip between my thumb and forefinger, still feeling the kiss she had just placed there. It had taken every fucking bit of restraint I had not to do exactly what I'd just described to her. I wanted to slam her against the nearest wall. My dick was yelling at the confines of my jeans and pleading for me to give into what we both wanted.

But apparently, we were both adults. I was in my mid-thirties and I presumed she was close to me in age, so we needed to communicate with something else other than our naked bodies. The only trouble was I wasn't sure how that went, it wasn't something I'd ever done or wanted to do before. All my best communication was done through songs and sex.

'Oooo, a hamper?' Her excited voice reached to me, breaking through my lust-filled thoughts.

'Ahhh, that's what they're called, I couldn't remember.' I walked around the furniture losing my wool coat, hat and gloves as I did so.

'You look gorgeous, Amy.' I took her in for the first time, skin-tight jeans that moulded over that fantastic ass of hers and a thick, cream sweater that had a large slash in the neckline, so it fell off one side of her, exposing her shoulder. My eyes were glued to that exposed shoulder as I realised it showed no sign of a bra strap. I was so fucking done for, as now I needed to know whether she was wearing one or not.

This woman and her underwear, or lack of, would be the fucking death of me.

Her chestnut coloured hair coiled over the top of her exposed shoulder and all I could think about was lifting it away so I could sink my teeth into her perfect, unmarked flesh. I adjusted my crotch and exhaled, making my feet move closer to where she was now lowering herself to sit crossed legged on the floor.

I sat down opposite her, effectively keeping her at arm's length. It took a hell of a lot of fucking effort.

Fuck, this was going to be a long afternoon.

'Go on then, release the straps.' She looked up at my choice of words and I smiled at her so she could catch my euphemism.

She smiled and shook her head at me, but the start of a blush was unmistakable.

The hamper lid lifted and for a few seconds I couldn't see her. I leant back into the couch behind me and bent one leg up at the knee to rest my forearm on it. I could hear the rustling of plastic and I finally heard a small laugh. The lid was closed a little and she was back in my view wearing a huge smile.

'Oh my God! Just how old are you?' I could hear the laughter in her voice at what she had found inside the wicker basket.

She then held up all my treats and waved them around in front of me. My stomach rumbled as I made out the Twinkies, Ding Dongs and Ho Ho's. She then disappeared, taking my treats with her.

'I'm thirty-four and all of the things in the basket are my favourite things from my childhood. I wanted to share them with you.'

The rustling sound coming from inside the basket stopped and she peeked over the top.

'Oh, I'm thirty-three, thirty-four next year. Tell me more about why these are your favourite things?' She smiled reassuringly at me.

I shrugged and stopped myself from crossing my arms over my chest. I didn't want my body language to make her think that I was pulling away. 'My dad was in the Air Force; my family came over here when I was three. Our favourite foods were flown in to us on a regular basis, because we couldn't buy them here. After each delivery, we'd have a picnic, even if the weather was bad…and you know England, it was often bad.' I surprisingly felt a smile attach itself to my face at the memory, and clearing the tightening feeling that sharing my memory was causing in my chest by clearing my throat, I carried on. 'When it rained, my mom would set us up on the living room floor.' I could see my family's happy smiles and even hear their excited voices. It was placating, but it was also too fucking much. I took a deep breath and stopped abruptly, fleetingly removing my eyes from hers.

It was as if she recognised I was uncomfortable and she pitched in just to help me out. 'So, where exactly do you come from? I mean I've read about some of these things but I've never seen them until now.'

'In case you hadn't realised... I'm American.' I looked at her again, she sighed at me and poked out her tongue. 'Put that away, before I come over and bite it.' Her tongue disappeared in a flash and I grinned at her. 'I was born in New Jersey, and lived in Nevada for a while when I was a teenager. Now, what are we eating first?'

'Well, I was born in London, but moved here when I was ten, when my mum decided that looking after her only child wasn't obligatory. Anyway, I'm very English and we always eat the sandwiches first.' I saw the look of pain flick over her face as she spoke of her past. Then she disappeared behind the wicker lid again.

Not realising it when I had packed up the food, I had given us a very useful barrier for when our "get to know each other" conversation, just got too raw and too fucking exposing.

'Go on then, unwrap them. They're peanut butter and jelly, my favourite.'

'Oh, okay,' she answered, although I heard by the tone of her voice that she wasn't convinced by the filling. I heard the greaseproof paper crinkle under her fingers. 'Are there any plates packed in here?'

'Oh, fuck!'

'Honestly?' she questioned, her head reappearing to smile her question at me.

'Look we're not all domestic Gods, ya know. Paper's better to eat off, anyway.'

She passed me a stack of sandwiches held in a piece of the paper.

'I think you've got that a little wrong, that's supposed to be newspaper, when you eat fish and chips.'

'It's guaranteed, Amy, there is no fucking fish in that hamper.'

'Wrong again!' She'd found a bag of my favourite Goldfish and was waving them around in front of my face.

'I know you find it hard to believe, beautiful, but although they're called Goldfish, they're really just cheese crackers.' I smiled the smile I knew all women seemed to love, the one that pulled slightly higher up one side of my face and showed off my one and only dimple.

My mouth suddenly stung as, with a smile, she threw the bag straight at my face and it caught me in my sarcastic mouth.

'Ooops, sorry.' Her hand came to her mouth and her eyes widened, but I saw the smirk on her face.

'Fuck.' My fingers came up to my lip and I pulled them away to see a small amount of blood on my them. I turned my hand so she could see the evidence on my fingers. 'You will *so* regret that.' I dropped my sandwiches unceremoniously to the floor.

I moved suddenly, sweeping the hamper out of my way with one arm, and grabbed hold of her legs, pulling them and her towards me in one movement. Wrapping one leg over hers I held her in place on her back where she had fallen. She looked at me expectantly, but she couldn't have been further from the truth. Before she knew what was happening, I'd pulled her fluffy pink socks off her feet and was running my tongue in between her toes.

'OH. MY. GOD... NO, just don't... THAT'S GROSS!' she implored.

Her body convulsed, her hands slapped the floor and her head rolled from side to side. She bucked as she tried to get me off her. I knew her feet were a no-no, from the first time I'd taken off her heels and she'd recoiled as I'd placed a single kiss on her sole.

'Do you give in? Do you wanna say sorry for making me bleed?' I asked as I pushed my tongue in between her toes one last time, just to watch her cringe.

'YES... I'M SORRY! ... JUST STOP!'

I stopped and with a laugh I sat back into my previous comfortable spot. I let my eyes run up and down the length of her. She was still lay flat on her back with her brown hair all around her. Her eyes were bright and her cheeks were flushed. With her possible bra-less chest rising and falling, trying to recover from my onslaught.

It was too much, fuck, *she* was too much.

I pushed myself forward and using the strength in my arms I began to crawl up the length of her body. I gently bit down through her jeans all the way up her legs, eventually reaching the mound of her pussy. I mouthed around the covered area, sucking and blowing warm air through the thick material, until I could smell her arousal through her jeans. Her sharp intakes of breath, and the unconscious way she lifted her hips for more, were like music to my soul.

'Amy, I'm obsessed with you. I've never wanted a woman as much as I constantly want you.'

I rested my chin gently onto her stomach and looked up and over her body, until finally her head lifted for her face to find mine. Her dark eyes were even bigger than normal and her chest was rising and falling sharply. Her hands came up to hold on to the sides of my face, and she ran her thumbs over my facial stubble.

'Why did you stop? I don't want you to stop,' she whispered.

'My first response would be, I'm fucked if I know. I want in that velvet-lined pussy of yours, right this fucking minute. But, I want more than just casual fun with you, Amy. For the first time, I'm willing to let my clusterfuck of a past go and move forward with you. I want to get to know you, beautiful, so I'm once again taking control. I want you to trust me with your life, your soul and more importantly your heart. So, it's down to you, are ya gonna let me in? Or are you gonna keep running from what we have here?'

A couple of minutes passed as we just looked at each other, my heart rate increased dramatically while I waited for her answer.

'I want to… I really want to find out what this is between us. I mean, I can't believe the way you make me feel.'

'Then don't think about it, just do it. My past would show you that I'm a selfish bastard, but you make me want to be more. I wanna be here for you when you need rescuing, I wanna be the one you turn to for the small and the big things in life, I wanna be the one you trust.'

'I'm just not sure, what I mean is… If I'm honest, I just don't see where this can go? You asked this morning for me to have a relationship with you. But you're American.'

'Yep, I am, and now you're stating the obvious.' I winked at her trying to put her at ease.

'How can we have anything other than a short-term arrangement? I live here and you're only visiting for Jack's wedding, and then you'll be gone.'

I felt my forehead crease as I frowned at her, just trying to work out what she was going on about, and then I shook my head at her.

'I'm not here for the wedding. I know a friend of mine's brother-in-law is getting married this weekend, but that's just a coincidence. I'm here on business and now it seems I'm also here for pleasure.'

I saw a small smile tease her lips in response to my answer.

'So, you won't be leaving next week then?'

'No.'

Her head fell back to the floor and she began to move her body under me in excitement. Making every limb of hers quickly fidget and dance.

I took in the look of excitement on her face and not being able to resist touching her in some small way, I lifted the bottom of her sweater and kissed the bare flesh of her stomach. 'What the fuck are ya doing, crazy woman?'

'I'm excited.' Then she stopped suddenly and her head lifted again to find me. 'But you're leaving soon though, right?'

'My business takes me all over the world, so yes I will have to leave sometime, but I would come back because you're here, and now I'm back in England I know it's where I'm meant to be. I feel at home here, you feel like home to me.' I raised my chin off her stomach and began again to move myself up her body, making sure we were as close together as possible. The swell of her breasts rubbed through my T-shirt and momentarily I closed my eyes to steady myself. 'In fact, beautiful, when I go away, you can come too. Then I'll always feel like I'm home.' I was finally face to face with her. I twisted my head and staring straight into her eyes, I began to slowly lower my mouth to hers. All the time I stared into her eyes I was trying to convey just how fucking serious I was about her. Our lips were about to touch and had the smallest fissure between them, when I saw panic come into those dark brown eyes of hers and I stopped dead.

'What's wrong?' I whispered to her, feeling my warm breath hit her skin and then return to me.

'I can't go with you.' Her head began to shake from side to side and I reluctantly lifted away from her. Her hands began to push at my shoulders to get me to move away from her.

I saw tears begin to pool in her eyes.

I moved my hands until they went underneath her and rolled onto my back, taking her with me until she landed on top of my body. I took her in my arms and held her tightly to me.

'Tell me why?'

Her body began to shake and I strengthened my hold around her, just so she knew I was there for her. I fucking hated women crying and I never knew the right fucking thing to do. It was something my sister had always used. But Amy crying was worse, much fucking worse, because I really cared about her. I wanted this woman, who held so many possibilities for my life in the future, to have everything, and I wanted to be the fucker to give them to her. But her sadness was hers and until she let me the fuck in, I couldn't help her and it killed me.

We lay there in front of the fire while she cried her heart out. It was as if she had been collecting the pain for years, I felt every tremble and shake of her body. Her tears flowed, soaking straight through my T-shirt to my skin. I held her close and every now and then I kissed the top of her head in reassurance. As her tears and her pain began to subside, I felt her body stiffen and her small hands grip either side of my body as if she was scared I would now let her go.

'Not going anywhere, Amy… cross my heart.'

Twenty-One

Amy

'**T**ELL ME.' I heard his voice through the broad chest I was lying on.

I exhaled and a shudder came over me as I tried to breathe properly. I needed to calm myself down enough to talk. I took a few more minutes and a lot of steadying breaths, finally my eyes began to focus. I stared out of the French doors to the lake beyond, using the beauty outside to calm my inner turmoil.

What must he think of me? I can't believe I just broke down in front of him.

'I'm sorry, what must you think of me?' I was worrying with the sides of his T-shirt as I spoke.

'I'm not judging you, Amy, far from it. I'd like to help if I can. Tell me about it?' His voice was wary, as if he was waiting for me to once again push him away and run.

I wasn't sure, could I? Could I explain to him, things that I didn't really want to admit to myself? Things that I didn't even vocalise to my cousins and best friend. Could I say how even at my age I was terrified of being left behind? And say how scared I was of losing the woman who had put her life on hold to bring me up, with more love than I had ever imagined existed.

'What a fucking asshat he must have been to let you go. Do you still love him?' I felt his body go tense underneath me as he spoke.

I sighed. 'You've got it wrong.'

'Yeah?'

'I'm not crying about a man. I've had relationships before, but I've always been the one to up and leave them. No one has ever let me go... apart from my parents.'

His body completely stilled, letting my words wash over him while he thought.

'Fuck, how stupid were they? I'll never understand what makes a parent in their right fucking mind, choose to walk away from their children... child?' I heard the anger and hurt in his voice and felt his hands rub my back to offer me comfort.

'And my nan who brought me up in the little shop you found me in, is now dying of vascular dementia, that's why I can't go anywhere with you. I would never, ever leave her when she needs me.'

'Amy, believe me, I would never ask you to.'

'Really? You wouldn't?'

I felt him shake his head in answer. 'Nah, we can work around it, I'll make sure that whenever I can be, I'm here.'

'That's possible? You're not just saying it?' He shook his head again, his stubble rubbed on the top of my head as he did so.

'And I'm so fucking sorry, Amy, it's the worst fucking thing in life watching someone you love dying. Your nan sounds like a fucking amazing woman. I'd be real honoured to meet her.'

'She'd love to meet you too, in fact meeting you would make her day.'

'Call it our next date then, I know how important she is to you and I know what it's like to lose people you love.'

I still hadn't lifted my head to look at Daniel. Somehow it was just easier this way, being held in his arms with my head lying over the steady rhythm of his heart. He held me like he might lose me and comforted me when he felt I needed the extra support, by rubbing up and down my back with his hands.

'You do?' I questioned.

I felt him nod his head. 'Yeah.' He huffed with acceptance of what he was bracing himself to tell me. 'My mom walked out on my dad when I was eight and took my little sister with her, so effectively she left me too. I was used to a loud, passionate home, full of life. When they weren't arguing, music was very often being played at full volume and they would dance together with me and my sister and then, just like that, my childhood home was silent. My dad died four years after she left from a massive heart attack. That's what the docs said anyway, although I'm convinced he died from a broken heart.'

'Oh, Daniel… I'm so sorry. What happened to you then? Did you go to live with your mum?' I was shaking my head with the unfairness of it all.

'She was already dead.' His voice was trembling, it was so full of emotion. He inhaled deeply underneath me, so he could carry on. 'I was twelve years old and back in America. It was a place I just about remembered, but it wasn't fucking home. I was in and out of foster homes, causing as much fucking trouble as I could to everyone around me. I'm not proud of that fucked-up teenager, but my life had turned to shit and the guilt of not being able to keep my family together and safe, weighed heavy inside me. I was spiralling out of control and I wanted to take everyone down to the depths of hell with me.'

I let go of his T-shirt and pushed my hands as far as they would go underneath his muscular back, just so I could hold him as close to me as possible in the position we were in. 'You were a child, how could you have kept two people together, who didn't want to be?'

'I could have tried harder…I should have done fucking more… maybe then they'd all still be here.'

I couldn't answer him. I knew what it was like to wonder… if I'd been a better daughter, if I'd tried harder, worked harder, been more perfect. Yes, I knew what it was like to think about the what ifs.

For a few minutes, we both gazed out of the floor to ceiling, arched windows. The snow had begun to fall once again outside. I knew he was watching it with me, as it swirled and skated over the frozen lake.

I was lying in a man's arms that I had only known for a few days, but I had never felt such a strong connection to anyone in my life before. I had told him things that to be honest I hadn't wanted to admit to anyone, even myself. It was therapeutic. I hoped it was the same for him. I wanted to, at the very least, be able to give him that.

'What happened to that young boy after the foster homes?'

'Military school.'

'Oh…' I wasn't certain if that was a good thing or not.

'It eventually did amazing things for me, after I stopped bucking against the fucking system.'

'Thank goodness. It sounds like you needed a break, and now you're back here.'

'Yep… Friends of mine talked me into coming back and now I've found you, I'm convinced it's the best fucking decision I've ever made.' He momentarily squeezed me tighter to him.

I smiled into the soft material of his T-shirt, feeling the muscles in my face react to the action. The salt left by the tracks of my tears had dried on my skin and it cracked as a wide grin took over me, reminding me just how far down I had let myself go only a short while ago. I needed to go to the bathroom to sort myself out. I began to move out of his hold.

'You okay?'

'I just need the bathroom.' His arms relinquished their hold over me and I rolled away from him to stand up.

I watched as he shifted himself to his former sitting position and offered me a small smile. 'Go on then, be quick. I'm determined that today you will eat, I'll get our food ready.'

Twenty-Two

Amy

WHEN I RETURNED, the atmosphere in the room had lifted. Daniel seemed relaxed as he watched me enter the room, he had placed more large logs onto the fire and it also roared its welcome. Music played softly in the background. Outside it had already started to get dark and I looked at the grandfather clock in the corner of the room as it began to strike out four chimes.

He followed my gaze.

'I know, the time has gone fast. Come on, let's eat.' I looked over at him.

In the short time I'd been gone, Daniel had moved all the cushions and the blankets off the settees, to make us a warm, cosy area. He had set up our food over by the picturesque windows, so we could sit and watch the last of the light disappear behind the lake as we ate. It was a beautiful, thoughtful and romantic gesture. I walked quickly over to him and took up the place he was offering me, underneath one of his large muscular arms, and pulled in tight to his body.

For a while we ate in comfortable silence. Then, far off in the background, from my coat pocket, came the sound of my mobile ringing its heart out. I knew I'd need to get to it quickly before it gave up. But knowing it was probably Winter or Lauren and still feeling unhappy with the fact they had abandoned me last night, I let the ring die away as it could only do on my extremely old, antiquated mobile.

'You could have answered it,' Daniel informed me.

'I know, but my mobile is so unreliable, the call would have died out here anyway.'

'That bad?' he questioned.

'Yes, like most of my life it needs a complete overhaul. But I'm hoping that this week's tips from the tearoom will be enough to buy a new one.'

I watched him mull over what I'd just told him. My precarious life was probably hard for him to understand, as he appeared to have all the trappings of someone who had money.

'Oh, fuck. I'm shit at this.' His arm released me as he began to stand.

'What's wrong?' I asked, immediately worried by his words.

I looked up at him, immediately comforted by the boyish grin on his face. 'I forgot the drink, hold on a minute. While I'm getting it, programme your number into my cell.' He flung me his mobile and I did as I'd been asked. I listened to him laughing at himself as he moved away. I heard the squeak of the hamper lid being opened somewhere behind me, then just as quickly he returned. Unceremoniously, I was moved until I was in the exact same place as before, as tight to him as possible. Once he'd got us comfortable, I passed him back his mobile and looked at the bottle he was holding.

'Elderflower cordial?'

'The one and the same, it's about the one and only English thing I like.' He winked at the look on my face.

'Huhhh hmmm.' I cleared my throat at him and poked him in the ribs, with the tip of my longest nail.

'Ouch!... Apart from you of course.' He winced and rubbed at the offending area.

'Oh, of course, apart from me,' I sarcastically replied. 'I love elderflower anything, but I was sort of hoping you might be about to ply me with alcohol, just so you could have your wicked way with me.' I turned my head to the side and looked up at him. He looked down at me, enveloping me with the depth in those gorgeous eyes of his. He appeared to ponder on my words for a moment.

'Nah, I'm not good with alcohol...' He looked at me trying to convey more intent than the words he was using. When I didn't shrink away or question his words he carried on. 'You don't need it either, you remember exactly how we feel together. I don't need to get you drunk or high to be able to seduce you.' He gently ran his fingers over my face, brushing my hair away from it and exposing my features to him.

'I'm a sure thing, huh?'

'Yep,' he replied.

'Sure of yourself aren't you, handsome?' I teased.

'Sure am, Ma'am.' He put on a deep southern drawl, using it to emphasise the words he used.

'Are you going to show me how sure?' I asked, curling a piece of my hair around my index finger. I was completely astounded by my own confidence with him.

'It will be my fucking pleasure and I know it'll be yours, too.' He rolled us as one, off the large dark green cushions we had been leaning against and on to the floor, with one easy movement.

I heard myself sigh as he adjusted his hold on me and his mouth came to find mine. He took exactly what he needed as his mouth crashed into mine. We had shared parts of ourselves that I didn't believe we had revealed to anyone else before. When our lips met, the feelings we had for each other felt even stronger than before. We had opened ourselves up to each other, and to the possibility that we just might have found someone to share the pain of our past with and hopefully the happiness of our future.

His tongue found mine as it swept firmly into my mouth, we teased and caressed each other with equal intent. Our mouths opened ever wider as we demanded more and more from each other, until our teeth clashed together in our frenzied rush. I moved my hands up to either side of his face and just held him to me. As his body rolled to the side of mine, suddenly his hands were everywhere on me, taking, demanding and tempting. His mouth left mine and I gasped for the air I so badly needed. His skilful tongue travelled down my jaw line and into the dip just below my ear.

'If you kiss my neck,' I whispered, 'I'm not responsible for what happens next.' I half smiled the words out and half gasped as his mouth immediately found the sensitive skin of my neck. My body began to instantaneously shake in need.

'That's fine… this, right here, is all on me.' I felt his breath hit my wet skin. Then he bit into the flesh on the top of my shoulder and my body ignited. I crossed my legs to relieve the ache that was building to a crescendo. I felt his fingers running down my neck, over the bare skin on my shoulder, until his hands cupped my breasts and his fingertips pinched and rolled my hard nipples. They were now so long and hard, I knew they were jutting out prominently, even through my jumper. Still he didn't let up, he left me with no doubt in my mind just how much he wanted me, how much he wanted us. His hands pushed at the hem of my jumper and the muscles in my stomach jumped to attention. Every nerve ending contained within me was brought to life, as the most captivating man I had ever met demanded I give him my all.

'I need you naked and I want you naked, now.' His mouth lifted slightly away from my shoulder and his voice somehow found me.

I didn't vocally answer him, but released his face and sat up. He bent his arm at the elbow and leant his head onto his palm to watch me. I took hold of the hem of my jumper and lifted the garment up over my body, then with a final flourish up and over my head. I shook my hair out and threw the garment on to the settee behind us. My bare breasts tingled as the cooler air hit them.

I heard his sharp intake of breath as the air travelled between his teeth, hissing as it did so.

'Fuck me, you're indescribable. Your choice of underwear, or lack of... blows my fucking mind.'

I knew it was taking every bit of his self-restraint just to lie motionless and watch. His breathing had ramped up and the bulge filling the front of his jeans was making my mouth water.

I lay myself back down beside him, refusing to let his eyes once again captivate mine, until I had completed my task. I released the top button on my jeans and began to shimmy them down, lifting my hips a little off the floor as I did so. I could feel his eyes on me everywhere and was pleased I'd thought hard about my choice of underwear. All there was between us now was the delicate scrap of lace between my legs. It took until my jeans were just above my knees for his restraint to finally snap. In one swift movement, he was now standing at my feet and yanking the ankles of my jeans towards him. They came off quickly and were thrown somewhere into the large room. His T-shirt followed rapidly and then he was in between my bare legs, sitting on his haunches in just his jeans. He was amazing, every time I looked at him my breath would catch and my heart raced. His body was a work of art, the tattoos adorning his body were stunning and showed every defined, worked-hard-for muscle on his incredible torso. I let my eyes wander slowly down him, relishing in the fact I was being given another chance to be with him. Finally, my eyes slowly swept over his abs and the start of what I had previously found to be an extremely well-defined V. My tongue on instinct flicked out to wet my suddenly dry lips. In my peripheral view, I could see him beginning to smile at my excruciatingly slow perusal. The top button of his jeans had been opened and I followed his happy trail of fine hair down to where it disappeared inside the button fly. I licked my lips again and swallowed down my building anticipation.

'I want to take my sweet fucking time with you, Amy. Then I'm going to fuck you so fast and deep, you'll be able to taste me in the back of your throat. I'm going to drive ya to the edge of insanity over and fucking over, until you can't remember your own fucking name... But you'll remember me and that from this moment on, you're mine.'

'Then get on with it, handsome. I have nowhere I need to be.'

Daniel shook his head and grinned at me, and it reached his eyes.

'Enough with the fucking sass, beautiful.'

I sucked in my bottom lip and smiled at him, promising him nothing. But knowing I would do anything to keep the lightness and strength of feeling here between us.

With his eyes still on mine, he placed his forearm under one of my knees and lifted it up, then he placed it back down at a right angle to the side of me. Effectively he had bent my leg and opened me up wide to him. I felt the air enter the small space where the triangle of lace had lifted away from me and I gasped, making him raise one eyebrow at me.

'So fucking sensitive.' His lust filled voice had deepened, and it stirred me deep inside.

He picked up my other leg by the ankle and placed it on his bare shoulder. His mouth then began its slow descent down my calf, as he kissed, licked and bit at my very needy flesh. All the time he spent teasing me with his mouth, his eyes held mine prisoner.

Very quickly my heart rate quickened and my body began to move of its own accord. My hips lifted and started to move in small, indignant circles. I was pleading with him, without using words. I wanted him, and I needed him to give me what I was silently crying out for.

'Keep still.' His words were quietly spoken, but his commanding tone made me comply. I restrained my hips and made sure the small of my back stayed fixed against the floor. It was sweet torture.

His tongue found its way to the back of my knee and I almost fell apart. I could hear the sighs and whimpers just tumbling away from my wide-open mouth. Not being allowed to move my hips meant that my head had started to turn from side to side. The more he licked into the cleft he had found there, the more my mind began to imagine his tongue had found its way to where I needed it to be. I began to expect the regular rhythm and the warmth he placed there. He knew and, watching and listening to my body, he moved himself away, to follow the path of the inside of my thigh. My core tightened to the point of being painful.

'How much do you want my tongue, Amy?' His breath found my skin and made my limbs begin to shake in expectancy.

'I want it a lot,' I nodded even though I wasn't sure he could see me.

'I'm not convinced,' he replied. My head lifted slightly to look at him with more intent. 'Tell me whatcha want me to do with my tongue.'

I felt my eyes widen as I looked at him.

'Tell me.' As he spoke one of his fingers ran gently over the top of the lace panel covering the bare skin of my pubic mound. As he connected with my enlarged clitoris, my hips bucked upwards and I moaned.

In my desperation, my embarrassment left me. 'I need you to part my lips open wide and to run your tongue inside them and over my clit.'

'Mmmm, that'll do.'

He pulled my thong to one side and gently opened my lips. The moment his tongue found my beaded clit, I was there, right on the edge. My hands found their way to his head and my fingers threaded quickly into his dark hair, holding him right where I wanted him to be. As he inserted one finger inside of me, my walls clamped down fast, effectively holding him in place. My orgasm was gathering strength in the small of my back. Lost in the tempo he was setting, my body answered every touch he gave me, so the moment he pushed his thumb against the nerve endings at my anus, I was gone. I'd never allowed anyone to touch me intimately there. It was erotic, and dirty, but most of all it felt exquisite. The light started to change behind my closed eyes and my orgasm shattered around me. As it rolled through me, I began to shout out to God, over and over.

As my catatonic state began to roll away, I could feel Daniel moving between my thighs as his jeans brushed over my now ridiculously sensitive skin. I watched as he pushed his jeans down over his hips, just enough to expose his heavy cock. I looked on, spellbound as he rolled a condom down his shaft. He put his fingers into the elastic side of my thong and tore it from my body. I gasped at the action and felt wetness once again pool at the top of my thighs. In what seemed like one flowing movement he pushed my legs open wide, purposefully fell over me, with his hands taking his weight on either side of my shoulders, and thrust his firm, steel-like cock inside of me.

'Oh. My. God!' I cried out.

As before, we both froze as the feeling of our connection travelled through both of us. I had never felt so much with anyone before.

'Feel me, Amy.' He thrust deep inside me again. 'Feel us! This here is fucking everything.'

'Oh God,' was all I could manage as he began to move.

'This and you were fucking meant for me.' He swivelled his hips and thrust again. Then I saw the look of determination come over his face, as he started what he had promised me earlier. He began a punishing pace that I fought hard to keep up with.

My arms on instinct found their way around his hard, muscular body and in no time at all I was careering towards the edge. Every muscle went tense. My fingernails dug into his bare arse as if I was trying to control his movements, but deep inside I knew I had no conscious control over his actions. In the short time we had been together, he was skilled enough to already read me like a book.

He was giving us what we both needed and wanted.

I was aware that some of his weight had come down onto me, freeing his hand to run down the side of my sweat-covered skin. It made my flesh react and turn to goose bumps where his fingertips had gently touched. He cupped my backside and squeezed my bum cheek with his large hand, before once again moving his hand to touch where are bodies were connected, as he wet his fingers in my arousal. With his fingers wet, they drifted backwards. The moment his thumb pushed through the tight ring of muscle around my anus, the most powerful orgasm of my life swept through my body.

Slowly, oh so slowly, I gradually came back down to earth.

My eyes flew open as Daniel shifted again, removing his cock from me and pulling off the condom. With both of his hands once again back beside my shoulders he began to push his cock backwards and forwards through my wet, sensitive folds.

'Look at us,' he demanded.

We both looked down at the movement between us. His cock was glistening as time and time again he rubbed the large head over my still throbbing clit. I grabbed hold of his flexed forearms.

'Let it go, beautiful.' His voice rasped as he grew nearer to his own release.

I felt my walls inside begin to flutter and almost on his instruction another orgasm crashed through me. I fought to keep my eyes open as I watched Daniel hurtle into his own.

'FUCK! ...YES!... Yes.' His words stopped and a deep guttural groan left his body.

My gaze drifted between his indescribable eyes and the depth of feeling I found there, to watching his cock as he emptied his seed all over me. His cum spurted again and again, up in between my breasts, over my stomach and pubic mound. I felt the liquid's heat wherever it touched me.

He was an erotic sight, still half dressed. My eyes were captured by the man between my legs. The same man who had made me come three times in succession. His tattooed body was now covered in a sheen of sweat from his exertion, making the colours on his skin even more vibrant. Like us being together made him more alive. I watched as some of his sweat dripped off him and onto me.

I wasn't sure of who I was when I was with him, but he made me feel sexy, he made me feel everything. With him still raised above me, and as his body came back down to earth, I moved my newly manicured fingernails in front of his face to catch his refocussing eyes. Then I swept my fingertips through his release on my skin and rubbed the moisture slowly over my nipples. I knew he was coming back rapidly with every movement I made. His body began to once again stiffen as his teal eyes watched my hand's progression. I felt him throb in response to my action. This small element of control over him was heady. I felt the heat of his cock as he grew hard once again. On a final flourish, I brought my fingertips up to my mouth and sucked them clean.

He lifted his gaze and found my eyes with his, a lopsided, cocky grin took over his face.

His mouth came back to mine, with so much force I was taken by surprise. He tasted himself and then broke away, licking his lips.

'You're as sexy as fuck, Amy. You'd better be ready for the long fucking haul, because I refuse to let you walk away from me, from us.'

I nodded and watching him cock his eyebrow in question, I answered, 'I am.'

'Good answer.' He pushed himself off me quickly and stood to his full, dominating height at my feet. His jeans fell further down his legs, until eventually he could step on the bottom of them, to pull his legs free of their confines. All the time his eyes swept up and down my body and the release he had spurted onto my skin. His right hand cupped his balls tightly and his left went slowly and methodically up and down his shaft. I heard myself gasp and bit down onto my bottom lip as I watched him.

'Like what you see?' he asked with a grin beginning to twitch at the corner of his lips.

I brought myself to. 'Errrm, maybe.'

'Too right you fucking do... but it'll have to wait for later. I need sustenance and so do you, it's going to be a long night.' He full on grinned and then moved away from my line of sight, and I relaxed back into the warm blankets underneath me. I heard the fire spit as it consumed the wood that he had just casually thrown onto it.

Then he was back with me.

He had found a few tissues to clean me up, and then he covered me up with a soft, gold throw. He pulled me to him and when I was comfortable lying in his arms he passed me over some bits to eat and we finally went back to the picnic we had started earlier.

'What is that?' I questioned after I'd swallowed a few mouthfuls of food. I watched him about to lower what looked like a fat, bumpy cucumber into his mouth. The totally devastating man next to me closed his open mouth and turned his head towards me. A thoughtful smile took over his face.

'Where are my manners?' he grinned. 'It's a dill pickle.'

He opened his mouth and lowered the pickle in between his full lips and then he sucked and pulled the pickle out whole from his mouth with a resounding pop. 'Let me share it with you.'

He moved quickly and I squealed as he flung himself under the throw he had covered me up with only a few minutes before. My legs were unceremoniously opened and I felt the calloused, cold skin of the pickle graze over my clit.

'Whoah,' fell from my mouth as I took a deep breath in.

His tousled head appeared from under the throw, with a look of amusement on his face.

'I dare you not to come,' he challenged as he bestowed a wink on me, and then he disappeared back under the gold throw.

I lay my head down with a thump and felt my eyes roll into the back of my head.

Really? I thought with a smile and as I began to gasp and moan at the sensations he was creating inside of me. *Oh heck, I was never much good with being dared, anyway.*

Twenty-Three

Amy

AS THE WATER from the shower cascaded down over my face and body, I thought about how fast the past few days had gone, but at the same time how long it felt like I had known Daniel.

In amongst our commitments, we had seen each other whenever it was at all possible. We'd kept ourselves away from prying eyes, as it seemed we both wanted to keep our new relationship to ourselves. It was as if we were far too scared to let anyone in to witness just how happy we were, in case we jinxed the situation. I hadn't wanted to share my time spent with him with anyone else, and it seemed he was just as selfish. So far, we hadn't spent the night together again. He had told me categorically that until he was certain that I wouldn't run, that was the way it was going to be. Although I received a text from him late on Tuesday night that made me giggle as I knew he was regretting his rule.

I'm in my bed and you're in yours. One of us is in the wrong fucking place.

On the Wednesday morning, I had been out for my regular boot camp workout. As we had rounded the perimeter of the communal park that surrounded The Manor, I'd been lagging behind the others. Running was *so* not my forte. I had been startled as Daniel had stepped out from behind one of the huge trees and using one arm only he had pulled me into him, effectively covering us from all prying eyes. I'd squealed like a schoolgirl as his large arms had enfolded me and his hard body had backed me up against the wide tree trunk. His cologne had invaded my nostrils, offering my frantically beating heart a sense of calm. His mouth invaded mine and for a few seconds he kissed me until I was breathless. As he broke away, he had rested his forehead against mine.

'I miss you,' he whispered and my heart soared at his simple words.

'I miss you, too.' I grabbed his hoodie and pulled myself back to him, before I brushed my lips against his to check if he was real.

'Are you sure you need this run, Amy? I mean, I could give you a more thorough all over body workout than running can.' He smiled his cheeky grin at me and I watched the mischief dance in his eyes.

'I know you could, but I've been thinking perhaps I've given in to you just a little too much already.' I ducked from under his arm quickly and began to run again, albeit backwards, away from him. 'Besides we're about to do a squat workout soon and I need to give these thighs a good going over.' His gaze travelled down to my Lycra-clad legs and then straight back up to my face. I watched a salacious smile break out behind his stubble.

'Giving your thighs a good going over, huh? I'm sure I'm the man for that job.'

I blew him a kiss as he watched me turn away. My heart felt lighter just for having seen and spoken to him for a few short minutes.

'Come on, Amy!' shouted Alastair, our P.T instructor, from at least a hundred yards ahead of me. I saw one of the other girls turn her head to look at me and I gave her a little wave. I turned around again as I pushed myself on and, running backwards, I looked back at the large oak I had been behind with him only moments before. There was no sign of him at all, it was almost as if I'd imagined him there. I spun around to face forward once again, before I had an accident, and put a glove-covered finger to my lips.

I couldn't have dreamt him when my lips still felt him.

It was now Friday.

The tearoom had remained at almost full capacity all week. With me running out to meet Daniel every available moment, I hadn't seen much of Lauren or Winter, but they too seemed to be otherwise engaged. *Or perhaps I was doing everything possible to avoid being in the same place at the same time?* When mine and Lauren's shifts had crossed, I'd gone out of my way to make myself busy and then had left as soon as possible.

I knew we would all catch up soon, Jack's wedding was tomorrow and we were going to the evening reception. Christmas was the day after and we were due to have our dinner up at The Manor, courtesy of Raff and Default Distraction. It would be interesting meeting them, celebrities weren't my favourite sort of people, not that I'd met that many. But I had come to that decision a long time ago, knowing that one very minor one in my life was way more than enough.

I couldn't ever remember feeling as happy as I'd felt when I'd woken up this morning. I'd hardly been able to contain my excitement as I'd got on with my work. The reason behind this was that I'd never had a weekend full of plans before. I was doing what my nan wanted me to do and it seemed to be what I needed.

At long last I was living, it was exhilarating. It was bloody fantastic and it was long overdue. I wanted to share the news with the woman who had brought me up. She deserved to see that her love and care for me had resulted in me finally being able to move forward.

I had just finished the lunchtime session at the tearooms and after pocketing my tips for the few hours I'd worked, I'd waved at the staff and taken my leave, shooting up the stairs to the side of the building. I needed a quick shower and to change my clothes. Daniel was due to pick me up in twenty minutes. The two of us were visiting my nan.

I was looking forward to seeing her. I knew she hadn't had the best of weeks and it hurt me to know I was having the best week of my life while she was struggling. Lauren and Mark had visited her on Wednesday and today was my agreed time slot. Our matriarch may be having a bad week but she still knew exactly how to keep us all under control, her previously issued instructions kept us all on our toes. Even with what was going on with her now, we weren't prepared to go against her wishes.

I pulled my brown jeans on over my shaved and creamed legs, feeling how sensitive my skin was at the thought of seeing him. The need to be as attractive as possible for him had become my upper most thought. It was a game I was playing, and one that kept me from dwelling too much on what else was going on in my life. It seemed he had appeared when I most needed him and I would be forever grateful. I pulled my new raspberry coloured jumper over my head. It was the same style as the cream one I had worn earlier in the week. I had seen just how much he had enjoyed the slashed neckline and the view of the bare skin on my shoulder. I wanted to tease him again with the small show of flesh. Looking in the mirror, I loosely wrapped up my long hair into a messy bun and applied a small amount of make-up. My skin seemed to have a glow of its own. Lastly, I spritzed my perfume into the air and walked through it.

I grabbed my leather biker jacket from behind the door and slammed it behind me as I carefully began to descend the wrought iron staircase, grasping the handrail tightly. The cold air rushed over the bare skin of my shoulder, as like a teenager I was carrying my jacket and not wearing it. I'd wanted to give him the full effect of the effort I'd just made, especially as that effort was all for him.

Finally, as my feet found the ground, I allowed my eyes to look at where I knew his vehicle would be parked. My heart skipped a beat the very moment he lifted his head from staring at the toe of his boot as he appeared to kick thoughtfully at the snow, and our eyes found each other's. His arms that had been crossed over his chest, opened and came down to his sides and he pushed his backside away from the bonnet. He began to walk towards me slowly, with his hands twitching at his sides. I walked slowly too, maintaining the connection between us and allowing him time to take me in. His eyes left mine as he swept his gaze up and down my body and even with distance between us, I could feel the now familiar spark ignite inside me.

We had known each other for one whole week. I knew it was absolutely no time at all, but to me it was already everything. I had known just how he would be stood there waiting for me. I already knew his mannerisms and could understand every unspoken signal of his body.

All at once, he was in front of me, gathering me up into his arms. Stood in the middle of the busy carpark, we blocked out everyone and everything around us.

'You take my fucking breath away.' He kissed me chastely, sealing our connection. Wordlessly he broke away and leading me by the hand he helped me up into his car. I settled immediately into the warm leather of the seat and watched as he jogged around the front of the car and jumped up beside me. The engine started and we began to pull away.

He picked up my hand nearest to him and placed it down onto where his well-fitting black jeans encased his muscular thigh, and I casually ran my hand up and down a little.

'Did ya phone?'

I looked over at him as he expertly drove us through the narrow country lanes, loving the feeling of safety I had with him.

'Yes, I spoke to Tina this morning, she's Nan's social worker. She said she'd have a chat with her. She'd warn her and the carers I would be bringing a visitor.'

I watched as his mouth twitched before he started grinning. 'She'd warn her I was coming? I'm not that bad.'

'Really?' I teased. 'Have you looked at yourself recently?'

He pulled his beanie away from his head, making his cropped hair fall untidily, and removed his sunglasses, revealing his beautiful eyes. Messy or not, he was simply stunning. Then he pulled down the visor and began to pull faces in the mirror. I smacked my hand on his thigh.

'Stop it... You know what I mean.'

He changed down a gear as we turned into yet another lane, on the way back to my village. 'Nah... I don't, explain?'

'Honestly? ... I know that you know what you look like.'

He shook his head smiling. 'Maybe? Or perhaps I want you to tell me.'

I sighed in exasperation.

'When women look at you, they see a guy who looks like he's just fallen off a billboard, or out of the latest GQ magazine, or maybe even come to life from their favourite porn channel.' He laughed out loud at my explanation. 'Men like you don't just turn up at our local care home. The nurses and carers, dependant on age, are either going to have a heart attack, or a bad case of very damp knickers after they catch sight of you.' I laughed at the look of horror spreading over his stubble-covered face and laughed at him.

'A *bad* case of damp knickers? Is there such a thing?' He laughed.

'Yes.' I sighed at his teasing and shot him a look.

'Mmmm... Thing is, Amy, I don't care what women see when they look at me. Looks are superficial, they're only skin deep. I only care what the one woman who has access to my heart and soul sees, when she looks at me. That woman in case you were unsure... is you.'

I heard myself sigh at his words as he picked up my hand from his thigh, turned it over and kissed my wrist. All my nerve endings sparked to life at the feel of his lips on my skin.

'So, what do you see when you look at me?' he questioned.

'I see you and you're the hottest guy I've ever met, but you're even more beautiful on the inside.' I didn't even think about the answer I gave him. The words were there ready and waiting on the tip of my tongue. No thought process was involved. I didn't put up my guard or even filter my words, I just spoke straight from my heart.

'Do ya know… I believe that's exactly what you do see? I can be myself with you, Amy, and after pretending to be someone and something else for over half my life, that knowledge is fucking everything to me.'

I kissed the top of my fingers and blew him a kiss and for a few minutes I just watched him as his concentration went back to the road ahead.

'Your nan, Amy. I wanna meet her, but I don't want to be the cause of any problems for her.'

I looked at the serious expression on his face and felt my forehead pull into a frown at his words. 'What? Stop joking around. You're coming, believe me when I say you're everything my nan has always wanted me to bring home and you're coming in.'

'Okay, I'm looking forward to spending time with her… she's brought up an amazing woman and I wanna say thanks.'

I looked at him, once again speechless at his words.

'Thank you,' I whispered to him and then I looked ahead again. Every feeling he conjured up inside me was now caught at the back of my throat, making it difficult to speak and forcing my eyes to fill with happy emotions. I managed to clear my throat just in time to give him the last direction. 'It's just over there on the left.' I pointed out of my side of the car.

He followed my pointing finger and a few minutes later he was pulling into the carpark. I started to shift in my seat as I got ready to get out, when his hand gently caught my arm to make me turn towards him.

'Tonight, you're staying with me. I have some things I wanna tell you about, and I want you in my arms when we talk.' He switched off the engine and looked at me with intent. 'Okay?' he questioned.

'Okay by me.' I'd hated growing closer to him over the last few days and not being able to spend the nights in his arms. I had my own reasons for wanting to spend the night with him, I wanted to show him that I no longer needed to run.

Our conversation halted. My eyes caught sight of the doorway as Tina opened it in welcome, she lifted her arm to wave at us and stood waiting. Daniel jumped out and was quickly around to help me down.

'Afternoon,' she greeted us as we walked in.

'Hi Tina, this is Daniel.' He held out his hand to shake hers. She took his hand and as they shook, I saw her take in everything about the devastatingly handsome man I had brought with me. I recognised. right at that minute, that I would have to get used to the way women stared at him. I swallowed down the sudden need to mark him as mine in some way, just so they could all see and never doubt that he belonged with me.

'I guessed as much. Nice to meet you, Daniel. Before you go and see Vera can you both follow me through to the office for a moment?' She gave me a smile, trying to get me to relax, but it was in vain. Her looking out for us and taking me to the office when I visited my nan, was not normal procedure. We followed her inside the small, well used looking room. She waved an arm to gesticulate that we could sit down and I followed her direction. Daniel stood behind me, holding on to the back of my chair as if he was trying to reassure me he was still there.

'Don't look so worried. I have a couple of things I need to discuss with you. Firstly, unfortunately Vera has another bladder infection. As you know it makes the dementia worse.' I nodded at her and sighed. These, like many other things, were becoming more frequent. 'And Dr. Carpenter and I were reviewing Vera's case yesterday, Amy. There is no easy way to say this, but we need you to prepare for the fact that her dementia has now worsened to the degree that she won't be coming back home in four weeks' time, as originally planned.'

I heard myself breathe in and out with shaky movements. I pulled my jumper further up my shoulder, to cover the flesh I had happily exposed earlier. I was suddenly feeling very vulnerable. If I was honest with myself, inside I had already known what she was going to say. When I had been looking after my nan, sometimes her dementia had been so bad she would let herself out of the shop at night and go wandering through the village in her dressing gown. She had at times, been a danger to herself and unfortunately to me. When I was down in the shop without her, I had to turn off the gas upstairs, so she couldn't cook something and then find that she had accidentally left the gas on. Although I had adapted to her needs, it was always in the back of my mind that one day she would take me by surprise and do something I hadn't worked out a contingency plan for. It was scary caring for her a times, but at other times it was so incredibly humbling and I really couldn't think of anything I wanted more in my life than to care for the woman who had given me her all.

'If I'm willing to look after her, surely that's up to me?' I pushed into her conversation.

'I'm afraid not, Amy.' Her voice now had a gentle tone to it as she tried to reassure me. 'Vera has left express instructions to the contrary. She had long conversations with us about her care and when she wanted us to step in to relieve you. To be quite honest with you, several things have happened over the last few months that have caused us to nearly intervene. We know how much you love her and she you. But having her here for the last two weeks has given us the time we needed to reassess her and now we have to go with her signed instructions for her care.'

'Yes, of course you do.' The happy emotional tears that had welled in my eyes earlier, now spilt rapidly down my cheeks as my pain and hurt raced each other to my jaw line. I felt the rings on Daniel's fingers as he began to rub my shoulders, trying to comfort me.

'I'm so sorry, Amy... we both know what a cruel illness this is. She has never wanted you to put your life on hold to care for her twenty-four hours a day.'

'But I would.'

'She knows that, Amy and that's precisely why she wrote down her wishes a while ago.' Tina picked up a tissue box and offered them to me. I pulled a couple from the top and let the conversation wash over me for a few seconds, while I wiped at my face.

A week had passed since I'd closed my nan's shop and at the time I'd had the feeling that it would be for the last time. Thoughts ran quickly through my head. I knew what I had to do now. I had to come to terms with her wishes and as soon as possible I needed to put the only home I'd ever known up for sale to pay for her care.

I wouldn't let her down.

I leant my head onto Daniel's hand as he continued to rub my shoulder in reassurance, and let his warmth embrace me.

'Tina, could you just give us a few minutes please?' I heard his strong, assertive voice break through my pain-filled haze as he addressed Tina and I watched her stand up from behind the desk she had sat down at.

'Of course, take all the time you need. I'll go and sit with Vera. Come and find us when you're ready.' I heard the door click gently shut as she left us.

Daniel moved around to stand in front of me. I put my hands into his front pockets and pulled him towards me as I rested my forehead against him.

Still the tears flowed. I sniffed, trying to clear the way to be able to form words.

'I don't know what to say to you? All I seem to do is cry. I'm so sorry, I know you didn't sign up for all of this. I'm high maintenance. New relationships aren't supposed to be like this.' I sniffed again, so I could carry on talking. 'I'm sure they're all fun and laughter and seeing each other in the best light, with none of life's complications?'

'Then those relationships are false, aren't they? Real life is fucking complicated, painful and sometimes it's almost too much to fucking bare. Unless you've got someone by your side to help carry the burden.'

I looked up at him in question and he gently held my face in his hands as he used his thumbs to swipe across my cheekbones, brushing away my tears.

'Amy, this between us isn't new, it's as old as time itself. I know you and you know me. My soul recognised yours the first moment I saw you and I know that you in turn recognised mine. I know deep down that I've found you many times before, in many different lives. And I fucking promise you, I'd search for you a million times over again. It doesn't matter where we live or what our names are. My only regret is not fucking finding you sooner in this lifetime... Now, come here.' He took hold of my waist and lifted me up into his arms. Once again, he was carrying me, although his feet remained still. He was holding me up as he supported me and offered me his strength. His arms had tightened around my body until we'd moulded together, almost as one. I buried my face into the layers of clothes at his neckline, and used the warm air coming away from his body to breathe in the smell of Christmas his cologne constantly reminded me of. I began to calm down as I felt the pulse in his neck beat out its reassuring rhythm.

'I'm here. I'm not going anywhere. Need me, use me and I'll get you through this... I promise.'

Twenty-Four

BRODY

'**TWENTY-ONE.**' **I** placed down my cards, with a pleased smirk on my face.

'I like a man who can play cards, Amy. You can hold on to this one.' I watched as Vera smiled at the woman I was quickly falling for.

Who was I fucking joking? I'd already fallen for.

Amy grimaced at her words and they shared a look between them that had probably been invented by them years ago. I found myself smiling as I witnessed their connection.

She was a wonderful woman, the lady we were spending time with this afternoon. Over the TV in her room at the care home, she had the day, date and month hooked into a frame to help her memory. For the first twenty minutes, she had asked the same questions. Amy had patiently answered the same thing over and over.

It was December.

It was Friday.

It was the day before Christmas Eve and yes, they'd had some snow.

Each time, Vera had walked over to the window and clarified her answers. The first hour had been painful. I'd been introduced to her several times over and then she'd look up again, regarding me like it was the first time we'd met and again she would ask who I was.

Around and around we went.

At one point, I'd seriously wondered if it had been a good idea, as me being in her room was causing her agitation and upset. That was hurting Amy, and it was the last thing I fucking wanted.

But for the last hour we had been playing Black Jack and she knew every move, her smiles and laughter filled the room around us as she beat our asses time after time. Her happiness was just what Amy needed right now and I was goddamn pleased to share it with them both

I heard my cell as it began to vibrate in my shirt pocket. The room was so warm that I'd removed as many layers as possible, just so I could cope with the heat. Much to Vera's amusement I was now in a thin T-shirt. While we had been playing cards she'd casually touch my forearms and trace her worn, soft fingertips on my tattoos, remarking as she did so on how I was making an old lady very happy. Every time, I'd grin at Amy and share her amusement and equally her embarrassment.

Standing up, I made my way to where the shirt had been thrown onto Vera's bed. I heard them put their cards down on the table and listened to their voices as they disclosed their card total and confirmed what I already knew, I'd won the hand. I pulled out my cell and looked down at the caller Id.

Fuck.

I closed my eyes. My hand that held the cell fell loosely back down, as my arm refused to lift it up to me anymore. With my back to Amy and as silently as possible I exhaled. Without even hearing her voice, darkness, guilt and pain began to burn the edges of my mind, exposing once again just how fragile I was. Instinctively, I licked around my lips, and tasted the alcohol that had been there many times before. I switched the ringer to silent and plastering a smile to my face I turned to the ladies behind me.

'I need to take this outside.' I walked back over to Amy who luckily had been looking down and hadn't witnessed my false smile. I placed a quick kiss down on top of her head as she nodded, and then I turned towards the door.

'Okay, don't be long handsome.' I heard Vera whisper to Amy, 'Who is he?'

'Daniel, Nan.'

'Don't be long now, Daniel. I'll miss the eye candy.'

'NAN!' I heard Amy shout as she jokingly reprimanded her.

'What? That's what you call good looking men these days, isn't it?'

I swung a last look over my shoulder. 'It's fine, beautiful. I'll take "eye candy,"' I reassured an embarrassed looking Amy.

I opened the door and as the cooler air from the corridor hit me, I drew in a deep reviving breath. Just before I closed the door behind me, I heard Vera semi whisper.

'I like him, Amy... I think he could be the one for you... and well the chemistry between the two of you... well, phew.'

I couldn't see them, but I heard the two of them giggle together like schoolgirls and even though the person on my cell only called when she wanted more fucking money or had a problem I had to sort out for her, a real smile swept over my face.

The cell rang off and then, just as I knew it would, it started again instantaneously.

The door clicked shut and I made my way a few steps over to a small seating alcove at the end of the corridor. My finger ready, I took a deep fucking breath before I swiped to take the call. I hated that even all these thousands of miles away from each other, she could always sense when I was happy, she knew almost fucking instinctively just when she should call to ruin it.

I still loved her, even after all these years. But with everything that had gone down between us, it was hard to see around it. I loved her, it appeared, almost as much as she hated me. Fuck knows what she wanted now?

Taking one more deep breath, I finally answered the ring that was becoming more irate with every second. 'Barbara.'

It took me more than thirty minutes to finish the call with her and then another ten fucking minutes to calm the fuck down. There was no way in hell I could deal with all the shit she had just piled on me, here. I needed to get back to The Manor.

At last I was pushing open the door to the room that contained the woman that centred me. I went in quietly and leant against the door, closing it with a quiet click. They had moved over towards the window and were sitting next to each other on a small couch. I watched as they turned the pages of an album and discussed the family pictures. I could see Amy knew I had returned, her body reacted to my presence and she gave me a little wave while she concentrated on her conversation with her nan.

'Ooooo, what's that gorgeous smell?' Vera looked up from the table and straight over to me. 'Oh, Amy, eye candy has returned.'

'Ladies.' I two-finger saluted them both.

'Nan... his name is Daniel.' She turned again and smiled at me, shaking her head a little at her nan's lack of filter, but I could see by the look on her face she was pleased her nan had remembered me from nearly an hour ago.

'Amy, can I have a word please?'

'Yes sure... Nan, I'll be back shortly.'

'That's fine, don't do anything I wouldn't do.' Vera burst out laughing and I smiled over at her.

I reopened the door and held out my hand, waiting for Amy to walk the few steps over to me. I was desperate to feel her small hand in mine. She eagerly skipped the last step and willingly gave me her hand. I relaxed straight away and took her out into the corridor behind me.

'Sorry, Amy, something has come up. Something I need to deal with.' As I spoke I pushed her up against the wall next to the door. With one forearm and hand flat against the wall, I trapped her within the confines of my body. I lifted her chin with the thumb and forefinger of my other hand and bent my head down to hers. I needed to taste her, selfishly I needed to rid myself of the taste of imaginary alcohol on my mouth. After kissing her lips, I placed my mouth gently down to her neck and sucked in a couple of places until she began to squirm and giggle in my hold. Just by kissing me back in return and with those few simple sounds she'd pulled me out of the hole that had once again threatened to engulf me. 'I know I said about us spending the night together tonight, but I need to make a few phone calls and fix some stuff.' I placed my mouth back to her neck again and felt her arms come tightly around me as her legs began to quiver. I removed my mouth and spoke to her, making my breath connect with the wet area on her neck. 'Sorry.'

'It's fine... we'll have other nights, won't we?' She said the right words, but I could hear the disappointment and question in her voice.

'Yeah, tomorrow will be the first night of forever.' I lifted my head to look at her. Her beauty hit me every fucking time. 'I promise.'

'I'll hold you to that...'

Twenty-Five

Amy

THE BUS HAD dropped me off as a request stop, at the end of the lane that led to The Manor. I needed to get back, to get myself sorted out for the lunchtime shift I was due to work today. We were then closing early to get to Jack and Lily's wedding reception. But I was enjoying the cold walk in the fresh air. I was attempting to clear my heart and mind of everything that had happened to me over the last week and I was in no hurry. I also knew that today I would be seeing Lauren and Winter, and after avoiding them for days I was bracing myself as I knew they would be full of questions.

Daniel leaving late yesterday afternoon had given me the opportunity to spend the evening with my nan, and I knew in my heart of hearts that it would probably be the last night we would spend together under one roof.

We'd had dinner together at Tina's insistence and then as the snow began to fall again outside of her window, I'd been convinced to spend the night with her in her room. It had been like old times. Each of us in a twin bed covered with a matching old-fashioned candlewick bedspread from our home. Nan had demanded that the beds were pushed together, and she'd held my hand as we had fallen asleep. She'd held my hand in hers, just as she had done for the first few months after I'd moved in with her all those years ago. I knew I would always remember her touch, and just how comforted and reassured I felt with my hand contained within her soft, loving one. She had tenderly rubbed her fingertips over my skin as we had wordlessly said our goodbyes.

Another chapter closed on both of our lives.

This morning I felt stronger, as emotional as ever, but stronger.

The tearooms were already lit up and offering me their welcome as I turned the corner of the Victorian wall and into the yard. Although I was still in yesterday's clothes, I went with my first compulsion and pushed open the door, even though the sign said closed. I stepped over the threshold and banged the snow off my leather boots and onto the bristled mat beneath my feet.

'Hi, anyone home?' I shouted into the warm, empty space.

'Back here.' I heard Lauren's voice coming from the office.

I hung my jacket up on the coat stand and moved towards her voice. I pushed the door open a little wider and smiled a small smile as she looked up to find me. She leant back on her creaking office chair and rolled a pen around between the fingers of both hands as her gaze swept up and down me.

'Well, I'm pleased you're still alive.' I heard the cross tone in her voice and grimaced at her.

'I know… sorry. I've, well I've…'

'Been avoiding us… I know. I'm sorry we left you on the settee by yourself, but we had only been gone for a few minutes, we'd been keeping an eye on you and then you just disappeared… for a while Winter and I were worried. Raff worked out what he thought had happened, knocked on his door and confirmed you were safe.'

'I know.' I didn't remember any of that and looked down at the floor just to compose myself. 'To be honest, I used the fact that you two left me there as an excuse to be angry with you… when really all I was angry at, was life. I just needed some space, with no questions coming my way, while I came to terms with everything that was happening.'

I watched her lean her head towards the kettle that was boiling in the corner of the office, in turn I nodded back and she stood up to make us a cup of tea.

'The only thing that's stopped us coming to find you to confront you, was that we knew you'd been doing your shifts here, as I saw you fleetingly before you deliberately avoided me. That and the fact your bed's still been slept in, occasionally.' She turned to me and waggled the silver teaspoon she was holding at me. 'I knew I could have forced you to talk, but knowing you as I do, I could see you needed some time. I take it that your former non-existent love life is suddenly alive and kicking? And you're still seeing him?' I heard the clink of the metal spoon on the ceramic mug as she turned back and began to stir our tea over zealously and then again as it was dropped on the tray.

'Yes, he's really helped me this week. In fact, I don't know what I'd have done without him.' I smiled at her, as she moved the few steps over to me and hugged me to her.

'I'm pleased for you, you deserve someone to take care of you. Mum and Dad rang this morning to tell me about Nan... they asked how you were taking the news, I couldn't tell them as I hadn't seen you to talk to. For the first time in all our years as cousins, I felt like I hadn't been around to help you when you needed me the most and I'm so sorry.'

Oh, dear God, I was crying again.

Holding each other close, I began to sob on her shoulder. I heard her sniff a few times and knew she was doing the same. For a while we stood close as we consoled one another.

'We know that Nan's will have to be put up for sale. Mum and Dad are going to ask you to move in with them, but you have a home here, don't you? My spare room is yours for as long as you need it to be. And you've remembered that The Manor is still looking for two deputy managers, haven't you? So, maybe it's finally time to put that degree of yours to good use?'

'Thanks, I'd love to stay here, thank you.' Firstly, I felt relief at her words, then I thought about the job possibility. 'God, how stupid am I? They are, aren't they? I'd completely forgotten about that.' I felt my heartrate quicken at the possibility that fate was showing me a path. 'I've done a lot of thinking over the last week, you would have thought that I would have remembered that? Lots of things are changing, Lauren. I know that some are heart breaking and extremely scary, but others I know are well overdue.' I peeled myself away from her and holding her by the tops of her arms, I looked at the woman who was almost like my mirror image, and just like Daniel had done for me several times over in the last few days, I wiped her cheeks dry with my fingers. 'I know that you, Winter and I need to start making some changes in our lives.'

With her eyes opening wider in question, she pulled out of my hold and went back to her tea making. Silence enveloped the room for a few minutes, a few minutes that felt so very much longer.

Lauren sighed before she began her answer. 'I agree, that sometimes we could *all* do with taking a few more chances, instead of staying in the comfort zone. But, *you*, Amy are the biggest culprit out of all of us and you know it!' She had agreed and accused me all at the same time. Her back was once again towards me as she started to stir our tea again, in over defensive swirls. The metal hit the ceramic mugs with such vehemence I was worried it would crack the sides.

'Maybe. I've realised that all of us need to start asking ourselves just how long we can go on blanking out the parts of our lives that have hurt us. We don't talk about it very often, but you know what I mean. This week I have been forced to question everything I ever thought I was doing to protect myself. I've tried to run away so many times, it's ridiculous and it doesn't work, the hurt and pain just follows. Having sort of accepted that, I'm worried that the three of us have been so busy being strong, independent women, showing everyone that we need nothing from the men that enter our lives... Well, let's say, I'm worried that we're so busy turning our backs on anything and everything, that we might miss what could possibly make us happy in the long run.'

She'd finished making our tea, but Lauren still had her back to me while she mulled over what I was saying. Her hands had come to rest on the side as she appeared to be casually looking at her painted nails.

'I one hundred percent agree with you,' she finally replied.

'You do?' I asked with a happy feeling beginning to bubble up inside me.

'Yes. But *you* need to make sure that *you* take in what you're saying and remember it. You're without a doubt the biggest offender of the three of us. *You* need to jump at the chances that come your way. *You* need to stop pushing away the chances of happiness, even if they're not quite what you first thought. Also, please for once remember not to tar everyone with the same brush... because they're not all the same as your mum.'

I nodded at her, but felt my forehead crinkle as I questioned her words. I knew I didn't agree with her, as I felt her and Winter were just as bad as me. But, I'd just lectured, so knew I had to let her do the same.

She carried on, 'I won't need to though, because I've stopped pushing, I'm taking my opportunity and I'm not running anymore.' Her voice gained strength as she suddenly turned and thrust her left hand out in front of me. As her fingers began to wiggle in front of me, I caught the sparkle of a tiny diamond on her ring finger.

'Oh my God! Rafferty?' My heart began to swell with happiness for her, until her hand was snatched back from mine, as if I'd burnt her with all the fires of hell with the words I'd used.

'NO... Toby proposed and I accepted. Another thing you missed this week.'

I felt around behind me for the seat I knew was there. Once I found it I sat down quickly.

She wasn't running, she was bloody sprinting.

'Oh.' I tried desperately to lift the tone of my voice and to put some sound of joy in there, but I knew it was in vain. I knew the smile I had quickly forced to my face, had become almost a grimace.

'You could at least be pleased for me,' she accused.

'Lauren, I love you… I am pleased, if you're happy then so am I.' I was in shock, he was *so* not right for her. But I had to remember that it wasn't my choice, I didn't have to marry the guy.

At that moment, the bell of the front door sounded as Winter burst into the tearooms.

Saved by the bell.

'I HAVE NEWS!' she shouted as she very quickly appeared in the doorway of the office. Her bright eyes found mine and she smiled, accentuating her already flushed cheeks as she barrelled into the room to offer me a hug. 'You're a sight for sore eyes, I must say. I'm so sorry about your nan… Are you okay?' she asked moving away from me and pulling her face into a severe expression.

'I'm fine.' I nodded back to her in reassurance. 'Come on, tell us your news.'

'I have been offered a HUGE job.' As usual, Winter gesticulated as she spoke, opening her arms up wide to emphasise the most important words.

'Go on then.' I smiled at her in encouragement. I was already pleased for her, just looking at her body language. I couldn't wait to share her news, and if the truth was told I was so pleased she had arrived when she had. I hadn't the words yet, to describe to Lauren how I felt about her new engagement.

'On a date, yet to be confirmed sometime early in the new year, wait for it…' She held up her hand to us. 'I'm off to Vegas. VEGAS! Can you believe it? Cade and the others have made me an offer I can't refuse. After the successful opening of The Manor, I've been offered the contract of opening the next three hotels. The first one is in Vegas. What do you both think?'

'Cade?' fell out of my mouth before I got it under control. As her eyes darted to mine once again, I spoke. 'That's fantastic news!' I congratulated her.

I'm not sure which one of us moved first, but soon the three of us were jumping up and down in each other's arms, trying to avoid crashing into the furniture. Our screams must have been loud enough to hear outside of the building as we celebrated and equally, I felt, commiserated with each other. For the first time I could ever remember since we had all been friends, the celebration, although acted out the same way as always, felt false. I wondered if they knew what my screams and whoops of joy were masking, and if their reactions were the same as mine.

Things were changing, I could only hope that all the changes would be for the best.

Twenty-Six

Amy

'**WOW, I DON'T** think I've ever seen a more beautiful bride,' I heard Winter exclaim as Jack and Lily entered the marquee hand in hand to thunderous applause.

She was right, Lily had appeared a little shyly from behind him in an emerald coloured dress. It was a fantastic choice with her dark hair and it made her green eyes pop. The deep, rich colour was so right for a winter wedding and with the white of the snow on the ground it was a fantastic contrast. But as I looked at her closely, I realised it wouldn't have mattered what she was dressed in, how much money had been spent on the flowers, or the amount of people invited. It was the way they looked at each other that gave her a luminosity that just lit her up. Sitting on Jack's shoulders in an outfit that matched his dad's, was their young son. The three of them together were an absolute picture and I was ecstatic to be sharing their day.

'You know how much I love the Carpenters, right?' I heard Lauren as she spoke quietly onto the side of her glass, trying to stop anyone lip reading her words.

Winter and I turned our heads further, to look at her in question.

'But, have you *seen* how well Jassy and Bella have done for themselves?' We both followed her eyes to the top table and looked at Jack's sisters with their husbands.

Winter and I laughed our answer.

Of course, I'd seen them around occasionally with their other halves. But to see them all in one place, with the men in dark grey three-piece suits, she was right, the testosterone was almost overwhelming. Especially hot in my eyes was Bella's husband, Nathan. He appeared to have already discarded his suit jacket, his waistcoat was unbuttoned and his tie had gone. Even through his smart white shirt, I could see his tattoos and I now realised just what those did for me. Unashamed as I was, I appreciatively watched him unbutton his shirt sleeves, then roll them up exposing his forearms and the said tattoos.

'Who would have thought that our small village would ever contain so many hot men all at the same time?' I heard Winter, as did everyone else stood around our table. She had never managed the art of whispering and although she had been born with a silver spoon in her mouth she hadn't, I had learnt years ago, been given a filter. I felt the others on our table look at her and smile.

I rolled my lips inwards, clamped down on them tightly with my teeth and supressed the sudden need to wet my lips at the view. Then I let a big grin take over my face at my internal thoughts. Sweeping my eyes up and down the top table I looked at them all again as Jack and Lily took their places in the middle of his family.

I had already known that all the men were devastatingly handsome, albeit in different ways. But I was now grasping, as I watched them, that it wasn't their obvious looks and money that made them that way, it was the way they looked at their wives. They looked at them liked the sun rose and set within them. It was the way they touched them like they might never be able to do so again. They kissed their fingers, whispered private thoughts into their ears to make them smile, and it was magnetising to watch. In return, Bella, Jasmin, Lily and Frankie came alight under their ministrations.

I thought back to Daniel and how he made me feel when we were together and the way he touched me with his flesh, his soul and, I now believed, with his heart. I understood, watching them, that I had a chance of having what they all had. My heart soared at the realisation I was falling in love with him. I looked at my friends standing clapping beside me and I wanted it for them, too. I said a silent prayer that one day they would also know what it was to be so adored by their soulmate and then realisation hit.

Toby didn't treat Lauren like that, he pawed at her like she was a possession and she in turn seemed to shrink away from his touch. I looked again at the ring on her finger. He owned his own business and was comfortably off, yet the diamond on her finger was a mere chip. It wasn't that I thought money could cement a relationship, it wasn't that at all. But surely, if he had found the love of his life and knowing that money wasn't really a problem, he would want to spoil her as such? Personally, I thought he would want to spend some money and effort on her.

I shook my head to get me out of my thoughts, as once again we sat back down at our table and began to listen to the speeches.

The evening rolled on and it was great to spend some real down time with Winter and Lauren. We didn't discuss anything deep, we didn't question each other's motives for our new choices, we just enjoyed each other's company. Knowing our threesome was about to be broken up for a while made it even more important to do so. The moment our conversation drifted towards anything remotely questionable, we would shake our heads at each other and go on as before.

After the speeches, the marquee had been opened outwards to one side. It had revealed another gas-heated area with a premade dance floor and after leaving our handbags behind at our table, we had been throwing some moves to whatever the DJ played. With all that was happening in our lives it was good to just have some plain, simple fun. I was pleased I'd chosen to wear trousers to the reception, I felt smart in the black, cigarette style. I'd worn an off the shoulder, Bardot top in a burnt orange colour to compliment them. I felt appropriately dressed, but comfortable enough to dance the night away.

Lauren touched my shoulder. 'Do you want another drink?' she mouthed as she lifted her cupped right hand up to her lips gesticulating, in case I couldn't hear.

'Please.' I nodded back enthusiastically.

Winter and I continued dancing to *Try* by Pink, singing to the words loudly. I looked around us, most of the wedding party were up on the dancefloor almost turning it into a family mosh pit. I soaked in the happiness.

At the end of *Try* the DJ, for the first time that evening, didn't blend straight into another song. Instead he took his mic in his hand and made an announcement. Winter and I stopped dead on the spot where we had been dancing at the back of the room and lifted our heads to listen to him.

I heard Winter groan beside me. 'Not more speeches?' she said a little too loudly. I reprimanded her by glaring and lifting my eyebrows at her.

'Okay, everybody. That's me for about an hour.' He grinned at our cries of 'Awwww.'

There suddenly seemed an influx of bodies carrying amps, microphones and drums on stands onto the large stage behind him. In a matter of a few minutes, the DJ had finished telling us what an awesome audience we were and how much we were going to enjoy the surprise set up by the best man Charlie and the groomsmen. I looked across at Jasmin's husband John as he nodded with reservation at the appreciative crowd on the dance floor. Then at Charlie, who in complete contrast was stood close to us in the middle of the dance floor, with his pint glass raised high in his hand, turning around full circle absorbing everyone's cheers.

'Mr and Mrs. Jack Carpenter, ladies and gentlemen, I give you… the one… the only… DEFAULT DISTRACTION!' The DJ stepped back at the same time his equipment was lifted away to reveal the bands instruments set up behind him.

I felt Winter grab my bare forearm, as in silence we watched the drummer, with his sticks raised high in acknowledgement, enter onto the stage first. The attitude that just exuded from his body was completely captivating. I didn't think I had ever seen a drummer with so much stage presence.

'Evening.' He bent to speak into a mic, placed to one side of the drum kit. He raised a green glass beer bottle up to the happy couple and pointed the neck at them. 'Congratulations, to the mad couple.' The crowd cheered and laughed at his words. He then took a swig and placed his beer on the floor.

While he was still standing, he began to start to tap out a beat on one drum. It seemed to be a beat that most people recognised instantaneously. He flung his leg high over the stool already in position and sat down, his other hand then entered the beat with a flourish. I watched as he closed his eyes and lost himself to his passion. The floor beneath my feet began to pulse as the crowd around me started to jump up and down to the rhythm. Butterflies began to dance inside my stomach, at the fact I was about to watch a band I had only ever heard of, perform.

I looked over at Winter as she watched the stage, her mouth was open and she seemed totally mesmerised by the man on the stage. I smiled as I realised she liked the foul-mouthed Cade much more than she had admitted to. As my body reacted of its own accord and started to join in with the increasingly loud stamping of feet on the wooden boards, I gave the recognisable drummer the once over. Dirty-blond hair and with his chin held high as he perused the crowd, he gave off an air of complete confidence. He was wearing heavy boots and his jeans were ripped to the point of almost hanging off him. A loose fitting, black vest meant you could see his worked-hard-for muscular frame and he was wearing more chains and wrist cuffs than I could count.

Winter was still beside me. I tried to speak to her but the marquee was filled with so many noises, it was in vain. I could see she was now looking behind us for Lauren. She obviously wanted a drink more than I had first thought. I let my body lose itself into the excitement around me.

The crowd grew louder as one by one the band members came onto the stage in an obviously well practised routine. I saw the man who had been waiting for the young woman in the tearooms a few days ago, come onto the stage. He carried his bass in one hand and he pushed it higher to show his appreciation to the excited crowd. He quietly took his place and started strumming the chords in time with Cade.

The atmosphere in the marquee grew to a frenzy as off stage the lead guitar started playing a well-known riff that sent the people around me wild. I watched in pride as our local boy Rafferty walked out, in his trademark leathers. He blew a kiss out into the crowd as his eyes wandered over the top of us all. I knew right at that minute he was searching for Lauren and when his eyes remained stuck fast in the doorway behind where we were jumping up and down, I knew he had found her. I looked over, to see her standing stock still, with her mouth wide open. Her fingers were turning white as her grip tightened on our three drinks.

I pulled my arm free of Winter's ever tightening hold, to go and help her out.

Standing in front of her, I used my fingers to tip her chin upwards and grinned at her as she closed her mouth. I wrestled one glass away from her deathlike grip, afraid that the three drinks would prove to be too much and that she might drop one.

'What a surprise?' I shouted over to her.

She just stared back at me.

I hadn't thought the crowd around me could get any louder, but the excitement in the air ramped up as the lead singer entered the stage. Hearing the screams, I turned around to face back towards the stage to watch as the tall figure entered from the right and walked onto the stage with a swagger that immediately spoke to my insides. I moved my head from side to side trying to see around the sea of jumping bodies in front of me.

The lead singer took his place in front of the mic that had been centralised to the front of the stage. He had a leather pork pie hat on his head and was looking down, I couldn't see his features around the brim. I joined in with the claps and cheers as the band stood complete in front of us. Looking around the bodies in front of me I took in the lead singer, well-fitting black jeans and a plain blue T-shirt that was ripped in places showing his many tattoos underneath. I looked at his hands cupping his mic and then to his ring-covered fingers.

I was suddenly aware of Winter and Lauren either side of me and I linked my arms with theirs in my excitement.

The crowd was already singing the words to the song that Default Distraction were playing and when the lead singer finally lifted his head, two-finger saluted at them and joined his amazing voice with theirs, the marquee erupted and they were all projected into a frenzy of excitement.

When he'd finished singing the note he'd entered on, his eyes opened.

His teal orbs found mine, and I disintegrated on the spot.

Twenty-Seven

Amy

I **LIFTED MY** glass to my lips. My hand was trembling but I was helped by the fact that my shaking limb was wrapped around Lauren's. She supported me as I poured the amber liquid down my throat in one gulp. Winter then prised the empty glass from my fingers and replaced it with hers.

In my shock, I downed that one too.

I could feel them both as they tried to make me go backwards to where we had left our handbags earlier, but my feet refused to budge. My eyes were focussed solely on Daniel and my head had decided to punish my stupidity by refusing to let me leave.

But he isn't Daniel.

For the life of me I couldn't remember what their lead singer was called. The only name that suited him at this moment was lying bastard.

His voice was captivating, his movements well practised and they were obviously achieving the desired effect on the crowd, as the noise in the room had increased to a crescendo. Watching him as he acted in front of them with a confidence that must have taken him years to develop, my heart sunk. As the second song went into the third, the third to the fourth, I slowly came to realise that the past week had been a complete lie from start to finish.

I wasn't normally this stupid.

Was I?

Anger flared up inside me and I stood there stoking it to the point of incineration. I wanted it to burn red hot. I wanted it to engulf me in its flames. I wanted to use that anger to cleanse my bloody stupid self. I needed it to completely envelope the hurt that had erupted from inside my heart. The same hurt and pain that was now flowing around my body. I could still feel his touch, hear his words and feel the way his body had sustained mine. I could still see the depth of those eyes and what he had tried to wordlessly tell me over and over.

But the Daniel I had met and nearly fallen for didn't exist, he hadn't told me the truth about who he was. So, everything we had been together was a lie.

The man on the stage making everyone fall for him with his stage presence, his voice, those damned good looks and that amazing body of his, had lied to me. He wasn't who he had pretended to be. He wasn't the man who had tempted me to trust him. As far as I was concerned he no longer existed, just another actor like my mum. He was, in fact, just another celebrity using people for his own devices and pleasure. I wondered how many other unsuspecting females he had duped into caring for him. He probably had many around the world, all thinking he was giving them his all.

My heart bled for them and myself.

Watching him on stage commanding the crowd, was mesmerising. Even now as I stood there rooted to the spot with rage erupting and flowing fast around my body, I had to admit he was the best looking man I had ever seen. His muscular body was honed to absolute perfection and it just begged "made for sex." I was at least fifty feet away, but my insides had traitorously sparked to life. My core was involuntarily aching and my knickers were damp. *Yes, there really was bad damp.* I was sure I would find my eyes dilated if I could see them. I watched him own every square inch of the stage the band were on, getting ever angrier with myself for allowing him to make me feel this way. I hated him for lying to me, and just to make things a whole lot worse I realised that I wasn't falling for him, I was already in love with him.

But, right at this moment in time, I was pleased to feel that anger felt the strongest of all the emotions coursing around my system.

I watched him as he sung, with his worried eyes fixed on mine. But I stared him out, no way in hell was I running away this time. He raised his eyebrows in question at me, and when I made absolutely no effort whatsoever to answer his unspoken question, concern overtook his expression.

Yeah, you should be worried.

176

The aversion to him, bubbling around inside me, was so intense because of the way he had used me, that I wanted to show him that I also wasn't who he thought I was. I wanted, if it was at all possible, to hurt the man inside his manufactured façade.

Without thinking about what I was doing, I jerked myself forward, effectively releasing my arms from Winter and Lauren. I pushed my way to the front of the stage, lifted my arms up high into the air and right in front of him I began to dance to the music.

Default Distraction played on and he continued to stare at me as I began to dance all over and around one of the male guests. I hadn't a clue who I was dancing with, and I didn't care. I knew nothing about the guy, other than he had smiled at me earlier. I knew that he wasn't my type, but I also knew that I hadn't seen him with another woman and that was enough. I needed a willing warm body and he seemed happy enough to be it.

Willing warm body looked pleased and the bastard formally known as Daniel looked bloody fuming. If inside my heart hadn't been slowly severing into a million pieces, I would have been ecstatic. On the rare occasion I fleetingly looked his way, I could see that he was becoming angrier. He had developed his facial tic and he had almost growled out a few of the words he was singing.

It spurred me on.

The whiskey I had just flung down me in rapid succession began to travel around my system. I clung on to nameless man's shoulders and rubbed my body over his. Finally, fuelled by the music and the alcohol in my system, I pressed my lips to his. The anger and alcohol that had been powering my actions suddenly abated at the contact and I pulled away from him like I'd been scorched. I moved quickly away, trying to smile an apology as I left. The crowds between me and my so-called friends parted gradually, and I pushed my way through.

Behind me, I heard the music stop and Raff saying they would all be back in a few minutes time. The DJ must have been waiting in the wings, as I heard his voice speak to the crowd on the dance floor as he got some tracks together.

I opened the door, hoping to leave it all behind and went out into the fresh air.

Twenty-Eight

Amy

A DECKING AREA had been created outside the marquee, to create a balcony in Jack and Lily's large garden. Even with gas heaters, twinkling lights and dark evergreen floral arrangements, it was empty and cold, but to me in my escape it looked welcoming. Luckily, even with the snow on the ground all around us, I managed to keep my shivering in check by wrapping my arms tightly around my body underneath one of the lit gas heaters. I stared out into the darkness just trying to compose myself as the last of the alcoholic buzz left my system. Eventually, I heard the footsteps behind me, but refused to turn around.

'There you are.' I heard Winter's voice. 'Amy?'

I spun around quickly. 'You two... you let me make a complete fool of myself. You both knew, didn't you?' I pointed an accusing finger at them.

'Yes, we both knew, but not initially,' Lauren admitted, dropping her arms straight down to either side of her body and showing me her open palms. 'We're sorry you found out like that.'

'I can't believe either of you could do that to me, and you call yourself my best friends?' I raised my voice at them as my emotions boiled up to the surface.

'We *are* your best friends, friends that want you to have a life. You know very well if we'd had told you straight away who he was, you would never have even got to know him, he wouldn't have stood a chance,' Lauren replied.

'YOU should have told me.' I pointed my finger at them both again, driving my point home, still accusing them, but in truth my voice was beginning to falter.

'Amy, we didn't know at first, we never caught a good look at him. But after we spoke to you in the drawing room, I put it together,' added Winter.

'You should have said, the moment you thought it was a possibility, the moment you found out. As my friends, you owed me that.'

Tears were coursing their way down my cheeks, probably taking most of my carefully applied eye make-up with them. As they watched my pain, they in turn began to silently cry with me.

'I talked to Raff about my suspicions and he confronted him. We were told that Brody had never lied to you, you'd heard Cade shouting out his surname when you dropped off the salmon at The Manor and jumped to conclusions. He was going to tell you who he was and we were asked to give him a couple of days to do it.'

So that was his name.

I was stood shaking my head at them and their pathetic excuses, when the lying bastard himself appeared behind them. He had come out into the freezing air of the night still only wearing what he had been wearing on stage. Steam rose off him and into the cold night air. His hands were pushed deep into his jeans pockets. My body felt his presence and started to rebel against what my brain was demanding of it. The way he made me feel when he was near me, was visceral. I was disgusted with myself when my breath hitched at the sight of him.

'Don't come near me,' I shouted over at him. I sounded like a woman on the edge, probably because that's exactly where I was precariously balanced. The emotions and anxiety running through my body were making me shake.

'I'm coming nearer, so you'd better prepare yourself. I need to hold you and from the way I can see you shaking, you need me to.'

'DON'T TOUCH ME!' My voice screeched through the cold night air.

His feet stopped moving and his shoulders slumped slightly in defeat. A long silent minute passed between us, then his eyes sparked alive in defiance. Once again, his feet moved forward until I found myself being spun around and engulfed in his arms. He held me tightly to him, his front to my back and together we stood staring out into the darkness. I wriggled around in his hold, until gradually I realised it wasn't loosening. An anguished sob tore from my mouth. Reluctantly, I found myself melting into his strong, hard body and under my breath I swore at myself for being so weak.

'What the hell do you think you were doing kissing that fucking asswipe?' I felt his chin move as he spoke to me and warmth spread through my body as he kissed the top of my head after asking me the question.

'Really? That's what you want to say to me? You lied to me and now you stand here with your arms wrapped around me, questioning me.'

'I never lied to you, Amy. But you've just deliberately tried to make me jealous, and it fucking worked. You're mine, no other fucker gets to go anywhere near you. Tell me you understand that?'

I couldn't form words in between my now more frequent sobs, so I just shook my head at him.

'What the fuck are we doing to each other? Look, you need to listen to me.'

'I NEED to listen to you? Who the hell do you think you are? Apart from some glorified rock God who thinks he can go around messing up people's lives.' My heart hammered in my chest as I allowed myself to pour all my hurt into anger.

'I'm sorry. I'm SO fucking sorry. I was gonna tell you last night, remember I said I wanted to talk to you? I was going to tell you everything as I held you in my arms.' He pulled me closer to him. 'I'm sorry I didn't get a chance to and I'm sorry you found out like this.'

'Of course you are,' I accused, in between taking in much needed deep breaths of air.

'Us playing here tonight was a last-minute thing, we were asked to step in for the band that had been booked for their wedding. They cancelled when the weather became so bad where they lived they couldn't get here. I tried calling you, but you know what your phone's like. Raff and Cade tried calling the girls too. My calls never went through to your phone and Lauren and Winter didn't answer or check their messages.'

'Yes, he's right, they did. My phone has loads of missed calls and messages on it.' Winter pushed into the fraught conversation. I suddenly remembered that my utter humiliation had an audience and I shook my head in despair. I could now see she had stepped closer to the side of us both, holding her phone out in front of her and waving it around in her hand. I turned my head and shot her a look, and she fell silent. I heard her feet on the boards as she hurriedly walked away.

How very dare she take his side?

'We were dancing, our phones were nowhere near us.'

'That figures.' I felt his leg bend behind me as he kicked the floor with his right boot. I knew he was fidgeting because he felt uneasy.

Raff and the others had appeared out on the decking. Hearing their voices and the sound of their boots banging on the wooden floor as they arrived, made Brody spin us both around. He released his hold over me momentarily and I saw his arms open up either side of me as he splayed his arms wide and pleaded with our audience.

'Goddamn it! Can you *all* give us some fucking privacy?' His arms came back around me as he spoke.

Initially no one moved, they all stood there looking between the two of us, trying to decide if it was all right to leave us to it.

'Come on, guys. This is hard enough,' Brody pleaded.

'Please leave,' I managed to force out. 'I need to hear all his excuses as to why he let me believe he was somebody else.'

I watched as one by one they filed back inside. The marquee doors closed behind them, but I knew they hadn't gone any further as I could see the colours of their clothing behind the translucent plastic panes.

I swiped at my face, clearing my tears and probably smudging the black further over my face.

'Go on then, you have five minutes.' I wanted to stay with him forever, but I couldn't handle any more pain.

'Fuck, Amy! We have a lifetime together, remember what I said when we talked?'

I shook my head at him, hearing my hair rub against his T-shirt. Of course I remembered. I remembered every minute of the last week and knew that I would for the rest of my life. But, I was not going to help him explain.

In the distance, I could hear Eric Clapton singing *Wonderful Tonight*. Brody obviously heard it too as almost unconsciously he started moving us both gently to the music. Reluctantly, I gave in to what I needed and held on to his bare forearms.

'When I first saw you, Amy. It was like being knocked over by a fucking freight train. I've told you already that I don't have relationships. But when I saw you, I wanted everything with you, children, the white fucking picket fence, hell I wanted the whole goddamn nine yards. We hadn't even had a proper conversation, but in my head you were already mine, are mine.'

'Were,' I corrected him and momentarily felt him flinch at my statement.

'I saw you and you saw me.' I was shaking my head at him, but he carried on anyway. 'Shout at me, scream, swear if you have to.' I knew he was saying the same words to me that I had spoken to him only a few days before. Although it felt like I'd lived a lifetime in those few days. 'Do whatever you need to do, because I'm not letting you walk away from me, from us.'

'That is not your decision to make,' I replied, sick to the back teeth of letting other people control my life.

He released me suddenly and spun me around to face him. His knees bent so he could get to my level and his eyes immediately found mine. Now I was stood without his warmth surrounding me, the shivers in my body started to get stronger. I could see the pain etched in his beautiful features, but I was more concerned with my own pain. I had hit self-preservation mode.

'Fuck! Amy, tell me what the hell I can do to put this right?'

I shrugged my shoulders at him and shook my head.

'I'm gonna try by saying what I should have said at the beginning.' He stood straight, pushed his hands back into his jeans pockets and momentarily looked down. Then his eyes came back up to find mine. 'Hi... it's really great to meet you, my name's Brody Daniels and... I'm an alcoholic. I'm in recovery, but I'll always be an alcoholic. I'm also in a band that you might have heard of.'

Momentarily, I was stunned by his honesty. I looked deep into his pain-filled eyes and I shook my head at him. My synapses started firing as things fell into place. 'That's why you wouldn't take me out for a drink.'

He nodded at me. 'Yeah, that's exactly why.' His hands came out of his pockets and my eyes watched as one by one he began to click his knuckles as he spoke to me. 'If I was a normal guy meeting you for the first time, believe me I would have fucking jumped at the chance. But I'm not, I'm far from normal.' His eyes pleaded with me to understand.

'Us taking over The Manor is down to them inside.' He threw one arm to the side of him to gesticulate Raff and the others. 'Even after all the years we've been together, unlike many in the same industry, we still genuinely care for each other. After I nearly drunk myself to death and various other things had happened to us, we came here in the hope we could all turn a corner. I love music, I love performing. But I hate the fucking life it brings with it. It's not real, it doesn't allow you to have anything tangible. When you didn't recognise me, it was like a breath of fresh air. You heard Cade call out my surname and just assumed that was me and I'm guilty of letting you believe it. For the first time in a long fucking time I could just be myself with someone new. It was honest and refreshing and you saw me, for me, when normally all people see is some fucking rock God.'

He stopped momentarily, letting me absorb what he was trying to tell me and took a deep breath to start again. 'People only want Brody Daniels, lead singer of Default Distraction, and all the things I can buy them with my money. Women open their legs for me because they want me on their arm, to open doors for them. What they don't want is the broken, damaged man I am and all the fucking baggage I carry, but you accepted me for me. You saw through my outer shell. It was fucking unbelievable when your heart opened and you invited me in.'

A loud sigh left his mouth, he shoved both of his hands through his hair and carried on. 'If being a former addict wasn't enough, I'm a member of a band, and in that band we've all learnt the hard way how much people want to be with us for what they can get out of it. Then I came across you. You're the most beautiful woman I have ever laid eyes on. Added to all of that, I could feel a chemistry between us that felt like it was off the charts. The fact you hadn't a clue who the hell I was and you still wanted to be with me, was the *best* fucking high I had ever experienced. You saw me, not my addictions, not what I could buy you or the money you could make by selling your story to the highest bidder and not all the mistakes I'd made... you just saw me. Can you understand why I wanted you to get to know me first?'

'Sort of,' I reluctantly admitted. 'I did see you, I saw more than you'll ever know. You rescued me, not just from the accidents I appear to frequently have, but mentally. But to find out you only let me in so far and that you refused to trust me, when I let you into my very existence wholeheartedly, is painful.'

'You thought I was rescuing you?' He spun away and his arms opened wide showing me his empty palms, emphasising what he was trying to get me to understand. Then he stepped quickly back. 'You literally saved me! I was so fucking empty inside before we met. I have so much fucking guilt and remorse inside me over my family, and how I wasn't able to help any of them. I used drink to numb the pain. I used drink to make me forget. I used drink, because most fucking days I don't even like me. I used drink just to get me through. But when I'm with you, I don't need alcohol, I only crave you. You're the only thing I'm now dependant on. But, I just needed to know that you wanted to be with me for me, that's all I'm guilty of this time.' He sighed loudly 'I know I was wrong, not putting you right as soon as I could and its fucking killing me that the pain we're both feeling here is on me. Before you make an impulsive decision about us, I need to tell you.' His eyes left mine for a second and then returned. His teal eyes implored mine. 'I've fallen in love with you.'

I absorbed every sentiment he had offered and closed my eyes momentarily as I sighed at the unfairness of it all.

'But I've fallen in love with Daniel. So, it appears we have nowhere else to go with this conversation.'

His head tipped back and he looked at the sky. I saw a tear roll down his cheek as he heard my words. He sniffed but made no effort to wipe it away. The teal eyes that I had always found so much beauty and depth in before, were even more stunning as they shone through the layer of liquid he forced himself to hold in.

I was an emotional creature, I couldn't help it. I felt for him standing in front of me. He looked as wrecked as I felt at the situation we were now in. God knows, I had wanted him to come up with some fantastic excuse as to why he hadn't told me who he was, so I could fall into his arms and everything would be okay, but it wasn't. He had done the one thing that I couldn't forgive him for. He hadn't been truthful.

'I opened up to you and you should have opened up to me. You could and should have told me everything when we were at Lake View.'

'I know and I'm so fucking sorry. I never wanted to hurt you, believe me.' Finally, his palm swiped across his face as he began to compose himself.

'The trouble is, Brody, I don't know what to believe and my heart can't take any more pain. I took a chance on you and I've had it thrown back into my face. I have no more chances left in me, my past has taught me not to open myself up for more hurt.'

'Amy, please let me prove to you, that I am the guy you saw in me. I've been more real with you than anybody in years. It's just a name, it doesn't change who I am inside here.' His closed fist hit his chest over his heart.

'I can't, because it does change everything. Deep down inside I never really expected you to stay with me, because I don't have that expectation of anyone. My dad didn't want me and my mum left me because the call of stardom was too strong for her to stay. I was a young girl constantly trying to be a better child, just hoping she might then be able to love me unconditionally. I wanted to be enough for her. Look at you, Brody you're a twenty out of ten, and I'm lucky if I'm a six, I could never be enough for you. It was a wonderful moment of illusion, dreaming that I'd found my soulmate, the man who would always be there for me. The man who would always rescue me. But all I'm left with now are doubts. What on earth would a rock star want with me? When he can have anyone.'

'You're not listening to what I'm saying. A great man once wrote that fame and fortune was only a passing thing, and he was dead on right, that's the rock 'n' roll life. I want real life and I want it with you. What a load of shit that is, all that "out of ten" crap. You are the most beautiful woman I have ever seen. I'm not your mum, I'm not leaving you. You're more than enough for me. That dream we both want is right there, Amy, in between us, it's not an illusion. All we have to do is reach out and grab it.'

I took a large side step around him. I needed to leave without touching him again, because suddenly I needed out of the large open space. The decking area was beginning to feel tight and constraining. With my sudden sideward movement, my ankle turned over as only mine could, causing me to stumble very slightly. His arm immediately came out and captured me. He pulled me close to his side, effectively stopping me from falling over. His cologne enveloped me and I instinctively raised my hand to hold on to his bicep. For a split-second I allowed my body to lean on him once again, to absorb the strength I needed, and my fingers sank into his bare, muscular arm. The warmth of his body and the familiarity of our skin touching, ignited the need in me that I had earlier refused to acknowledge. The pull was too strong and I turned my head to look at him. His hand came up and he brushed a small piece of my hair away from my face and looked in my eyes. Knowing it would be all so easy to stay there in his arms, I pulled myself away quickly and tried to recover from his touch. I walked a couple of steps and then froze when he spoke again.

'Right here, right this fucking minute, you might be walking away from us, Amy. But, this isn't over. I *refuse* to let you go.'

I turned to look at him one last time. He had turned away to look back at the dark of the garden, it appeared he was unable to watch me leave. Stood all by himself with his back to me, I could see his hands were once again pushed down deep into his pockets. His broad shoulders had sagged in defeat. From the back, he looked like a young boy who had lost his whole world. I felt my heart trying to break out of my chest as it begged me to forgive him and take him into my arms, but my head refused. I needed him to understand that this wasn't right, this whole sorry situation couldn't just be forgiven and forgotten.

'I trusted you. I let you in and I did it all too fast. I mean, who falls in love in a week? That was my stupidity, that was all on me.' A huge audible sob wracked through me again. 'You even bloody promised me. When you knew that I hated promises,' I called over to him.

I forced one foot in front of the other, as I made myself walk back inside.

'Amy, this isn't over, there's so much more we need to say. I'll give you some time, but all the while it remains unsaid, you and I will always be unfinished business. I won't let you walk away from us forever.' I heard the desperation and pain in his voice and it hurt me way down deep inside.

I let out a soft sigh of acknowledgement at his words. 'The trouble is, there is no us.'

Twenty-Nine

Amy

I **PUSHED OPEN** the door and heard the familiar tinkling of the
bell above it. I let out a long exhale, expecting to feel the peace and
contentment I was craving. Twisting myself around, I lifted a hand
to wordlessly thank one of the Carpenters' security who had helped me
and offered me a lift as Default Distraction had once again taken to the
stage.

I had heard Brody's voice as he had started to sing and as he'd lost
himself into the words of the song. I stayed long enough to hear him
singing about regret, about not taking chances and not saying the words
that needed to be said and when I heard the words about not taking a
chance on a relationship because it was too risky, I knew he was
singing to me.

I had escaped to the only place I wanted to be. I watched the car
pull slowly away and the lane around me fell into almost complete
darkness. I locked the door behind me and slid the large bolt across.

When everything had crashed around my ears less than an hour
ago, I needed to be at the one place I would always call home. I felt to
the side of me and switched on the fairy lights, which gave me enough
light to walk to the back of the shop without breaking my neck, then I
turned on the light that led upstairs to the flat. The light flooded into the
back of the shop through the gap between the open door and the frame.
I looked around hoping to find the sense of calm I desperately needed,

but it was nowhere to be found. The place was cold and smelt of damp in the week I'd been gone and that worried me. It strangely seemed to mirror my life. It was ridiculous how quickly our home had started to fall apart in our absence and the same could be said of me.

I was wearing my coat but a shiver overtook me. It seemed everything in here was destined to remind me of him. I made my way back to the door to turn off the fairy lights, but remembering it was Christmas day tomorrow, I pulled back my hand. Then I saw the gloves left in the window and my mind went back to one of our first meetings. I ran one finger over the yellow pair with the daisies on, and without thinking I placed them on my cold hands.

I turned and walked upstairs to our flat.

With the open fire lit in our small living area, the room now had a warm orange glow to it. I glanced around the familiar space and smiled as my eyes ran quickly over everything. The room was furnished in odd, mismatched furniture. In fact, not one piece matched anything else in the room and that was just the way my nan liked it. She had often told me everything had memories, either from her life with my grandad or of a well-loved relative who was no longer with us.

I had closed the burnished gold, velvet curtains on the bay window and wrapped a fleece blanket around myself. I'd placed a hot water bottle in the small of my back and held a hot cup of cocoa in my gloved hands as I stared into the flames, looking for answers.

Only a week ago, I went out looking for excitement and looking to live, now I was craving the familiar and comforting things in life. I'd had a hot bath, changed into an old pair of pyjamas and was now curled up in the one armchair in the room, with my legs tucked underneath me. In the background, I had turned on my nan's old record player. The beautiful sound of Eddy Arnold and his melodic voice singing *Make The World Go Away* was playing on repeat. The record was my nan's favourite and I had it playing over and over as I imagined her and my grandad dancing around the large table that dominated our living room. It wasn't something I'd ever witnessed, but my uncle had described it to me and my cousins so many times, I could see it in my mind's eye. I sipped at my cocoa and saw them laughing and holding each other tight, happy in their own small world.

Eddy finished singing and the needle ran quickly to the centre, creating the familiar crackling sound, before the arm came back over, the needle reconnected and he started singing all over again.

I had never felt so alone in my life.

Tears fell down my face and I did nothing to try to stop them. I was grieving, I missed my nan, I missed my steady unchanging life, I missed Lauren and Winter, but most of all I missed him.

I missed bloody Brody Daniels.

My life was changing and I was shit scared, but I was determined to meet it head on. I realised how much I needed this time to myself as so much had happened over the last week.

Seriously, was it only a week? I shook my head at the realisation and allowed myself to carry on sobbing. I sobbed in anger at my dad wanting nothing to do with my pregnant mum. I sobbed at my mum selfishly leaving me. I sobbed at my nan's illness and the fact I was now losing her too. Finally, I broke my heart at having had a week to see the wonderful possibility of a future. A future with a man I believed I could have had a lifetime with and then just as quickly having had that fleeting dream ripped from my hands.

It took me just under an hour to compose myself, but that time was clearly the best time I'd ever spent on myself. As the sobs that had ripped through my body began to pass, I began to understand that I felt stronger for the time to think and the time to cry. I blew my nose loudly and wiped my face dry with my hands. Then with a sudden need to get my head sorted out, I released the fleece blanket from around myself and stretched towards my nan's old walnut bureau. I lowered the desk part and snuck my hand into the small gap I'd made, grabbing at the pen and notepad I knew I would find there.

Starting at the beginning and with tears still rolling down my face, I began to list everything I needed to sort out and achieve.

I intended to live the life I wanted, the one I was convinced I was supposed to have, and as far as I could see, I was the one stopping myself achieving just that. I was determined that things were going to change and they were going to change tonight. My pen flew over the paper quickly, in my round, recognisable handwriting. The list included sorting out the shop and flat and putting it on the market as soon as possible to give my nan what she needed. My CV needing updating and that was high up on the list, as was applying for one of the positions at The Manor. The more I thought about it, the more I thought the job was made for me and it would keep me here, where I needed to be. Even if the place would always remind me of him. My pen had hovered for a while, the nib seemed desperate to write the words, but I held back. Somewhere, although still unwritten on the white paper in front of me, was sorting out how I felt about Brody. I wasn't sure how I was going to achieve it, or at this moment exactly what priority it should take. So, I refused to write it down. But before I could start to move down my numbered list, I had to start with number one and I was going to do it today.

Placing the pad and pen down on the dining table, I prepared myself to do something I never ever thought I would do. I walked out into the chill of the landing to where the only phone in the flat was located and I allowed my fingers to flick through my nan's name and address book. I found the S and opened the page with force, sending the blue faux leather cover onto the table with a bang. I stared down at the number I'd already looked at a few times before when I was younger, on my birthdays and at Christmas. Taking a deep calming breath, I let my eyes connect with the numbers. With my other hand shaking, I picked up the receiver and then pressed the corresponding buttons on the phone.

The phone at the other end rang several times. I watched as my fingertips, exposed in the gloves I was wearing, started to turn white under the pressure of clasping hold of the receiver too firmly as I waited.

'Hello.' A female voice hit my ears. It was a voice I allowed myself to remember sometimes in my dreams.

'Hello, Mum.'

'Amy?'

'Yes, it's me... I phoned to wish you a Merry Christmas.'

For a few seconds the line was void of words, although I knew she was still there. Finally, she spoke again.

'Merry Christmas to you, too.'

I took a deep shaking breath to prepare myself for what I needed to say next, what I simply knew I had to say. 'I wanted you to know that I'm at last strong enough to forgive you for leaving me.'

'Thank you, Amy.' Her voice wavered with emotion.

'Although, I'll never be able to forget.' My voice grew louder with the words I was speaking, as my courage overtook my fears.

'I know, Amy. I'm so very sorry for letting you down.' Her reply came back quickly as if she had gone over this moment many times in her head.

I placed the receiver back down, without asking any questions, without even saying goodbye and walked back into the comfort of our warm living room. I closed the door behind me and leant my back against it. I wasn't sure what would happen to our relationship now I had broken the ice after many, many years. But if I was honest with myself, I wanted nothing from it or her. All I needed was the release from the tight constraints that it had always held me captive with, and I selfishly hoped I could now move forward with my life.

I walked over to the paper on the table and struck through number one on my list, feeling an immense sense of achievement. I'd done what my nan had asked. I had finally let go.

The church bells struck, indicating the end of midnight mass. I knew that friends and neighbours would now be making their way home down the lane, chatting as they went about their Christmas plans with family and friends, just as my nan would've been doing right now if she were here. I walked over to the window to watch them, just needing to feel close to someone.

I pulled the heavy curtains open and looked down to find no one there at all, I was obviously too late. Stupidly, I began to fill up with tears at the situation, at my self-inflicted misery. I was just about to drop the curtains back into place when a movement in a large, dark car across the lane caught my eye.

I just knew.

In the space of a millisecond, I just knew.

I could feel him there, I could feel him offering me his strength, his remorse at our mutual pain and when I closed my eyes fleetingly, his strong arms wrapped around me offering me comfort.

I no longer felt alone, because I knew that I wasn't.

My heart skipped a beat as I brushed my gloved hand over the glass, clearing a circular space through the condensation on the window. As the wool squeaked across the glass, I could now clearly see Brody sitting in his car staring up at me. Even in the dark of the night, with only the dim light in the lane, his teal coloured eyes found mine. That simple connection filled me up inside, making me feel whole and complete.

Our eyes met and for what seemed like forever we just stared at each other. I wasn't going to invite him in, not because I was still angry with him, but because he was right, I needed time. He appeared to understand, as he made no move to open his car door. But knowing he was there, checking on me, offered me the comfort I needed.

I huffed on the clear glass and wrote in large backward facing letters, "FRIENDS?"

I watched him squint and then slow blink as he read the word and then he wrote back on his window. "FOR NOW."

Tentatively I lifted my hand at him to say goodnight. Pressing two fingers to his lips he blew me a kiss. I dropped the curtain back into place realising how right he was, we were unfinished business.

As I got myself ready to collapse into bed that thought made my heart lighter and the dull ache of loneliness began to dissipate slightly.

Thirty

BRODY

WITHOUT THINKING IT through, I decided to spend the night as close to her as possible, across the lane from her nan's shop.

I'd left the wedding reception after learning from John Edwards that one of his security had dropped her off at home. There was no thought process, no decision to be made. I had driven straight there. I knew she needed time and although it hurt like fuck to be so close but so far away, I had to give her some space. She was right, the last few days had been a fucking whirlwind. I'd never fucking thought I'd fall in love, like ever, and there was no goddamn way I would've ever believed it would happen to me in the space of a fucking week.

In seven days, the woman locked in above that shop, had totally consumed me.

I had never felt this way.

I was one seriously lucky bastard. I knew that if it meant I could have her in my life I could really start to live. Not the false fabricated life of a celebrity, but the real life of a man who loved a woman with everything he was, with his whole heart and soul. To be loved in return for just being me, was something I'd been unconsciously looking for since my dad had died. I concluded that if she could love Daniel, she could love me and that was the one thought keeping me going.

Staring up at the flat as I sat there gave me some comfort. Through some wider gaps at the top of the curtains, I could see what I presumed were flames from a fire, dancing on the ceiling. I didn't know how long I could cope sitting out here in the fucking freezing cold, but I was determined I'd stay for as long as I could.

It was my punishment for fucking up.

The nearby church bells had started to ring out, I looked at my watch and saw it was just before one a.m., and now Christmas day. I exhaled a long sigh at the realisation that for the third Christmas in a row, I'd be sober and without even knowing it, she'd helped me achieve it. A sense of pride took over me. Within a few minutes, people began to walk past my car as they left the church and went back to their homes with their loved ones. Up and down the lane, front doors closed around me.

Not for the first time since I'd been back in the UK, I thought how very fucking lonely I was. Money could buy everything if you had enough of it and yeah it was awesome to be able to own the house or car you wanted. I knew I was a fucking lucky bastard travelling the world in a private jet. I also knew how goddamn lucky I was having the money to pay my bills. But, it couldn't buy you love, happiness and peace of mind.

Amy held all of that for me.

I pulled my beanie down as far as it would go and pulled the collar from my jacket up as high as it would stand. I fished around to the side of me and pulled out the gloves she had given me the first day we met and pushed my hands inside of them. A smile crept over my face as I held them in front of me and looked at them. It had only been a week, but that solitary week held some of the best memories of my whole life.

Just as I'd begun to recline the seat, a movement coming from the curtains caught my eye, and there she was. It was a relief to see her, although she looked young and vulnerable framed by the Victorian window. Her body froze and I knew she could feel my presence. I only hoped that knowing I was here gave her the comfort it had given me as I'd sat here. I watched her hand, in a yellow glove, as it went around in a circle cleaning the pane of glass and then our eyes met. I knew then that every time our eyes found each other would always be like the first time. For a few minutes, we just looked at each other as we tried to convey exactly how we felt. In my head, I claimed her yet again as mine. But, I made no move to demand she let me in, I didn't deserve it.

The ball, as they fucking put it, was now well and truly in her court.

BRODY

I watched as her lips parted and her mouth opened to steam up the clear space on the glass. In the steam, she wrote out the word "FRIENDS?" I blinked at the word and then swallowed at the sudden constriction in my throat.

How the fuck am I supposed to be her friend?

But goddam it, I'd accept anything she was offering right now. I replied that I'd accept it, but only for now.

It was my sole objective in life to get her back.

She lifted her yellow gloved hand and waved cautiously. In response, I blew her a kiss. She looked emotionally spent staring out of the window, but as a small smile slowly crept over her face, it offered me all the hope I needed. Sitting out here as close to her as I could get, I had been unknowingly waiting for a sign. A sign of what I hadn't a fucking clue, but that smile meant for me was fucking everything.

As she dropped the curtain back in place and severed our connection, I settled back into my heated seat for the night, with the knowledge that she had accepted we weren't finished.

This was just an interval in between sets.

This was the end of the beginning.

Thirty-One

Amy

THE DOORBELL RANG again. I picked up the pillow from beside me, placed it over my head and squeezed the edges to my ears, to blank out the noise.

It had to be a joke. No one would be visiting this early on Christmas morning.

The fear of God suddenly swept through me and I sat bolt upright in bed. Listening, I could hear the bell again. Whoever it was they were bloody persistent.

Maybe something's wrong with Nan?

What if I hadn't replaced the phone properly last night?

The worries quickly penetrated my mind and throwing the pillow away, I jumped up and off the bed all in one movement. My head pounded in disgust at my sudden change in position. Ignoring its protests, I made my way out of my bedroom as fast as my legs would carry me. Unusually, but luckily for me, I was still wearing the pyjamas I had put on last night after my bath.

I flew down the back stairs as I heard a knuckle knock on the window. My hand connected with the door and I pushed it open quickly, anxious to see who was so eager to wake me. The door banged against one of the counters and in my head I could hear my nan's silent reprimand about being careful. I looked at the shop window and my feet stopped as I came face to face with Lauren and Winter.

The expressions on their faces said it all, the grimaces and small tentative waves to me, showed me how remorseful they both felt.

I walked through the cold shop and slid the large bolt across. Opening the door, and stepping back quickly, I watched as they hurried to be the first through the gap to take me into their arms. Them both holding me close brought back all the emotions of yesterday. As soon as I could I pulled myself away.

'Enough, it's making me too emotional and I've no more tears to cry after yesterday.'

'We're sorry, Amy,' Winter offered.

'I know.' I picked up their hands with mine and looked down to where I held them. 'I know you did it because you wanted the best for me.'

'Absolutely, and we still do,' Lauren added.

'It was all just all too much.'

'Come on, let's go upstairs and you can tell us about it all.' Lauren spoke and I nodded in agreement.

We sat on my nan's large feather bed, surrounded by soft cushions and blankets, for over two hours, eating chocolate biscuits and drinking tea. I fidgeted with the lace on her quilt cover as I told them everything that had happened to me over the last week from meeting Brody downstairs to seeing him last night. Being the friends that they were they sat and listened. The last thing I showed them was the list I had written out.

'I'm so bloody proud of you, Amy,' Lauren had declared after running her eyes over my writing and realising that number one had been struck through.

'Now you've done it and stepped out from under her shadow, how do you feel?' Winter asked as she stared at the piece of note paper in her hand,

'The words you have just used, are precisely how I do feel. You need to try it sometime.' Winter's eyes found mine and the pain that she always kept so well hidden ran fleetingly across her blue eyes. I broke the moment and grabbed their hands again, and pulling them both backwards, we fell onto the comfortable bed in an unglorified heap.

'Thanks for coming over. I really appreciate it.' I spoke as I looked up at the ceiling.

Lauren moved fast, sitting up to look down at me. 'After what happened, where else would we have gone to?'

I turned my head to look at her, feeling guilty. 'I know we should all be at The Manor now having Christmas dinner.'

'Oh, I cancelled that hours ago,' Winter replied and caught the expression on my face. 'Don't you dare feel guilty, let them all stew in their own juices today. And don't feel guilty on my account, I've suffered the stuffy parents for long enough. As far as I'm concerned, Raff and the boys can have them today. I've got better things to do.'

We stayed there for a minute or two just laughing at Winter's words. As our laughter died down, my head escaped the here and now and I began to revel in the company of the women who I knew would always have my best interests at heart, even if I didn't always understand the way they went about it.

The bed began to move as Winter leant over to pull her small handbag up off the floor by its long strap and started to rummage inside it. I saw a small silver pen in her hand and heard the click as she pushed the nib out.

'May I?' she questioned.

I looked at her holding my list in one hand and her pen in the other.

'You can, but know this, the moment you two make a list I *will* be adding to it.' I smiled at them both.

'Agreed,' she replied and I felt Lauren shifting beside me to look at what Winter was about to do.

'Agreed, I think,' Lauren added.

We both watched as Winter wrote.

Brody Daniels?

'Well played, Winter.' Lauren added her agreement at the two words she had added.

'I know, and I will once I've sorted myself out first.' I stopped speaking as my stomach grumbled and I sent one hand down to hold it out of habit.

'That's fair enough, Amy. Changing the subject, perhaps we had better think about what we're eating today?' Lauren laughed as she spoke.

'As far as I remember, I've only got fish fingers and waffles left in the freezer for when the grandchildren visit Nan.' I looked at them both knowing what excellent chefs they were and laughed at the expressions on their faces.

'It's food, it'll do,' Lauren declared.

BRODY

With a stomach full of fish fingers and waffles, the three of us decided to go and visit Nan for the afternoon. It certainly wasn't the normal food we would have eaten for Christmas dinner, but it had been a far from normal Christmas. Somehow I knew, deep down inside, that trying to have a normal Christmas with everything that was going on in my life would have been impossible. I couldn't have gone about the normal rituals of our family Christmas, not this year and not without my nan.

Perhaps fate had played a part in giving me this quirky sort of Christmas instead.

Winter had spied a small gift for me underneath Nan's Christmas tree, almost as soon as we had walked into her room. It had no tag on it, but Nan remembered it was from "eye candy." We had all laughed with her as she began to describe what exactly eye candy looked like and then laughed even louder at her declaration of what she would do to him if only she was twenty-five years younger. Eventually, she had gone on to ask his name and we had looked at each other in silence not quite knowing what to say.

'Daniel, Nan,' I answered.

'Really? I'm sure he said his name was something else this morning?'

'Brody?' Lauren questioned.

'Yes.' She looked up and smiled at us all. 'That seems more like it. Brody suits him.' When she had caught the looks on our faces, she had countered. 'I might have got it wrong, you know me. I'm such a clutter head these days and I've probably slept since then. Anyway, whatever his name is, it doesn't matter. I mean what's in a name? I just know that I like him.'

The conversation had gone on around me for a few minutes as I took in what she had said, and I realised the words she had inadvertently spoken were true. It didn't matter what his name was, I liked him too. More importantly, I was in love with him. Even after all the hurt of yesterday, I knew the feeling was still there threaded into the very depths of my heart and soul.

I peeled through the layers of gift wrap after picking at the tape with my fingernail and eventually broke through the cellophane paper inside, to find a new phone. I knew that although Nan and the girls were talking, they were all watching me out of the corner of their eyes. I took the lid off the box, pulled the phone out and switched it on. I hadn't understood until that moment, just how much I had needed clarification that he was still thinking of me. Being who he was, it had gone around my head several times during the night that he may have decided, as he had driven away, that I was just too much like hard work. I pressed the button and the screen sprang to life.

I looked over it quickly.

The date and time had been set, which pleased me as it took me forever to work out how to do things on anything new. As my eyes swept over the phone again, I saw that he had even put up a screen saver for me. The picture he had used had been taken last week. It was a picture taken at Lake View of us huddled together under the fleece blanket, the two of us were looking out at the lake lost in our thoughts. You couldn't see our faces, and I hadn't realised he had taken it, but I knew it was us. My heart broke open just a little bit more at the loss of not having him that close to me now, holding me. I took a deep breath and used the passcode he had left on a scrap piece of paper for me to find and opened the main screen. I could see one message sitting in the inbox, and for a few seconds my finger hovered over it.

'Amy. Come on tell us, what does he say?' My eyes snapped up to Lauren who was holding Nan's hand. I hadn't comprehended until then, that their conversation had completely stopped.

I placed my finger to the green icon and watched as it revealed his words.

Amy
Happy Christmas.
Hope you like your new phone?
Now we can never miscommunicate again.

Love Brody
xx

I read out his message to them all after I typed back a very simple reply.

Happy Christmas
Thank you for my present.

Then I switched it off and concentrated on my day with my nan and the girls. Inside I recognised that I felt happier and more content. He was still with me, at least for the time being, and it made my heart full to bursting at the thought that the two of us just might make it out of the shit hole we had inadvertently fallen into.

We shared out our other gifts, laughing as we did so at our pact the previous year to give the money we would normally spend on cards and presents to contribute towards buying a donkey for a third world village somewhere. And we had, back in August.

'I don't understand, why have you all only got one present for each other?' Nan questioned. 'We're not back in the war, are we?' I saw her glance at the date above her TV.

'No, Nan,' I began, as I mulled over just exactly what I was going to say to explain it to her.

'Nan, we all contributed to buying a donkey, that's why,' Lauren tried, and by the look on Nan's face, I could see her explanation had immediately crashed and burned.

I saw Winter place a hand over her mouth to stop the laugh that wanted to fly out.

'A donkey? What the bloody hell are we going to do with a donkey?' My nan's voice raised as she looked around at all of us in astonishment.

'Nan, it's okay…'

'It's not okay. We live in a flat. We don't even have a yard to put it in,' she interrupted.

'We decided that we would contribute towards buying a donkey for a village in the third world,' I put in quickly, hoping it would ease her concern.

'So, there is a war on? You've just said there wasn't.'

I looked around at the others, pleading at them with my eyes to try to find a way out of the conversation that was fast becoming stressful for her and us.

'No, Nan. There is no war,' replied Lauren slowly, hoping it would help with the confusion in the room.

'But you just said third world,' she muttered indignantly.

'You're right, Nan, we did. Let me explain, last year the three of us made a pact not to waste money on gifts when so many other people have nothing. Instead we contributed money towards buying a donkey.'

I let my words settle for a few seconds, then added more. 'That's why we only have one gift for each other today.'

'Uh huh, I see.' She spoke quietly and the words she used let me know that she didn't understand at all.

It was days like this that really confirmed to us just how confusing everyday life was becoming for her. The lighter days when we laughed gave me and I'm sure her comfort, but these situations brought you back to earth with a bump.

Silence filled the room and Winter jumped up. 'Right, okay, let's distribute and open one at a time, shall we?'

'Oh yes. I love Christmas presents.' Nan's face broke out into a wide smile and I knew that the rest of us breathed a quiet sigh of relief, that for the moment we had diverted another upset.

I unwrapped my presents from the girls and found matching lingerie sets. I smiled my thanks at them and remembered just how much pleasure Brody had discovering what I was wearing under my clothes. I had brought them both their favourite perfume and we had bought Nan cardigans, chocolates and an audio book, in the hope that she might be able to follow it.

But of course, it was Nan who had stolen the show. Winter, Lauren and I had matching gifts and after checking her notes for the day, she had us open them together. She had made black A3 papercuts for us all and then she'd had them framed in a glass-fronted pale wooden frame.

The tags on the gifts read,

I wish you all love.
Love Nan.

The words she had chosen for the papercuts resonated around my head.

Be with someone who can understand three things in you:
the sadness behind your smile.
the love that enflames your anger.
And the reason behind your silence.
Be with someone who accepts you for you.

As we read the words she had creatively displayed for us all, she explained that she wanted us all to have the sort of love she had found only once in her lifetime. She assured us that although she had found it only once and lost it almost thirty-five years previously, that once-in-a-lifetime love would be forever enough.

That evening, after spending time playing cards, we had left her happy. I hugged her to me as we said our goodbyes and she whispered in my ear.

'I'm still not sure about having a donkey, Amy. Maybe you'd better have a word with Dr. Carpenter, perhaps his Jack could have it at his farm?'

I pulled out of her arms and looked at her again.

'Good idea, Nan. I'll do just that, don't worry.'

'You're a good girl, Amy. Don't forget how much I love you. See you soon.' I hugged her to me again, never wanting to let her go.

Thirty-Two

Amy

Five weeks later

THE PHONE RINGING for longer than was necessary, caught my attention. I looked up from my antique desk to the doorway, wanting to hear the already familiar, "Good morning, The Manor. How can I help you?" And sure enough, there it was, the friendly voice of Maria, one of the receptionists, answering the call. I carried on listening with a smile growing on my face.

'Yes certainly, may I ask who's calling?' A pause followed as Maria listened to the reply. 'Thank you, Barbara. Unfortunately, he's not here at the moment. He is due back in a few days.' Another pause from our end and then. 'Yes, certainly I can do that for you. Thank you for calling, goodbye.'

I liked her politeness and made a mental note to check that all the receptionists came across as professionally as she did.

I forced myself to look back down to the high-class magazine's review of The Manor. It was supposed to be consuming all my attention and I tried to focus on the words, when all I really wanted to do was to spin my chair around in giddy excitement. Today was the first Thursday in February and was also the first day in my new job. It had to be said, I was feeling very pleased with myself. I was now one of the deputy managers of The Manor, amongst other things my main responsibilities included making sure our level of customer service was second to none.

My life was changing and I was extremely proud that I was the driving force behind the change. I was still working through the list I had made in the flat, but I couldn't believe what I had achieved so far.

The shop and house had been sold. Two weeks after Christmas, it had gone on the market and although the estate agents had warned me that property sales were always slow in the New Year, it was snapped up by a property developer. The estate agent said it was unheard of to see something go so quickly and for the full asking price. I wasn't stupid, I had my suspicions as to who had bought the property. But I hadn't been able to get an answer to that nagging question. Default Distraction had gone back to the U.S. to attend some impromptu awards show in Los Angeles a couple of days after New Year. I had then been away training in London, after being offered the position at the hotel. Now I was back, but Brody and Cade were in Las Vegas. Apparently, he told me when he texted, they were meeting Cade's family to iron out some problems with the new hotel.

Lauren, Winter, and I, had moved past our fall out, as we had many times before. We had come to terms with the fact that we had differing opinions on things, because our pasts would always make us look at things differently. We were now back to the teasing, supporting and accepting level of our relationship. We all knew the moment any of us needed the backup of each other, whenever life smacked us in the face, we would drop anything to be there for each other. It was called friendship, and I felt badly for those that didn't have it. I didn't understand how they could move through life without its backup.

In a few weeks, I'd achieved so much. Nan was safe and well and provided for, and it was a huge weight off my mind. Her beloved furniture had been split up amongst the family and given to the local charity shop after she'd announced, "I don't want all that old crap in here." I'm sure it made her day when she still managed to surprise us all. Everything apart from her old record player and albums had gone. She now had all brand new furniture that filled the room she now permanently occupied at the care home.

I had moved into The Manor, as accommodation was provided as part of the package deal in my new role as one of the two Deputy Managers. I was shocked at how easy it had been to leave the only place I had ever really called home. But as I had locked the door for the final time on the shop, I knew it was time to move on. Truth be told, without my nan there with me, it just hadn't felt right anymore. My room at The Manor was bright, modern and comfortable. The only trouble was it was just a few doors away from the room Brody kept as his own. I knew he wasn't even in the country, but walking past the door several times a day meant he was always at the forefront of my mind. Who was I kidding? He had claimed that place as his own and nothing was shifting him.

My list had nearly been completed, apart from the one thing I had refused to write down on the paper in the first place. But as Winter had, every time I picked up the now dog-eared piece of paper to cross something off, his name and the question mark next to it jumped off the page at me, demanding that I gave it some attention.

I needed to work out what to do about my "friend" Brody.

He had texted me daily, sometimes more than once, since I had received my Christmas present. The texts had started off inhibited, like we were strangers getting to know each other, because in a way I supposed we were. Slowly, over the days and weeks that followed, we had become more relaxed with what we wanted to share with each other. Eventually, our messages contained all the little things you would share with your best friend. My days now started with me waking up and sending him a "Good morning" text. While he was in the U.S., with the time difference between us, I would wait a few hours until he replied. During each day, we shared all the funny and annoying anecdotes we could think of with each other, and then at night we would make contact again to wish each other good night. In a nutshell, he had become the person I contacted first when I wanted to share anything at all.

I still missed him, because quite simply in that short week we had spent together, I had fallen in love with him. I only hoped my "friend" was still available to move forward with.

A knock at my door brought my attention back to the here and now.

'Come in,' I answered.

The door pushed open and I looked up to find Maria behind a huge bouquet of the brightest coloured mixture of flowers I'd ever seen. The vibrant colours immediately lit up my sparse looking office.

'Miss. Harper, these have just been delivered for you. Aren't they simply stunning?'

'Wow! They're gorgeous. Could you put them on the side table please?'

I got up from behind my desk and followed her to the table, eager to read the card I could just see poking up from the top of the foliage.

'Thank you, Maria.' I watched as she smiled back at me and then vacated the room. After putting my nose down to smell the perfume wafting up to me, I plucked the small white envelope from its hiding place. Hurriedly, I tore the envelope open and pulled the card out from inside.

Morning Beautiful

I just wanted to wish you a great first day in your new job.

I know I fucked up.

I hope you've had enough time to do what you needed to do.

because I'm back in a few days and I'm more than ready to claim what's mine.

This fucked up mess between us ends, no refusals to listen and no more walking away.

I won't live without you, because I can't.

Brody

Just reading his words made my heart accelerate and my stomach turn over like a washing machine on the spin cycle. I ran my finger over his words, then because no one could see me, I clutched the card tight to my chest and let out a muted squeal of excitement. Everything we felt for each other was there, right there. We had only known each other existed for all of six weeks and only spent one of those weeks together, but the strength of feeling I had for him barrelled around inside me, demanding to be let free. Unlike my mum, he was returning just like he had promised. I texted him immediately, thanking him for his gift. I didn't mention the words he had written, as I quite simply didn't know what to say.

He hadn't forgotten me, he was coming back.

I looked at the flowers he had sent and grasped just exactly what all the bright colours reminded me of, they reminded me of his tattooed torso. My whole body buzzed with excitement at the thought of seeing him again.

My door knocked again and before I answered, I tucked the card back into its envelope.

'Come in.' I tried to sound professional, but knew my voice was just slightly off.

'It's only us.' The door flew open, banging the antique, ceramic handle against the blue and silver, silk papered wall and I winced, hoping it hadn't marked. Lauren and Winter, as always, pushed around each other to get through my doorway first.

'Calm down. I'm not going anywhere.' I laughed at them both as they crossed the threshold and then stood in the room turning around slowly, taking in my magnificent work space.

'My God, they certainly pull out all the stops when you're fucking one of the bosses, don't they?' Winter opened our conversation as she pulled a chair further away from the desk in preparation to sit down.

'Shhhhhhhh.' I placed a finger to my lips as I took in that the door hadn't fully closed behind them. I looked at them both and shaking my head I silently reprimanded Winter for her choice of language. I walked behind them and pushed my office door shut with a bang. Then I turned around to face them, leaning my back on the door as I did so.

'Firstly, I'm at work. You both understand that, don't you?' I nodded at them enthusiastically and put my hand down to check that the door was sitting snug against the frame and that it was firmly closed. I really didn't need the reception team being party to what was probably going to be a pretty base conversation. 'And just so you both know, I'm not fucking anyone right at this minute. So, this fantastic office is just down to me, thanks very much.' I smiled broadly at them both.

They laughed and enthusiastically nodded their replies to me. 'Secondly, both of you better come here for a hug before you sit. I've missed you so much.' I pushed myself away from the door and opened my arms wide, gathering them both to me and squeezing them for all I was worth.

'Have you been working too hard as usual, Lauren? You look tired.' I squinted at her as our grip on each other began to loosen and I took in her pale complexion.

'Oh, you know me, probably,' she replied with a small smile and a shrug of her shoulders.

Lauren looked over at Winter as they positioned themselves at the chairs on the opposite side of my desk and spoke to her as they sat down. 'And, Winter, I'm sure you'll be exploring all the perks of shagging the boss very soon. I bet twenty pounds you'll have an office all of your very own in Vegas within a month of being there.'

Winter answered her with an overly pronounced tut and a shake of her head.

God, I've missed these two.

'What you're implying, Lauren, is *so* not going to happen… maybe I'll just marry one of those uptight prigs that my mum and dad keep trying to force on me instead?' She burst out laughing at her own joke.

'I'm not sure that even being married would put Cade off you, Winter. In fact, watching the way he acts around you, it just might make you even *more* interesting to him, if that were at all possible.' I put in my two pennies worth.

'He can look, but not touch,' Winter announced. 'I have much higher standards than some bloody drummer. Anyway, we came to talk about you, Amy.' I watched as she crossed her legs, almost on instinct at talking about Cade.

'We've just seen Raff outside and he told us that Brody and Cade will be back in a few days. So, when are you going to remedy *that* situation?' Lauren pushed into the conversation as she leant herself comfortably back into her chair, looking extremely pleased with herself.

I walked away from the door, choosing to go the long way around behind them, so I could gently touch the flowers that Brody had sent.

It was a gesture that wasn't missed by my audience.

'Those are from him, aren't they?' Lauren questioned as she followed my every move, twisting herself around in the navy blue, fabric-covered tub chair.

I smiled, found my way back behind my desk and sat down. I knew that my face gave me away completely. I nodded at them both and pushed the small card across the desk for them both to read. I watched as they read his words, swivelling a little from side to side on my chair in my excitement.

'That's damn hot, Amy! He's coming back to claim what's his… Whoah.' Winter was pretending to fan her face as she spoke. 'Who would have thought it, our Amy bringing the lead singer of one of the biggest bands in the U.S. to his knees.'

'It does read that way, doesn't it? I don't mean the on his knees stuff, but the fact he's coming back for me?'

Their heads lifted from the card they were reading over and over in perfect synchronisation and their wide eyes found mine.

'YES!' they both yelled over at me in agreement, smiling from ear to ear at my stupid question.

'There is no mistaking what he's written on here. Get your best underwear out lady, he's reclaiming what's his!' shouted out Winter, a little too loudly.

I grinned back at them.

'I can't wait to see him, I can't tell you how much I've missed him.'

'You don't need to tell us, we both know. So, when are you next off? I'm sure once he gets you in his grip, he's going to want to keep hold of you for a while,' Lauren asked.

I looked at her smiling. 'It's a great job. I work four days and then have four days off. It gives me time to see Nan…'

'It gives her days to spend in bed fucking Brody,' Winter added, talking directly to Lauren.

'So, occasionally if I need a day off from The Fairy Garden you might be able to cover me?' Lauren questioned.

'Not so you can fuck Toby, she can't,' added Winter.

'Winter!' I scolded. 'Of course I can, Lauren, as always just let me know.'

Ignoring Winter, Lauren carried on, 'We're so proud of you, Amy. You've had so much thrown at you. You came through the other side and now you have a future to look forward to. If I didn't love you so much, I'd envy you.'

I felt my forehead crease as I looked at Lauren smiling at me and thought over her words. When would she see that she needed Raff back in her life? I hoped it would be soon.

The girls left me soon after our conversation, and I went back to work determined to do what was required of me. I managed to complete my day's work in half the time. Thoughts of Brody coming back in only a few days kept the adrenalin flowing around my body.

Thirty-Three

BRODY

'**T**HERE YOU GO, asswipe.'

I opened one eye to see Cade holding an opened bottle of still mineral water. I adjusted my position, sat up and uncrossed my arms. Holding out my hand, I took the bottle from him. I hadn't been sleeping, I was just lost in my thoughts as I listened to the engines of the plane.

'Cheers,' I toasted, clinking my blue glass against the brown of his beer bottle.

I took a mouthful of the cool water, put it down beside me and watched Cade take a seat opposite.

'So, let's go there, shall we? We've known for two whole days and we left McCarran airport over two hours ago and you still haven't said a word about it.'

I sniffed, exhaled and put my leg up. I placed my ankle on my opposite knee and started tapping out a tune on my protruding ankle bone.

'Talk to me!' Cade moved suddenly, leant forward and knocked my leg down with his hand. 'Don't shut the fuck down, I've seen it before. We know where it leads.'

'Fuck off, Cade.' I righted my leg, glanced quickly at the shiny drinks cabinet behind him and then looked away. I knew what he meant, but for the first time ever, I felt absolutely no compulsion to go there. I knew exactly what I needed to take away the guilt and pain. All I wanted was to be buried balls deep in Amy. I only hoped she still wanted me there. Amy had messaged me to say thanks for the flowers I'd sent. She hadn't however mentioned what I'd written on the card and it was a worry, as I'd meant every single damn word I'd written. I turned my wrist over to look at my watch, we had at least eight more hours in the air. It was too fucking long.

'Not going anywhere, man. Let me in,' he demanded, immediately expelling the picture of Amy that I had in my head.

'What can I say? What do ya want me to say?' I threw my arms wide open and felt my tic begin to spasm above my cheek.

'Look, I know Nico can be an asshat, but he's my brother. Inside he's a good guy, you don't know him like I do.'

I burst out into what sounded like manic laughter.

'Right... Then you tell me how the fuck you would feel if your baby sister just married into the mob?'

I watched as he slowly raised his eyes to mine and then as his fingers started to tap up and down on his knee. It was a sure way to tell his anger was ramping up.

Bring it on. It wouldn't be the first time we'd gone for each other. I carried on. 'And not just into the mob. Oh no! ... But the head of the fucking mob. Perhaps even the head of five fucking families, like in The Godfather,' I added, knowing I was being an asshat. I spoke the words so vehemently I saw my own spittle leave my mouth.

'He's made the family business legit and you know it.'

'Your brother's a fucking killer and you know it.' The air between us crackled.

I knew I was being unfair to Cade, but at this moment I didn't give a flying fuck. He had walked away from his family's business a long time ago, wanting nothing to do with any of it. He had made his money the same way I had. When we'd met nearly twenty years ago, the two of us owned nothing, except a love of music and a troubled fucking attitude. We rented a run down, filthy dirty apartment together, right on the edge of the strip itself and some days we didn't even eat. Together we'd played in some real shit joints just to get our name out there. The only thing he'd kept was the Morello name, and mostly they'd left him alone and let him live with his decision. We'd all heard the stories that came our way, as soon as people found out who the fuck he was related to. Yes, the Morello family were now running completely above board, but I knew how the fuck they'd got that way. Nico Morello was a man who liked the thrill of violence far too fucking much to give it all up completely.

Now that same man was married to my baby sister. He was thirty-five years old and she was thirty-three. There was a two-year age difference, but over one hundred in life experience. She told me he was good to her, and he offered her the security she needed. When I'd asked her if they were in love, she'd stuttered before she answered me and I knew the answer she gave was a lie, just by that simple show of anxiety.

I jumped up and started to pace up and down the aisle in between the carefully positioned groups of seats. As I got close to the bar area, I allowed my fingers to brush along the walnut edging and then pulled them away just as fast.

'What really has me fucking riled is we didn't even need to be in Vegas. There wasn't anything wrong with the hotel. So, your brother is a fucking liar, too.'

'It's obvious why he did that, isn't it?' I looked at him as he stared back at me, his eyes opened wide with disbelief and he shook his head.

I looked away and carried on walking around.

'Is it?' I questioned, with my back turned on him.

'For fucks sake, Daniels, get your head out of your ass. She can't get you to be in the same room as her. You're so eaten up with guilt that isn't yours to own, that you've pushed her away. He lied for her sake and that's what tells me that their marriage stands a chance of fucking working. He lied about business, to get you to come and listen to what she wanted to say.'

I stopped walking and looked at Cade. The bastard was sitting back, relaxed in his seat, showing me just how confident he felt. He really believed he had everything all fucking worked out and that was the bit that got to me.

Cade never had shit worked out.

'You need to let her live her life, Daniels. He'll take care of her now.' His voice was quieter, offering me the sense of calm I'd not felt in the two days since I'd found out.

'You can't know that for certain. How the fuck will he deal with her?' I asked.

'I'm convinced I do. I know him, better than he thinks and I've thought of nothing else for two fucking days. He'll help her, because her vulnerability calls to the brother I know and love, the one he keeps hidden and buried deep down inside. This could be good for them both. My mama always used to say he was a man who needed a wife and now he's got one. Maybe my brother is just the sort of man she needs in her life. For far too long you've bailed her out. She's not your little sister anymore, she's a grown woman and she deserves to live that way. Let's face it, you've tried every other fucking thing and it hasn't worked, how many hundreds of thousands have you spent bailing her out and paying for rehab?'

'It's only fucking money and I'd have spent everything I ever made to make her happy.'

'I know, man. But it's just fucking money and, Brody, love goes so much fucking further than money ever could.'

I sat back down opposite Cade and stared at him, trying to take in everything he was saying.

'How long has she been giving you shit because you'd moved on with your life and she couldn't?' he carried on.

I laughed out loud again. 'She couldn't have been more fucking wrong, could she?'

'But now you have. You've got Amy and, fuck me sideways, if you don't realise what you've got there in that woman, then you're far more fucking stupid than I ever thought. As soon as we touch down, you go and make it right between you. You do whatever the hell needs to be done, so you don't lose her… You, Daniels are an ugly fucker and God knows what the fuck she sees in you, but with her by your side you can conquer all your fucking demons.'

'Yeah, that's the plan.' I felt the previous anger at his words wash away and a small smile take over in its place.

I watched him nod his head and tip his beer right up to horizontal, as he drained the dregs. The air between us had cleared.

'Let her and Nico give it a try. All your sister wants is for you to give them your blessing and then back the fuck away.'

I felt my tic begin to relax. 'Cade, you honestly think your brother could be what she needs?'

'Yep.' He put another beer bottle to his lips and took a glug. 'You've tried to protect her for far too long, she needs to stand on her own two feet. She really needs to be the woman she was meant to be, not caught in some fucking time warp as Brody Daniel's dependant little sister. How long have you held on to that little girl that you swore to protect?'

I shrugged my shoulders at him and replied, 'Too fucking long.'

'That pinky swear has been holding you both back. It's time to let the fucking poison go.'

I sat back into my seat and exhaled. I watched a smile sweep over his face as he took in that he'd got through to me.

I hoped he was right, but would I give them my blessing? Fuck no. I'd seen marriage first hand, and that one look was enough for me.

Thirty-Four

Amy

MY THIRD SHIFT of the week was going to be over in less than an hour. I had one more day to do, then I was off for four whole wonderful days. I was enjoying my job more than I ever thought possible, but I was looking forward to some down time. The last few weeks had been a whirlwind, emotionally and physically, with no break in between. I needed to see my nan and for the past eleven hours, although I had been working hard, my whole body had been buzzing with the expectation of seeing Brody today.

Surely, the first place he would come to, would be the hotel? I could only hope.

I'd been given permission to hang the framed papercut that my nan had given me for Christmas, on my office wall. I'd been waiting impatiently for a maintenance guy and was now currently standing on one of the tub chairs in my office, shoeless and on tiptoes. I held the frame in the exact place I wanted it to go. I made a small pencil mark on the wall and lowered the frame gently to rest on top of the polished cabinet below it. Bending over, I reached to pick up the hammer and picture hook I needed to complete the job.

A wolf whistle behind me stopped me in my tracks.

I closed my eyes, feeling the sound as it entered through my back and zipped around my body, lighting up every nerve ending.

'Woman, you blow my fucking mind.' Without moving a muscle, I kept my eyes closed and took in everything about the voice I had just heard. It was deep, warm and slightly rasping, which not only told me who it belonged to, but also just exactly what I was doing to him bent over in this position. Slowly, I picked up the tools I needed and forced myself not to turn around. I carried on with the job in hand, using it as an excuse to hold on to the moment for a few minutes more. I felt like I'd been waiting for this for a lot longer than I had and I wanted time to appreciate it.

As I banged the picture hook into place, I could picture him in my mind's eye. I knew without turning how he would look in his trademark torn jeans and a fitted T-shirt. All the time we had been apart I had been trawling social media looking for pictures of him, I had even saved a few on my laptop. I inhaled quietly and took in the smell, bergamot, spices and the unmistakable smell of Brody all mixed together, and unwittingly I licked my lips in response. I bent again to lift up my frame, still refusing to turn.

As the frame found home, I heard his voice again.

'The words in the frame are very moving.'

I ran my finger over the black font in front of me, tracing every loop and stroke my nan had painstakingly cut and took in a deep breath.

'Nan made it.' And then I voiced the biggest fear I had. 'You really came back.'

'You got my flowers, Amy. The card said I was coming back.'

I felt the start of tears begin to fall from my eyes and down over my cheeks. I lowered my head a little and watched as they dripped silently onto my new cream blouse.

'I'm so sorry. I need to know if you can forgive me?'

I nodded my head in response, unable in my emotional state to form words. I felt the sigh of relief that left him, deep down inside me.

'Get down from the chair and turn around, Amy,' he demanded as his voice gained in strength. I recognised the tone he was now using on me.

Such was my body's response to his words and the way that he said them, that I became aware of my body beginning to shake. There was nothing anywhere near the same height as I was, so all I could hold on to was the flat wall in front of me. It wasn't nearly enough to help. I didn't hear him move, I only felt the moment his large hands positioned themselves onto either side of my waist. He turned me slowly until we were finally facing each other.

I wanted to look at him properly, to take all of him in. I wanted to sweep my eyes up and down his beautiful body, to check he was real.

But, as his eyes bored into mine, they held mine captive. I knew he was trying to speak the words he understood I needed to hear, but he couldn't find the language for. When I didn't move from his hold or protest about it, his lopsided grin took over his face, his dimple appeared and his teal eyes began to sparkle. I couldn't hold back anymore. Still standing on the tub chair with his hands firmly grasping my waist, I looped my arms over his shoulders and pulled him to me. His forehead nestled between my breasts and I held on to him for dear life. I felt him sigh in what sounded like contentment, his warm breath filtered through my sheer blouse, connecting with the wetness of my teardrops and then finally with the bare skin of my chest. I lowered my head to his and, running my hands through his slightly longer hair, I breathed him in.

In the back of my head I heard all the harsh words I had spoken last time we had seen each other. What I didn't know then, but realised now as we stood in silence holding each other close, was that loving Brody was unlike anything I had ever experienced before. I now understood that being with anyone else was not an option, it would be settling for second best. Loving him was so much more than anything I had ever imagined. It had been painful in the past and no doubt at some time during our future together would be so again. But to love so strongly and deny myself being with him, wasn't a possibility. Even in the position we were in now, the chemistry between us felt fervent and explosive, our bodies spoke to each other even when we hadn't the words to express how we felt. He was my life, I needed him more than I needed air to breathe. I was moving forward and I wanted him beside me as I took every step.

His head moved in my hands and I lifted my head up and away from him. His eyes came up to once again capture mine, just like they had the very first time we had met.

'I've missed you.' I spoke for the first time and I saw the moment my words resonated inside his head. His eyes filled with tears and he sniffed to make sure they stayed put.

'I told you, you and I were unfinished business, beautiful.' He cockily smirked at me.

'You did.' I bent down and placed a kiss on his lips.

The chaste kiss between us sparked a connection like I had never felt before. In that millisecond our skin connected, my body ignited and became alive. It was like I had been hibernating all the time we had been apart. My body, heart and soul wanted to live. They wanted to experience the absolute bliss they knew only this man could give me. He had awakened me and I wanted more, so much more from him.

'I have so much to say, Amy, and I don't know where the fuck to start.'

'Then just tell me that you love me. I need to hear you say the words when we're not emotionally overwrought.'

He released his hands from my waist and wrapped his arms around me, then I felt my stockinged feet leave the tub chair. He lifted me and then gently lowered me, not all the way to the floor but enough so our eyes were at the same level. Secure in his hold, I placed my hands either side of his face and moved my thumbs over the stubble beneath them, silently offering him encouragement.

'Amy Harper, I love you.' I felt a wide smile stretch over my mouth and more tears fell down my face. 'I've loved you since the moment you fell over your suitcase.'

'Stop it.' I laughed at his words.

His teal eyes sparkled in amusement and his beautiful grin enveloped the most handsome features I had ever laid eyes on.

'I told you before and I meant every fucking word. When I first saw you, it was like being hit by a train. We hadn't met, we'd never spoken a word to each other. But I loved you instantly. I love you, Amy Harper. I know that my feelings for you will only get stronger. I love you, Amy, now and forever. Now, it's been too long since you kissed me properly, I feel like a fucking starving man.'

For a few seconds, we stood there breathing each other in, getting closer and closer. His eyes began to narrow, questioning me and daring me all at the same time. I wanted the moment to last forever, to be able to see his need for me so blatantly obvious and so deafeningly clear. Those few seconds were mine to control. I knew he would never take what he still wasn't sure was freely given. I watched as his lips parted and his tongue swept out to wet them, tasting my breath on his skin.

Until, unable to deny myself any longer, my lips hungrily found his and conjoined with a force so strong that my heart instantaneously pounded in reaction. Our mouths opened wide immediately as we consumed each other with a powerful need. All our hurt, fears and dreams poured into the very basic connection. Our tongues caressed each other's and equally demanded. I could taste his regret and his pain, equally I made sure he could feel my hurt and anger. But most of all, I made sure that without a doubt that he could feel my love.

My hands released his face and found their way to the back of his head to thread into his hair. His hold on my body increased slightly, as if he was trying to show me that he would never, ever let me go. The kiss that had been mine to control when it started, changed in direction until it was his. He kissed me until we were both breathless and then he reluctantly pulled away. Our foreheads rested together as he gradually released his hold over me and allowed my feet to eventually find the floor beneath them. I moved my arms around him, sneaked them up the back of his T-shirt and held onto his muscular back, needing to be as close to him as possible.

Momentarily, I closed my eyes and tried to take in enough air to speak.

'I love you, Brody Daniels,' I whispered as I looked up at him.

His body stiffened, his eyebrows lifted in question, and his eyes flew open to find mine. Then a slow smile broke over his face.

'Say it again,' he demanded.

I inhaled a wavering breath and spoke again as I breathed out, 'I love you, Brody.'

His head tipped back and he looked up at the ornate ceiling in my office. Then it came back down to find me. He pressed his lips to mine in a loving kiss and then once again broke the connection to create a small fissure between us.

'I always knew you fucking did, it was just you I had to convince.'

I shook my head at the cocky bad boy holding me in his arms and knew at that very moment I had found the home I had always been looking for. I realised for the first time that home wasn't a place, it was a feeling.

'We still need to talk and I think we need to start at the beginning.'

I nodded and looked to one side of him at the clock on the wall. 'I finish in fifteen minutes and I'll need a further fifteen to freshen up.'

'You know, I know who owns this place, I can get you off early.' I watched the grin I loved so much slide over his face.

'I'm sure you do and can, but it's not happening.'

'Nah?' he questioned me disappointedly.

'No. Now, as much as I hate to say the words, you need to let me go. You can however take me in your arms again when you pick me up later from outside the front of The Manor. It can be like a real date.'

'A real date, huh? Okay.' His nosed wrinkled up and he grimaced, like a kid being asked to do something that they really didn't want to do and then his arms fell away from me. Without touching me again, he pressed his lips to my forehead and lingered there for a few seconds. I watched as he then turned and walked towards my door. 'I'll see ya around, beautiful.' He two-finger saluted me and smiled.

'Not if I see you first,' I retorted and he froze with the sudden realisation that he although he was hearing the words for the first time, they were the exact words I'd breathed into the night air, the night he had put my case into my nan's car.

The loud laugh that abruptly left his body wrapped around me, enveloping me with love and all the possibilities of our future together.

Thirty-Five

Amy

TEN MINUTES LATER, I left my office. I peered around my office door and out into the large, open-plan reception area. Brody was nowhere to be seen. Good, I wanted to get up to my room to take a quick shower and to change out of my work clothes.

'I'm just off then, Maria.' I smiled at her.

'That's fine, Miss. Harper.' She turned her head to look at me. 'Can I ask, was that Mr. Daniels in your office earlier?'

I felt my eyes open wide at her question. 'Yes, it was,' I answered.

'Oh, so he's back. That's good to know. I have a few messages for him. A lady has been trying to get hold of him. I'll make sure he gets them.'

'Oh, okay.' I smiled back at her. The relief that all she wanted to talk to me about was messages, was evident in my tone. I didn't want the staff knowing about us just yet. I could do without them thinking I'd slept my way into the deputy manager position.

I watched her look away to go back to her work, effectively severing our connection. 'Have a nice evening.'

'Yes, you too, Maria,' I called back as I started up the main stairway that split into two at the top. I took the left side towards the west wing.

As soon as I felt there was no one around me to witness the display, I stopped walking demurely up the stairs and pulled my fitted skirt up a little. I could then take the stairs two at a time. I had all of fifteen minutes to shower and change. I ran down the corridor, unlocked my door and flew into my tidy room. As soon as the door clicked shut behind me, I started to hurriedly pull off my work clothes. I picked them all up in the heap they'd fallen in and without sorting them through, I dropped them into my linen basket.

In the space of five minutes flat, my hair was twisted up to keep it dry and I was soaping my body in the white musk body wash that I kept for special occasions. I jumped out of the shower with one eye still on the clock. I brushed my teeth, creamed my body and pulled out the underwear I needed and my rust dress from my wardrobe. It was made of jersey fabric, with a V-neck, fitted waist and full skirt. I loved the way it felt on me. The material hugged me in all the right places and fell over my curvaceous hips. It was smart, but comfortable and offered me a sense that I looked good for the man I loved. I pulled on my long brown boots and quickly sprayed on my perfume. I then had all of two minutes to put on some make-up. Brody had seen me at my worst, I now wanted him to see me at my best. I hastily swept on some brown eye shadow and reapplied my mascara, as I tried to make the most of what people said was my best feature. I added a little blusher, not needing much as my cheeks were already flushed in excitement and brushed on some lipstick.

I stood back and took one final look in the full-length mirror in my room as I ran a brush through my long, wavy hair and grabbed my wrap and bag. I left my room and walked slowly back to reception, taking long calming breaths as I willed my frantic heartbeat to slow down.

Finally, I came to the main staircase and I walked slowly and carefully down the left side holding on to the banister, hoping that I wouldn't come a cropper and end up a bedraggled mess at the bottom of the stairs, as only I could.

Reaching the bottom, I let out a small sigh of relief.

I draped my wrap around my shoulders and walked towards the large oak doors that formed our entrance. The doorman opened the right-hand door for me and I stepped out.

I took in the sight in front of me and opening my lips a little I took in some of the cool air. But it wasn't the crisp, cold evening that took my breath away. It was the sight of Brody that stole it and threatened never to give it back.

His Defender was parked to the right of the main entrance. I could see it through and around the granite columns, but Brody I could see more clearly. He was leant against his vehicle in exactly the place he knew I would look for him the minute I stepped out.

I stopped dead in my tracks to take him in. I had never seen him dressed in a suit before. I felt my mouth fall open into a gawp and hurriedly closed it, but not before he noticed and smiled at my response.

The man looked like he'd stepped off the cover of a high-class, glossy magazine. His hair was tidy and being held in place with some sort of product, his stubble had been trimmed and the deep blue of his suit made the blue in his teal eyes sparkle. If that wasn't enough, the suit looked as though it had been tailor made to fit him. I took him in from the bottom up. The straight-legged trousers fitted perfectly and sat on top of his black Chelsea boots, where his ankles were crossed. I continued to move my eyes up this incredible man's body. I caught a glimpse of a smart, black leather belt where one button at the bottom of his waistcoat was undone. A crisp white, button-down, collared shirt was underneath, which had the two top buttons undone, revealing more tattoos, and he had rolled up both sleeves. His suit jacket was being held by one finger over his shoulder.

My eyes moved between his tattooed forearms, the rings on his fingers and then back up to where his Adam's apple bobbed up and down as he swallowed. He was trying hard to gauge my reaction. The silver in his large wristwatch glinted in the light being sent out of the windows of The Manor and finally snapped me out of my drool fest.

Eventually, my eyes landed on his face. I blinked, trying to rid myself of the fact my eyes had suddenly gone dry, from staring so hard.

'Are you coming any nearer?' He smiled his question at me as he pushed his body away from the side of the car, shaking his legs to make his trousers fall exactly where they should be.

'Holy hell,' fell from my lips. Still, I stood frozen to the spot, just looking at him.

'Amy, if I have to come over there to get you, I'm warning you just fucking once, I will pick you up and carry you back inside. I don't give a fuck about who sees us. All I know is my room in there, is nearer than the place I planned on taking you to tonight.' One eyebrow lifted at me in question.

'I'm coming. I just need to tell you first, you look amazing,' I managed to force out of my mouth.

I watched him smile as I slowly stepped closer to him.

'Thank you, and so do you, Amy. You always look good enough to eat, but tonight...' He stopped talking as I finally stood in front of him. He took one of my hands in his, lifted it up and turned it over. He pressed a slow kiss to the sensitive flesh he found at my wrist and it travelled straight to my core. Before he lifted his head again he breathed in my perfume. His head lifted and his eyes opened to find mine. 'But tonight, Amy, you look spectacular. You, woman, intoxicate and consume me... We need to get into the car so we can get moving, I'm already having to sing in my head to keep my dick under control.'

I burst out laughing at his words and moved behind him as he turned and walked me the few steps to the passenger door, leading me with one hand. He pulled it open, threw his jacket onto the back seat and still holding one hand only, he helped me up into the car. The door closed and I watched him put his hands in his trouser pockets and walk with his usual confident swagger around the front of the vehicle to his side.

I pulled the seat belt down over my shoulder as he jumped into the car.

'Here, allow me.' He leant across me, flooding all my senses at once with his physicality. I felt my core begin to ache and wetness hit the top of my thighs. I noticeably gasped as his mouth brushed the skin at the V-neck of my dress.

He abruptly moved away, the engine started and he began to sing, 'Ten green bottles hanging on the wall.'

As the car pulled away, I sang with him. Between singing and laughing we eventually made it to our destination.

I looked at the building we had pulled up outside. I was sure I recognised it, but not the driveway we had driven on to get there. Brody walked around to open my door and offered me his hand.

'So, if I told you that tonight I was the big bad wolf, would you still want to come inside?' He smirked at me.

I laughed back at him.

'It's okay, big bad wolf. I trust you. I know all there is to know about your *badness*.' I took hold of his hand, got down from the car and felt the gravel crunch under my boots.

'Oh, Amy, I can assure you that what you've experienced so far, is just the tip of the fucking iceberg.' He winked at me, then let his gaze sweep up and down my body and he licked his lips just to drive his words home. 'Come on.'

We walked down a short path covered over by trees. The path was well lit in the dark gloom of the winter's evening. Everything looked old, Victorian, but at the same time brand new. I could feel the frown on my forehead as I looked around questioningly. Eventually, we came to the navy glossed door that I recognised. I released his hand, turned around on the spot and took in my surroundings.

'We're at Lake View.' It wasn't a question, but a statement.

'Yep, we are. From the moment I came here with you, I knew it was the place for us.'

'The place for us?' I questioned, not quite able to believe what I was hearing.

'Yeah, the place for us. Is that okay?'

'You want us to live together?'

'Once it's finished, yeah. Whatdaya think?'

I grabbed hold of his hand once again and squeezed it tightly. 'I think I'd like that. I'm just not sure how you've managed all of this in five weeks?'

'Money, Amy. It speaks, loudly.'

'It must do. I wouldn't know, never really having had any.' I shook my head, trying to comprehend everything he was saying.

'Come on, let's go in.'

I nodded and walked in the door after he pushed it open. It was just like I remembered from being here last time. I loved the place, nothing had changed, except the damp smell had gone. I removed my wrap and threw it over the back of the nearest settee. Then I focussed all my attention back to him. He closed the door behind me and turned to face me. As he started to speak, I really wanted to concentrate on every word he was saying, but all I could think of was what he had told me he wanted to do to me against this wall, last time we were here.

'I've had plans drawn up to turn it into a family home and they've been working on it all the time we've both been away. There's loads more to do, but the main room is still habitable...' I watched as he stopped speaking and crossed his arms over his chest, showing me his well-defined muscles encased in the white shirt and shook his head from side to side.

'You aren't listening to a fucking word I'm saying, are you?' He grinned at me and leant towards me, resting one bare forearm against the wall next to me, making my body move instinctively up tight against the cool wall.

'I was trying to, but being here with you, made me think,' I answered and offered him a smile.

His head dipped to kiss the side of my neck and I gasped at the contact. My body was already on fire for him.

'What were you thinking about?' he questioned as his breath caressed my needy skin.

I let out a sigh as his teeth nipped my ear lobe and then swallowed so I could speak.

'When I was here before a breathtaking man told me a story about all the things he wanted to do to me.'

'Oh yeah?' I felt him smile against my neck. 'Perhaps you'd better tell me that story. I mean, you're already in a house in the woods, with the big bad wolf. So, tell me the rest of the story, Amy.'

I crossed my legs in anticipation, merely trying to quench the need that was building inside me as he continued his ministrations on my neck. His other forearm came down beside the other side of my face and he lifted his head to stare deep into my eyes. He shifted his legs and pushed his knee in between my thighs, effectively opening my legs once again. I watched as he took in a deep breath. He inhaled the smell of my arousal and I watched his pupils dilate as we stared at each other.

'Tell me, and start at the fucking beginning,' he almost growled out. 'Once upon a time...' He started speaking, as his knees bent and his hands ran quickly down the sides of my body, until they reached the bottom of my dress. He lifted my dress high up to my waist and his knees bent again, to take him further down. As he took in the fact I was naked from the waist down, 'FUCK ME!' fell from his lips.

I couldn't help but smirk at the look of wonderment on his face. Eventually his eyes came back up to meet mine. Just by looking at me that way, he gave me the confidence I had never had with anyone else.

'Sorry, Brody, you've got it all wrong. In the story he fucked me, not the other way around.' I grinned at him as the look of devilment landed on his face and he raised one eyebrow at me in response.

'Oh, Amy. You really don't know what the fuck you've got yourself into, do you?' He laughed and then grinned at me. 'In five short fucking minutes from now, I'm gonna have you screaming my name so loudly, they'll hear you back at The Manor.'

'Is that a dare?' I questioned, pushing my tongue into my cheek as I did so.

'No... It's a fucking promise,' he retorted.

In one burst of movement his hands found my waist and he lifted me up, pushing my shoulders firmly against the wall behind me. My legs were unceremoniously placed over his shoulders and my body was pushed higher up the wall. I gasped as he blew over my sex. 'You, beautiful, have far too much fucking sass. Eyes on me while I lick it and then fuck it out of you.'

I tried, really I tried. But as the first sweep of his tongue connected with my needy flesh, my eyes rolled into the back of my head and I was gone.

He was wrong, it only took three minutes and Lake View was filled with my voice screaming out, 'Brody,' over and over again.

Thirty-Six

Amy

I **HAD SLEPT** for a while wrapped up in Brody's arms, but the heat coming from him was immense. He was lying on his back with one arm bent underneath his head, his other arm was holding me tight to the side of his body. One of my arms was trapped underneath his and the other was draped over his broad chest. I was reluctant to move, enjoying how we felt together and not wanting to disturb him. So, I moved my leg a little and gently tried to flap the quilt off one of my feet. Finally managing and feeling the cooler air circulate around my exposed skin, I let out a sigh.

I settled back down and relaxed, trying hard to go back to sleep. It was no good, I was awake now and my brain had switched on, running over everything that had happened yesterday evening and into the early hours of this morning. Thank goodness I only had one more shift to do today, I knew I was going to be feeling the effects of only having had a couple of hour's rest.

The evening had started with him living up to every expectation I had of him as we relived the story he had told me a few weeks before. Dinner had been brought out to Lake View from The Manor's kitchens and we had sat laughing, joking and enjoying each other's company as we ate.

Then he had taken me to bed once again. I had no complaints, the man was extremely talented. But, now I wanted to know all the things he felt he needed to tell me. Wriggling free from his hold I propped myself up on my left elbow and stared down at this man who had stolen my heart.

'I can feel you staring.' One sleepy looking eye opened slightly and peered up at me. In response, I smiled down at him.

'Sorry, I can't sleep.' I pulled the arm that I had placed over his chest back a little so I could trace a colourful tattoo he had on his chest with my finger.

'I know, I can feel you fidgeting.' He opened his other eye and smirked at me and caught my moving hand in his.

'I can't sleep because I know we still need to talk, Brody.' My heart started to accelerate.

'Yeah,' he answered me as he began to pull us both further up the bed and onto the vast number of pillows behind us. 'I know what I need to tell you, but where do you want to start?'

I heard the hesitation in his voice and decided to start the easy way. 'Well, I need to know, did you buy my nan's shop and the flat above?'

'No, sorry, Amy. I didn't even know it had gone up for sale.' I could see the concern in his eyes as he answered me.

I had thought all along he had and had been willing myself not to be too upset if his answer was no. Surprisingly, when his answer came, it didn't affect me like I thought it would. I could hear my nan's voice in the back of my head saying, "out with the old and in with the new." Knowing I had living with Brody at Lake View to look forward to, made it even easier to accept.

At my silence, Brody spoke again. 'Do you want me to make an additional offer to who has?'

'What, offer more money to whoever bought my nan's place?'

'Yeah.'

I thought for a moment, looking around the room in Lake View that was going to be used as our bedroom. The walls were bare waiting to be decorated, the huge four poster bed that we were currently in, was sitting in the middle of the room and the only other furniture in the room was the still-blazing open fire.

'No, it's fine. I really don't. I know your heart is in the right place offering to buy it for me, but I don't need to look back. You've just given me you and this place. It's our chance to move forward.' I snuggled back down next to him to carry on and he kissed the top of my head offering me the strength to do so.

I felt his arm squeeze me tighter to him as he heard my answer. 'I wish I'd met you sooner. The way you look at life is so fucking refreshing. I'm sure you'd have been able to stop me making some pretty huge fucking mistakes. You're the second person in two days that's reminded me that there's more to life than fucking money.'

'What do you think made you turn to alcohol?' I realised that I was now holding my body taut as the words left my mouth. I wanted to know the answer because I needed to know what made him tick. But, I was unsure how he would feel providing an answer, if he even knew the answer.

'Mmmmm…' he took a deep breath as I continued to hold mine. 'I started drinking young, because it's what everyone else was doing and then because it helped to dampen down the pain inside me. I told you how my mom had left my dad when I was eight, didn't I?'

'Yes,' I replied.

'Our home wasn't the same as other kids had. Sure, every now and again we had a happy day, but in the main it was fucking miserable. My dad loved her, but she didn't love him anymore. Mom took prescription meds to dampen down the pain of being homesick and with someone she didn't want to be with, which meant she generally couldn't function. My sister and I were caught in the crossfire of two adults pulling in different fucking directions. Most days it was scary and hard, others it was terrifying and fucking painful.' The exhale that left his body was long and loud, like he was expelling his torment with his words.

'Oh, Brody. I'm so sorry for you both...' I could picture in my head two small and scared children. 'But, why is it that you feel guilty for not looking after your family.' My arm that had been lying relaxed on his chest moved, until my hand made it across to the other side of his body. I wanted him to feel me holding him.

'The worst of my guilt comes from letting down my sister. I was her big brother, Amy. Through all the crap that was going on with our parents we stuck together and got each other through. I swore to her that I would make everything better, that everything would be okay. The day my mom packed up to leave my dad she wanted to take us both with her back to America. Trying to stop her leaving, I told her I refused to go, thinking she would see sense and stay. Instead, she drove away with my sister crying in the back seat. If I close my eyes I can still see her balled up fists hitting the back windscreen as she cried for me and dad.'

I moved away from his hold, leant over him and placed a kiss over his heart as I tried to take away his pain.

'I never saw my mom again, as she eventually took too many of those fucking tablets and checked out. For a while, I even blamed myself for that. You know, if I'd have gone too I could have stopped her, and all that shit. After she died, my sister went to live with our aunt and never came back. I stayed with my dad and watched as he gradually went downhill, eventually his heart broke and carried him away. Drink hid all of that for me, it dampened down my pain, smoothed down the rough edges of my guilt and carried me into oblivion. It wasn't until Luke's wife died and I was threatened with my own mortality that I had the guts to try to stop.'

I let his words wash over me and lying across his chest I held him even tighter to me.

'What happened to your sister?'

'She grew up and hated me even more for not keeping my promise to her, she felt I'd abandoned her and moved on with my life. All she could see was, I was rich and successful, so I had to be happy, right? We were as close as siblings could be one minute and then the next she hated me.'

'Where is she?'

'She stayed in America. I know where she is when she asks for more money to cover her debts or when I manage to convince her to go into rehab. I've just seen her for the first time in over five fucking years, in Vegas.'

'That's good.'

'I'm not so sure about that, she's just newly married and I refused to give her my blessing.' The hurt in his voice was evident.

I sat up quickly and looked down at him. 'Why?'

'Marriage, I've got no time for it.' I felt myself tense at his words, he realised and his eyes left mine. 'I saw what it did to my family.'

'Brody, I was married once, we were both young and naive. It wasn't meant to be but, looking back, I can see it was what I needed at the time.'

'You've been married?' he asked.

'I was. We were fresh out of university, with all the hopes and aspirations of two people in their early twenties. What we forgot to ask each other, was what we both wanted out of life. It very quickly became evident that we wanted two entirely different things.'

'Go on,' he encouraged.

'He only wanted a career and I wanted a family. We parted amicably when we realised we'd made a mistake.'

'I'm sorry, that's sad.'

'It was initially, but six months down the line, I knew it was for the best. It helped me understand who I was. I understood that I couldn't settle for anything less than what I wanted. You know, this marriage might be just what your sister needs. You can't control everything in life, Brody and I'm sorry if I sound harsh, but you can't throw money at things hoping that it's going to solve all the problems.'

I lay myself back down over his chest and his hand regained its place in the middle of my back, staying firmly in place as he thought over what I had just said. I decided to try to make the atmosphere a little lighter in our room. 'I wanted to say thanks for turning up and parking outside the shop, after I left you at the wedding.'

I felt him relax underneath me once again.

'It was the fucking least I could do. It killed me letting you walk away. I needed to be as close as possible to you and that seemed like the only fucking option I had.' His hand began to gently run up and down my back as he caressed me and just like that, we were back.

'I made a list on Christmas Eve, of all the things I needed to sort out in my life.'

'Yeah?'

'It was hard walking away from you, but I needed to find myself first, before I could take the time to work out what we were to each other. I phoned my mum that night, after years of having nothing to do with her. I forgave her for leaving me, because I knew I had to take that step first, before I had any chance of working out how I felt about you. To find you out there offering me solace meant the world.'

'I need to sort this out with my sister, don't I?'

'I think so, the two of you need to make your peace.'

'Thank you, Amy. You make me want more from myself.'

'It's what we do for each other, Brody.'

I cuddled further into him and watched the dying embers of the fire. He removed his arm from behind his head and wrapped both of his arms around me, holding me like he would never let me go.

'You need to sleep, you have work at seven, don't you?'

'Mmmm, hmmm,' I agreed as my eyelids finally closed.

Thirty-Seven

Amy

I **LOOKED AT** the clock in my office, as I walked in for only the second time today. It was already gone eleven and I was desperate for a coffee. I was only four hours into my twelve-hour shift and fatigue was already washing over me. I kicked off my shoes as I walked behind my desk and let out a sigh of relief, as my bum found my seat.

'What a bloody day.' I spoke out into the empty room. I sank further into my chair and closed my eyes, trying to absorb the absolute bliss of the silence.

A knock at my door had me sitting back up almost immediately.

'Come in,' I replied as cheerfully as I could manage.

'I've brought you a cup of coffee, Miss. Harper. I thought you might need it. It's been a busy morning, hasn't it?' I heard Maria's voice as she entered the room and then I saw her smiling face. She, unlike myself it seemed, was the ultimate professional.

'Hasn't it just, Maria. Thanks, that's just what I needed.' I looked at her as she placed the cup down on my desk.

'Can I get you anything else?' she offered.

'No, thank you. The coffee is perfect.' As if to show her exactly how perfect, I lifted the cup to my lips and sipped at the hot liquid. I watched as she left my office with a nod and pulled the door closed behind her. As I held the cup to my lips, I thought back to this morning. The worst thing about living where you also worked, was that someone was always bound to see you when you crept in thirty minutes before your next shift, wearing last night's clothes.

As Brody pushed open the night door and strode in I followed him, praying that the reception area would be empty. To my complete relief, I couldn't see or hear anyone. Brody, noticing the same, had turned on his heel and spun around to capture me in his arms.

His mouth immediately found its way to my neck.

'How much are ya gonna miss me today, beautiful?' He spoke to me in between biting at my exposed skin.

I let out a sigh and closed my eyes. He had been inside me only an hour previously and already my sore, tired body wanted more. 'Too much,' I whispered back, hanging on to his biceps tightly. 'The Manor is very nearly booked to capacity from today, that means I'm going to be far too busy to have my head full of you.' I smiled as I spoke to him.

His head lifted and his mouth spread into a lascivious smirk. 'It's not your head that I want full of me, Amy. But it'll do til later.'

I looped my arms around his shoulders, in an attempt to say goodbye, before our luck run out. We'd talked on the drive here about how I would prefer that we didn't shout it from the roof tops that we were an item, not just yet anyway. He didn't see a problem with anyone knowing, but he had promised to keep his mouth shut for the time being.

Just as I was readying myself to say goodbye, he abruptly dipped me backwards. At the sudden change in position I let out a squeal and a giggle.

'Ssshhhhh,' he reprimanded and righted me instantly at my loud response.

'Good morning, Miss. Harper.' I heard the bright voice of Maria as I watched her in my peripheral view stand up from behind the long counter.

'And just like that our secret is out,' he whispered in my ear before he released me.

'Good morning, Mr. Daniels,' she continued.

Separating myself from Brody, I smiled my hello to her and with a flush of embarrassment taking over my face, I made my way to the main staircase.

I heard Brody behind me, chatting away to her like he hadn't a care in the world that she'd just caught us. It reminded me how different our worlds were. He was used to people scrutinising his every movement and I hated being the centre of attention. But, I grasped, it didn't faze me. I knew what we felt for each other was strong enough to get us both through.

BRODY

'I have some messages for you, Mr. Daniels. They arrived while you were away,' I heard Maria say.

As I continued up the staircase, I thought back to last night and how it felt to sleep in his arms and a flurry of excitement overwhelmed me. I decided to take one last look at the man who had systematically taken over my life in six short weeks. He really was everything I had ever dreamt of and so very much more. I swept my eyes over him, observing him in secret from the curve in the staircase. Brody took the messages from her and after flicking through them all, I watched as his face contorted.

He placed the pieces of paper into his back pocket.

'Thank you, Maria. If any other messages come for me, I'll be at Lake View, and you can probably get me there.'

I watched as he walked away to personally oversee the home he was creating for us.

The day seemed to surprisingly drag. I had dealt with a few minor issues already, and I had made a note of all the things that it appeared some of the staff might need retraining on. I had comprehended very quickly, that it was one thing operating a five-star hotel when you only had half of the rooms full, but today we were nearly full and a few little things here and there had slipped. It was only to be expected as the staff were still finding their feet, but I was determined it would be teething problems only and that it wouldn't become the normal.

The sound of a woman's voice reached my ears through my half-opened doorway and my ears pricked up. I was just finishing up a call to a supplier, but found myself once again in awe of Maria's professionalism.

'I'm sorry, we just don't have a room of that size available and we won't have for the next six nights.' I heard her begin to offer something else, but I couldn't concentrate on what it was as my phone call equally needed my attention. I blocked my free ear with my finger, so all I could now hear was the voice on the phone. I replied in all the right places and finally ten minutes later I replaced the receiver. Now free of the call, I listened once again, focussing on finding Maria's voice in the bustling reception area.

'Thank you. There's your ID back. Yes, of course we can do that for you. I'll just call a porter and he'll take your bags up for you.' Her voice sounded a little flustered, but it appeared her exemplary customer service had yet again sorted out another possible problem.

I looked back down at my IPad and systematically went through the list of things the manager had wanted me to attend to on my shift. It was nearly completed and I felt a sense of pride that I still had over an hour to deal with the last few tasks.

My door being fully opened without being knocked on, drew my attention up from my desk to watch Maria quickly arriving through the gap.

'Maria?' I questioned with concern at her harassed looking expression.

'I'm sorry to be rude, Miss. Harper, but I need to talk to you about something.' She closed the door behind her and immediately gained all my attention.

'Are you okay?' I gently asked. 'Would you like to take a seat?' I could feel my forehead creasing with concern.

'No, thank you. I don't think it would be right. In fact, you may well tell me to mind my own business.'

'I'm intrigued,' I replied, 'please carry on.'

'I'm sorry, but as you know, I saw you with Mr. Daniels this morning.' I watched as her fingers grabbed on to the back of the tub chair she was stood behind and I nodded at her.

'Yes, you did,' I agreed.

'I know I'm speaking out of turn here, and I can only hope you'll forgive me, but I believe that women should stand up for each other and have each other's backs so to speak. My marriage broke up recently because my husband was having an affair. When I confronted the other woman, she swore blind that he had never mentioned he was married and I believed her.'

I leant back into my chair. I wasn't sure where this conversation was going but I was convinced I wasn't going to like the outcome. 'I think you need to get to what it is you're trying to say.'

'An American lady has just tried to book into The Manor, when I explained to her that we hadn't the room available, she told me that it wasn't a problem as her name was Mrs Barbara Daniels and I could put her into Brody Daniels' room.'

Married?

My ears were ringing with her words, they went around my head again as I stared at her in disbelief. My heart was pounding in my chest in panic as I forced myself to think her words through, because there just had to be an explanation.

'Barbara?' I questioned as my synapses started firing. 'Didn't she leave him a message before?'

'Yes, several.' Her voice was quieter as she answered me and I watched her look down to the floor. The room was uncomfortable, we didn't know each other well enough to be having this sort of conversation.

'Thank you, Maria,' I forced out of my mouth. 'Please close the door on your way out.' She turned immediately and vacated the room, closing the door quietly behind her once again.

Every single variable, possibility and thought swirled around my head as I replayed her words. Although my heart refused to believe it, my head always came back to the same answer. With anger fuelling my actions, I pulled my phone out from my jacket pocket. My fingers shook as I typed out the letters.

You gave me this phone so we would no longer miscommunicate. So, I'll say this loud and clear. Understand this, I will accept a lot of things, but I will never be the other woman. IT SEEMS YOUR WIFE HAS JUST ARRIVED!

Thirty-Eight

Amy

FOR A FEW seconds my finger hovered over the send button, until finally as my body began to shake with the pain erupting inside me, my finger connected, and it was gone. Then I switched my phone off, no longer wanting any link to him. Now all I had to do was make my escape. I wasn't going to break down in here, I refused. Feeling more ill than I could ever remember, I completed my tasks for the day and emailed the general manager. I lied, like it seemed everyone else did around here. I explained that as I hadn't taken my lunch break today and had an emergency dentist appointment to attend, I would be leaving early. It took me all of twenty-seven minutes to put my plan into action and I did it all from the cellular enclosure of my office.

I grabbed my coat from the stand and taking a deep breath I placed my hand on the ceramic handle of my door. The spring squeaked as it turned and the catch released, and summoning up all my courage I began to open the door.

'AMY!' Brody shouted out as he entered the building. I heard the shout echo around the large reception area.

My heart reacted immediately, pounding with familiarity and hurt.

'Where is she?' I knew he'd arrived at reception as his voice sounded nearer. 'Where is Miss. Harper?'

Taking a deep breath, I pulled open my door and braced myself to face him. 'I'm here, come in.' It was the last thing I wanted to do. I'd planned on being gone before he arrived, but I was *not* washing my very dirty linen in public, no way. I stepped back inside and instinctively made my way behind my desk. Within seconds he was through the door and we were enclosed within the four walls.

'Look at me,' his voice demanded.

I looked up in my own time and stared him down with every ounce of fortitude I could find. 'I'm looking.'

The sight in front of my eyes made the heart that I had just imprisoned, melt a little. He was wearing clothes that were covered in paint. His hair looked dusty and unkempt. Realisation hit me that he had been working on Lake View with his own hands. Our conversation about doing things with love rather than money, had not fallen on deaf ears. Finally, I plucked up the courage to look into his eyes. They were narrowing as he silently questioned me and his tic above his cheekbone began to flicker, with either uncertainty or anger.

'No, you're not looking, Amy. You've already run the fuck away,' he accused as he lifted his square jaw and crossed his arms over his broad chest.

'I've just found out you're married, what the hell do you expect me to do?' I tried to tear my eyes away from his, but he held them captive.

'I'm not married, I've never been married. I'll never be married. You need to hear that and absorb it. Didn't you take in what I said last night? My parents' marriage was one too fucking many for me to be part of.'

With my head shaking from side to side I carried on. 'Then who is she? Who would book themselves into your room as Mrs. Daniels.'

'Believe it or not, I don't have fucking x-ray eyes,' he sarcastically came back with, as his arms uncrossed and he pushed his hands into his jeans pockets, inhaling deeply. 'Although, I've got an idea who it might be. Do you have a name?' he questioned.

'Mrs. Barbara Daniels.'

'There isn't a Mrs. Barbara Daniels, she doesn't exist. I do have a sister called Mrs. Barbara Morello. So, come with me and let's confront this situation head on.' His voice was now calmer and his head tilted to one side as he dared me.

I shook my head indignantly.

I watched his eyebrows raise at me in question. 'Listen to me, very carefully, Amy. We can do this the easy way or the hard way, it makes no fucking odds to me. We are not going around in fucking circles anymore. You're not running away from this. You're not running away from me or us.'

'I'm not running. I don't run anymore. I promised myself,' I answered.

'Then prove it.'

I stood my ground staring him down.

'Enough,' Brody growled and shaking his head at me, he propelled himself forward. It appeared that every bit of his self-restraint had snapped. With that one word and two large steps, Brody was around my side of the desk, wearing a face that looked thunderous. Instinctively I moved away, only to be grabbed by the hand and pulled back until my body firmly collided into his. His arms wrapped quickly around me. He had cleverly aligned our bodies so we were facing each other, with my arms pinned in between both of us.

'DON'T…' I began to shout out.

'I know, don't fucking touch you. That's getting old don't you think? And it's also too fucking late, Amy.' I could hear the anger in his voice.

Without any more conversation he picked me up and unceremoniously threw me over his shoulder. I punched him as hard as I could on his lower back, but he didn't even flinch. I heard the squeak of my door being opened, then we were through and out the other side. I squeezed my eyes tightly shut.

'Miss. Harper?' I heard Maria question. 'Are you okay?'

I couldn't answer her. The busy reception area had suddenly fallen into an almost complete silence as we made our grand entrance. I couldn't imagine what we looked like. I closed my eyes and stayed still as Brody once again climbed a set of stairs with me over his shoulder. As we turned the corner to go to the left, leaving behind our audience, I spoke again.

'I can't believe you just did that.' He didn't reply at first, but kept on striding towards his room.

Then as we stopped outside of his room he spoke calmly. 'Oh, you better believe it, I've had enough of all this shit.'

I heard the metal of his rings rap hard on the door. When he heard no movement from inside, he shouted out, 'BARBARA!'

The door was pulled open and he marched us inside.

'Finally, I've got your attention.' I heard a female voice reply from behind me.

'Yeah, you could say. What the fuck are you playing at?' I felt the words rumble deep inside his chest before he spoke them.

BRODY

I hit his back again, reminding him of where I still was. At last Brody pulled me back over his shoulder and placed my feet firmly on the ground. I refused to look up at him. He had placed me in a situation that I had no idea how to handle. I was majorly outside of my comfort zone. Embarrassed and angry, I turned towards Barbara.

The woman my eyes found, was blonde and willowy in stature. Her clothes were expensive and they made her look almost as perfectly put together as Winter. The only differences between the two of them was the anxiety that was plastered all over her beautifully made-up face and the way she constantly rubbed at her hands, with nerves. I felt for her, whoever she was. I continued to move my eyes up to study her face. My body sagged with relief the moment I looked at her eyes.

Instantly, I knew exactly who she was.

Tears of pent-up emotion spilt rapidly down my face. I felt Brody's arms wrap around me tightly from behind and he pulled me back into him, bent his head down and kissed my neck as he breathed me in. As his mouth lifted away he started to speak.

'Amy, I'd like to introduce you to…'

'Your sister,' I finished for him. 'I'm sorry I ever doubted you.' He squeezed me tighter in reply to my apology.

I watched as the woman in front of us grimaced. 'Hi, Amy. I'm so sorry. I never meant to upset you.'

'Hi,' I managed to answer, as I wiped the tears on my face away with my hand.

'What did you think you were doing, coming here and booking into my room using that name?' Brody asked from behind me.

'You drove me to it, Brody. I wanted to talk in Vegas, and you left. I've sent messages and phoned, you ignored it all. I won't live like this anymore. I've been working for eight long months, to get me to a place where I can see a future for myself. You can't ignore and bury our past any longer. For my own sake, I won't let you.

Silence filled the room.

'Sissy, I don't know how we got here. Just how the actual fuck did we get from A to B?' It wasn't really a question, but a declaration of disbelief. I could feel Brody's head shaking from side to side.

'I don't know all the answers, not yet. Nico has paid for me to see a therapist who's been helping me…' Barbara began to reply.

'I paid for you to see loads of therapists, what makes this one different?' Brody asked her. I could tell he wasn't accusing her, but trying to understand.

'The difference is, Brody, Nico comes with me.'

'Nico Morello?'

'Yes, Nico Morello, my husband.'

'You don't even know who he is,' he accused as his anger flared again.

'You're wrong, I know exactly who he is and he knows exactly what he's married.'

The deep sigh that left the man behind me, vibrated his hurt and pain through me.

'If he can offer you what I couldn't or wouldn't, then he's a better man than I believed him to be. So, it's what I always thought all these years, all of this is down to me.' I heard the disappointment in his voice and brought my hands up to cling on to his biceps. I needed him to know that despite how he had brought me here, I was now very much with him.

'It's not down to you. I know that for years I told you it was and I'm sorry. Brody, we followed a pattern that was drawn out for us, a path that we just couldn't see past. But there is a fork in that path now, we have a choice which way we choose to go. And I, for one, don't want us to be these toxic people anymore.' Barbara wrapped her arms around herself and I truly felt for her, standing there all alone. I leant myself further into Brody in response, as she carried on. 'Cade told me you'd fallen in love, Brody, and I couldn't see how it was possibly true. But, I can see it now. I'm sorry if I've caused all this trouble, but I had to see you and this was the only option I thought I had left. I booked in as Mrs. Barbara Daniels, because I *am* married, but until you give me your blessing I won't accept Nico's name.'

The sigh behind me was loud, as he audibly sounded his disappointment in himself. I gripped his arms tighter, pressed my fingers deeper into his skin, making sure his hold stayed put and I tried to offer him my strength.

'I was wrong, Barbara, and in so many ways... I'll give you both my blessing. I hope that you'll be happy together, and I sincerely pray that he gives you everything that Amy offers me,' Brody answered and I felt his face come down onto the top of my head as he breathed me in again.

'Thank you, Brody. That means so much, I just can't tell you,' I heard Barbara say.

I released my hold on his arms and he took the cue to let me go and to go and hug his sister. I sat down on the edge of his bed and I watched them hold each other. I could hear as they whispered their apologies to each other.

'I'll give you two a bit of space, I'm sorry I doubted you.' I stood to leave the room. I wanted to hold him in my arms. We were moving forward, slaying the ghosts of our pasts and doing it together. My heart was full to bursting and I needed to show him exactly that. But it could all wait for now.

'Don't go, don't leave. I have something I want to ask,' I heard as I stood from the bed.

'You two go ahead, I need some fresh air anyway,' Barbara offered.

'Thanks.' He smiled his response to her.

I watched as she grabbed her coat and walked out of the room, smiling at us both. Her anxiety had lifted the moment her brother had taken her into his arms. The door closed behind her and I turned around to face the man I loved. As I did so, he simultaneously fell to his knees in front of me.

'Brody?' I questioned as I felt my mouth open in shock. I tried and failed to pull him back up by grabbing his hands in mine. It was pointless, there was no way I could move him. He turned my hands around, lovingly kissed both of my wrists and then gazed up at me. I fell in love with him all over again.

'Amy,' he started and I held my breath, not knowing what to expect. He smiled a shy sort of smile at my reaction and I bent down to chastely brush my lips on his in reassurance. 'Amy, when I stood in your office earlier, taking in your anger, I read the words your nan created for you. It was as if she was speaking to me. I know that sounds crazy.'

'It doesn't sound crazy to me. She often speaks in my head, too,' I revealed to the incredibly serious, but sweet man on his knees in front of me.

'I want you to want to be with me. I want to be the one you spend the rest of your life with. I want to be the one who rids you of your sadness, so that you can smile again.' I watched as his lopsided grin swept over his face and his voice changed to a more playful tone. 'Hell, I know I can enflame your anger, take today for starters. But, I also want to be the man you have passionate make-up sex with.' He offered me a wink and I smiled back at him. 'I know sometimes we'll argue to the point of you ignoring me and still, I want to experience that with you. I want to be the father to our many children.'

'Many?' I laughed a little, as I questioned him.

'Yes, Amy, many,' he replied. I could see the previous tension he had held in his body falling away, the more he spoke. 'FUCK! I read those words she made for you and I know I'm that man. I want the white picket fence and the whole goddamn nine yards with you. So, what I'm down here officially asking is... Amy Harper, will you live with me for the rest of your life.'

I burst out laughing at his words and flung myself into his arms. 'Yes!' I shouted out.

With my sudden momentum, he collapsed backwards, taking me with him. I placed my hands on either side of his face and kissed all over his smiling lips, until he whispered to me.

'Then, beautiful, this isn't the end of our story, it's just the end of the beginning.'

Epilogue

BRODY

Five years later

I'D DUMPED MY bags in the hallway and after calling out and getting no reply, I followed my nose. It led me through to the back of our house, to the open-plan kitchen and family room. Standing at the door, I took in the woman who owned every single fucking part of me. She was busy in the kitchen, with the full view of the lake behind her. Not for the first time, I thought to myself just what a lucky fucking bastard I was. If someone had ever told me I was going to fall in love, just by seeing someone through a shop window, I'd have told them that they must be fucking high. But, she had come into my life and rocked my world. Here we were, five years later and I couldn't imagine what my life would be like without her. I was a better man for loving her and I could only hope she felt the same way about me.

Quietly, not wanting to disturb the view in front of my eyes, I walked in and sat down at the breakfast bar. I knew I should let her know I'd arrived home, but hell, for these few peaceful minutes, I just wanted to watch her, like I had the first time I saw her.

I'd missed everything about her in the time we'd been apart. Three weeks away from my family these days, was my fucking limit.

I studied what she was doing and knew I was comprehensively fucked.

Amy was baking, fucking baking, when she knew exactly what the smell of flour on her skin did to me. I watched as she moved around, taking in the way her supple body looked in her black leggings and fitted vest. Her chestnut coloured hair was up in a ponytail and the skin on the back of her neck showed a sheen of moisture that just called for my fucking attention. I watched as she wiggled her hips around to the music she was playing in the background. A huge part of me loved the fact that she listened to me singing whenever we were away on tour. I knew that she missed me, as much as I fucking missed her. Skype sex was hot as fuck, but it only took the edge off the need I had for her, my woman, the one that I wanted twenty-four hours a day, every single fucking day.

I licked my lips at the sight of the cakes she was icing. I could smell the peanut butter from here. She knew they were my favourite and I knew that they were being made especially for me. But, the unsurpassed view was of her, bending over to place another tray into the oven in front of me. I couldn't see any panty lines and I started my game of guessing just exactly what she was or wasn't wearing underneath her clothes. My fingers twitched along with my dick, as I imagined running my hands all over that ass and finding out.

The best sort of women were cooks in the kitchen and whores in the bedroom. Fuck me, those sexist bastards were right. I was the lucky bastard who was on the receiving end of all her handiwork.

My expanding dick meant that I was now fidgeting as I rested my ass against the edge of the stool. I always knew that I found watching her baking erotic, but the sight of her and the neat baby bump she was carrying, was fucking killing me slowly.

I fucking loved her being pregnant. It spoke to me in a primeval way.

As her voice joined in with the chorus of one of the love songs I'd written when we were first together, a huge fucking grin broke out on my face. I cringed as she missed the high note and started to laugh at her.

My secret was out.

The moment she heard the sound behind her, she spun around. The knife that she'd been using dropped unceremoniously onto the granite worktop with a loud clatter and she flew towards me. I took in the sight of her face, tendrils of hair had fallen out of her hair tie, her cheeks were flushed, her eyes alight and her face was dusted in flour, as only hers could be. I realised that I'd never loved her more.

'You're home!' she shouted, as her bare feet flew over the slate floor to reach me.

I shifted my ass off the edge of the stool and matched her step for step, until at last we were touching. I lifted a piece of her hair off her face and placed it behind her ear. Instinctively, her arms went around my neck as she pulled me closer. My hands found her ass and I lifted her up, to place her exactly where I needed to feel her and her legs wrapped around my waist.

A groan left my mouth as the warmth of her pussy rubbed against my hard dick.

'Yep. I'm home. You miss me?' I kissed the tip of her nose and watched her.

She pulled away and looked at me like I was stupid and I grinned at her, watching as her dark brown eyes darkened further. 'Desperately. Woman in her second trimester here.' The words stopped and her mouth crashed into mine and I met her half way. She demanded and I let her take. Her tongue swept into my mouth and I met it with equal fervour. The pace she was setting started to quicken and small moans left her mouth. Finally, I took control, refusing to be rushed, as I wanted to savour every moment of our reconciliation. I pulled away and rested my forehead against hers.

'Don't you dare pull away, Daniels.' Amy rolled her hips, making her warm pussy rub against me. It caused a dull, painful ache inside my balls that was so strong it felt fucking dangerous. I exhaled and raised my eyebrows at her words.

'Turn the oven off and take me to bed,' she demanded.

'I'd love to, beautiful. But aren't you forgetting a couple of small things?'

'I'm seriously forgetting how much I love you the longer you talk and insist on making me wait.'

I laughed out loud at her words.

I moved one of my hands, knowing she was gripping her thighs tight enough around me. I wanted to tease her a little bit more. I ran my fingers up her back and stroked her neck. Her skin changed in the wake of my fingertips. I loved watching her react to me, it never got old. As her eyes closed and she leant into the feel of my hand, I couldn't hold out any longer.

'Where are the boys?'

Her eyes opened and she smiled a slow, lazy smile at me.

'Aunty Barbara has taken them for a few hours. We're all by ourselves.' I knew I loved my sister, but I'd never loved her more than when she was in the U.K. offering her babysitting services. It had taken us a long time and a lot of therapy to come through our twenty-odd years of hurt, but it had been worth every single fucking piece of heart rendering pain. I had her firmly back in my life. Between her, Amy and the boys, and the guys in the band, they had put me back together, piece by very broken piece.

'Well that puts a different swing on things, why the fuck didn't you say before, beautiful?'

'You never asked.' She grinned back at me.

Amy

The three weeks he'd been gone had almost been painful. I missed him with every bone in my body. After five years together, my heart still leapt when I saw him. Even after having two children already and with another on the way, the very moment he gave me that look, or used a certain tone of voice, I would move heaven and hell just to fall into his arms.

Barbara had taken Felix and Max off my hands a couple of hours previously. She knew Brody was due home this afternoon and it had given me an opportunity to make sure I was ready for him. I had soaked in the bath, shaved and creamed my skin. Then I'd pulled on comfortable clothes, knowing that he didn't give a rat's tail about what I was wearing. I'd brushed my hair and without putting on a scrap of make-up, I'd gone down to the kitchen to bake his favourite cakes.

I was sure my nan was with me on days like today. I felt so close to her when I baked and I was convinced I could feel her love surrounding me as I made food for my own growing family. Dementia had finally taken her two years ago, the only thing that consoled me about her loss was the fact she had stayed with us long enough to see I was happy and settled. I could still remember her soft skin on mine, as she touched our first baby bump and felt him kick her in response. She had left us, but her love and words of wisdom still echoed in my heart and my head. She was the one who had shown me how to be a mum, and I had made a vow to myself that our children would never be short on the love and encouragement that she had shown me.

Feeling a little emotional due to pregnancy hormones, I turned up the volume on the radio to let Brody's voice wrap itself around me.

All the time Brody was away I listened to Default Distraction, as it made me feel closer to him.

Stood in the kitchen getting more and more excited by his imminent arrival, I was now singing at the top of my voice. The man I loved had the sexiest bloody voice. I knew I was a mess of hormones, but thinking about him being here soon and listening to him as the music reverberated around the kitchen had my core aching with need. My breathing was unsteady and my skin was so on edge that goose bumps had started to appear on my arms. I laughed to myself at just what the thought of him could do to me.

The song that was playing was one of my favourites by the band and had me singing out loud. As the chorus came around again I put my heart and soul into every word.

Deep, melodic laughter hit my ears and I spun around so fast, I dropped the palette knife I was using.

And there he was. I let my eyes sweep up and down him, taking him in and inhaling deeply to find his spicy cologne.

'You're home!' I shouted out in disbelief. Without thinking any further, my feet moved of their own accord and flew over the tiled kitchen to where he was pushing himself off one of the stools. Our bodies connected and I exhaled a sigh of relief. He moved some hair off my face and I looped my arms around his neck as he lifted me up into his arms.

My pregnancy hormones had taken over and I shamelessly rubbed myself over the hardness I just knew I would find. The groan he released was almost too much to bare.

'Yep, I'm home. You miss me?'

Was the man stupid?

'Desperately. Woman in her second trimester here.' The time for talking was over. I crashed my mouth into his and took everything I needed.

The next few minutes were a blur, I demanded and he controlled. I thought he might never give in to what my body was pleading of his. The conversation went back and forward between us, until suddenly the look in his eyes changed when he found out we were home alone.

Finally, we were moving. I wrapped my arms tighter around his neck and gripped his waist with my thighs. He strode towards the oven and switched it off. I could now only feel one of his hands on me and it wasn't nearly enough. I heard the rustle of a cupcake wrapper and moved my head to look at him squarely in the face.

'You'd better not be thinking about food?'

He grinned back his response to me. 'You needn't worry, the only thing I'm eating, Amy, is you.'

'Promises, promises,' I teased.

At my words, his teasing, relaxed demeanour changed to one of a man on a mission and I couldn't help the sigh of relief that left my mouth. I clung on for all I was worth as he strode back across the kitchen to the breakfast bar. The sound of his boots thumping on every piece of slate was like music to my ears. His hold on me changed as he kicked a couple of the boys' toys out of our way. Slowly, he lowered me backwards until I was lying on top of the cool, granite worktop.

'Okay?' he checked.

I nodded at him and sucked my bottom lip into my mouth in anticipation.

'Lie still, I'm getting these clothes off you.'

I exhaled a trembling breath. I placed a hand either side of me to check exactly where he had placed me and then held on to the edges of the granite. Brody stood in between my legs and pulled his T-shirt up and off his body and then lovingly placed it under my head. I heard myself gasp, as I took in everything about his gorgeous torso and my eyes went down to watch him release the top two buttons of his jeans. It was then I knew he was playing me at my own game. Very tidy manscaping met my eyes and my core tightened as I realised he was commando. I let my eyes run all over his body and his nipples hardened under my perusal. I knew he was watching my reaction as I took him in and I licked my lips at the sight of him, showing him just how he affected me, as if he could ever be in any doubt.

'Hold on, beautiful.'

His hands found the waistband of my leggings and I lifted myself a little to accommodate him. As he pulled them off my feet, I relaxed into the inevitable.

He leant over and kissed our neat, twenty-four-week bump and he spoke something to the baby that I didn't quite catch. The look of wonderment on his face was everything to me and as our eyes found each other as he lifted his head to look at me, it filled me up inside. I knew I could and would never get enough of this man. I watched as his bright teal eyes clouded over momentarily with emotion.

'You're fucking stunning, Amy. Remind me to keep you pregnant forever, it's my fucking favourite look on you.'

He moved up, hovering over me and his lips gently brushed mine. His tongue softly licked the seam of my lips and then pushed its way inside, as his mouth consumed me. His desperation for me was fuelling his every movement. I released the edges of the worktop and threaded my fingers through his hair and held him to me. His lips left mine and travelled down my neck. I could hear my own breathing quicken as he descended further, until the feelings he was drawing out of me made my hands intuitively grab hold of the worktop again.

BRODY

My vest top was hurriedly pushed up and over my breasts, and one of his hands made short work of the clasp on the front of my bra. The material fell away and my nipples pebbled as soon as the cooler air found them.

'I need you to suck them,' I murmured to him. 'I've been dreaming of feeling your mouth on me for days.'

He instantly moved and his wet flesh connected with where every nerve ending in my body had collected. I arched my back and groaned at the exquisite sensations he was creating inside me. He moved between both of my large, extended nipples, pulling them into his mouth and sucking them hard as he released them. My body followed the pace he was setting, desperate for it to be enough to send me into the orgasm I so badly craved. But he could read my every movement and just when I felt I was going to explode into orbit, he removed his mouth from me and my back sunk back onto the cold beneath my back.

'No,' I mumbled.

'Don't worry, beautiful, I'll get you there.'

A sound hit my ears and after three years of being a mum, my body went immediately into full alert.

'Nothing to worry about, it's just I didn't want all this going to waste. I thought I could dirty you up a little.' He salaciously smiled down at me.

I smelt the peanut buttercream I'd made for the top of Brody's welcome home cupcakes, as he began to spread it over my nipples. I gasped as he ripped the tiny piece of elastic at the side of the thong I had worn especially for him and with his finger loaded with cream, he wiped it all over my sex. I lifted my head and opened my eyes to watch him decorate my body with his favourite boyhood flavour and then I almost cried out loud as I watched him place his finger into his mouth to suck it clean. He had taken a step back to admire his creation, and smiled with the knowledge that he knew he was driving me crazy.

Two can play at this game.

I dropped one hand in between my open legs and found my engorged clit with two fingers and began to offer myself the friction I so desperately needed. I fought to keep my eyes on his as I silently dared him to do something.

'Not happening, Amy, I'm gonna be the one who makes you scream, not you.' His voice had deepened to the point of a growl.

Game on.

The sound of his voice spurred me on and my fingers sped up. I was so very close. I watched the moment he couldn't hold himself back anymore. His body moved quickly, his hands took hold of my knees as

251

he parted my legs further open. Then his head fell between my thighs and he ran his warm, wet tongue through my soaking wet lips. My back arched off the worktop as I reached the precipice of the ecstasy I so badly needed. Bursts of colour hit the back of my eyelids as my orgasm rolled through me and I fell off the cliff into free fall.

'Brody, Oh God!... Brody!' I screamed out enjoying the rare opportunity to be as loud as I wanted.

Just as my orgasm began to ebb away he moved again, pulling his cock free of the confines of his jeans. Holding on to my thighs and steadying me he opened me up wider and then drove his steel like hardness inside me. The orgasm that had been dying away, immediately sprung back to life with every slow thrust of his hips. His mouth came down to my needy nipples and he sucked off the cream he had just placed there. With his hands holding on to my waist keeping me safe, I forced my head up and watched the scene in front of my eyes, as he picked up the pace and plunged inside me again and again.

This is what I had needed, this is what my body had been craving. The feel of us together had my eyes filling with tears and I closed them, overcome with emotion. But as his cock began to pulse inside me unevenly, I opened them again to watch the man I loved as he found his own release in the confines of my body.

'FUCK! Amy. Yes.'

His hands remained firmly holding my waist and his body slowed, eventually stilling as he tried to control the aftershocks that were careering through his body. I wasn't sure how he was still managing to stand after what I'd just witnessed. Eventually, his breathing slowed and his eyes refocussed on mine.

I smiled up at him and he grinned back at me, exposing his dimple.

'Well, rock God, that was good for starters, but I'm ready for the main event now,' I teased.

The laughter that left him was music to my ears.

'Really?' he questioned. 'And as it so happens, so am I.'

I looked at him, taking note that his grin had gone and that it had been replaced with a more serious expression. One of his hands left my waist and he appeared to fidget in his jeans pocket. I heard myself inhale as he pulled out a small black ring box. My eyes opened wider as I stared at him waiting for an explanation.

He took a deep breath and then got out the words I knew he'd been practising over and over in his head, the way he did with all new songs. 'Amy, I want no more regrets in my life. You've been by my side every step of the way for five years, we've had Felix and Max together and now have Louis on the way. I can't imagine life without you, because I would have no life without you. Sharing a lifetime together will never be enough for me to show you how much you mean to me. The three years of therapy sorting through my shit have given me the chance to reconsider the whole marriage thing. I now want it, I crave it, but only if it's with you. I'm a sexist bastard, I know it. I want to see you pregnant with our child, with my ring on your finger. You complete me, you make me a better man, with you I've come full fucking circle. Amy Harper, will you marry me?'

Completely stunned, I watched as he flicked open the ring box lid to reveal a stunning teal coloured topaz surrounded by diamonds. My mouth was wide open and tears spilt down my cheeks.

'YES!' I shouted out, lost for any other words.

He picked up my hand, placed the ring onto my finger and placed a kiss over the top.

Then he pulled out of me, pushed his jeans down with both hands and kicked them off his feet. I watched smiling as they dramatically flew through the air. His hands came back to lift me up off the hard granite surface beneath me and he held me as tight to him as our baby bump would allow. For a few minutes, we breathed each other in. Once I was high enough in his arms with my legs once again wrapped around his waist, he began walking towards the stairs.

'Carrying me again?' I teased.

'Yep, over the threshold and into the rest of our lives.' He placed a loving kiss on my mouth and looked at me as we carried on moving. 'Oh and, Amy, that fucking sassy mouth of yours is going to get you into trouble,' he rasped out.

'Is that a dare?' I asked.

'No, but it's a fucking promise,' he retorted.

He strode into our master suite and placed me down gently onto our bed.

'Eyes on me, beautiful, while I fuck the sass out of you.'

'Always,' I sighed.

THE END

Coming Soon

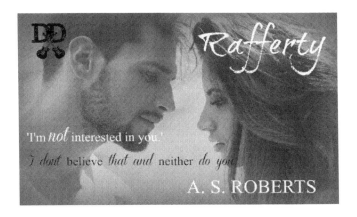

'I'm *not* interested in you.'
I don't believe *that and* neither *do you*
Rafferty
A. S. ROBERTS

Chart topping U.S. rock band, Default Distraction, have everything money can buy…

RAFF
But I don't.
I've got money, women, and the fans' endless adoration.
But none of it's enough.

I have one distraction, and I can't forget her.
I shattered all our dreams, when
I walked away from our world,
to conquer the music world.

But now, I've got one fantasy,
One wish,
One desire.
Lauren.

And she wants nothing to do with me.
Those broken pieces I crushed,
she doesn't want mended.
But when a cruel twist of fate puts her back in my arms,
I'm not letting go.

LAUREN
He was everything,
everything I ever wanted and needed.

When he walked away, he took a piece of me with him,
a shard of pain that I never thought would heal.
But I worked hard, and piece by agonising piece, I almost rebuilt my
life.

Now, he's back and wants only one thing.
Me.
He wants my forever.
Something I can't promise.
I won't give in, I can't cling to the past.

This time, there's more on the line, even more than my shattered heart at
stake.
And forever isn't really that long anyway.

31004929R00157

Printed in Poland
by Amazon Fulfillment
Poland Sp. z o.o., Wrocław